The Bestiary

Books by Nicholas Christopher

FICTION

The Bestiary (2007)

Franklin Flyer (2002)

A Trip to the Stars (2000)

Veronica (1996)

The Soloist (1986)

POETRY

Crossing the Equator: New and Selected Poems, 1972–2004 (2004)

Atomic Field: Two Poems (2000)

The Creation of the Night Sky (1998)

5° (1995)

In the Year of the Comet (1992)

Desperate Characters: A Novella in Verse (1988)

A Short History of the Island of Butterflies (1986)

On Tour with Rita (1982)

NONFICTION

Somewhere in the Night: Film Noir & the American City (1997)

EDITOR

Walk on the Wild Side: Urban American Poetry Since 1975 (1994)

Under 35: The New Generation of American Poets (1989)

The Bestiary

A novel by

NICHOLAS CHRISTOPHER

THE DIAL PRESS

THE BESTIARY
A Dial Press Book / July 2007

Published by
The Dial Press
A Division of Random House, Inc.
New York, New York

Book design by Francesca Belanger

The Dial Press is a registered trademark of Random House, Inc.,
and the colophon is a trademark of Random House, Inc.

Library of Congress Cataloging-in-Publication Data
Christopher, Nicholas.
The bestiary : a novel / Nicholas Christopher.
p. cm.
ISBN: 978-0-385-33736-6
1. Bestiaries—Fiction. I. Title.
PS3553.H754 B47 2007
813.'54 22   2007008337

Printed in the United States of America
Published simultaneously in Canada

www.dialpress.com

BVG   10 9 8 7 6 5 4 3 2 1

for my wife, Constance,
for her dedication to this book, from beginning to end

✳

ALEXANDER THE GREAT: Which is the most cunning of animals?

INDIAN PHILOSOPHER: The animal which man has not yet discovered.

—Plutarch, *Parallel Lives*

. . . I have handled other rarities, plum-sized pearls from Ceylon & chimes stirred to music by light & rose windows tinted by a blind glazier, but none so wondrous as the illuminated book filled with all manner of unnatural & fantastical beasts refused entry to the Ark by Noah when he set sail in the Great Flood. I acquired this book from an Antiquary's widow on the Island of Rhodes & presented it to the Doge of Venice, to whom I was a royal Emissary in the year of our Lord 1347. Now, as we know, the first bestiary, called the Book of Life, was a natural history of all the beasts delivered unto the Earth at the Creation. Only God Himself saw the original, but its offshoots were transcribed & scattered in monasteries throughout Christendom. Over many centuries, divers monks and scholiasts attempted to consolidate these bestiaries, but one fugitive volume eluded them & came to be called the Caravan Bestiary *after an Alexandrian Greek smuggled it by Caravan across the Libyan Desert. Compiled by many hands, this book of lost beasts, that were left to their fate in the Flood, was composed in Aramaic, & appended in countless tongues—Armenian, Arabic, Coptic, Greek, Latin, Provençal & our own French. Many times the book has surfaced & been lost, & in pursuit of it, men have suffered torture, imprisonment, & death at the stake. The book itself avoided the Inquisition's fires. But by the year 1255 no man alive had seen it, or could claim to know of men deceased who had, & so it was said to have disappeared forever. . . .*

—Duc D'Épernay
Paris, 1368

I

THE FIRST BEAST I laid eyes on was my father.

At all hours his roars reverberated, breaking into my sleep, rattling the windows. When he entered my doorway, he filled it. That was my earliest impression: he was bigger than the door. And he came from far away, smelling of the sea, snow fringing his thick coat and woolen cap.

We lived in four dark rooms. I shared a room with an old woman, my mother's mother. My father slept in the room across the hall, tossing on the rusty box springs, snoring loudly. He was a restless sleeper, getting up many times in the night, his footfall heavy on the creaking boards. Then there was the kitchen, a low-ceilinged room with a black stove and a round table where my grandmother fed me.

When shadows moved through those rooms, brushing my skin like mist, I could hear their subtlest workings. Sound was my primary sense. The world seemed to be coming to me through my ears. Water trickling through wall pipes, steam knocking in the radiator, a mouse scratching, a fly buzzing. In sleep my grandmother's breathing was punctuated by a whistle from the gap in her teeth. Everything else out of her mouth was a whisper. She whispered to me continuously, as she must once have whispered to my mother.

I believe my grandmother was telling me things, and when I came to understand words, they were already embedded in my consciousness. Dates, names, places that could not have arrived there by any other route. My grandmother's history, my mother's—the story of their lives, which I had just entered, a character in my own right.

My mother died in childbirth.

That was when my father began to roar. In my first year, this was how I knew him. Then one day he fell silent, as if he had dived into a deep pool inside himself from which, in my presence at least, he never truly emerged.

THERE WAS A DOG AND A CAT. The first nonhuman beasts I would know. The dog was my grandmother's. He was a German shepherd, black with a tan muzzle, named Re. He slept at the entrance to my room, like a sentry.

The cat had no name. She was orange, with white stripes and golden eyes. When she came to the windowsill from the fire escape, my grandmother fed her kitchen scraps. Sometimes the cat curled up beside me and slept. I remember her warmth, her small breath on my arm, the ticking of her tail against my ribs.

At night my grandmother held and rocked me, stroking my head or singing a lullaby. Her own bed felt far away in the darkness, like a ship across a deep harbor. Mostly I was alone, the window to my left, the door before me, the ceiling overhead lined with plaster cracks—a map of some nonexistent place I studied.

A part of us never leaves the first room we occupy. Everything I was to hear, see, or feel first took shape in that room. It was a world— with landmarks, climate, a population—splintered infinitesimally off the bigger world. The air was dark blue. It moved. Was ruled by currents. Ripples. Fevers of motions.

I felt the spirits of animals. In the instants of entering or leaving sleep I caught glimpses of them: an upturned snout, a lizard eye, a glinting talon, the flash of a wing. Hooves kicked up sparks by my cheek. Fur bristled. Teeth clicked. I heard pants. Howls. Plaintive cries.

And at dawn they were gone.

Тhe first imaginary animal I ever saw leapt out at me from my father's back. He was shirtless, shaving in a cloud of steam with the bathroom door open, when I came up behind him. Inked in blues and reds—with flashes of yellow—the tattoo looked alive, undulating with every movement of my father's muscles, from his shoulders to his waist.

It was a sea serpent. A long scaly body with a horse's head. Flaming mane, fiery tail fin, bared fangs, glowing eyes. A terrifying hybrid. It was surfacing through cresting waves, beneath clouds torn by lightning, with foam streaming off its back.

I cried out, and my father wheeled around, shaving cream on his chin and his razor frozen in midair. Kneeling down, he patted my cheek and reassured me that there was nothing to fear. I didn't agree. To this day, it is the most fearsome tattoo I've ever seen.

"It scares away evil spirits when I'm at sea," he said.

To me, it was an evil spirit.

My father was the man who shoveled coal into the furnace on a freighter. His name was Theodore. His hands were huge, his arms and shoulders knotted like wood. His back so solid it had once bent a knife blade when he was jumped in an alley. He had black eyes, curly black hair, and a thick, close-cropped beard. His eyebrows met above his hooked nose. He wore a heavy medallion on a chain around his neck. When I first saw images of pirates in a picture book, I thought this was what he must be.

Usually he was away for two months at a time. When he came home, even after he had bathed every day for a week, the coal dust still adhered to his hair, his skin, his breath. He would be talking and a black wisp would trail the end of a sentence.

Ports he visited in one year alone: Hamburg, Marseilles, Singapore, Murmansk, Caracas, Montevideo, Sydney. He sailed through the Panama and Suez canals, around Cape Horn and through the Strait of Magellan. He followed the equator across the Indian Ocean from the Seychelles to the Maldives.

Sometimes he sent a postcard from a foreign port. Only one of these has survived, yellowed and crumpled: a tinted photograph of the open-air fish market in the harbor at Tangier. Rows of sardines gleaming silver on rickety carts. The sun casting webbed shadows through the nets hung to dry. A man in a kaftan beating the ink from squid on the seawall. As a boy, I could almost smell the harbor. From the stamp on the other side a man in a red fez gazed out severely. My father's laborious print, in watery ink, turned pale brown over the years. He was a man of few words, written or otherwise.

> *Arrived Friday, leave Tuesday for Alexandria. Raining.*
> *—Theodore Atlas*

His name signed in full. The card addressed to "Atlas," and then our street address.

His parents, married as teenagers, had emigrated from Crete. Their village was perched in the mountains of the interior, amid jagged cliffs, deep ravines, and pine forests. Its inhabitants were like the man Odysseus was told to watch for when he traveled to remote lands carrying an oar—a man who, never having set eyes on the sea, would ask him if the oar was a winnowing fan. These Cretans were farmers and goatherds who never ventured more than ten miles from the houses in which they had been born and would die. My grandparents were an exception.

They settled in the Bronx and died before my father turned sixteen, his mother of diphtheria, his father in an accident on the docks. Like me, my father was an only child, and he had no other relatives in America. Having to support himself suddenly, he dropped out of school. Already over six feet, he could pass for eighteen. He might have become a stevedore, like his father, but instead went to sea, signing on to a freighter flying the Colombian flag, bound for Lisbon.

He had only seen the Atlantic from Jones Beach and Far Rockaway. Just as his ancestors had lived within a tight radius of their village, he had rarely left the South Bronx and only once—a week in the Catskills—been out of New York City. The open sea stunned him. His father had told him that only the sky above the mountains in Crete was bluer, so close to the mountaintops you could reach it by scaling the tallest tree. My father claimed to have done just that on his first visit to his parents' village, several years after I was born—the most expansive statement I ever heard him make.

Still, however, nothing he ever said or did in those days compared in scope to his tattoo. I never really got used to it. And I never forgot that it was there, so at odds with the drab inexpensive clothing that covered it.

When I asked my father about it one day, he told me he had been tattooed in Osaka, Japan. He said he was twenty-five years old at the time. Which meant my mother had lived with it. I wondered what she thought when she saw it for the first time—if it frightened her, too— and how she felt sleeping beside it at night. Even among Japanese sailors this particular tattoo was uncommon. The image was so ferocious that many regarded it as a challenge to the sea gods, which could as easily provoke as appease them.

I encountered the tattoo twice more in my life. The first time was on the docks in Tokyo, where I was boarding a ferry. Three young Japanese sailors, shirtless in the afternoon sun, were awaiting a dinghy that would return them to their ship. One of them turned into the wind to light a cigarette, and there was the sea serpent on his back, vividly colored. I stopped and stared, moving on only when the sailors stared back.

The second time, some months later, I was in the jungle, certain that I was about to die. The tattoo was on the back of a man who was framed by burning palms, holding a machete. He had a red bandanna tied around his head. For a few seconds, the tattoo hovered before me, the man's sweat running down his back like rain onto the rearing serpent. I thought that tattoo would be the last thing I saw in this life. Then an explosion shook the earth. The man was engulfed in fire. The flames danced on his back as if it were parchment, crumpling the skin, devouring the serpent, before the man was swept up into the air.

M Y NAME IS XENO. The name my mother had chosen for me. She was sure I would be a boy. She was Italian, exposed to Latin in the Catholic Church, and I like to think she derived my name from *xenium*, a Latin word for "gift." But when I asked my father about it, he claimed she had gotten the name from a faded billboard across from their apartment on Tremont Avenue, advertising "Xeno's Eye Drops," a product already long gone in 1950. "She liked the sound of it," he shrugged. "A fancy name." He made it clear he hadn't approved. And, in a dismissive tone, added, "In my people's language, *xenos* means 'stranger.' "

In my mother's family, the second generation descended from immigrants, the men had names like Steven and Edward—Anglicized from "Stefano" and "Edoardo" on their birth certificates. A dreamy, romantic sort, my mother would not have surprised them by naming me "Marcello" or "Rosanno," but no one could understand "Xeno," a name that conjured images of praetors and centurions in ancient Rome. Obviously my father had never explained (or been given the opportunity to explain) the old billboard. And what could he have said, when, in fact, it made little sense to him. My mother was uncharacteristically adamant about the name, and my father adhered to her wishes, duly recording "Xeno" on my birth certificate. Xeno Atlas.

I grew accustomed to my father's absences. It was all I knew. Over the years, he signed on to longer and longer voyages. But I also knew it would have been difficult to have him around all the time. His temper was volatile, his moods quicksilver. Which is not to say I didn't get lonely. Loneliness was at the center of my childhood; from it proceeded all I was to become.

When he met my mother, Marina, in the electric glare and clatter of a street fair, my father was thirty-two and she was nineteen. Just out of high school, she was working in a record store. He courted her for eight months, they eloped, and ten months later I was born and she was gone. He was a man who shared few feelings, but I knew he had been grief-stricken. Even as a small child, I sensed my mother's death was the worst thing that ever happened to him—altering him more profoundly than the loss of his parents. For over fifteen years—half his life—he had been on his own, living closemouthed and tightfisted, on ships and in furnished rooms. Then, out of nowhere, he had fallen in love, and after a spell of brief, apparently intense happiness, had lost everything. He still had me, but I was less a product of his happiness than a reminder of his anguish. His take on the situation was anything but subtle: I had lived and she—the great love of his life—had died. And he resented it bitterly.

My mother was one of three children of a widow named Rose. Rose Conti was a small woman with a tight bun of white hair, thin lips, and a long nose. She had a small mole beside her mouth which in her youth marked one end of her smile. Her ears were pointy, the lobes too small to accommodate earrings. My father always addressed her as "Mrs. Conti." Among the aunts, uncles, and cousins on my mother's side, there were plumbing contractors, electricians, a funeral parlor director, and the one prodigy, my uncle Robert, a certified public accountant who had graduated from night school. None of these relatives ever approved of, or accepted, my father. Whether their rejection of him catalyzed my parents' elopement or whether the latter had incited this vast rebuff after the fact was a murky point. On this, as on so many matters, my father and my grandmother held opposing views. It was amazing after my birth that they were able to coexist under the same roof. For my benefit they maintained a remarkably effective truce. I never heard a cross word pass between them, despite the fact that their dislike was mutual and unyielding.

Their typical conversation went like this:

"I'll be back in two months," my father would say. "The bills are paid. There's four hundred dollars in the bread box. Do you need anything else?"

The tin bread box, a blonde girl with a basket of wheat painted on its slide-up door, was where my grandmother kept money, never bread. "How about that you tell O'Dowd the landlord to fix the faucets in the bathtub," she would reply. "Sometimes they both run hot. Maybe that's how they work in Ireland. But Xeno could get scalded. I told O'Dowd plenty of times, but maybe he's going to listen to you."

"I'll speak with him."

Throughout my childhood, I never met anyone else in my mother's family, and they made it clear they didn't want to meet me. After my mother eloped, all of them, including my grandmother, severed contact with her. Their list of grievances was long: she had been married in secret, outside the Catholic Church, by a justice of the peace; my father, poor, practically a greenhorn, was at the base of the social ladder; and, worst of all, he wasn't Italian. They were a hard-bitten, intolerant lot. "He could have been a Jew, or colored," one of her nastier cousins remarked. "Otherwise, it couldn't be worse."

The day before my mother's funeral, my father informed the family of her death. His intermediary was an Armenian priest, the brother of a shipmate, who returned grim-faced from his mission. The sight of an Orthodox priest had merely fanned their anger. My grandmother was the only one of them to attend the funeral. She broke down, and the following day she turned up at our door carrying a suitcase filled with baby necessities. She looked hard at my father, and without a word began caring for me. She seemed to take this as a given, her unquestioned duty: her daughter was dead and there was a newborn infant. That trumped all previous history.

At times my grandmother's silence—toward my father, in particular—resounded in our small apartment as loudly as his voice. Unfortunately she died when I was eleven, so I never heard, through adult ears, her full and true take on him. All I had to go on was innuendo, tiny shifts of expression, intimations of what was not being said. Between my grandmother and my father there was not so much a gulf as a desert, stark and measureless. Even if each of them, with the best intentions, had set out to cross it, the chances are nil that they ever would have met. And they never did.

M Y GRANDMOTHER had strong connections to the animal spirits in the house. At times I thought I heard her talking to herself in Italian, only to realize she was conversing with creatures invisible to me. When I inquired, she muttered words like *lupo, struzzo, drago,* which I soon learned meant "wolf," "ostrich," and "dragon." She believed these spirits were everywhere. Billions, trillions, of animals had come and gone on this earth, she liked to say, so how could it be otherwise. Their bodies returned to dust, but their energy must remain behind, finding new vessels, new outlets.

When we went for walks in the park, she talked about the animals she saw embodied in other people. The animals those people had been in previous lives. She believed they displayed the vestiges of these lives—the man with bovine eyes, the woman with a rodent's teeth, the sheepish, catty, and pig-headed among us. There is the cliché about people who resemble their dogs; or is it the other way around? Does it become impossible to say after such resemblances have been passed back and forth long enough? In crowds my grandmother picked out wolves and vultures, rats and tigers. "*Piccioni,*" she murmured, as we left the park, pointing to a stone bench where, in gray coats, with darting beady eyes, pigeonlike old men were tossing bird seed to pigeons. Never much of a churchgoer, my grandmother was a pagan at heart. Maybe literally so.

Her parents were Sicilian, from a mountain town southwest of Messina. She was born there, and before they emigrated to America, her father bought and sold mules. Her grandfather was a woodsman. He chopped down trees, hewed them, and sold the wood in nearby villages. He married a woman he met deep in the forest, who told him she was the runaway daughter of a priest. Some villagers said she was not Christian at all, but a *dryada*—a wood nymph—attached to a pagan coven.

Her name was Silvana. She had red hair and black eyes. Though she wasn't able to read or write Italian, much less Greek, she could recite from memory pre–Homeric hymns celebrating Artemis and Hera. They flowed from her like music. No one could explain where she had learned ancient Greek, last spoken in eastern Sicily in the third century B.C. when it was an Athenian colony. My grandmother remembered her father telling her how as a boy he had scoured mountain caves for mushrooms with his mother. She would add them to a stew of field onions, yams, and blue turnips, cooked over a fire in a black pot.

My great-great-grandmother Silvana had even stronger connections to the animal world, living as she did in the wild. However embellished or distorted they might have become over several generations, the stories about her always boiled down to the same elements: small animals followed her without fear; birds alighted on her shoulders; wild beasts refrained from harming her; and somehow she knew how to communicate with all these creatures in their own languages.

I didn't know about the rest of it—I never saw a sparrow perch on my grandmother—but I was sure this last power of communication had been passed down from her own grandmother. I knew, too, that it hadn't continued on to me. Perhaps one of my American or Sicilian cousins was the recipient. That I was attuned to the spirits around me was enough. I took it as an extension of my grandmother's powers. A gift.

On countless nights after tucking me in, my grandmother retired to her bed and told me animal stories, punctuated by sound effects, out of the darkness. I heard about the one-wingèd stork that flew over the Alps and laid an egg from which an entire city was born; and the serpent that ate the moon and spat out a skyful of stars; and the black bear that fell asleep on a mountaintop and awoke a hundred years later in the same spot, now a tiny island in the sea, and turned himself into a whale. All of this was accompanied by sound effects—growls, beating wings, birdcalls—so authentic that I always imagined my grandmother as the animal in the story. Often a fantastic animal, like the ones found in her stories; an animal, that is, no longer, or never before, or soon-to-be found in nature.

Late one night, after she finished one of her stories, the stray headlight of a passing car shone through the window and I was stunned to see, not my grandmother, but a red fox, with a ring of white fur around its neck, stretched out on her bed.

I cried out, and Re started barking. A moment later, the lamp came on and there was my grandmother, sitting up in bed. She was wearing a red nightdress, with a white shawl around her shoulders.

"It's all right, child," she murmured, coming over and laying her palm against my cheek. "You were dreaming."

I shook my head.

"Yes, you were dreaming," she nodded.

I turned onto my side and she rubbed my back and sang a lullaby.

The next morning I found a white whisker on the floor. Re's whiskers were black, and it was too long to have come from the cat that visited us. I saved the whisker, keeping it inside a silver music box that once belonged to my grandmother. When you raised the lid, and saw yourself in the mirrored interior, that same lullaby played.

WᴴᴱN ᴍʏ ɢʀᴀɴᴅᴍᴏᴛʜᴇʀ grew infirm, my father hired a young Albanian woman to take care of me. Her name was Evgénia. She was thin and pale, with sharp features and straight black hair. Her blue eyes shone brightly in her pale face. She spoke softly, with a strong accent. A neat dresser, she favored plain dresses and cardigans and rubber sole shoes. Outdoors she always wore a hat.

My grandmother told me Evgénia had lost her entire family when the Nazis overran Albania. Evgénia herself had escaped into Macedonia, then Turkey, and using what money she had, bribed her way onto a passenger ship bound for America. That was all my grandmother knew, for it wasn't territory Evgénia liked to revisit. At first, my grandmother was wary of Evgénia, as she would have been of any outsider. But Evgénia won her over. She never shirked her duties, cut corners, or complained. She didn't allow me to leave the house in clothes that were not clean and pressed. She never lost her head. And she was a good cook. In short, we were lucky to have her. Yet, though quietly good-humored, she remained a mysterious sort of character, and by her own peculiar logic, my grandmother found this comforting, reasoning that such a person would be self-involved, not inclined to meddle.

It was true that Evgénia was a private person—averse to small talk, comfortable with silence—but she was not selfish, and I never knew her to be dishonest. More trusting of children than adults, she was, in fact, a very tender woman, without whose devotion my own childhood would have been far rockier.

In time I learned more about her, but at first there were only these facts: she was unmarried, lived alone in Brooklyn, took three subways to get home, learned English at Berlitz, and had come to us through an agency, with excellent references.

She didn't touch alcohol or tobacco, but she drank many cups of black tea during the day and for lunch always ate a salted cucumber and a hard-boiled egg.

When I asked why she never varied her lunch, she replied, "Eggs give you energy, cucumber refreshes the spirit."

That was one of the few times she referred to the spirit, my grandmother's favorite topic.

Evgénia came into my life when I was eight years old. The previous year we had moved into a bigger apartment. Again it was dark, with most of the windows facing north, but I had my own room finally. My grandmother occupied the room beside it, through a door which I liked to have open when I slept.

Every Sunday Evgénia helped my grandmother into her best black dress and took her downstairs to a gray sedan idling at the curb. From the window I watched a stocky man in a brown suit help her into the front seat. He had a pencil moustache and thinning, slicked-down hair combed across his large head. This was Robert, my mother's older brother. He would drive my grandmother to her sister Frances's house for dinner with the rest of the family, including her many other grandchildren, nieces, and nephews.

Once I heard my grandmother remark to Evgénia that she wanted to take me along. "But Robert, my son, won't allow it. One day he's gonna have to," she added defiantly.

That day never came.

I was not to meet Robert's children, his brother's children, my great-aunt, nobody. He never relented. I had enough of my father's pride and anger to tell my grandmother the feeling was mutual.

"I don't want to meet any of them," I said bitterly, "especially him. If they hated my mother, and now me, I want no part of them."

My grandmother looked pained, furrowing her brow. Usually she confined expressions of feeling to her eyes—just a glance or a flicker to clue you in. She didn't defend my uncle, or herself, didn't offer excuses, but neither did she give me the satisfaction of agreeing outright.

Warmer hearted than anyone else in her family, she nevertheless would not speak against them—especially under my father's roof.

Yet, to the end, she defied them by remaining with my father and me when she could have been living with her sister or one of her sons. Her other grandchildren saw her for a few hours a week, while she devoted most of her time to me.

I could console myself with this knowledge, but, in truth, the ongoing rebuff from my mother's family hurt badly. As I grew older, and understood better how cowardly, how insane, it was to punish a child for choices his mother made before he was born, I knew my instincts had been correct and I was better off having no contact with these people.

E VGÉNIA ARRIVED at dawn and left at dusk, except on Sundays. After I dressed, we gave Re his morning walk, down Webster Avenue where the shops were opening, the grocer stacking pyramids of fruit, the old man at the Chinese laundry ironing in the window. Then she heated me milk with honey stirred in, and toasted rolls already buttered, and joined me at the table with her first cup of tea, to which she added a spoonful of blackberry jam. At eight o'clock she sent me off to school with two quarters for a hot lunch at the cafeteria.

Evgénia and I got along well, and I came to trust her implicitly. When she thought I was out of line, she called me "Effendi Xeno," raising her voice a notch. Outside the house, away from my grandmother and father, she relaxed out of her role.

During our walks, she liked to talk about the birds we spotted: the thrushes, bluejays, doves, and cardinals that lived nearby, in the New York Botanical Garden. She could identify every type of cloud, from cumulonimbus to altocumulus. "And highest of all," she said, "the cirrostratus you can only see from the mountains. In my country, people say angels make their wings from those clouds."

"Do you believe in angels, Evgénia?"

She hesitated. "No. But that doesn't mean they don't exist."

Sometimes, sitting on a bench outside the candy store, sipping Cokes, we played the game of guessing people's occupations, the nature of their errands, and their destinations. It was a game I liked because, without conclusive answers, our conjectures took on lives of their own, entertaining us long after the person had disappeared. Evgénia was good at it. From the way she picked out and assembled details, I sensed she had seen more of life, across the social spectrum, than she let on. Maybe more, at thirty-two, than she had wanted to see.

At dinner she read me human interest stories from the *Daily News:* a French balloonist had sailed over the North Sea; a doctor in Antarctica had removed his own appendix. "You'll like this one, Xeno," she said one night: " 'When the floodwaters reached Memphis, a dog and two pigs were observed sailing down Davis Avenue in a small boat.' "

At first the new apartment was as stark as the first, but one day, offhandedly, my grandmother suggested Evgénia try sprucing it up.

"Some plants, you know. Get fabric, too, and I'll sew new curtains."

"Any particular colors?" Evgénia said.

"You pick."

Evgénia fixed up the place far more than my grandmother had expected, trying to make it cheerful for me. She hung white embroidered curtains in the kitchen. In my room she laid a red comforter on the bed and replaced the drab muslin curtains with bright green ones imprinted with jungle animals. She bought a Persian rug for the living room and placed jade plants and potted palms around the house and a spider plant in the front window. She put white lampshades from Woolworth's on the old ceramic lamps that flanked the sofa. Across from it she set a fishbowl with fantails, their ribbony fins a turquoise swirl. In the front hall she hung framed photographs of alpine vistas: the Himalayas, the Andes, and her native mountains, the Albanian Alps.

Isolated and unsociable long before she came to live with us, my grandmother seemed oblivious to such amenities; but, even for her, my father's neglect of his (and my) surroundings had had its limits. He never treated any house I shared with him like a home. He came and went as he saw fit, carrying his essentials in a seaman's trunk. Over time, the ships he sailed on were fueled by oil, not coal. He was elevated to boatswain, supervising the engine room. It was still hard physical work, but now he was also responsible for a team of five other men. He told me some of the places he visited, but without a trace of romance or adventure, without mentioning the sights he must have

taken in—the Southern Cross shimmering on the horizon, mountainous icebergs, volcanic islands enshrouded in fog—and the marine
creatures, from flying fish to narwhales, he encountered. I got all of
this from books, which I read in hopes of getting closer to him. When
this didn't happen, I grew even more resentful, as always happened
when I tried too hard with him. That terse postcard from Tangier was
my father at his most outgoing. He believed displays of enthusiasm,
spontaneous emotion, jarred your inner compass and diluted your focus. And what was it he was so focused on?

For many years we had no television. My grandmother wouldn't
allow it. Her reasoning was simple: "They want to control your
dreams." It was not a political conspiracy she feared, but the fact that
such an onslaught of visual information, ingested so rapidly, must corrupt the imagination, crowding out the naturally acquired imagery of
life. For her this was a visceral, not a philosophic, issue. When I persuaded Evgénia to help me buy a small black-and-white portable late
in my grandmother's life, we kept it in a closet. I watched it surrepti-
tiously in the kitchen. The picture was cramped, the sound tinny. I
favored the old cartoons—old even in the 1950s—in which the pro-
tagonists were animals. They weren't so much fables, like Aesop's—in
which a turtle outfoxes a hare or a fox is tricked by a stork—as conventional human comedies in which animals stood in for people. A pig in
coveralls who ran a general store was beset by troubles: a hectoring
wife and lazy son (also pigs), a sneaky clerk (ferret), cranky customers (hippos), an unscrupulous competitor (wolf), and pesky mice (in
cameo roles as real mice) who foiled cat burglars. These cartoons were
testaments to my grandmother's notions about the animal natures of
people, with animals functioning directly as those archetypes. I
wanted to share the cartoons with her, and one day I got up the
courage to do so. I thought as a younger woman she might have seen
them at the movies, where they often preceded the main feature. She
hadn't, and after watching a couple, she got hooked, and the television
was awarded a permanent place in the living room. Now, in the
evenings, I was able to watch the *The Lone Ranger* and *Tarzan* and
some Yankee games.

My school was a boxy brick building on a busy street. I was dazed at first by the commotion of a large public school. Socially it was a relief to be one of many, to lose myself in the stream of bodies in the hallways. The classes were full, and during recess about two hundred children crowded the playground. I was good at sports, but indifferent to my studies. I grew bored easily. As an only child in an insular household, I had grown accustomed to devising my own forms of entertainment. Rote lessons and the memorization of facts left me cold.

I frequently got into trouble: listening to a transistor radio through an earphone, reading comic books, chewing gum. In truth, I wanted to be caught out because the punishment usually got me out of the classroom, even if I did have to stand at attention in the hallway. My rebellion took other forms. I could write with either hand, and when my teachers insisted I restrict myself to one hand or the other, I did it all the more. A couple of times I got myself sent home early, claiming to be sick, but Evgénia saw through my lies and scolded me. After that, if I got restless, I cut school altogether.

In the cafeteria we sat at long Formica tables beneath fluorescent lights. The menu was the same each week: chicken à la king, macaroni and cheese, meat loaf, spaghetti, fish sticks, and Jell-O embedded with fruit cocktail for dessert.

In the playground I hung out with a group of boys who were also troublemakers. My nickname was X, of course, which I shared with a big ruddy Irish kid named Xavier, a known bully who was a grade ahead of me. For the audacity of allowing myself to be called X, he challenged me to a fight. He was a head taller than me, but other boys had heard him taunt me, and I wasn't about to duck out. He was strong, but clumsy. He didn't throw punches, or even kick. Instead he came right at you and applied a crushing headlock until you begged for mercy. He demanded I renounce the nickname X. "Tell 'em never to call you that," he growled. I refused (though I didn't even like being called X), and he squeezed so hard that my face turned blue. The other boys grew alarmed, shouting at me to give in, but I wouldn't. My eardrums were pounding, and my nose started to bleed, and when he released me finally, I collapsed. For days I plotted my revenge. It came a week later when he waylaid me again, eager to work me over. My father once told me that in a fight, even with someone bigger than you, the trick is to break his nose: the shock will stop him cold. Xavier pushed me against a wall and closed in, a twisted smile on his face. I let him think I was scared. Then, as he leaned down to hook my head under his arm, I planted my feet and punched him in the nose as hard as I could. "Fuck you!" he sputtered, and I hit him again. This time the cartilage crunched. Blood spurted. And he dropped to his knees, wailing. I pushed him to the ground and pinned his chest with my knee. "Don't ever come near me again," I shouted into his face. And he never did. Nor did anyone else pick a fight with me.

It was at school that the loss, and ongoing absence, of my mother felt most acute. Because of my erratic performance and bad behavior, my various teachers had asked to see my parents. I always managed to deflect them when I said my mother was dead, my father was at sea, and my grandmother was sick. I took a perverse satisfaction in watching their faces when I recited this litany, but it didn't compensate for the hollowness I felt. It was especially painful when I began thinking of my teachers in relation to my mother. They were all women, about the age she would have been. Knowing my mother's face from a handful of photographs, I looked for resemblances. My third-grade teacher, Mrs. Borodin, was most similar, with wavy brown hair and dark brown eyes. I wished I could see her, just once, outside of school.

One day I lingered after class and asked if she would take me home for dinner. She was startled, but kind enough not to embarrass me, even as she turned me down.

"I have a husband and two children, Xeno," she said, "and I need my time with them. It wouldn't be fair . . ."

It wasn't fair, either, when she wrote a letter to my father, expressing her concerns about me, including this incident. My grandmother got wind of the letter and grew cross with me, as she rarely did.

"How could you do such a thing?"

"What did I do, Grandma?"

"Asking the teacher to give you dinner—like we don't feed you here."

It didn't occur to her (or if it did, she squelched the thought) that maybe this had more to do with the fact her own family never deigned to meet me, much less invite me to dinner.

Her pride was hurt, and that cost me a beating. My father, who happened to be home at the time, had been content to rebuke me in passing when he read the letter; but hearing my grandmother's complaints, confronted by the shame she so obviously felt, he got angry too—at her as much as me. He whipped off his belt, and lifting me by the collar, lashed me across the buttocks. I was furious, but I wouldn't give him the satisfaction of crying out.

That night I went to bed, and choking back tears, tried to figure out how I could run away. I'd steal some money from my grandmother's purse and pack food in a bag. Then I'd ride the subway to Penn Station and take a train west, high into the mountains, or stow away on a ship to a deserted beach, where I'd find a fisherman's shack with a stove and a bunk, and never come back. Or maybe that ship could leave me in a place even more timeless and remote where, however briefly, I would share my mother's company. My mother as someone I could touch, not just a photographic image or a phantom of my imagination or the name that on rare occasions slipped from my grandmother's lips. *Marina.*

When I awoke hours later, I saw something perched on my windowsill. Its wings, tail, and spiky crest were silhouetted against a yellow moon. I was frightened but also thrilled when I realized it was one of the two griffins that graced the parapet of the First National Bank, which I passed on my way to school. They fascinated me, lifelike, forever poised on the verge of flight. I always looked up to see if they had moved (they never did). Now one had come to my window. Or was I still dreaming, agitated by the day's events, my mind in a ferment?

As a child, the poet William Blake claimed to have encountered a tree filled with glittering angels. When he reported this to his parents, his father beat him. I didn't make that mistake: I knew better than to risk another whipping.

At the bank the next morning the griffins were in their usual positions, stony wings enfolded, on opposite ends of the parapet. It seemed something was different—that one griffin's head was tilted left now instead of right. I couldn't be sure, but in a world of infinite metamorphoses—only a fraction of which we're privy to—who can cleanly separate the fantastical from the commonplace? Who would want to? Blake went on to encounter more ominous angels, and at the age of thirty-three wrote that there are vast worlds closed off to us by our five senses; that, entombed within the cavern of the self, we look out through narrow chinks.

Perhaps, I thought, that griffin flew off to a new perch each night; or it may have returned to my own window many times while I slept. As with the fox, I couldn't be sure whether I had been gazing into, or out of, the world of dreams. I did know that this had been a seminal moment in my life. If nothing else, I had learned that the monsters we suspect are at the door (or window) might in fact be there—and sometimes we even see them.

M Y FRIEND BRUNO MORETTI kept a menagerie. He lived in a two-family brick house with his parents and sister. His father was a captain in the Fire Department. His father's brother was a policeman who occupied the other half of the house with his wife and four children. The two halves of the house were identical, like a Rorschach test, each with a yellow front door, blue shutters, and a cement walk through tidy rows of azalea bushes.

Bruno was sickly. He had been born with one lung and barely survived a bout of meningitis. Everyone in his extended family indulged him. He had one sister, Lena, who was a year younger. Lena was very pretty, with braided blonde hair and deep gray eyes. I had a crush on her. I had never known anyone—especially another child—with so much reserve, such an aura of mystery. Even Evgénia seemed easier to read.

Both of us outsiders of a different sort at school, Bruno and I had grown close. I was always welcome at his house. In the summer, the Morettis had weekend barbecues in the common backyard. We ate hamburgers and hot dogs, corn on the cob and mickies—Idaho potatoes tucked into the coals to roast. An AM radio blared top-ten hits. The younger kids ran through a sprinkler. Bruno's mother and his aunt, bleached blondes who kept up a steady chatter, set out salads and side dishes on the redwood table. I welcomed the commotion, just as I did at school. I felt like a prisoner on furlough, away from the apartment where my grandmother was rapidly becoming a ghost and my father's presence was even less substantial.

Bruno and I spent a lot of time in his room, with his animals. Bruno was slight, with wispy brown hair and small hands and feet. He walked with a limp and wore thick eyeglasses. He suffered from

migraines. As with his one eyelid that drooped, these were aftereffects
of the meningitis. He had premature lines on his forehead and nearly
transparent skin, and at times his lips were so white it seemed as if no
blood were reaching them. He was by far the smartest kid in our class.
A whiz who every year took first prize at the science fair.

A number of creatures—some in cages, others roaming freely—
cohabited in his room: two parrots, a lizard, a cockatiel, a monkey, a
ferret, a family of tortoises, and two black cats that had been rescued
from a junkyard. They were surprisingly harmonious. The cats and
tortoises frequently beat a path to Lena's room, and the ferret liked to
sun himself on the windowsill in the hall.

On his walls Bruno had tacked up pictures of extinct or soon-to-
be-extinct animals he had cut out of nature magazines. The Hawaiian
crow, the yellow ibix, the Talbot hound, the Comoros dolphin, the
Carpathian vole, and the spotted squirrel of New South Wales comprised the first of six rows of pictures. It was a painful gallery: the
doleful headshots resembled the grainy photographs of the newly
dead in newspapers.

Bruno and Lena knew all about each of these animals: habitat, ex-
tant population, food supply, and predators, which invariably meant
man, either by his actions or neglect. The Hawaiian crow, for example, was being wiped out by a combination of sugarcane pesticides and
California blue jays—recklessly introduced to the islands—that raided
the crows' nests for eggs. The ibix was being poached for its lush
feathers in Brazil. Bruno received newsletters from animal rights organizations and was taken to their gatherings in the New York area by
his father, a red meat eater who I didn't think had lost much sleep over
the Carpathian vole.

Lena wanted to be a veterinarian. Bruno's ambition was to become
a field biologist. For my birthday he gave me a gift subscription to
the magazine *Animal Habitat,* which featured articles on topics such
as the night vision of the Tasmanian quoll and primate epidemics in
the Sumatran rainforest.

Lena and Bruno showed me what caring for an animal really
entailed, nursing a two-week-old mouse with an eyedropper and cooling

down a monkey with a high fever. Once I watched Lena bandage an iguana's foot, deftly wrapping gauze and affixing tape even while the animal squirmed in her arms. She not only helped her brother with his animals, but in the basement spent many hours tending to a group of her own. They were animals too sick or injured to be kept at shelters: cats stricken with leukemia, birds with broken wings, a poisoned squirrel on the mend. There was a set of cages along the wall, a table, a sink, and shelves Mr. Moretti had built, stocked with medicine and bandages.

Lena was born with a big heart. In Bruno's case, I think his own physical infirmities had made him simpatico. He sometimes fell asleep at his desk, the dinner tray his mother had prepared untouched beside him. But what he lacked in stamina, he made up for in patience. Bruno was the most directed person I ever knew. His focus rarely strayed from flesh-and-blood animals, their plight in a hostile world and the tough scientific work that might save them. He had little interest in their imaginary incarnations. Yet once he had had a powerful vision himself which he shared with me.

"When I had meningitis," he said in his high-pitched voice, "my fever hit 105. I saw an animal with three heads and a body that was lion in front, goat in the middle, and dragon in the rear. The heads of those animals, off a single neck, shot fire. I started screaming. My father ran in and said I was hallucinating. But I'll never forget it."

A few years later, I would find the chimera featured in a book about fabulous beasts. Only one chimera ever walked the earth, in ancient Lycia in Asia Minor, where it devastated the countryside. It was killed by the young adventurer Bellerophon upon his wingèd horse, Pegasus—itself a magical creature. All that survives of the chimera is its name, which has devolved into a common noun, signifying the impossible or fanciful. But the chimera embodied a fiercer truth, which soon enough I would learn for myself: our illusions can ravage us as mercilessly as violence or disease. And the illusions of others, when they take on lives of their own, are even more dangerous.

Every year my father seemed to have more money. The size of the check that arrived each month became large enough to elicit even my grandmother's approval. He didn't suddenly begin to dress better or modify his other habits: twenty-cent cigars, cheap beer, riding the subway and never taking cabs. I found his stinginess with himself oppressive, and swore that when I had my own money I would deny myself nothing. Once I overheard him say on the telephone (to whom, I didn't know) that, having stashed away his savings, he hoped to buy shares in a freighter. It sounded like a pipe dream for a lowly seaman, but I realized he had bigger ambitions than I'd thought. He would never discuss them, but perhaps they were finally being realized.

My tenderest memory of my father is a weekend when we happened to be alone and I came down with the flu. My grandmother was away and Evgénia had the week off. Overnight my fever climbed to 104. I kept slipping in and out of sleep, but whenever I opened my eyes, my father was sitting by my bedside. Supporting my head, he raised a glass of water to my lips, laid cold washcloths on my brow, and made me drink a tumbler of cod liver oil and hot lemon juice (the sailor's cure) every few hours. When the fever broke after two days, I opened my eyes on Evgénia sitting in the same chair; my father was out somewhere, and I wondered if it had all been a feverish hallucination. My mother must have known that side of him, I told myself, or she wouldn't have married him. I had mixed feelings, for it was painful to know he could be that caring when he wanted to.

He was away from home more than ever, yet he returned from his voyages with smooth hands and the faintest tan. When I asked him about this, he seemed surprised I had noticed, then replied blandly that he was supervising more and exerting himself less. In this, as in all matters, he had a disarming method of keeping you uninformed: he maintained a silence so profound that when he did share a few elusive facts, it felt like a deluge, until later you realized he had told you nothing.

When he did come home, he visited his doctor or dentist, paid bills, and slept long hours. I usually received one full day of his attention. On a typical outing, we ate breakfast at a diner before attending a soccer match on Randall's Island or a track meet at Fordham. He didn't care for conventional American sports, and was bemused by my interest in baseball. His passion was Greco-Roman wrestling. Not the crooked circus of professional wrestling, but the "pure sport," as he called it, still practiced by gifted amateurs. He saw it as a true contest, mano a mano; a manly pursuit, for athletes and spectators alike. Outside of collegiate competition, there was little Greco-Roman activity in the United States. Around Christmas a meet was held at Madison Square Garden, but my father was rarely home during the holidays. So we went to exhibitions at a small athletic club in Queens.

Flimsy folding chairs and two tiers of benches surrounded the ring. The room was dimly lit and poorly ventilated, smelling of sweat and liniment. The spectators were hard-core aficionados, all male. They drank Turkish coffee and smoked oval cigarettes. I never saw my father so engaged by any activity—or so talkative. He watched intently, commenting on the various holds, the precise footwork and positioning. He referred to the wrestlers by nicknames, "the Goat" and "the Ram," which they both lived up to. The Goat had nimble goatlike feet and, yes, a blond goatee, while the Ram, with unruly red hair and short legs, snorted loudly.

In the ancient Olympics, my father informed me solemnly, wrestling had been second in importance only to the discus throw.

"The wrestlers were naked, with olive oil rubbed on their bodies," he explained. "They wrestled outside in the sun. Back then, it was part of a boy's education: you practiced every day, just like grammar and numbers."

As we took our seats, he explained the basics. "See, the ring is perfectly square, twenty-four feet on each side. Most of the action takes place in that circle in the center. No holds allowed below the waist. No holds using the legs. No tripping. It's all balance and leverage. Agility. Endurance."

The day we saw the Ram battle the Goat, my father pulled at his moustache and told me all the reasons he favored the latter. "Quicker hands . . . superior shoulder strength . . . lateral mobility—plus, he's got the killer instinct."

"How can you tell?"

"Look at his mouth. He never opens it. He breathes through his nose. Stokes his anger. Gets a fire going inside, but stays icy on the surface. That's the sign of killer instinct."

I wasn't sure, even at age eleven, that I agreed with this formulation; but I was interested if only for the fact that, in making it, my father revealed more of himself than usual. I noted, too, that, when animated, he expressed himself with the metaphor he knew best: coal stoking.

He was right about one thing: the Goat was the more powerful wrestler, pinning the Ram, a more muscle-bound man, in less than a minute.

For dinner we went to a nearby restaurant called Samos, run by two brothers from that island. Their specialties were octopus stew and stuffed peppers. They served retsina from the barrel and ouzo in blue shot glasses. Blown-up photographs of Samos's landscape covered the walls. Also an illuminated beer ad in which Miss Rheingold 1961, wearing her crown, stood beside a faux waterfall that appeared to be flowing. The place was packed. The air thick with smoke. My father ordered me the peppers and for himself grilled bass and a glass of wine.

We were in a corner booth. I was surprised to find that he actually knew several people on the premises. A furniture salesman in a plaid jacket who patted me on the head and introduced himself as Artie. And one of the brothers from Samos, named Manny. And, finally, a

tall seaman with a buzz cut named Gus. I remember them clearly because they were the first men with whom I saw my father socialize.

He was his usual self, though I did glimpse another part of him—if
only a sliver. With Artie, who was also a habitué of the athletic club,
he continued the wrestling patter, and he and Manny bantered about
the food. But it was Gus who interested me the moment I realized he
and my father had been shipmates. Another first. When Gus referred
to their sailing into Caracas at night, pictures opened up in my head:
flickering lights, murky piers, a windswept harbor.

Gus called my father Teddy, which I'd never heard anyone do.
Though at ease, my father maintained his usual reserve, sipping his
wine while Gus threw back several ouzos and chain-smoked Lucky
Strikes. Gus was already a little tight when he joined us. The more he
drank and talked, the more restive my father grew. He was still under
the spell of the wrestling, which he didn't want broken. Besides which,
he didn't feel safe around people who veered, conversationally or
otherwise. Also, I was there.

Calling for the check, my father ordered me to finish my dessert, a
thick rice pudding, while he went to the men's room.

"Yeah," Gus continued, "your old man and me have seen some
places. Down in São Paulo an old woman read my future in chicken
tracks. You know how?"

I shook my head. He leaned forward, his breath like kerosene.

"I give her five bucks. She wets down the dirt and has two chickens
walk around while she talks mumbo-jumbo. Then she reads the tracks."

"How?"

He shrugged. "How should I know?"

"Maybe it's a kind of alphabet."

"Maybe." He lit another cigarette. "You're a smart kid, huh?"

"What did the tracks say?"

"Eh?"

"About your future."

He blew a string of smoke rings. "That I'd have three kids and live
to be ninety." He snorted. "Maybe the second part will come true."

"Do you have kids?"

"Nope. Don't like 'em. Present company excepted," he added half-heartedly. "Anyway, for five bucks the old lady didn't tell me much." He laughed. "For another ten she said she'd cook me the chickens."

I tried to conceal my disgust. "Did she read my father's future?"

"No, he didn't want no part of it."

"No part of what?" My father's voice came up behind me.

"I was telling him about the old lady in Brazil who read the chicken tracks."

My father grunted and examined the check. "Put on your coat, Xeno."

"You got a smart kid here, Teddy."

My father nodded while counting out some bills.

"You never talk about him." Gus was looking at me, smiling, but his eyes were cold. "I don't know why not."

"Come on," my father said to me.

"Hey, one for the road, Teddy?" Gus said.

My father shook his head.

"Suit yourself. So you're in town until Friday. Then you go home?"

My father stiffened. "Then I *leave* home. I'm shipping on the *Hecate* for Barcelona."

Gus looked away, nodding vigorously. "Yeah, that's what I meant."

"Goodbye," my father muttered, clutching my arm and leading me from the restaurant.

On the sidewalk he tried to head off my questions. "Sometimes that's what sailors say when they're putting to sea: 'going home.' "

Speeding through the subway tunnel beneath the East River, I was thinking hard about this. "Do you think of a ship as home?" I asked him.

Without missing a beat, he said, "You'd better think that way about your ship when you're in the middle of the ocean. But, no, I think of our apartment as home."

I didn't believe him. I decided to be as direct as I'd ever been on the subject. "Even though you're on ships more than you're here?"

But he didn't bridle. "Yes," he replied, staring at the lights that flew by.

"Why did you get mad at Gus?" I said.

Asking my father a question like this, however innocently, was usually out of the question. It wasn't that he got angry when you probed: he just clammed up.

This time he looked at me. "Never trust what a man says when he's drinking."

This was not an answer to the question I had asked, and he knew it. But that was all he was going to say.

The door between us had been jarred open a crack, and I had hoped to open it further. But, just as quickly, it closed on me. A few days later, my father set sail. And that same evening, while my grandmother dozed on the sofa and Evgénia prepared dinner, I realized how much it had hurt when Gus said my father never talked about me.

MY GRANDMOTHER DIED on a snowy December night. Only the cause of death was unexpected: she was being treated for kidney disease and intestinal disorders, but she suffered a massive heart attack. She had had her spleen removed the previous winter, after which her sister Frances urged her to move in with her once and for all. My grandmother refused: our apartment had become her home, and sensing that the end was near, she said she wanted to die there.

She rarely left her room that last year. I sat at her bedside for hours at a time, with Re at my feet, beside a table cluttered with pill containers, tonics, tinctures, ointments, lozenges, and a Thermos of blackberry tea, which she believed superior to all her medicines. She sat propped up with a heating pad at the small of her back and packets of herbs beneath her pillow.

Cataracts had set in, but though her vision was darkening, she refused surgery. At first, she continued to watch the morning soap operas. Or she stared out the window at the shadows that shifted, like pieces of a jigsaw, across the building façades. Finally, though, she could only listen to the television. And even when the room was sunlit, all she could see was a vast spiderweb—*una ragnatela vasta.* As her condition worsened, she often lapsed into Italian.

"*I ragni stanno facendo . . .*" she murmured. *The spiders are spinning . . .*

In her mind's eye, however, she saw clearly. She described to me a panther that walked on its hind legs and addressed her in a language she had never before heard but understood completely; a burning salamander that exploded into a rainbow; an eyeless crow with one white and one black wing threading a forest.

"*I demoni,*" she whispered.

The demons that inhabit this world—*to whom the world belongs,* as she once told me—were now everywhere, in all their manifestations.

"No, Xeno, they've been there since the world began," she corrected me, "but now I can see them clearly. The panther—*la pantera*—most of all. He stood right there at the foot of the bed."

I looked at the spot. "What did he say?"

"Ah," she smiled. "Things I wished I knew before, that I can tell you now. So you'll know them all your life. First, he explained why I could understand him. He said before men started their killing ways, they spoke the same language as all the other animals. There was no boundaries between them. Then the worm of cruelty burrowed into man's heart. The animals needed to protect themselves, so they made up their own languages that only their own kind could understand. The same thing happened when men started killing other men. Everyone felt safer talking their own language. They still do."

She sipped her tea.

"Next he told me that there are animals like the phoenix—*la fenice*—that can only live in the world one at a time. You can't be more alone than that."

I was about to pipe in about the chimera, but she was getting short of breath and I didn't want to interrupt her.

"He said there are other animals like that," she went on. " 'The lost animals,' he called them, that didn't make it onto the ark at the time of the Great Flood. One day these animals are gonna be discovered, and all of their stories told, and the great mysteries will come clear." She closed her eyes. "That panther promised me that soon my spirit's gonna move on. If you're lucky, it doesn't live on in heaven—forget all that—but inside another creature on earth. Otherwise, it becomes a lost soul, like one of those seabirds that tries to fly to the moon but instead falls into what my grandmother Silvana called *il mare di tempo*—the sea of time—and never returns. When I was a girl, and we went to

Messina, we waited in the dunes all night for a look at those birds. I don't have to wait long now, Xeno, no matter where I'm going."

"Don't say that, Grandma." I choked back tears, but she was happy with the thought, and she pulled me close and kissed me.

That last night, I was eating a sandwich in the kitchen when I heard a glass break in her room. Then Re started barking. Evgénia had just stepped out the front door, on her way home, and I cried out to her as I raced down the hall.

At my grandmother's door, I stopped cold. Her bed was empty. Re was barking at the window, where the red fox I had seen years before was slipping out onto the fire escape, into the snow.

I turned to Evgénia as she reached my side, and when I looked back into the room, the fox was gone and my grandmother was lying in bed. Her head was tilted and her mouth was open. Her face was white as powder. Shadows from the lamp swam up onto the bed-clothes. The tea from the broken glass was spreading on the floor-boards.

It felt as if my own mouth was filling with sand. I was shaking as I ran over and laid my head on my grandmother's chest, listening for her heart. Evgénia took hold of her wrist, then pressed her neck, searching for an artery.

"I think I hear something!" I cried, but Evgénia shook her head and hurried away to the telephone.

What I heard was my own blood pounding in my ears. I sank to my knees sobbing and at the same time felt as if I were floating far away from myself, that room, my grandmother's body. Despite her bitter-sweet feelings toward my mother, and her strange ways, my grand-mother had been the great constant in my life. I became inconsolable. If it hadn't been for Evgénia, I don't know what I would have done. She was the only one I had to fall back on in those terrible days, and she came through for me.

The ambulance took my grandmother away. And then her family— the family of Rose Conti—prepared to bury her. She was theirs now. And I was not invited to the funeral. Even if my father had been around, I would not have been invited.

Evgénia was outraged. "I won't allow it," she declared.

She had never said such a thing before. Not in all the years she had watched my grandmother's family shun me.

It was Uncle Robert, of course, who made the funeral arrangements. Now, if only for a few seconds, I would see him up close, I thought.

Two days after my grandmother died, Evgénia had me put on my one suit, itchy gray wool, with a black knitted tie that she bought me. She put on a black dress herself. Then at three o'clock, in sharp sunlight, we took the No. 14 bus up Webster Avenue to Cichetti's Funeral Home. The front room, visible through the glass doors, was a kind of fake living room. It had sofas, a Persian carpet, and dim lamps. A poor reproduction of some landscape—trees along a river—hung over the fake fireplace. The air was dusty, waxen, and I didn't want to draw it into my lungs.

Outside the room where she was laid out, my grandmother's name had been tacked onto a board in white letters, like the ones they used to spell out the daily menu in my school cafeteria. Evgénia took my hand and we went in. There were no other mourners present at that hour. The perfume of flowers from various bouquets was overpowering. She was lying in a rosewood casket lined with lavender silk. They had put a blue dress on her and fixed her hair and applied makeup to her face. I had heard people say that, freshly laid out, people look as if they are sleeping; but she didn't look like she was sleeping, she looked dead. It brought me up short. I didn't shed tears by her casket. I don't remember feeling anything at all. In the suffocating stillness of that place I was sure if I looked at my wristwatch—a tenth-birthday gift from my grandmother—I would discover that time itself had stopped.

The funeral service the next day was at Saint Anthony of Padua Church, on another bus route. Wearing the same suit and tie, with Evgénia at my side, I entered the church near the end of the service and sat in a rear pew. My grandmother's closed casket was up at the altar. The priest, flanked by acolytes, was praying over it in Latin. I glimpsed the backs of my relatives' heads, including the children, my cousins, one of whom, a girl about my own age, had the reddest hair I'd ever seen. Once I had seen her in the rear seat of Uncle Robert's car. This was Silvana, named after my great-great-grandmother the dryad; of all my cousins, she was the one my grandmother had most wanted me to meet. "Because you're so much alike," she once remarked. "And she's going to be a great beauty, too." But, thanks to my uncle, I hadn't met her, and now I probably never would. I started to cry again, and for the next half hour I looked around that church, the stained glass, the icons of the saints, the flickering candles, through a veil of tears. And I never did see Silvana's face.

Evgénia comforted me as best she could, keeping her arm around my shoulders, stroking my head. She had done as she promised, and then some. Her courage and audacity did not extend to marching me down the aisle to take my "rightful place," as she called it, in one of the first three rows, reserved for family. Nor would I have wanted her to make this sort of scene; I doubt either of us could have handled the consequences. So, as the service wound down, we walked out of the church, past the hearse and limousines, back to the bus stop.

Some years later, I would discover the location of my grandmother's grave at Sacred Heart Cemetery in Yonkers. But that night, I thought back to the first time my grandmother had taken me to my mother's grave, a few miles to the east, in Mount Vernon. Chosen by my father, her gravestone was a modest slab of marble. Her name and dates were plainly chiseled, and in the upper corner there was a flying fish at the center of a rosette. My grandmother didn't approve of the site, beside an iron fence at the end of a long row of graves. Down a slope of tall grass, traffic hummed on a busy road. Exhaust fumes rose through the trees. My grandmother didn't like the flying fish, either. She said it was a symbol of resurrection for Greek sailors. "Marina wasn't a sailor," she muttered, resentful of this final intrusion by my father. What she wanted to say, and refrained on my account, was that my mother wasn't Greek, but Italian—a distinction to be strictly maintained, even after death. I traced the letters of my mother's name—their edges sharp beneath my fingertip—while my grandmother got to her knees, pulled weeds from the dirt, and planted geraniums. I thought of my mother lying face-up below my feet. Was she just a skeleton now, or was it too soon for that? I noted the dates on neighboring gravestones. Most were for old people. One was for an infant. My mother might have liked that, I thought, since she hadn't had the chance to be with her own child. I realized that if I had died with her, I would have been buried in that place, too. Later, when my grandmother and I walked out the gates and down to the train station, I was glad to have visited, but I wasn't sorry to leave.

I had often asked my grandmother what my mother was like. One night, when she was ailing, she answered more frankly than usual.

"Your mother," she said, squinting across the room as if she might discern her in the shadows. "She loved to dance. At weddings she was the best dancer. She had plenty of friends. When she got married, she was still just a girl. I hoped she would have a nice wedding herself. I thought I knew her." She shook her head. "I didn't, really, and I can't forgive myself for not going to her after she run away."

My grandmother had given me a handful of snapshots of my mother. They were taken before my mother met my father. If he had photos of them together, or of my mother alone during their brief marriage, he had kept them to himself or destroyed them.

In four of the snapshots, taken on a rooftop against a smoky winter sky, my mother looked pensive, staring past the photographer. Was that a friend, or one of her siblings? She was wearing a brown coat and matching beret. The wind was fluttering her long hair.

In the fifth snapshot she looked happy. Wearing a white bathing suit and a sailor cap aslant, she was eating cotton candy at Jones Beach, mugging for the camera. A locker key on an elastic band was fastened around her ankle. She was tanned. Slim. With nice legs. She couldn't have been more than eighteen. On the boardwalk beside her, elongated by the late-afternoon sun, there was an unusual shadow: the photographer, from the neck up, with a large bird perched on his shoulder. The bird had a curved beak and long, forking tail feathers. A distinctive crest—a row of spiky tufts—that ran down its neck made me think it wasn't a parrot. Aside from the bird, there was nothing to distinguish the photographer; not even his height could be ascertained from the shadow.

I had studied this snapshot many times, weaving stories around it:

That the man was a stranger who, upon request, photographed my mother with her own camera.

That he was a boyfriend who happened to own (and take to the beach with him) an exotic bird.

That the bird belonged to a sailor whose cap she had put on (a seafarer who predated my father?) . . . or a vendor (of cotton candy?) . . . or a Gypsy fortune-teller whose booth my mother had visited and learned—what? Judging from her smile, not the fact that she wouldn't live to see her twenty-first birthday. No, in that snapshot, with glowing limbs and bright eyes, she looked as if she would live forever.

The night of my grandmother's funeral, Evgénia stayed in my father's room. And I sat awake in my grandmother's room with Re, who rarely left my side that week. I opened the silver music box containing the white whisker and listened to the lullabye my grandmother used to sing to me. Then I lit the candle that had replaced all the paraphernalia on her bedside table, and Re stared at the window where the fox had disappeared.

THE DAY I had to leave Re with Bruno, a fierce storm hit the city. By three o'clock a foot of snow had fallen. It was so dark the streetlights had come on. Cars were skidding into intersections. Buses weren't running. Re and I walked east, into Bruno's neighborhood, cutting through U.S. Grant Park, onto DeMott Avenue. I ducked my head against the wind and guided Re away from the deeper drifts. In my knapsack I had his food bowl and plaid blanket.

When my grandmother died, the cover she provided for my father's neglect went with her. However comfortable the apartment, he couldn't just leave me alone there, with Evgénia coming in forty hours a week and no one else around on weekends. There could be no pretenses anymore about that aspect of my life. Evgénia had remained with me for several months, but when my father asked her to continue as a live-in caretaker, she declined. Whatever the particulars of her private life, she wasn't willing to give it up. To my surprise, one morning my father woke me with the news that I would be enrolling in a boarding school in Maine. "There's no alternative," he said flatly, stalking from my room with his heavy gait, meaning there would be no discussion, either.

It also meant that Re needed a new home. He and I had become closer than ever. At fourteen, two years my senior, he was ancient for a German shepherd. His strength was ebbing, his vision dimmed, his hind legs stiff with arthritis. That day, he tugged at his leash, for he knew the way to the Morettis' house and enjoyed visiting the other animals. The fact Re was so happy there was the only thing that offset my despair at having to give him up. I had been sick over it for weeks. The Morettis' home was full of strays, and now Re would join them.

They were taking him in unquestioningly, just as they had taken me in. As always, Re sensed what was coming: the previous night he had crouched on my bed and watched me pack. When I slipped under the covers, he laid his forepaws across my ankle and wouldn't lift them until morning.

Now, as I rang the Morettis' doorbell, at least his spirits seemed to have improved, even if mine had not.

Lena let us in. By that time, more than the family comforts and the menageries, my primary delight in visiting the Moretti household was her presence. I brushed the snow from my coat and she gave me a towel to dry Re.

"Here's his bowl," I said, removing it from the knapsack. "And he likes to sleep on this blanket."

"He'll sleep in my room. By the radiator. Can I hang up your coat, Xeno?"

"I can't stay long. I'll just say goodbye to Bruno," I said, starting up the stairs.

I only had a few hours before my father and I were to go to Grand Central and board the train for Boston. At our apartment, my bags were lined up in the hallway and the furniture was covered with sheets.

I found Bruno hunched over his terrarium, feeding the lizards live roaches. In the ultraviolet light he appeared even paler than usual. While my physical capacities were growing as I entered puberty, Bruno's were diminishing. To the list of his afflictions could be added the fact he was going deaf in one ear. I wished that I could lend him some of my own strength.

At that moment, I was overwhelmed by all the things I wanted to tell him. "I'm not just going away, Bruno. I'm losing my home, and Re along with it."

"Re will always be your dog. And Mom told you you can stay with us anytime, not just Thanksgiving and Christmas. I mean, if you're not going to be with your father."

At the Morettis', if nowhere else, I had ceased to be embarrassed by the instability of my life with my father.

"Don't worry, I'll take good care of him," Bruno said as we headed for the stairs.

Passing Lena's room, I felt a tap on my shoulder.

"I'll be right with you," I said to Bruno, who was already descending.

Lena pulled me into her room and closed the door.

Her eyes twinkled in the half-light. "I wanted to say goodbye, too," she said.

I had been in her room many times, but never in such an intimate way. In the silence I could hear the clock ticking on her bureau. Her bed was neatly made, her white curtains open to the falling snow. There was a brass statuette of the Egyptian sphinx on the bureau, a gift from her maiden aunt who had traveled down the Nile with a tour group. Lena was very attached to it, especially after reading about the sphinx. She wasn't one for riddles, but I knew she must feel an affinity for the sphinx's subtler qualities, its unshakable repose.

She smiled at me. Her hair smelled of lavender. Her skin glowed. Around her neck she wore a gold locket, engraved with her initials, that I had never seen before.

I couldn't take my eyes off it.

"Do you like it, Xeno?"

I nodded.

"It opens," she said. Holding it between her thumb and index finger, she released a tiny catch. "See?"

The locket was empty.

She clicked it shut. "Will you come home at Easter?"

"I hope so." I hesitated. "Lena, will you write to me?"

"Of course. And you do the same."

Bruno was calling me from downstairs.

"I'd better go."

Her lips parted, but she didn't speak. She stepped up close and kissed me on the lips, long enough so that I could taste it. My first kiss. Then she opened the door with a small smile.

Saying goodbye to Re, I didn't linger. He rested his head in my lap, then followed me to the door with his eyes. We both knew we wouldn't see each other again. I had never felt worse about anything.

Mrs. Moretti insisted on driving me home. In her station wagon she was a good driver, fearless on the icy streets. She had the radio on low. Nat King Cole was singing.

Mrs. Moretti was not yet forty. But, having had two children so close together, combined with the stresses of her husband's profession and Bruno's health, she seemed decades removed from the slender young woman in the wedding pictures that adorned her mantelpiece. Her blonde hair was streaked gray, her eyes radiated wrinkles. Still, I could see Lena's pretty features in her own.

While she concentrated on her driving, I stared out my window at the dark flakes spinning past. I felt my throat close up, not just on account of Re and Lena; or the fact I was going away; or that I wished Mrs. Moretti could be my mother, too; but because I kept thinking that if my mother had lived I would not be taking this train into the night. I would not have had to endure my father, accompanying me in a double-breasted suit and expensive shoes (he had real money now: I was not even a scholarship student), unusually talkative, even upbeat, insisting this was the best thing that had ever happened to me. He seemed in a hurry. He hastened my farewell to Evgénia, not comprehending, apparently, that I wasn't saying goodbye to hired help, as he was, but to a person dear to me, and with her, an entire portion of my life. Someone who had seen to my daily needs, escorted me to the doctor, taken me shopping for my clothes; who had taught me, by example, to prize my dignity and never pretend I didn't know right from wrong. While he tramped upstairs for our suitcases, I hugged Evgénia by the street door, feeling the rough wool of her coat on my cheek for the last time, and her cool fingers in my hair, and though I wasn't crying, I saw that she was—the only time I ever saw her cry. Then she kissed my forehead and was gone. And two hours later my father and I were rushing north, with the same snowstorm following us, from Boston to Portland to the Canadian border, the wind howling, the darkness deepening, and the temperature dropping below zero at our destination. At a desolate, windswept train station we got into an overheated taxi and rode through a forest to the all-boys boarding school where I would spend the next five years. By the following afternoon, my father was gone and I was ensconced in my dorm room gazing over that vast forest. The trees were glazed with ice. Crows huddled on the upper branches. Isolated in wilderness, the school felt like a prison. Stone buildings with Gothic spires and slate roofs, Spartan dormitories, antiseptic classrooms, immaculate grounds. I hated it. But I learned some hard lessons there that would serve me well, and that I would fully appreciate only after I had departed.

Mrs. Moretti pulled up before my building and switched off the radio. Drifting snow had buried the fire hydrant at the curb.

"Take care of yourself, Xeno," she said, leaning over and kissing my cheek.

I smiled at her, thinking of Lena kissing my lips.

Then I got out and waved, watching her taillights disappear in the dense static of the storm.

2

I FIRST HEARD OF THE *Caravan Bestiary* when I was fifteen years old, and it changed the course of my life.

It was my history teacher, Mr. Cletis Hood, who told me about it in his office one afternoon in my third year at school. That meeting came about because of a lesson several months earlier in which he had mentioned the mythological phoenix in passing, during a discussion of Henry VIII.

Tall and fit, with a wasplike waist, crew cut, and cropped beard, Mr. Hood was at the blackboard rocking lightly on his heels, as was his custom. He always wore a bow tie and a vest. His shoulders were so straight that if a level were laid across them the bubble would be perfectly centered. His voice was equally measured, deep enough at times to sound as if it was echoing within him. He was telling us about Henry's only son, Edward, on whom I became fixated. Known as the "boy-king," Edward was ten years old when he inherited the English throne in 1547. Guided by a regency council, he ruled for six years, and was coming into his own when he died of tuberculosis. His father had been a large man. Tyrannical and secretive. Brooding. Often absent. Though my father fit that description nicely, it was the fact Edward's mother, Jane Seymour, had died in childbirth that made him feel like a kindred spirit. Queen Jane was a great beauty, vivacious, and much younger than her husband. Edward was her only child.

"English monarchs had elaborate crests," Mr. Hood intoned. "Queen Jane's was of a phoenix, a bird reborn from the flames of its own pyre. After his coronation, Edward added a motto to his mother's crest: THAT ANOTHER MAY BE BORN."

My hand shot up. "Sir, were there other imaginary animals that became important in mythology and history?"

"Dozens of them," he replied, glancing at me over his glasses, for he was not used to being interrupted.

"Where can I find them?" I persisted.

"In the library," he replied tartly.

I rushed through my dinner that evening and went to the library. I hadn't spent much time there before. It was impressive, for a secondary school: a huge room with high rows of bookshelves on both the ground floor and the mezzanine, where a faculty monitor sat at a small desk. Despite the grim oil paintings of retired headmasters and the darkly curtained windows, the silence and solitude made it one of the more welcoming places on campus. On the walnut tables, brass lamps cast a succession of amber pools. It was at one of those tables that I began my journey.

First, I pored over every book I could find about Edward, skimming the central issues of his brief reign—war with France, the publication of the first Book of Common Prayer—and searching in vain for additional information about his mother's crest. By the time I moved on to the phoenix, it was ten o'clock and the library was closing.

I carried a satchel of books back to my dormitory: *Zoological Mythology, Mythical Monsters, The Phoenix & the Dragon,* and *A History of the English Bestiary.* Lights-out was strictly enforced at eleven-thirty, and this was the first of many times I got into trouble when the floor monitor caught me reading with a flashlight. I was reading about the phoenix. From my grandmother I knew that there was only one phoenix in the world at any given time. But that was all I knew.

Soon I was discovering countless other imaginary animals—more than I ever expected. Some were obscure, others more visible than we know, all of them vivid. Over time they had passed in and out of our human reality—like the ghosts in folk tales that retreat into mirrors and, when light strikes the glass just so, can be glimpsed.

In the years since my grandmother's death, my connection to the world of animal spirits continued to ebb—as if its source of energy were gone. There had been no apparitions like the griffin for some time.

The subject of imaginary animals had been an essential part of my child-hood, my earliest perceptions, and suddenly I was finding books de-voted to it—books which clued me to the fact that it was a subject at all.

Bestiaries, they are called. I learned that a bestiary is a compilation of real and imaginary animals, the categories frequently blurred. The animals are described in words and pictures, and often framed in alle-gorical terms for the virtues and vices they supposedly share with hu-man beings. The first formal bestiary, a kind of scholarly scrapbook, was assembled by monks in the tenth century. They drew on many sources, but primarily the *Physiologus*, written in Greek by an anony-mous third-century Egyptian. Soon he was known by the same name as his book, for "Physiologus" in Greek means "naturalist." His book contained forty-nine animals. He himself was part of a line that stretched back through Aristotle, Ctesias, and centuries of anony-mous chroniclers to the caves of the earliest men, whose gods and myths were inspired by the beasts they encountered daily, as hunters and hunted—and in their dreams. The first bestiary also drew on the fantastical miscellanies of Physiologus's contemporaries, Aelian and Saint Ambrose (except for Aristotle, all of these names were new to me), and the seventh-century encyclopedist, Saint Isidore of Seville, who devoted the twelfth book of his *Etymologiae* (which I discovered in translation in the library) to animals. In short, the bestiary was in constant flux, layered with Ethiopian, Syriac, Anglo-Saxon, and, espe-cially, Armenian additions until the original text had been absorbed beyond recognition. From the eleventh century on, the bestiary's off-shoots were copied by hand, translated from language to language, ever expanding, until they contained hundreds of entries. The last such copy was made in Iceland in 1724. After that, scholars worked to recover and preserve manuscripts around Europe. A few scoured the mythologies of other cultures—Polynesia, South America, the Far East—and uncovered similar compilations, even more remote in time and composition. A handful searched for undiscovered bestiaries and unknown beasts, fabulous and otherwise.

I discovered that the phoenix originated in Heliopolis, where it was called *benu*—the Egyptian word for "date palm." The Greek word is *phoinix*. It was atop the date palm that the bird built a nest of cassia, spikenard, and cinnamon in which it immolated itself and was reborn from the ashes. Or, as the Egyptians observed: the bird's tomb became its cradle.

The Christians believed the phoenix was granted immortality because it was the only creature that did not eat of the forbidden fruit. The Greeks declared its life span to be a Great Year, the time required by the sun, moon, and five planets to orbit the cosmos: 12,994 common years; after each such cycle, the history of the world repeats itself to the last detail under the planets' influence. The phoenix mirrored this process, with comprehensive images of human history encoded in the intricacies of its plumage. (As if those feathers held the data of a million computer chips.)

This was heady stuff, unlike anything I had ever encountered. During those first weeks, I stayed in the library every night until the lamps were extinguished. Returning to my dorm, drunk on these words and images, I felt as if the animals I'd just read about were peering down at me from the evergreens and steeples and the darkened classroom windows.

The first bestiary I studied was a well-thumbed facsimile edition. The original, illustrated with woodcuts, had been compiled by thirteenth-century monks at the Abbey of Revesby in the north of England. Like the *Etymologiae*, it was kept in the library's restricted room, which I could only enter with the head librarian's permission. The library also contained a battered Oriental bestiary—part of a collection of Oriental texts bequeathed by an alumnus. Its first entry was the three-tailed Chinese fox that lives a thousand years, like the phoenix, and mounts to heaven after sprouting six more tails. I was excited to learn that, during its long life, this fox can assume any human or animal form by striking fire from its nine tails, bowing to Ursus Major, and balancing a human skull on its head. I also read about six-legged antelopes, an eight-legged horse (similar to the Norse Sleipnir that could gallop on clouds and ocean), an ostrichlike bird with three hearts, and a dog like Cerberus, with one hundred heads and a serpent's tail.

Every night I took copious notes, yet struggled to comprehend the context of what I was reading. I knew something about animals, but not much about history. I threw myself into the latter with a passion, to the detriment of my other studies. In science, math, English, my grades dipped; but in history—and Latin and Greek, which had become essential to my study of it—I went to the top of my class. I also excelled in zoology, a sparsely enrolled elective.

After three months in which I had used all my free time to read up on bestiaries, I approached Mr. Hood one day after class. I thought I had gone as far as I could on my own, and I wanted his advice. He was grading papers, but after I told him what I was doing, and what I wanted, he studied me with new interest.

Capping his red pen, he asked, "Why are you doing this, Atlas?"

"It's something I want to know about, sir."

"I can see that. But why?"

Now my palms were sweating. "I just can't get it out of my head."

"Since I mentioned the phoenix?"

"Before that, sir. I just feel like it's taking me somewhere."

This answer seemed to surprise him. But I saw he approved of it, even if he didn't yet know what to make of me. "All right, Atlas, I'll do some digging and see if I can come up with any suggestions."

A few weeks later, he asked me to come by his office after lunch.

A former Marine captain, Mr. Hood had been at the school for six years. He was known as a blunt taskmaster, outwardly humorless, hard on students foolish enough to come to class unprepared. Needless to say, he wasn't popular, but he was respected as a good teacher. An inspired one, if you ignored his outer shell and listened to what he was saying. He taught ancient and modern European history and the advanced Latin class, including medieval Latin. Rumors about him abounded: that, grievously wounded in Korea, he had two artificial limbs; that he was once married to a South American dictator's daughter who committed suicide; that his two children were killed in an automobile accident; that he was independently wealthy and taught on a whim.

His office was spare, with few of the personal touches evident in other faculty offices. Instead of family photographs, he had pictures of historical figures he admired: Alexander the Great, Charlemagne, Captain James Cook. The only mementos were a tomahawk and his Marine battalion's flag, a black eagle ringed with red stars. The bookshelves contained only the texts for his courses, not his personal library. The ashtray cradled a meerschaum pipe. Out the lead-paned window, on the main athletic field, a groundskeeper was laying down yard lines for a football game.

On this day Mr. Hood wore a yellow bow tie and a brown herringbone suit.

"Sit down, Atlas," he said, by way of greeting. "And tell me about yourself."

It was an obvious request, but I hadn't expected it. I assumed he would be all business, as he was in class.

"I guess I'm interested in history."

"You guess? There doesn't seem to be much doubt about it."

"No, sir."

"What have you read recently?"

"I'm reading Solinus's *Gallery of Wonders*."

He raised an eyebrow. "Not in Latin?"

"No, sir. I tried, but I'm not ready for that."

He sat back in his swivel chair, and I thought maybe I'd gone up another notch in his estimation. "I read Solinus a long time ago," he said. "I remember that he drew a great deal on Pliny."

"I didn't know that. I've never read Pliny, sir."

"I expect you will by the time you reach my Latin class," he said drily. "Now, the last time we spoke you told me your interest in all of this is long-standing."

"Yes, sir. Not in bestiaries—I didn't know about them."

"I understand that. In animals, and animal lore. Why?"

How could I tell him that, on one side of my family, I was descended from a wood nymph; that birds perched on her shoulders and wild beasts grew tame beneath her touch; that my grandmother could channel animals' spirits. "My grandmother," I said. "She used to tell me stories about animals."

He raised an eyebrow. "Including phoenixes and the like?"

"Especially those animals, sir."

He mulled this over, then said, "You're from New York."

"The Bronx, sir."

"And your father is a seaman. Navy?"

"No, sir. He sails on freighters."

"Any brothers or sisters?"

I shook my head. "My mother died when I was born."

Now it was he who was caught off guard. His eyes softened, but without missing a beat he said, "I know you've studied the Revesby bestiary. I have something for you." He took a large green book from the desk drawer. "In your explorations, have you come across the Hereford bestiary?"

"No, sir."

He handed me the book. "You have now," he smiled.

It was an old facsimile edition—much older than the Revesby facsimile—bound in faded green cloth, with a leather spine. I hadn't expected this, and when he saw how pleased I was, his smile widened. The book was heavy, the pages thick. I opened it to a woodcut of an animal with the body of a lion, a man's head, and a scorpion's tail; the facing page was covered with two columns of dense medieval script, beginning with these words: *Manticora, ab India leo saeva astutusque . . .*

" 'The manticore,' " I translated aloud, " 'a ferocious and cunning lion from India . . .' "

"Very good, Atlas." He leaned forward, laying his palms on the desk. "I've learned a few things since we last met. I spoke with a friend who's a curator at the Folger Library in Washington, then corresponded with a friend of his who's a medievalist at Yale. Listen carefully now. Through the Dark Ages, monasteries were the repositories of Western knowledge. The Renaissance began when that knowledge was disseminated. I knew that several dozen bestiaries had been produced in England around the time of the Revesby. I knew that they were fairly similar. But the Hereford took me by surprise. Until last week, I too had never heard of it. It was compiled at a remote monastery on the Welsh border around 1390. It's unique and exciting, not because of the main text, or the fine woodcuts, but because of its short, astonishing prologue. The prologue begins solemnly enough, reiterating the dogma to be found in every bestiary: the Holy Ghost authored two books, the Bible and the first bestiary, and because the latter was lost long ago, all subsequent bestiaries are fragments of the original." His eyes lit up. "But then the monks veer off, spouting outright heresy. Apparently these fellows were Gnostics who had severed their ties with the Church. They believed that the Bible, too, was incomplete, missing large pieces—'secret books' like the Gospels of Thomas and Philip, and the *Book of Jubilees*. More importantly, they asserted that the complete Bible and the intact original bestiary comprise a universal history which is, in fact, the only true history of the world; if read in tandem, in their entirety, they would offer up the same knowledge a man could otherwise acquire only by reading all the other books ever written."

My head was whirling. "But that's impossible."

"One would think." He opened his arms. "We are, however, in the realm of the miraculous. A leap of faith is required, Atlas. In this case," he added ruefully, "one that can never be tested."

"Why not, sir?"

"The Hereford monks allude to a bestiary far more valuable than their own. They call it the *Caravan Bestiary*, without whose contents the original bestiary, and therefore that universal history, can never be complete." He paused, good teacher that he was, to let this sink in. "This fugitive bestiary was an incendiary work, at one time known only to the powerful—princes and churchmen—who believed in its latent power, and to scholars who secretly passed it among themselves. Whatever its implications for them, it was, first and foremost, a compilation of the animals lost in the Great Flood."

A chill ran through me. "The ones that didn't make it onto Noah's ark," I interjected, recalling the story my grandmother told me when she was dying.

"That's right," he said, bemused that I would pick up on this so quickly. "Over the centuries, many hands contributed to this book, enlarging and refining it, until it disappeared in the thirteenth century.

Many conventional bestiaries were lost or destroyed, but because they overlapped so heavily with surviving bestiaries, their contents were not lost. But the *Caravan Bestiary* was one of a kind. Its contents were irreplaceable. Insofar as I could discover, many scholars continued to search for it—some as recently as the 1920s. None of them found it. The most serious were Niccólo Cava, a philologist at the University of Bologna in the mid–nineteenth century; Michael Brox, an Austrian theologian who was murdered in 1891; and Amanda Faville, a French art historian (and, briefly, the fiancée of Oswald Spengler) and an expert in illuminated books after the First World War."

"But why is it called the *Caravan Bestiary*?"

"The monks don't say. They indicate that, earlier in its history, it may have had other names, or no name at all."

"Was the theologian murdered because of this book?"

He put a match to his pipe. "Brox was murdered at the time he was searching for the book. The circumstances may be totally unrelated. He may have been killed in the course of a robbery or a quarrel. I only know that he was murdered in Istanbul, Turkey. Most of his papers that were published posthumously dealt with Near Eastern religion, his specialty. But in several letters he mentioned the *Caravan Bestiary*. He believed it had been burned by the Inquisition in Seville, Spain, in 1191. Among his unpublished works is an essay on the bestiary that can only be read in the library stacks at the University of Vienna. Niccólo Cava was a more obscure scholar. He was convinced the book was in Italy, in the hands of the Catholic Church. He searched for ten years, antagonizing a lot of people. First he believed it was hidden in the cathedral at Ravenna, then Orvieto, and Naples, before settling on the Vatican itself. He spent the rest of his life battling the authorities for access to the papal vaults, which of course was never granted. In the end he accused the Pope of ordering the book's destruction and was promptly excommunicated. He was also fired from the university. Finally, there is Madame Faville, the most interesting of the three and the most successful."

"Did she come close to finding it?"

"Hard to say. She did fill in a huge gap in the book's history, tracing its whereabouts from 950 until its disappearance on Rhodes in the thirteenth century. Those are the centuries of the eight Crusades, during which the book was spirited around the Mediterranean, from Gibraltar to Cyprus, by pirates, soldiers, smugglers, and scholars. Madame Faville was a cautious and meticulous researcher. Yet she grew so confident she would find the bestiary that in 1921 she began a book documenting her search. She never finished it. Rhodes was a dead end. She was sure that the bestiary never left the island intact. So, you see, they all concluded that the *Caravan Bestiary* had been destroyed, but each had a different explanation for how and where it happened."

"What was Madame Faville's explanation, sir?"

"I wish I knew. I found out as much as I could for you, Atlas. It's an incredible subject, deserving of the time and energy you're giving it. But now you're on your own." He started packing his briefcase. "And I have a class in five minutes."

I stood up reluctantly; I had so many questions. "Thank you for your help, sir."

"It was my pleasure."

I held up the facsimile of the Hereford bestiary. "I'll return this as soon as I can."

"No, you won't." He opened the door for me. "It's a gift, from me to you."

I was very moved. Not since Evgénia had anyone taken such a close interest in me.

"I know you'll make good use of it," he said, starting down the hall.

"I will, sir. Thank you."

This was a fateful encounter for me. Mr. Hood's generosity and encouragement would carry me a long way—to places he could never have anticipated.

THRILLED BY ALL I'd heard, I was determined to undertake my own quest for the *Caravan Bestiary*. I wasn't entirely sure what that meant, but later realized it was one of those rare instances in which a youthful enthusiasm that could have evaporated instead grew more powerful each year. Even the fact I was a schoolboy with no credentials ended up working to my advantage: who else in his right mind would have had the hubris even to contemplate such a project—searching for something that had disappeared seven hundred years before I was born—undaunted by the failures of expert predecessors and ignorant of the obstacles before him? I now know how fortunate I had been, not just to have a man like Mr. Hood come into my life, but to have learned of the *Caravan Bestiary* when I was so young, equipped with vast stores of energy and little knowledge of the world.

I began reading more voraciously than ever. By way of their bibliographies, indices, footnotes, and appendices, each author led me to other authors—and other creatures. For example, in *Mythical Monsters*, published in 1884, Charles Gould, the Royal Geological Surveyor of Tasmania, refers to the geographer Strabo's description of "nocturnal serpents with bat wings"; then to Strabo's source, the Greek naturalist Megasthenes; and, in a footnote, to a chapter on flying snakes in *Folk Lore of China* by Dr. N. P. Dennys of Singapore, who in turn credits a monograph on fantastic herpetology by Hans Spuyfel, a Dutch professor in Jakarta. Though I would learn more formal research methods as my education progressed, I never abandoned the eclectic approach that seemed to suit my subject matter. Perhaps the more rigid, academic mind-set of those who preceded me had helped to doom their efforts. They were professionals, trained to be skeptical, while I was an enthusiastist, open to all possibilities and unencumbered by obligatory doubts. I was bound to make a lot of errors, but, by taking chances, and following even the most far-fetched leads, I was also liable to get lucky. As Mr. Hood had pointed out, when it came to the *Caravan Bestiary*, the miraculous ought to be embraced, not discounted. Pursuing such an elusive prize, you walked a road bound on the one side by history and on the other by a luminous, shifting terrain defined by faith as well as facts.

All my reading served a single purpose: I was keeping a notebook in which I recorded all the beasts I thought might be in the *Caravan Bestiary*. Inclusive to a fault, I tried to keep my entries short and precise, focusing—in the spirit of bestiaries—on the animals' most unique characteristics. Unable as yet to venture into the world, I decided that one way of searching for the bestiary was by attempting to re-create it.

In my juvenile script, in red ink, my initial notebook entry read:

THE PHOENIX
A large bird with feathers the color of fire.
Like fire, it is sustained by air alone, and neither eats nor drinks.
It lives in paradise, and every thousand years dies and is reborn.

And is known by many names. The Bird of the Sun. Of Fire. Longevity. Resurrection.

The Bird of Assyria, Arabia, the Ganges.

A bird with iridescent wings and eyes blue as the seas it could cross, flying for nine days and nights without rest.

The Bird of Incense. Spices. Music.

With a song so beautiful it was the basis for the first musical scale.

Its journey always ended in Egypt—in Heliopolis, the City of the Sun, atop a golden temple.

The Egyptians deified it, with a grand title: the Lord of the Long Cycles of Time. They chose as guardians of the temple pilgrims that had followed the bird from India.

Over the years I filled twenty-eight notebooks with descriptions and drawings of other such animals. Different sizes and colors, some of these notebooks were bleached by the sun, others warped by rain-fall. Their pages were stained with tea and whisky. One was charred in a hotel fire in Corsica. Another barely survived a flooded basement in Siena. That very first notebook, which I bought at a general store in Maine, had a green marbled cover and unlined pages.

Meanwhile, my everyday life at school continued. Few of my fel-low students were from blue-collar families. I may as well have hailed from one of the outer planets. I divulged little about my family out-side the fact my father lived abroad, which was intended to explain why I was one of the few students who never received a visitor on homecoming weekend. After that first train trip, my father hadn't set foot on the school grounds again. (Even on my graduation day, years later, I would leave immediately after the ceremony; I couldn't bear to sit alone, or attach myself to one of my classmates' families, for a last celebratory luncheon.) My tuition checks arrived on time and my ac-count in the school bank remained balanced. And every so often I re-ceived the usual three-line postcard from some far-flung port—but never a letter.

I had to follow a rigid schedule: wake-up bell at six, chapel, break-fast, first class at eight, lunch, more classes, phys ed, dinner, study hall, and bed. We wore jackets and ties at all times; were required to ad-dress faculty members as "sir"; were not allowed to speak to other stu-dents during class. And so on. I rebelled by isolating, much as I had in elementary school, where I had been lucky to find a real friend like Bruno. At boarding school I had many acquaintances, but no close friend. I gained the respect of my classmates by remaining silent and detached. Because of my childhood, this was not a difficult niche for me to carve out. Required to participate in a sport, I joined the archery team, which felt more like a collection of solitary competitors. I used to think solitude was my natural element, from the moment my mother simultaneously deposited me in the world and abandoned me to it.

I only knew my mother's image from that handful of snapshots which I now kept in my grandmother's silver music box, along with the white whisker. Many times I had studied my mother's face with a magnifying glass. I failed to identify the shadow of the bird on her shoulder. One day I took the snapshots to Jones Beach and tried in vain to determine their exact location using some blurred landmarks—shrubs, a bench, a lamppost—in the background of each. What did I expect to find? My grandmother had preached to me that the spirit of every creature to walk the earth was still among us. I felt my mother was nearby when I was most alone—lying awake at night, riding in a darkened train, descending an empty stairwell at school.

In Mr. Hood's ancient history class he had us memorize passages out of Livy and Herodotus. I was entranced with the latter: his incredible descriptions of animals such as the giant silver ants that fought elaborate wars in the Libyan desert; and in Book IV, the catalog of Scythian tribes like the Melanchlaeni, who all wore black cloaks, and the Budini, whose entire population had red hair and gray eyes. I also chose Mr. Hood as my adviser. I was a regular visitor—maybe the only visitor—during his office hours. His other advisees were assigned to him because they hadn't gotten their first or second choices. In addition to helping with my bestiary research, he actually offered me real-life advice, culled from philosophers like Diogenes: "To be saved from folly, Atlas, you need either kind friends or fierce enemies."

Mr. Hood was considered a loner himself among his more convivial colleagues. He lived alone in one of the faculty cottages by the river. Every morning he canoed or kayaked six miles. When the river was frozen, he used the rowing machine in the gym. For relaxation, but with a kind of religious fervor, he built and refurbished bark canoes, working out of a shed on the riverbank. One morning when I visited him there he explained how to construct a twelve-foot canoe.

"First, you strip bark from a silver birch," he said. "Unlike elm or hickory bark, birch bark doesn't waterlog. For the frame, you use spring cedar. I choose to work only with the tools available to the Malecite Indians who lived around here: an ax, a peeling tool, and, most importantly, a crooked knife." He handed me a knife with a bulbous grip and a V-shaped blade. "Ever seen one before?"

"No, sir." I balanced it in my palm and touched the tip, sharp as a scalpel.

"It was peculiar to Maine. That bent tip is for carving and shaving the rib boards and planking. My canoes don't contain nails or tacks. I pitch them with sap from a black spruce. Then I decorate the prow with porcupine quills. The Malecites considered a canoe incomplete, unprotected, without an insignia. I've used a fox and a lynx. Their favorite was a rabbit smoking a pipe."

I laughed. "It sounds like a cartoon."

"It was supposed to demonstrate their calm in the face of adversity."

Most afternoons after his last class, Mr. Hood retreated to the rocking chair on his porch, a pipe clamped between his teeth, a book in hand, and his white bulldog at his feet. Blind in one eye, Polyphemus was named after the cyclops in *The Odyssey*.

My own dog had died a month after I went away to school. In his cramped hand, Bruno reported Re's last days to me:

He didn't want to leave Lena's room. But he got short of breath climbing the stairs. We took him to the animal hospital, and saw two vets, and they said, "He's just old." They wanted to keep him there, but I said no. He didn't want to stay, and I knew you wouldn't have wanted him to. The next night he stopped eating. We brought food upstairs, but it was no use. He stayed in Lena's room, and she never left his side. In the morning, he went over and stretched out by the window, watching the snow fall. He fell asleep like that, and then Lena saw he had stopped breathing. I'm sorry he couldn't be with you, Xeno. We did all we could. Lena's been crying ever since.

Lena wrote me her own letter:

My mother says the best way to die is in your sleep. It's because she's afraid my father will die in a fire. I don't believe there is a good way to die. I hate that Re died. But he was peaceful in the end. I know how much he loved the snow. . . .

Two weeks later, Bruno sent me Re's ashes. I opened the package in the bathroom, away from the other boys, tears flooding my eyes. The ashes were in a tight gray packet the size of a brick. I couldn't believe my dog's bodily self had been reduced to that. Bruno also sent along Re's leather collar and the medallion imprinted with his name, my name, and my old address. I placed them and the ashes alongside my grandmother's music box in the trunk under my bed. Now Re's spirit had joined hers and my mother's.

Throughout my stay at that school, I felt his presence, not as a shadowy mist, but a weight that shifted gently at the end of the bed, or a rustle in the shadows, or a brushing against my leg when I walked in the woods.

I N MY SENIOR YEAR, just before I turned seventeen, Gina Moretti's worst fear came true when her husband was killed in a fire.

One December morning Frank Moretti's engine company responded to a four-alarm blaze at a Bushwick paint factory. He was the first man in, off the truck ladder through a top-floor window. Some beams gave way and the ceiling fell, trapping him behind a wall of flames. Two other firefighters recovered his body and got out just before the floor collapsed. Bruno phoned me at school, as distraught as I'd ever heard him. "Xeno, my father's gone," he said hoarsely, then broke down. It was during exam period, and I was in a daze that afternoon, going through the motions on my physics final.

I boarded a Greyhound in town, and riding all night, making connections in Bangor and Boston, arrived in New York at nine A.M. on the morning of the funeral. I had slept maybe two hours. I changed into a fresh shirt in the men's room at the Port Authority Terminal. Then I took the shuttle to Grand Central and the No. 6 train up to the Bronx. It was bitter cold. Mounds of dirty snow lined the curb. I lit a cigarette and walked down the old familiar streets to Saint Anthony of Padua Church, where my grandmother's funeral was held.

A crowd was gathered in the sunlight. Two battalions of firefighters, in dress uniform, were standing in formation. The fire commissioner was there, and the mayor, surrounded by a claque of politicians: city councilmen, a state senator, and the dapper silver-haired man who had been our congressman since I was a kid. He was Italian and every Sunday attended mass, rotating between the three Catholic churches in the district. Because of the mayor's presence, cops were out in force, and there were reporters and photographers, in addition to all the people from the neighborhood.

I was scanning the crowd for the Morettis when two limousines rolled up in front of the church. The mayor and fire commissioner waited by the first limo as the driver opened the rear door and Mrs. Moretti stepped out. She was wearing dark wraparound glasses. Her brother-in-law, Carl, in his police uniform, followed her, then Bruno, slump-shouldered, and Lena in a long black coat. Carl's wife, Irene, emerged from the second limo with their children. The mayor held Mrs. Moretti's hands and spoke to her as if they were the only two people there. Then she took his arm and they climbed the steps. Everyone else followed, including Mr. Moretti's entire squad, who later, while a bagpiper played "The Battle Is Over," would carry his casket out to the hearse. As I made my way through the crowd, my eyes never left Lena. Her long blonde hair partly shielded her face. Her eyes were downcast. She was pale, like a phantom of her real self, which at that moment was somewhere else.

I walked to the front of the church, and there was the flag-draped casket, floating in a sea of flowers. Bruno stood up and embraced me. He felt even thinner and shakier than usual.

"I'm so sorry," I whispered into his good ear.

He gripped my forearms and his eyes filled with tears.

I hugged Mrs. Moretti. Her body was stiff, her cheeks cold as marble. I saw my face reflected in her dark glasses.

"Thank you for coming," she said in a husky voice, touching my cheek. Her lips were quivering. She was heavily sedated.

Suddenly I was standing before Lena. Her eyes were empty. I held her close, then sat down beside her.

When the priest appeared, crossing himself before the altar, she started to sob. "Oh, Xeno," she murmured, squeezing my hand.

After the service, at which the fire commissioner and Carl Moretti delivered eulogies, and the burial on a windy hillside at Sacred Heart Cemetery on Long Island, we went back to the Morettis' house. A photograph of Mr. Moretti in his uniform was propped on the mantelpiece beside the wedding pictures. There was liquor and coffee and platters of catered food. Mrs. Moretti sat in her husband's easy chair, quiet and dignified, though I saw how red her eyes were now that she had removed the dark glasses.

"How is school, Xeno?" she asked when I approached her.

"I don't know," I said, choking back tears.

She smiled. "You came a long way. Have something to eat, even if you're not hungry."

She was right; all I'd eaten in the last twenty-four hours was a doughnut and a candy bar at the Bangor bus station.

I hadn't seen Bruno since we entered the house, and I found him up in his room, sitting on the edge of the bed.

I sat beside him. The water filter was bubbling in the aquarium. The ferret was scratching around under the bed. "Your father would have been proud of you today," I said.

He shook his head. "My father was so strong. I'll never be like him."

"Maybe not physically. But you're like him in every other way."

"I wish that were true," he sighed. "I thought it went well at the church."

"It was a beautiful service."

"Uncle Carl rambled on too long."

I shrugged.

"He was maudlin. It was all about him."

"He's upset."

"He's juiced," he said with uncharacteristic vehemence. "He drank his breakfast."

"You need to rest, Bruno. Why don't you lie down for a while?"

"No." He stood up slowly. "My place is downstairs with my mother. I just needed to catch my breath."

Carl was still drinking. Everyone could hear him holding forth in the kitchen, swearing profusely. Mrs. Moretti was about to confront him when Irene stopped her.

"This isn't your problem, Gina," Irene muttered, flushing with embarrassment.

She strode into the kitchen. There was a moment of silence. Then two firefighters emerged sheepishly, drinks in hand. We heard Irene say, "What do you think you're doing?"

Carl shouted, "Get out of my face. Go home!"

Without another word, she did just that—out the back door, and around to her own front door.

Carl left too, slamming the back door, and moments later his car screeched out of the driveway.

Mrs. Moretti didn't pretend nothing had happened. "I'm sorry for that," she said to the firefighters sitting around her.

The man closest to her was a bald, square-jawed captain named Ralph DeFama, who had risen through the ranks with Frank Moretti. They had been avid Polar Bears—the swim club whose members plunge into the ocean in winter—and I remembered the day Lena joined them at Coney Island, remaining in the frigid water as long as the men and afterward telling me she would never do it again.

After everyone left, Mrs. Moretti retired to her bedroom, and Lena and I went out to the backyard. We sat on a redwood bench on the patio and smoked my Camels. Frozen snow blanketed the lawn. The stars appeared. It was the first time we had been alone all day.

At sixteen, Lena had grown into quite a beauty, tall and strong, with lovely skin. She had been flourishing at school: first in her class, popular, a varsity swimmer. She was close to her father. The shock waves from his death would keep hitting her for years. Her sphinxlike qualities, the tranquil poise that was so attractive when she was thirteen, were already obscured by weariness and grief. Lights still flickered in her gray eyes, but they seemed a long way off.

It pained me to see her like that, but I didn't try to draw her out.

"I understand you want to help," she said, blowing smoke into the darkness, "but I can't see anything in front of me right now. All those people. I just want my father back." Her eyes softened. "I'm glad you're here, Xeno."

I took her hand. I wanted to hold her.

"You know, around my father, Carl controlled his drinking. He wouldn't have become a cop or bought his house if it weren't for Dad. Now he's going to be nothing but trouble."

She was right about that.

The day after the funeral, Mrs. Moretti collapsed. It took her months to get back on her feet, and by then her hair was turning white.

Back at school, I dozed off during the last of my final exams, and turned in my English term paper, which I had completed on the bus. But I wasn't concerned about my studies. And I couldn't stay focused for long on the misfortunes of the Moretti family. I had to deal with the ongoing crisis of my relationship with my own father, which seemed never to approach resolution.

WHEN I FIRST went away to school, I only saw my father at hotels or furnished apartments which he would sublet for the one month I wasn't at summer session. Even for him, this became too irregular—or too inconvenient—and so, in my third year, he bought an apartment in Boston that became my nominal home. It was really a mailing address.

A sign of my father's continued prosperity, the apartment was in a block of expensive brownstones canopied by maple trees near Kendall Square—a far cry from our old Bronx neighborhood. Yet the furnishings were equally drab and heavy and, like every apartment he'd ever chosen, the air itself felt dark. An inky mist seemed to hover just below the ceilings. There were two bedrooms, and a kitchen overlooking a bare yard. The kitchen was equally bare. Except for the groceries purchased for immediate use, the cupboard was occupied by the same yellowing box of kosher salt, a dusty bottle of vinegar, and a tube of toothpicks. It wouldn't surprise me if they were still there. My father visited several times a year—the same routine he had followed in New York. Except the rest of the time the apartment was unlived in, or else I was there alone.

Alerted to his arrival by the usual terse postcard, I would make the five-hour train ride to meet him. Sometimes it was around a holiday weekend, but never at Christmas. With the Morettis I had always alternated between Thanksgiving and Christmas, so every other Christmas Eve I was a regular at the headmaster's house, one of those students (the others were invariably from foreign countries) who didn't go home. We dined stiffly with the headmaster and his family, made small talk, and felt—at least I did—like intruders required to give command performances. I was at once jealous of the headmaster's children and repelled by their stiflingly good manners. I also felt sorry for them. Already residing in a fishbowl, they were no doubt irritated by our presence during one of the few times the campus emptied. My table conversation was limited; since I wasn't from Switzerland or Saudi Arabia, the family was politely curious about my background, unusual name, and Greek and Italian ancestry, which was exotic in those parts.

The rendezvous with my father were lonely enough, but the time I spent alone in Boston was worse, especially in August when the summer sessions ended. It was because I was such a summer school regular, accumulating credits, that I was able to graduate from high school a year early.

When I did see my father, he asked perfunctory questions about my schoolwork, but since he had no interest in books or learning, and I had no desire to share my newfound passions, those discussions went nowhere. We dined out and passed most of the meals in silence, the conversation limited to the food before us, the weather, and the day's headlines. Once when I asked him—affecting a tone of clinical inquiry—about our long silences, he readily attributed them to his years in ships' galleys.

"At sea you don't talk much over meals," he explained, as if this had any bearing on our circumstances in a steakhouse in the North End.

The fact is, nothing had changed since I was a boy: he was disinterested, I was angry, and the rift between us had only deepened. I never succeeded in penetrating his opacity, emotionally or intellectually. I had to admit that, despite my education, his was the stronger mind; he could always repel me.

Finally I felt so defeated that I decided I had nothing to lose by confronting him. I asked why he bothered crossing the ocean to see me at all.

"You're my son."

"Then why can't I visit you in Europe?"

"I've told you, my life there is all business. I'm never in one place for long."

I didn't understand how anyone's life could be all business.

"I have a place in Athens," he went on, "where I hang my hat. But it isn't a real home. I still spend a lot of time on ships."

"This apartment is also a place where you hang your hat. And it isn't a real home, either."

"Then why not get together here?" he asked with mock innocence.

Our conversations had achieved a new level of absurdity.

When I questioned him about his life, he remained guarded and elusive. The litany was always the same: he had the place in Athens; he owned several freighters; he was often at sea. He kept his office on one of the ships, he said, not in some airless building in Piraeus. "Unlike most shippers, who sit on their asses, I still like to handle a rope and a wrench," he added self-righteously. Most of his business now was in Africa and the Far East.

It wasn't clear how he had put together such an enterprise. Thrift and hard work were his ready mantra, but as I got older, that seemed an awfully facile explanation. I wondered where he had acquired the business acumen to invest his small savings so shrewdly while expanding so fast. And who had assisted him? Did he have partners? Patrons? He wouldn't say. Nor did he ever express pride in what he had accomplished. To him—despite the fact he had started out as a coal stoker with a ninth-grade education—that would have been effusive, boastful, against his code. Anyway, he never would have shared such thoughts with me. His idea of intimacy was to offer me a medical report, also superficial: blood pressure up; left shoulder arthritic; bone spurs in his heel. His more serious problems, dry cough and shortness of breath, he never discussed. Obviously the years of breathing coal dust in confined spaces had taken a toll on his respiratory system. It sounded to me like emphysema in the early stages, but when I asked about it, he insisted that the cough developed when he quit smoking, because his lungs were purging themselves. "A doctor in Malta told me so," he said solemnly.

Behind these meager facts loomed the question of the life he really led in Europe—the central mystery of my childhood. I had always assumed there must be some correlation between his efforts at concealment and the magnitude of the facts being concealed. Why would he work so hard to hide something small? I had my fantasies: that he had remarried; started another family; maybe taken a mistress? But why would any of those scenarios necessitate a double life? And why would he have to keep me away at all costs, especially as I grew older? I figured he possessed the guile to pull off a large-scale masquerade of that sort, but I didn't credit him with the necessary imagination. Or maybe the explanation was simpler: not a double, but a single life, a dreary reversion to his earliest model: remote, friendless, built—as he insisted—around work. Maybe he was being honest when he said that it would be no different seeing him in Athens as in Boston—or Bombay or Lisbon. Every place in the world essentially becomes the same when you are that isolated.

Outwardly, incredibly, I could detect no clues about the life my father led during the roughly 340 days of the year I did not see him. He dressed better, had plenty of money, ate in better restaurants, but, still, he felt like the same man who inhabited my earliest memories: humorless, taciturn, giving me all I needed materially, yet displaying little generosity of spirit, toward me or himself. Whatever he had lived through, and suppressed, and however that had transformed him internally, he kept hidden. At that he was masterly.

All the while, for seventeen years, he had consigned me to limbo. I refused to remain there any longer. I wanted out.

I got my opportunity—if you can call it that—just after Mr. Moretti's funeral. My father summoned me from school. He had rented us rooms at the Devon Hotel, near Central Park South. I was surprised; it would be the first Christmas I spent with him in many years. It was not the way I wanted to return to New York just then, but his invitations arrived infrequently. And I wanted to see what he had in mind.

On Christmas Eve we set out from the hotel, up Seventh Avenue, into a freezing wind. Other people were doubled over, but I tried to emulate my father, who, having endured the harshest conditions on the decks of North Atlantic freighters, strode unbowed, erect. The snow crystals froze in his moustache and on his eyebrows, yet he didn't flinch. His black overcoat, taut across the shoulder blades, barely contained his bulky frame. His thick wrists protruded from the sleeves. His gloveless hands were clenched.

Though I'd grown several inches in the previous year, I realized I would never be his size. I would make it to six feet, but no taller. And though I was strong, I was slim; I wouldn't have his big arms or barrel chest. I had my mother's hair, and her lighter coloring, and set far apart over a nose with a small bump and the right cheek more sharply planed than the left, her eyes, too, the same dark brown. My grandmother used to tell me I looked like her younger brother, Ennio, who had been killed in the First World War. She showed me a bleached picture of a handsome man in an Italian Army uniform, cap pushed back, cigarette between his fingers, smiling wryly beside a fountain.

My father and I had dinner in a gloomy Turkish restaurant. Blinking colored lights framed the window in which a scrawny fir tree was draped with tinsel. The meze were displayed on a side table beneath a fake wreath: eggplant dip, turnip pickles, stuffed grape leaves, and sardines. My father drank two large rakis—unusual for him—but his outward demeanor never changed. I had baklava for dessert while he puffed a cigar, eyeing me absently. Then we walked across Fifty-first Street to Rockefeller Center.

At the rink, Rimsky-Korsakoff was blaring from the speakers. Floodlights illuminated the towering Douglas pine, adorned with thousands of bulbs, a silver angel poised at the summit. A children's program was under way: skaters costumed as animals spinning in formation, brandishing torches, performing tricks. There were tigers, lions, a moose, a walrus, but the best skater was a golden bear. He was juggling red balls. With each circuit of the rink, he tossed the balls higher, never dropping any or losing his rhythm, even when he leaped through a series of hoops. After taking a bow, he led the other animals off the rink and a wave of human skaters replaced them.

I remembered what I read about bears in the Hereford bestiary:

Bears eat ants when they're sick from too much honey.
And a dying bear sings.

My father and I stood at the brass railing before the Christmas tree. He hadn't said a word since dinner, and now he started talking.

"I used to come here with your mother. She liked to skate, you know."

I didn't know, of course, because he had never told me.

"Most of the time she skated at the rink on Merrick Avenue," he went on. "The rink was next to the elevated line, so the trains kept drowning out the music. She had always rented skates. For Christmas I bought her a pair, but she only wore them a few times. They were white with red laces." He looked at me. "She had to stop because she was pregnant." He turned back to the rink. "She said she'd skate again after you were born."

He might as well have punched me in the stomach. Had he brought up the taboo subject of my birth because he wanted a contrite acknowledgment, once and for all, that if it hadn't been for me, my mother would be alive?

He could have saved himself the trouble, I wanted to shout. But I didn't have the courage to call him on such things. The anger I nursed ran so deep, and our relationship was so tenuous, that I was convinced if I lashed out, the consquences could be irreversible. My great fear was that my father was waiting for just such an opportunity to cut what remaining ties we had.

The wind made my eyes water. As I gazed at the skaters, most of them young, wearing brightly colored scarves and gloves, my anger ebbed into a familiar sorrow. My mother, I thought, had once been one of them, at her death just a few years older than I was that Christmas. My conception of her, drawn from the wispiest of vapors, had evolved over the years. I had come to think of her almost as a peer—one who happened to live in another time—whom I could relate to, not as my mother, but as another teenager. It was a paradox that the older I got, the less remote and timeless she seemed. My father, on the other hand, had become more of a stranger than ever.

"The last time we came here," he was saying, "we stayed until all the other skaters left. Then we watched the ushers sweep the rink and shut the lights. And she said, 'I wish I could stay here forever.' That's how happy she was."

I looked at him. "And you, were you happy?"

He nodded. "I was."

"Why are you telling me this now?" I asked.

He seemed taken aback. "Because we're here."

"And if we weren't, you wouldn't have told me at all."

He shrugged and turned up his coat collar. "We're here. And now we should go."

That was all he was going to give me. And that was the end for me.

A month later, I severed what little contact I had with him, telling myself—with more anger than conviction—that for once I was abandoning him. I did it by postcard.

Dad:

I won't be meeting you in Boston anymore. It's too painful for me to see you when I know you keep me out of the greater part of your life. That was hard enough when I lived with Grandma and Evgénia. Now it seems impossible.

    Yours,
    Xeno

I sent it to his post office box in Athens, and two weeks later received a postcard in reply:

Dear Xeno,

I am sorry you feel that way. The apartment will remain yours to use. Until further instructions.

    —Theodore Atlas

D URING MY LAST SEMESTER, drugs were readily available at my school. It was 1967, and even in Maine we could find whatever we wanted. Until then, I hadn't been much interested, but after Mr. Moretti's death and the break with my father, I started smoking a lot of grass. Occasionally I dropped acid or mescaline. I was unhappy, but I also felt liberated. In the apartment in Boston, I could get high whenever I wanted and play music as loud as the neighbors would tolerate. I wandered the city, hanging out in the Commons, eating Mexican food, and going to the art houses to watch interminable European films, or, when I was stoned, a movie house in Chinatown where Taiwanese flicks were shown without subtitles. I met girls at the coffeehouses in Cambridge and lied that I was a Harvard student; in eight months, I actually would be an incoming freshman. Sometimes I got lucky with these girls. It helped that I had my own apartment downtown, twenty minutes away on the motorcycle I'd bought when I turned sixteen, a red 350cc Yamaha.

Earlier in my adolescence, I had few such opportunities. Locked away at school, I was limited to making out with the girls bussed in for dances from our sister school, eighty miles away. For anything more satisfying I would have to leave the campus, as I did just after my fifteenth birthday, traveling to Bangor one weekend with my archery teammate, Nathan Forman. His father owned the local Cadillac dealership. When he worked there the previous summer, Nathan went after the bookkeeper's young secretary, Marie, who had slept with half the salesmen. When Nathan told Marie I was coming home with him, she let him know her best friend, Polly, would be open to a date with me. Which translated into the four of us taking two adjacent rooms in a motel. At eighteen Polly was very much the older woman. She was built like a farm girl, wide hips and big breasts, but with the pallor and the tired eyes—already—of someone trapped in a factory town. My strongest memory is of the cubes rumbling in the ice machine outside our door while she guided me inside her. After which I took my first shower with a girl, soaping her back, watching her rinse her stringy hair. Beaded with steam, her skin looked even paler. Her cheeks were blotched. Later we were joined by Nathan and Marie. We sat on the bed smoking joints and drinking beer. We ordered in a pizza. Afterward Nathan and I drove to his parents' house and went to sleep in his room, where I took his brother's old bed.

One snowy night in my senior year I dropped acid with two girls from Tufts whom I met at my dealer's house in Somerville. We rode the subway back to my apartment. I put on a stack of LPs: Hendrix, the Dead, Cream. The first rushes of acid came on—sparks of color shooting off of objects, sound elongating. One of the girls went out for food and instead returned with a bunch of people. By then, we were tripping hard. I didn't like having so many strangers in the apartment, talking, smoking grass, but I fell into conversation with one of them, a tall man around thirty with a red beard and a bandaged hand. I couldn't say what he looked like exactly because his face kept turning to red clay, melting, and reconfiguring itself.

We sat at the dining room table. He chain-smoked Spanish cigarettes and said he was a reporter for *Mother Jones*, just returned from Spain.

"I was in the Pyrenees with ETA, the Basque separatists. They make the Weathermen look like fucking Boy Scouts. Their bombers are called *los felinos* because they're elusive as wildcats. I was blindfolded and taken to their ace bombmaker. C-4 packed with drill bits is his specialty. During our interview, there was an explosion in the next room. My guide was killed." He held up his bandaged hand. "I lost this."

I was staring out the window at the snowflakes glinting in the streetlight.

"You don't believe me?" he said, and to my horror he began

unwrapping the bandage. Round and round—there was no end to it, and no hand in evidence underneath. I expected blood to gush from the stump of his wrist.

Finally I found my voice, at the end of a long tunnel. "I believe you."

"No, you don't." Nearly the entire bandage was coiled on the floor.

The front door slammed. The girls from Tufts and the other strangers had left after cleaning out my father's liquor cabinet. When I turned back to the journalist, he was gone, too, his cigarette smoke hovering across the table. The radiator hissed. Then I heard a sharper hiss: that discarded bandage was now a cobra, rearing up, with a darting tongue.

For the rest of the night, the cobra never left me, even as I moved from room to room, switched on all the lights, and opened windows, drinking in the icy air. At dawn I ended up back in the dining room, stiff and exhausted. The cobra remained by the door, watching me, poised to strike, until it dissolved in the first light.

THAT SPRING, before graduation, I went for a walk, and as usual felt Re beside me. It was dusk, and I had just entered the thick woods north of the grounds. In the forest to the south there were trails on which science classes began field trips. Eventually the trails met at a dirt road with a furrow of grass down the middle that led to the state road. But the northern woods were virgin, off-limits, running straight into New Brunswick and beyond. No houses, no roads. They were the beginning of the wilderness.

The wind was swaying the treetops. The clouds were tinged violet. Underfoot the pine needles were damp. Night was falling—owls began to hoot, bats swooped—but I kept walking. That afternoon I had cut my classes and holed up at the library with my facsimile of the Hereford bestiary. I was still clutching it under my arm.

The first animal in the Hereford was the bear. A woodcut depicted it standing by a lake, with raised forepaws, beneath a ring of stars. It reminded me of the bear at Rockefeller Center.

Soon it was pitch-dark. I might have been two miles from the school—or two hundred. I had never felt so intensely alone, with such a mixture of fear and exhilaration. Finally the wall of trees opened onto a clearing. The Milky Way spanned the sky. To my right, the moon shone on a lake where something broke away from the shadows on the bank: a bear, on its hind legs, with forepaws extended. Within seconds it disappeared and a smaller animal—a fox!—emerged from the same shadows, sniffing the air before darting into the woods. Like the Chinese, the Hereford monks believed the wiliest foxes could transform themselves into other animals, including man.

The monks offered advice to anyone foolish enough to try trailing such a protean creature.

The fox can leave tracks in one direction while traveling in another.

They didn't explain how the fox managed that feat, nor did they identify the song a dying bear might sing.

3

I WALKED OUT of the forest into a scorched field. The wind licked at me like fire. The soil was smoking beneath my boots. In bomb craters, twenty feet across, rainwater was boiling beneath the noon sun.

I was in a place ruled by the beast.

Province of fire, Year of the Rat, I had scrawled on a postcard that I kept in the cargo pocket of my pants. On the other side of the post-card, a Vietnamese girl in a red dress and flip-flops stood astride her bicycle before a pagoda. Hibiscus flowers were clipped to the spokes of her wheels. Her black hair flowed over one shoulder. She was gaz-ing into the distance. I often examined her image and looked into her eyes. Before I returned home, I wanted to meet her. I knew the post-card had been printed during French colonial times, that the girl must be much altered by the years—and the war—or else dead.

If the latter, why should that stop me? In the previous months I had come to realize that there were schemes of life and death more comprehensive, and far subtler, than anything I imagined—zones in which the living mingle with the dead: fighting, embracing, even falling in love. At certain times and places these crossovers are not the exception, but the rule. I was in such a place.

Increasingly the travel became one-way—terrifying numbers streaming from life to death. The dead overwhelming the living, de-manding that we join them. Like everyone around me, I felt isolated, helpless. Between us and the rest of the world was an ocean of water and—infinitely vaster—an ocean of time.

I stopped beside a thicket to study my compass and map. I was a quarter mile from coordinates 11°27'49" N, 106°39'08" E, the location Murphy had radioed in to Central Command. Murphy was dead now, back in the forest, his legs in one place and his torso in another after he tripped a land mine. I had been about ten yards from him and my first impulse was to run; but I resisted it, and tried to block out the image of his guts plastered on tree trunks as I zigzagged to the forest's edge, scanning the ground for packed dirt, leaves— anything that could conceal a trip wire. Murphy's radio had been destroyed, too, before he received confirmation of his message. But still I was waiting for help, my ears peeled for the *chop-chop* of an approaching Huey. I was the only one left, with nowhere to go. All I could do was wait.

Across the field, bare trees lined a ridge. Their foliage had been blasted away. They looked like fence posts. Seeing dust kick up beyond them, I dived into the thicket. A man clutching a rifle appeared on the ridge. Eight more Vietcong followed him. They wore baggy green fatigues and straw hats. Two of them carried an antiaircraft gun.

I lay flat and didn't breathe. Didn't blink. I couldn't swallow the dry knot lodged in my throat.

I was in the Signal Corps, stationed in the hills east of An Loc near the Be River. We were just twenty-five miles from the Cambodian border; between us and it there were two U.S. Army regiments, a brigade of South Vietnamese Army regulars, and a dozen Special Forces units. We were a C&C unit: communications and cryptography. We had radio receivers, transmitters, scramblers, Teletypes—all high-tech for that time. There were eight of us. The emblem on our sleeves was a bear clutching a lightning bolt. For four months we had lived and worked in a pair of glorified hootches, oblong wooden buildings erected in two days and nights by the Corps of Engineers. It had a name: L Base. We had an outhouse, an outdoor mess beneath a corrugated roof and a showerhead behind the mess for one-minute showers. For anyone in-country, these were deluxe accommodations. Indeed, the four grunts out of Ba Ra who shared our quarters and guarded the site considered it a plum assignment. Because the tree canopy was so thick, by day we operated in a constant twilight. At night the clatter of birds was deafening. And before dawn it grew so quiet I could hear the bamboo ticking miles from our perimeter. Sometimes in the darkness it felt as if we weren't really there, while the enemy was everywhere—owning the darkness.

In basic training, after shaving my head and conditioning me to do fifty push-ups by my bunk at reveille and teaching me to take apart, clean, and reassemble my M-16 hundreds of times until I could do it blindfolded, the army had discovered that with my college education, speed-typing abilities, and (added bonus) skill on a motorcycle, I was suited for the Signal Corps. Once again my nickname was X. I encrypted and decoded messages: troop movements, bombing runs, surveillance data. I also served as a motorcycle courier, dispatched to forward positions at Loc Ninh and Bo Duc. Even the army's stripped-down Harleys were tricky to handle on the rough dirt roads, but the fact I could ride one at all was what saved my life. The war had spilled over into Cambodia. Every morning we woke to the F-15s flying their sorties out of Saigon. One day in April we received an urgent message: three North Vietnamese Army armored divisions, equipped with Russian tanks, had crossed the border and joined up with a VC brigade. They were overrunning Binh Long province, routing the troops that had been our buffer. We had twenty-four hours to evacuate L Base and make for the army garrison at Tay Ninh City. The grunts had already left to join the remnants of their company, retreating from a massacre at Ba Ra. Six of our men would flee in a truck, with whatever equipment we didn't destroy. Our captain, who had been burning papers in a pit, handed me a pouch of the most sensitive remaining material and ordered me to ride on ahead.

"The extra hour may make a difference, Atlas. Return this to me at Tay Ninh, or give it to the commanding officer. And take Murphy with you."

Murphy was a tough kid from Oakland with an eagle tattooed on the back of his head. His specialty was unscrambling radio signals. Drafted on his nineteenth birthday, he was counting on the army to pay his way through electronics school when he got out. He wanted to work at a radio station. Not just any station. "KNEW in Oakland— country music 24/7—or KMPX across the bay."

He climbed on the bike behind me. We were wearing our flak jackets and helmets. I had the pouch under my jacket, with the strap around my neck. Murphy slung our rifles over one shoulder and a PRC-6 radio over the other. We both wore holsters with standard-issue Smith & Wesson .38s. On his belt Murphy also had a pair of canteens. Two more canteens, C rations, and our ponchos were stuffed into the bike's saddlebags. A three-gallon can of gasoline was strapped onto the rack behind Murphy's seat.

We set off at noon. Even then the road was dark, the bamboo on either side thirty feet high, the dust coating our goggles. Murphy was reading the map, directing me. I was familiar with the two main roads, Highway 9 to Tay Ninh and Highway 13 to Saigon, but with the VC moving south so fast, we avoided them. We rode hard for a couple of hours, fording streams, cutting through rice paddies, weaving in and out of the forest. We began to hear gunfire ahead. Then we heard it behind us, too, and finally on all sides. Until then, with the throttle open and the wind at our backs, I could tell myself we were escaping danger. But we were riding right into it. Since I was a child, I'd always known I could die young, like my mother—that it might really happen. But for the first time I believed it.

Murphy was scared, too. When we came to a river with a bombed-out bridge, he squeezed my shoulder and shouted, "Go back to that last crossroads."

I spun the bike around and backtracked about a mile. We stood at the center of the crossroads and drank from one of the canteens. Dust and exhaust fumes had burned my throat. Murphy pushed up his goggles and pored over the map. It was a new map, updated and sent out to all command posts by our own unit the previous day.

"We go that way," he said, nodding to the right. "It's the only road that's blue, not red." A red road was off-limits at all times. "Every fucking cow path in this province is gonna be red by tomorrow. I just hope Kamazine didn't fuck up when he made this one blue." Kamazine was the guy in our unit who had updated the map.

"Which is the shortest route to Tay Ninh?" I said.

Murphy pointed to another road. "That one."

I thought about it. "I say we take the blue road."

Our captain and Kamazine and the four other members of our unit would be killed at that same crossroads an hour later when their truck was hit by a mortar shell. Soon afterward, twenty miles to the west, Murphy and I were ambushed. We never saw the VC that shot the bike out from under us. We were thrown and lucky to land in high grass. The VC kept strafing the road and we crawled through the grass and then began running, heads down, stumbling, falling, gulping for air, certain that without the bike we were dead. Without our rifles, too, which Murphy lost when we were thrown. We still had our .38s, and he had held on to the radio and one of the canteens. We ran without stopping until the gunfire grew faint, and then collapsed in the brush beside a muddy river.

It was over a hundred degrees. I tried to catch my breath, but it was like drawing fire into my lungs.

"They should've fucking gotten us out sooner," Murphy shouted, slapping the mosquitoes from his neck. "There was no recon over Cambodia? No one saw three fucking armored divisions?"

We were scraped and bruised. My lip was cut and I pressed my sleeve to it to stop the bleeding.

"How many assholes were asleep at the wheel in An Loc and Saigon?" he railed.

"Here, Murph." I had a Snickers bar in my pocket that I split in half.

He shook his head.

"It's all we've got."

He spat. "You think we're gonna take on Charlie with these pistols—like Wyatt Earp?" He tore off his flak jacket. "And this fucking thing won't be worth shit in a firefight."

I let him go on. It was his way of dealing with his fear. How did I deal with mine? I felt like throwing up. I tried to think about something else—anything. The transistor radio I had as a kid: it was red, with a single earplug that hurt my ear, tiny serrated dials for volume and tuning, and a circle of numerals that lit up. Like Murphy, I was loyal to certain stations. WABC. WMCA. I thought of my favorite disk jockeys: Cousin Brucie, Scott Muni, Jack Spector. I tried to hear the songs they played. *Bye Bye Love. Money. You Can't Catch Me.*

"I don't want no KIA after my name," Murphy snapped.

Killed in Action. Maybe he was right; maybe that would be the next station we heard: *WKIA.*

We finished the water in the canteen, refilled it with river water, and dropped in iodine tablets. Then we popped some salt tablets and washed them down. My helmet that weighed five pounds felt like twenty. My flak jacket was like lead. Sweat was streaming down my back.

Murphy jumped up suddenly. "Fuck this, too!" he shouted, flinging his helmet into the river. I saw his eagle tattoo for the last time before he pulled an Oakland A's cap, green with a gold brim, from his pocket and put it on as his helmet floated away through the reeds.

That had been nineteen hours and about twelve miles ago, across the roughest terrain I had ever seen. And Murphy had been right: his flak jacket and helmet could not have saved him when he stepped on that mine.

I still had the pouch under my flak jacket. And I still had my .38, which I slipped from its holster when that VC platoon descended the ridge and fanned out in my directon, heading for the forest. I had seen men die, but in my eight months in-country I had shot at no one. A bottomless silence was welling up beneath me. Maybe it was this that would carry off my spirit, I thought, when, in a few moments, my body was dead. Before that happened, before they killed me, would I kill one of them? Was that the only choice left me?

They were ninety feet away, moving in a broken line. Their leader was a wiry man with a goatee, bare-chested, a red bandanna knotted around his head. He was carrying a machete and staring at the thicket that concealed me. I'd heard reports of soldiers recently captured and executed, their heads affixed to spikes to frighten villagers who might collaborate. And other soldiers who, prior to interrogation, were stripped and doused with gasoline while their captors tossed lit matches at them. And—the worst—prisoners strung from trees with ropes, a canvas bag filled with rats fastened tightly over their heads.

As the men came closer, it struck me that I had another choice: put the pistol to my skull and—

Red Bandanna jerked his head up and shouted, pointing at the sky. As he turned, I saw the tattoo covering his back, a sea serpent in a storm—my father's tattoo. Then there was a thunderclap, followed by an explosion that rocked the earth. A wall of fire swept past me. Red Bandanna, his men, the trees—everything was consumed as I flew into the air myself, into the flames, tumbling, flailing, blacking out.

When I came to, I was sprawled out far from what remained of that thicket—a mound of ashes. My uniform was in tatters, my skin black. One boot was gone. Dirt filled my mouth. All my bones felt broken, but in fact it was my left arm and two ribs that were cracked. And there was a hole in my left side—the size of a cigarette pack—caked with blood.

It was twilight. Many hours had passed. Maybe an entire day. Spitting dirt, I raised myself up onto my right elbow. That was as far as I could go. If any of the VC had survived, they couldn't be doing much better. Body parts were scattered around the field. The old craters had been supplanted by two others, many times wider. In the largest a severed leg was dangling a sandal. The red bandanna was floating in a puddle of blood.

The bombs dropped—probably from an F-15—had saved my life. But when I thought of Murphy radioing in our coordinates, my terror deepened: had he somehow—by giving the wrong code or having his message garbled—called in an airstrike rather than a search and rescue? If so, no Huey was ever going to come and I was going to die right there in the mud.

I closed my eyes and waited for that stillness to return and carry me away. Instead, a trapdoor opened and I started falling, arms and legs extended, weightless suddenly, down a long shaftway. The walls were on fire. Lights flashed, stars exploded. Then there was nothing but darkness, warm and velvety. I landed in a room with bamboo walls and a slow fan, on the softest feather bed imaginable. It smelled of jasmine. Fruit glittered in a bowl. A caged bird was singing. I turned on my side and that girl in the red dress rolled into my arms. She was naked now, with a hibiscus flower in her black hair. Her eyes were closed. She parted her lips and I kissed her. I felt her breasts compact against my chest. Her fingertips running along my back. I slid on top of her and as I entered her she opened her eyes. They were black glass, reflecting, not my image, but a beast with a long face, wrinkled forehead, and pocked cheeks. In the recesses of its close-set eyes stones were suspended—like holograms.

The Revesby bestiary says a man can foretell the future if such a stone is placed under his tongue.

The stone and the beast had the same name: *yena*, which means "hyena."*

But the man who dreams a hyena, the Revesby monks noted, has no future: he is so far along the road to death that he doesn't leave a trace—no footprints, no scent—and soon becomes invisible. Not even his screams can be heard.

I was four months shy of my twenty-second birthday.

*THE HYENA
An animal that is male one moment, female the next.
A tomb robber.
Like all hybrids, it was banished from Noah's ark.
After the Flood, it reemerged—the union of a mad dog and a graveyard cat—to feed on the corpses of the drowned.

*

A DRAGON TOWERED over me. With one claw it had seized a serpent, with the other a fox. A tiger was crouched behind it, ready
to spring. A monkey watched wide-eyed from the shadows.

They were jade statues, so lifelike I was sure I detected movement
among them: a fluttering eyelid, the twitch of an ear, a ticking tail.

I was in a sprawling basement room. Candlelight flickered off the
low ceiling. The floor was packed dirt. No walls were visible, just
darkness flowing off in every direction. High above, I heard a bell
ringing, muffled but purely pitched. Like a temple bell.

In addition to the animals, there were statues of the Buddha,
his mother Maya, the goddess Kwan-Yin, and the Zen patriarchs,
Bodhidharma and Huiko. Mara, the Evil One, was carved in cinnabar, as was his army of wingèd demons. And there were myriad statues
of creatures in monstrous transition between lives: a beetle metamor-
phosing into a squirrel, an eel into a lizard, a snail into a sparrow.

Scanning the statues, I discovered I had living company as well:
two men in orange monks' robes sitting on stools with fishing poles.
Between them was a basket, a net, and a stick of incense from which
smoke threaded upward. Were they crazy? I wondered. Then I heard
a gurgle of water and, through the shadows, made out an underground stream that wound across the room.

The monks paid no attention to me. I was lying on a canvas cot beneath a thin blanket. My left side was throbbing. My forehead was
hot, my lips cracked. I tried to lift my hands and discovered that I was
tied to the cot, like a prisoner.

That bell rang again. I called out to the monks, but still they didn't
move. Then I heard someone come around on my left: it was a panther,

walking on his hind legs. His eyes were topaz, his whiskers silver. He had a human smile.

And it was in a human voice, soft and deep, that he addressed me, speaking a language I had never heard before. On her deathbed my grandmother could understand every word this panther said; maybe the fact I couldn't meant I wasn't dying.

The panther held up a sheet of black paper, swirling with white shadows, and studied it. Then one of the monks caught something in the stream. It was not a ghostly fish that flashed on his line, but a disk of light that spun across the room and hovered over me, growing so large and bright I had to close my eyes.

※

WHEN I OPENED my eyes again, the light was blinding. A machine was whirring beside me. Needles were taped to my arms, and fluids flowed to me from IV bags, one red, one clear. My wrists were fastened. The air was cold. A circle of masked faces was staring down at me, still as statues, only their eyes moving. Their smocks and caps were white.

Through padded double doors, I heard gurneys rattling off an elevator.

One of the surgeons was holding an X-ray up to the light. He was rail-thin, with long fingers.

The anesthesiologist, in a green smock and tinted glasses, appeared and checked his canisters.

"Ready?" he asked.

The surgeon nodded.

A nurse touched my leg reassuringly. "You're going to be okay," she said.

The anesthesiologist raised a cup over my nose and mouth. "Start counting backward from one hundred," he commanded.

"Where are we?" I mumbled.

"Honolulu," the nurse replied.

"See you in four hours, soldier," the surgeon said.

It took them that long to pick the shrapnel out of my rib cage and sew me up again. Several pieces lodged in the bone itself remained.

Even now, my ribs ache on cold nights. And I have never been able to sleep on my left side again.

I HAD BEEN MISSING for thirty-six hours before the Huey picked me up near Dok Lo. Deep in enemy territory, I was nearly given up for captured, or dead. The Huey was already returning to Da Nang when they spotted me. I had lost a lot of blood, and my dog tags were gone, but I still had that document pouch around my neck.

After surgery, I was in bed for five days, and then a wheelchair for a week. My side was heavily bandaged and my arm was in a sling. The army hospital was overflowing. The fighting had intensified all along the Cambodian border and the worst casualties were being ferried in to Honolulu from Saigon. Men missing arms, legs, eyes, skin. Two beds down, with a catheter up his nose, there was a gunnery sergeant whose jaw had been blown away; beside him, a sniper with hooks for hands whose entire face had to be rebuilt. Worst of all were the men who had stepped on mines and were missing everything from the waist down. Murphy, if he had been a little luckier, or unluckier, might have been one of these. I was aware how fortunate I was just to know I would walk out of that place under my own power. But at night, when everything was magnified—the press of bodies, the sti-fling odors, the groans and screams—this was small comfort.

The patient in the next bed was a black kid from the Chicago projects named Monroe who had gotten religion. Monroe had lost an eye and a foot. With his remaining eye he scanned the Old Testament prophets and mumbled their words. An orderly gave him a book of Emanuel Swedenborg from which he began copying significant passages: *In Hell we find the most destructive creatures constantly at war: the viper, the scorpion, the rat—and man, first and foremost.*

The Tripler Army Hospital is on a bluff in the foothills of the city,

just above Salt Lake. When I wasn't so groggy from painkillers, I liked
to be wheeled out onto the cement terrace with the potted palms.
Sitting under an umbrella, I cadged cigarettes from the nurses and
gazed out over the Pacific, at the big clouds, the distant waves, the twi-
lights in which everything slowly went silver. I had plenty of time to
think—maybe more time than I wanted.

Those forty precarious miles I had traveled from L Base to
11°27'49" N, 106°39'08" E were only the last leg in the hectic line my
life had followed in the previous years.

In my junior year of college, I was drifting. Taking drugs. Bored,
not so much with my studies (not surprisingly, I had majored in history and classical languages) as with studying itself. I decided to drop
out to do some serious drifting, to see the world. Instead, I was promptly
drafted, and dispatched to a part of the world I had no desire to see.

When I enrolled in college, I gave up the apartment downtown,
with its bad karma, and moved across the river to a smaller but sunnier
place near Central Square. Eventually a girl named Nathalie moved in
with me. She was from Denmark, the daughter of a diplomat. We met
in a seminar on ancient exploration that began with Pytheas, the Greek
pilot who sailed to Iceland, and Hsuan-tsung, the first Chinese to
cross India. Nathalie was a traveler. Using her father's overseas post-
ings as springboards, she had trekked in the Andes and the Gobi
Desert, sailed a ketch solo in the Windward Islands, and kayaked in
the Seychelles. I never told her my own father had been a seaman.

However, in the city, Nathalie led a sedentary existence. If she
wasn't venturing into wilderness, she didn't go out much at all. In this,
as in all things, she alternated between extremes. She might work for
a month straight, fueled with speed and cigarettes, or be idle for weeks
on end, drinking rum late into the night. One constant was her appetite for Moroccan hashish. She obtained top-grade stuff from a
friend in Copenhagen, via the diplomatic pouch at her father's embassy. We broke chunks off the sticky bars imprinted with yellow
Arabic letters and smoked them in a hookah filled with crème de
menthe. The green liquid bubbled and the smoke filled my lungs with
a tightening rush.

We read aloud from De Quincey and Lautréamont. We played recordings of Tibetan chants. I bought her a book with one hundred color plates of Chinese dragons. River dragons, sky, thunder, fire, fish, horse, and treasure dragons. Scarlet dragons that circle the sun and silver dragons that sleep on the mountains of the moon. The one-headed, two-bodied *t'ao t'ieh* that never stops eating and eventually will consume the whole earth. And the reclusive *ti-lung*, which hides among the stars in spring and on the seafloor in autumn. Because the dragon population in China is so large, it is assumed dragons have established their own shadow government. The foremost ministry is the Treasury of Waters; its divisions include a Supreme Council, a Body of Dragon Ministers, and the Departments of Sweet Waters and Salt Waters, which in turn contain countless subdivisions.*

We studied the dragons in the glow of a lamp with a red lightbulb. On the dresser incense burned in the hollow stomach of a brass Buddha. The bedspread was a purple batik cloth that Nathalie had picked up in India. It depicted Vishnu and Lakshmi floating inter-twined among the stars in various stages of coitus. Sometimes we stayed in bed for an entire day. The apartment was overheated, filled with tropical plants, the curtains drawn on the sour New England winter that we both hated.

My father subsidized all this from afar, relieved, I imagined, just to authorize a monthly check and have me out of his hair. A lawyer in Athens named Pericles Arvanos actually wrote the checks.

Nathalie had black hair cut short and full, combed back—like raven's wings—over her ears. She was trim, and stronger than she looked. Her eyes were harder than the rest of her face, and her lips were full. She exuded the air of someone who had been around, who could look right through people if she wanted to. She was a wonderful

---

*THE CHINESE DRAGON
The pearl under its chin is the source of its power.
It exhales burning clouds that rain fire upon the earth.
The first emperors were descended from 3,000-year-old dragons.
At death, the emperor ascended to heaven on a dragon's back.

lover. A voracious reader, always ready to stay up all night talking. She liked to wear lizard cowboy boots. Sewn with colored beads on the back of her buckskin jacket was the ravenous wolf Fenrir and his brother, Jormungard, the Norse serpent which, like the Greek uroboros, encircled the great ocean that bounded the world. Shackled with an invisible chain (composed of a stone's roots, a woman's beard, a fish's breath, and the sound of a cat's footfall), Fenrir was destined to break free at the twilight of the gods, Ragnarøk, to swallow the sun and moon.

Nathalie was sly. An accomplished liar. Capable of stealing, too. Once in a Chinese restaurant when we were short of cash, she lifted a man's wallet. She was adept at charging long-distance phone calls to defunct numbers, and managed more than once to secure an airplane boarding pass without a ticket. Her lies were about getting what she wanted, when she wanted it. But sometimes she lied merely to embellish a slow evening when we were with someone she didn't like. Usually another woman. She didn't get along well with women. "For what?" she would say. "I like to be with men."

For one year and seven months that meant me. I had never known anyone like her before. Even more than her worldliness, it was the fact she was unafraid to focus only on what interested her that drew me to her. Wily and fast on her feet, she seemed much older than the other girls I had dated. She was impervious to others' opinions. In that respect, I wished I had been more like her. But I was thin-skinned; behind my isolating, and the barriers I erected, I cared what people thought about me. A part of me felt guilty about shutting them out. For Nathalie that was never a source of ambivalence.

With Nathalie I learned that you can be in love with someone even when certain things about them repel you—in her case, dishonesty and cynicism. And that such a person can make you happy even if, fundamentally, she is unhappy herself. At the same time, I did not delude myself that Nathalie and I would be together long. I never allowed myself that luxury with anyone.

One day Nathalie got word that her sister had been in a car accident on Majorca. She was in a coma. The family had her flown to

Denmark, and Nathalie joined them. When her sister died, Nathalie was devastated. She phoned me at three A.M., her voice scratchy through the static.

"I want to be there with you," I said.

After a long silence, she said, "That's not a good idea." I could tell she had been drinking. "I need to be alone for a while. Anyway, I'm not coming back to school anytime soon. Just mail me half our stash."

When I didn't reply fast enough, she raised her voice. "Okay?"

"Sure."

And she hung up.

I wedged the hash into a hollowed-out textbook and packaged it carefully, along with the book of dragons.

Soon afterward, I traded in my Yamaha for a silver 750cc Triumph Bonneville, powerful enough to travel the interstate, and set out for California. Officially I was on leave from school for a semester, so I assumed my draft status—student deferment, II-S—would remain unchanged. I followed an erratic route, south to New Orleans, north to the Dakotas, and south again to the Mexican border. By the time I reached San Francisco, I had grown a beard and smoked the rest of the hash. As arranged beforehand, I crashed with a friend in his apartment near Alamo Park. In mail forwarded to his address I found a letter from Nathalie inviting me to join her on Corfu, and a notice from my draft board with a different sort of invitation. My deferment had been canceled and I was reclassified I-A. Opposed to the Vietnam war, with no desire to kill or be killed for something I didn't believe in, I dropped methedrine for a week and for two days drank Ex-Lax. When I went in for my physical, I was sleepless, strung out, dehydrated, but still I passed. I could have fled to Canada—or Denmark, where Nathalie insisted I could make a life for myself—but I wasn't ready to renounce my citizenship and live abroad. For better or worse, I was an American; because I had no family or roots to speak of, giving up that particular connection would be even more painful. So instead of basking in the Ionian sun with Nathalie, I soon found myself in the dark jungles near An Loc. She thought I was insane. In our last phone call before I shipped out from San Diego, she shouted, "I will never forgive you, going over there." And she never did.

The day before I was released from the hospital in Honolulu, a major with red hair and unblinking eyes paid me a visit, accompanied by an aide who stood at attention. The major's name tag read CAPELLO. I knew why he was there; I had been expecting him.

"Private Atlas," he said, "it is a privilege to honor your service to our nation."

The aide snapped open a briefcase from which Major Capello took a small leather box. He pinned a medal to my robe and shook my hand. It was a Purple Heart. Nearly everyone in the ward had received one; if you were wounded in action, it was automatic.

As I studied George Washington's cameo on the medal, the major surprised me, taking out a second box. He made a little speech, which concluded, "For valor in combat above and beyond the call of duty, in Trang Province, Republic of South Vietnam, on the twenty-second of April, 1972, I hereby award you the Silver Star. Congratulations."

This was not something everyone got. And when you did get it, you knew why. I had to ask.

Major Capello looked at me skeptically, then leaned closer. I smelled tobacco on his breath and saw the groove on his lower lip where he planted his cigarette. "It was the pouch. You brought it home under fire."

The pouch. Of course. In the end, Murphy, the motorcycle, the radio, my rifle, even my uniform—everything else I'd set out with that day was gone. I'd stayed alive and I'd held on to the pouch, and they didn't give you a Silver Star for staying alive. "May I ask what it contained, Major?"

He raised an eyebrow. "You don't know?"

I shook my head.

He hesitated again. "Phoenix," he whispered, his eyes more unblinking than ever. "There were dossiers . . . operational details."

Operation Phoenix was an assassination program run by the CIA. The targets were not soldiers, but citizens alleged to be Vietcong sympathizers. Forty thousand of them had been executed by U.S. Special Forces. By war's end, twenty thousand more would die. Most CIA informers were petty criminals or corrupt officials on whose word entire families were killed if a single member was accused of aiding the communists. What I had been carrying was a new list of intended victims.

In June 1972 I may have exited Vietnam without shooting anyone, but I knew now that I had assisted in the killing of hundreds of people. Nathalie had been right: just getting inducted, becoming complicitous in something I detested, I was sure to end up tainted—and miserable. I didn't know just how miserable.

For years I made myself read everything I could find about Operation Phoenix, from transcripts of congressional testimony to the lurid paperback memoirs of assassins. It was my attempt at expiation. But it never gave me relief.

MOLOKAI WAS ONCE an island of sorcerers. They tattooed their bodies with the images of beasts. They shaved their heads with sharks' teeth. They could assume the shape of lizards. Their eyes were smoke. And in the oily smoke of palm fires they divined the future. Because of them, the warriors of Maui and Oahu, perpetually at war, avoided Molokai. The sorcerers' armies were composed of ghosts. When the sorcerers died off, the ghosts remained, roaming the island.

Molokai is still said to be a haven for ghosts—especially the ghosts of soldiers. I'd come close to becoming one myself, I thought, stepping off the prop plane from Honolulu in a driving rain. As I crossed the island in a rental car, through forests choked with mist, I wondered if I would encounter Murphy's ghost. If so, would his two halves be rejoined? Would he be a transparent version of himself, or just a coil of that mist, whispering by?

After receiving my medical discharge, I made a reservation on a flight to San Francisco—then thought better of it. I had wanted to get as far from Southeast Asia as possible, to ease back into civilian life, but realized I had a better chance of doing so in Hawaii, where things were more laid-back. I checked into a sleepy motel on the north shore of Oahu. For the first time in ten months, I ate alone, showered alone, and had my own bathroom. I tried not to drink a lot, though I wanted to; I stayed away from weed, which was readily available; and I cut down on the painkillers the doctors had loaded me up with. In my nightmares I was still riding on that motorcycle with Murphy, but he was just a skeleton pressed up against me; or I was back in that field, scrambling as the napalm hit; or sitting on a freezing C-130 transport with hundreds of other soldiers, stiff as statues, forced to return to Vietnam for another tour of duty. These dreams became so torturous that—in vain—I invoked Baku, the Japanese spirit known as the "Eater of Dreams." With a lion's head, tiger's feet, and horse's body, Baku resembled the chimera or the manticore, but was a beneficent spirit. If a sleeper awoke from a nightmare and cried, "Baku, eat my dreams," Baku would do so, and the sleeper, relieved of his burden, would drift off serenely.

Mr. Hood, my old history teacher, had invited me to Molokai. He had retired to the island two years earlier and lived in a ranch house on a rough stretch of its southern shore. Catching my name in the newspaper, in a list of newly decorated soldiers, he had sent me a letter, care of the army. I was surprised to learn that he was in Hawaii, and even more surprised that he would invite me to be a houseguest. He had offered me crucial encouragement as a student, but we had never socialized—not even a cup of coffee in the school cafeteria. We met in his office, never his home, to discuss coursework and my research, not personal matters. To the end, he was formal and reserved. So I did not find it strange when we fell out of touch during my freshman year in college.

Approaching his house, I felt for a moment as if I were back in Maine: he was on the lanai, holding a book at arm's length and puffing a pipe. His dog Polyphemus was asleep at his feet. The dog was thirteen, and I was halfway across the lawn before he rose stiffly, to sniff me out. He was nearly as old as Re when he died. The lawn ended at the beach, about thirty yards away. There was a one-man kayak propped against a tree. And on a low platform, under construction, a forty-foot canoe.

Mr. Hood looked much as he had when I walked into his classroom seven years before. Thin waist, rough hands, powerful shoulders and arms from his daily rowing. The crow's-feet were deeper beside his blue eyes. His beard was grayer. The crew cut was gone. It was disconcerting at first to see him with longer hair, well over his collar. It too was grayer, with sprays of white on the sides. But he seemed far more at ease. The tropics evidently agreed with him more than the Frozen North. Or maybe he too was just glad to have left the school.

"Welcome," he said, and we shook hands.

I had been wondering if he had invited me out of loneliness. Or if, having always liked me, he could now befriend me as an adult. More importantly, I had become a fellow vet. Whatever his motives, I was gratified: at school, after all, he had learned a great deal about me, while I knew little about him.

He picked up my bag and led me into the house. The guest room was cool and quiet, with darkly lacquered Chinese furniture. There was an empty antique birdcage. A sliding door opened onto a terrace in the garden. Blackbirds were singing through the louvered windows.

He got a plate of walnuts, cheese, and crackers from the kitchen and set it out on the lanai. Dropping ice into two glasses and pouring us Irish whisky, he saw that I was admiring the canoe under construction.

"I was taught the Phoenicians were the greatest seafarers ever," he said, handing me my drink. "But they were day-trippers compared to the Polynesians, who roamed the Pacific in canoes like that. Fifteen hundred years ago, they sailed here from the Marquesas Islands, across seven thousand miles of open sea. They believed the first canoe was built by a warrior named Rata. After he rescued a heron from the jaws of a sea serpent, the heron taught Rata the art of canoe-building. Rata visited dozens of islands, passing on his knowledge. As in Maine, I'm only using indigenous tools—an adz, a mallet, a machete—and ironwood and palm from that forest. The Polynesians could build a canoe in five days. I'll have this one seaworthy in three months."

"Where will you sail?"

"Only as far as Oahu," he smiled. "I'll enlist some rowers in town."

We sat down and I lit a cigarette. He refilled his pipe. The surf was rough and the first stars were flickering.

"You should call me Cletis now," he said simply.

Then he told me something of his history—more in twenty minutes than I had learned in five years at school. First he put to rest the rumors I'd heard, ticking them off with a grimace. His wife was not a suicide: she had died of a heart attack at forty; he had never been court-martialed; none of his limbs was prosthetic; and his children had not died in an automobile accident. The most outlandish rumor, that his father-in-law had been a South American dictator—"President-for-Life of Bolivia for three years," he said wryly—was true. And he did have an independent income that allowed him to give up teaching and live wherever he wanted and do what he liked.

"I am attempting that one book," he smiled thinly, "which some-one like me saves up to write. A specialized topic that accommodates digression."

He was writing about the cities Alexander the Great founded, and named after himself, when he swept across Asia.

"There were eighteen Alexandrias," he explained. "Alexander chose the sites himself: in Persia, India, even Siberia. Only the Egyptian Alexandria survives. In Scythia, Alexandria was a city of sandstone towers. By the Indus River, it was a sprawl of canals, with houses on stilts. The Babylonian Alexandria contained a zoo, with exotic animals from around his empire. Kabul, Afghanistan, was one of the Alexandrias. And this should interest you: Alexander also named one city, Bucephalia, after his horse, and another, Peritas, to honor his dog."

The previous year, I doubt I would have heard all this with such a jaundiced ear; but, sipping my whisky, watching the breakers burst against the reefs, I told myself that, for every city he founded, Alexander must have razed ten others, and for every animal placed in a zoo, thousands more were sacrificed to his gods. In Vietnam, in the Year of the Rat, people were eating rats. And the only construction project I'd seen was the lengthening of airport runways for bigger, deadlier bombers. Still, after my grim stay in Honolulu, Mr. Hood's conversation was a tonic. Having been wounded in combat himself as a young man, he knew that enthusiasm for anything—except survival—was in short supply where I had been.

"There's my theme," he went on, "built on a contradiction: Alexander is the only conqueror to have left in his wake a string of new cities while waging an active military campaign. He explored deserts and rivers no European had ever seen. He had radical notions for a king, allowing the tribes he defeated to govern themselves, adopting their customs and dress, conversing with their priests. He made a Bactrian princess, Roxane, his queen, and rewarded his soldiers when they too married Asian women. When he visited the Temple of Ammon-Re, the reclusive priests, who had no idea of his identity, hailed him as a god. He began to believe this himself." He smiled. "He's a tough subject to keep up with. My book will take years to write."

"Is that why you moved here?"

"It's one reason." He relit his pipe. "This house belonged to my wife. After she died, I couldn't bring myself to stay on alone. I didn't want to rent or sell, so I closed it up."

"That's when you started teaching."

"Yes. It was a way to start over. To stay sane. It was the only real job I ever had outside the military. But I always knew I'd return here. I just didn't think it would be this soon."

Of all the reasons I had imagined for his moving to Maine, a broken heart was not one of them. I felt bad about that now. "When did your wife die?"

"Twelve years ago." He saw my surprise, and added, "To me, that doesn't seem long. Not long enough."

"I'm sorry."

He shook his head. "We had a wonderful run. In Spain, Mexico, here. Here best of all. This was our only real home. Then one morning, coming up from the beach, I heard Polyphemus barking. Marion had collapsed in the garden. I rushed her to the hospital—too late." He leaned over to pet the dog. "He was just a year old when she rescued him on the road. When he and I returned to the island, it was as if he had never left. He went right to his favorite spots in the house. He slept on her bed." Mr. Hood sat back slowly. "Marion had a weak heart, and it finally gave out."

My grandmother used that expression when she spoke of my mother. "Her heart give out," she would sigh. I wasn't sure what this meant exactly until I discovered that, because my birth was complicated, my mother had hemorrhaged suddenly, gone into shock, and died of cardiac arrest.

I watched the smoke from my cigarette waft into the vines above Mr. Hood's lanai. The moon was high. Mercury was visible, too, unblinking among the stars. After coming and going several times, Polyphemus had nudged open the screen door and retired.

It was close to midnight when I told Mr. Hood about my stint in the Signal Corps. My side ached, as it did whenever I sat for too long. The surgeons had warned me it would be this way for at least six months, until my wound healed fully.

Mr. Hood listened carefully, and after a long silence, said, "Livy tells the story of a courier in the Galatian campaign who overcame countless obstacles—dangerous terrain, hunger, enemy patrols—only to discover that the message he delivered included his own death warrant. That's an extreme example, but soldiers are always kept in the dark. In war, you think you know some fraction of the story, including your own story, when you know nothing. When, in fact, there is no story. If you had lost that pouch, the army wouldn't have told you anything. If you had known what it contained, you might have been tempted to lose it, and no one the wiser."

"Don't think that hasn't occurred to me."

"But you didn't know. You couldn't." He leaned forward, placing his palms on his knees. "Phoenix is shameful. This war is lost. But that doesn't mean it's over."

"It's over for me."

He knew better but—out of kindness, I'm sure—didn't correct me.

Instead, he pointed at the half-built canoe. "To the Polynesians, canoes were living spirits. Canoe-building is a healing art. I built my first canoe when I returned from the Philippines. I worked on it for three months. After going to war, the hardest part isn't coming back to other people, but to yourself. Some people can't." He looked away. "My son Roy fought in Korea. He made it home in one piece. He seemed all right. Then, a week later, he was gone."

It was his son who had committed suicide.

He shook his head. "Roy tried to hide it, but I knew things weren't right. I'd seen it in other soldiers. Still, I felt powerless. He couldn't—or wouldn't—discuss what happened to him the way you just did. My daughter, Katie, blamed me for that." He poured himself a last drink. "She was right. He and I had never talked much, not really, and that was my responsibility. She also blamed me for pushing him into the Corps. I didn't push him, but I didn't discourage him either. She lives in Spain now. We haven't talked since her mother died. Marion never got over Roy's death. For us, it just kept rippling. It's still rippling."

I was stunned to hear him talk like this. And to learn how much pain he'd been carrying. "I'm sorry," I said, touching his arm.

"I thought hearing this might help you."

I looked at his lined face, the washed-out eyes. "Is there anything I can do for you?"

"You already have," he said quietly.

We sat back and looked out at the sea. On the horizon, the lights of a passing ship were just disappearing.

"Xeno, what about the *Caravan Bestiary*? Last I heard from you, you were still researching."

"Yes, I filled a lot of notebooks, trying to reconstruct the bestiary's contents. Before I was drafted, my goal was to learn all I could and lay the groundwork so I could search properly." I hesitated. "I need time now, before I get back to it. Everything I read in college confirms what you told me years ago."

"Oh?"

"Brox, Cava, and Faville were probably right: the book was destroyed. All the evidence points to it."

"But you're still not sure."

"I just don't know. The Catholic Church really wants it gone, and then one day—it is gone. Does anything really disappear without a trace? Part of me says yes. I've seen it happen . . ."

"And the other part?"

"Tells me I need to find out for myself. In the real world."

He smiled. "I told you back then: it may not be in the real world that you'll find answers."

"As soon as I finish school, I'll start looking."

"You're going back, then."

"Yes. I was a junior when I left. I need three semesters' worth of credit. I'd like to cram it into a single year. And at the same time try to pick up where I left off with the bestiary. I got very interested in Brox. I read about his unfinished essay on the bestiary; probably there's nothing there. But I want to see for myself. Like Cava, Brox was convinced the bestiary had been hidden away in Italy for centuries before it was destroyed in Spain. But he didn't think it had been in the Vatican, or that the Catholic Church was involved."

"Good. The sooner you get back to it, the better."

"For starters, I thought I would go to the public library in San Francisco, and maybe Berkeley."

Mr. Hood stood up and put the bottle and our glasses on a tray. "We have some good libraries in Honolulu. You're not leaving for a couple of weeks. Why not start here? I know some people at the university library in Manoa. I can give you an introduction."

When I retired to the guest room, rain was drumming softly on the roof. The leaves in the garden were dripping. I stepped outside, under the canopy of trees.

That postcard of the girl with the bicycle was the only item I had carried during my tour of duty that survived. Everything else was gone, including my three photos—of Nathalie, Lena, and my mother (at Jones Beach)—and a Saint Francis medal my grandmother had given me. The postcard was bloodstained now, and my message to myself was gone.

Province of fire, Year of the Rat.

I put a match to the postcard, and holding one corner, watched it burn: the girl's red dress and black hair, the hibiscus flowers, the pagoda. The wind caught the ashes in midair and blew them into the rain.

I went back inside. Shadows flitted around the empty birdcage. I took my pills and checked my bandage. I got into bed and eased onto my right side, wedging a pillow behind my back to make sure I didn't turn over.

THREE DAYS LATER in Honolulu, on a steaming hot morning, I sat in the Asia Reading Room on the fourth floor of the Hamilton Library. Arrayed before me on the teak table were the fourth volume of the ancient Chinese *Bamboo Books*, an illustrated edition of the *Annals of Lakes and Mountains*, and a seventeenth-century Tibetan bestiary in which the renderings of the animals could only be appreciated with a magnifying glass: the snow leopard, the eagle, and that bizarre humanoid, the yeti (later, unfortunately tagged "the abominable snowman"), which was once a commonplace in the Himalayas. I also had the famous commentary on the *Bamboo Books* published in 1865 by the English Sinologist James Legge and a pile of books from the classical Greek collection on the second floor. Except for a Japanese scholar huddled over a scroll and a professor with a white beard dozing in the corner, I had the place to myself. A frieze from Angkor Wat, of monkey gods battling demons, was hung on the far wall. Two glass cabinets were filled with Han Dynasty ceramics. The prophet Milarepa, ringed by dancers, beamed down at the professor from a silk tapestry.

Mr. Hood had made a phone call and written a letter of introduction to the Hamilton's associate director, his friend Joseph Tamasho (mentioning that I had just returned from Vietnam), and—presto—I was issued a library card with full privileges. A slight, moustached man with impeccable manners, Mr. Tamasho wore a madras jacket and white shoes. He offered me tea and showed me around the library himself.

The reading room was comfortable and the stacks well organized. Scents of plumeria and yellow ginger wafted in from the garden.

There was a café across the courtyard that served good Kona coffee and sandwiches. Nevertheless, for the first two days I couldn't concentrate. But for the rustle of pages and the purr of the air-conditioning, the room was practically silent. It made me restless. I caught myself staring out the tinted windows. In the jungle I had not even been able to get through the pulp mysteries and Westerns we passed around; focusing on a scholarly text now seemed impossible. I flipped through book after book, pausing over passages that caught my eye. My C&C work, encrypting and decoding, had required concentration, but of a mechanical sort. There was nothing stimulating about encrypting dozens of messages like *Alpha Red rendezvous Delta Blue, J Quadrant.* To preserve my sanity, I had had to shut down selective parts of my mind; opening them up again was not so easy.

This only intensified my despair. I was ready to thank Mr. Tamasho, return my library card, and move on. Then an entry in an encyclopedia of Greek scholiasts broke through my paralysis. The encyclopedia was compiled by a sixteenth-century rabbi from Fez, Jakob Ben Chaim. The entry was for the peryton, a high-circling bird—often mistaken for a hawk—that is among the most ominous of lost beasts. The rabbi discovered it in the trancription of an anonymous treatise, one of the 500,000 volumes lost when the Great Library of Alexandria burned down in 48 B.C. This is his description:

> *It possesses the head and forelegs of a deer affixed to the torso of a bird. Geron of Chios reports that Perytons are the souls of lost wayfarers, especially soldiers, who have died far from home. If a man is unlucky enough to glimpse this creature, it means he himself is lost, and in danger of being transformed into a Peryton. The Peryton is always encountered as a large bird casting the shadow of a man.*

Perhaps the power of suggestion, abetted by my painkillers, was at work when late that afternoon I walked across the city and visited the Foster Botanical Garden. There were few people around. Steam rose from the ferns beneath the banyan trees. With their long bills the cranes in the pond tossed water onto their feathers. There was a couple necking in a gazebo. Near the Orchid House, in a maze walled by hedges, I came on an intersection in the paths where a man's small, watery shadow was undulating on the flagstone. He must have been perched high in a tree around the corner—a gardener, pruning branches, I thought. But when I rounded that corner and squinted into the glare, I saw only a large bird streaking off a kapok tree, disappearing into the clouds. It may have been a hawk or a petrel, but I took it as a warning that, coming from where I'd been, if I wasn't careful, I could get very lost very fast.

Maybe I needed to be jolted. That night I slept for twelve hours and awoke with a terrible thirst. I drank several glasses of cold water, and was still thirsty. But I could breathe again. Something had snapped free inside me.

I bought a notebook to replace the nearly empty one I had lost in the war. When I returned to the library, I made my first entry:

THE PERYTON
Originally from the continent of Atlantis.
It nests in caves on the Rock of Gibraltar and subsists on soil and salt
    water.
If it kills a man, it regains its true shadow.

I dove into my reading with a new sense of purpose, making original entries and expanding old ones. With the phoenix, for example, I discovered a rich mythology across many cultures, from Sumatra, where the *Garuda* dwells in an underwater cavern, to India, where the *Samandal* is kept in a maharajah's crystal cage. My favorite was the Japanese phoenix, the *Ho-ho* (named for its cry); Rijo, court astronomer to the Emperor Toba, took what we call the Fourth Dimension for granted when he wrote in the *Imperial Annals* of 1137 that "it is well known the Ho-ho can fly across time and space and in a single hour visit the same man in his cradle and on his deathbed."

In another Japanese chronicle, I found a cousin of the peryton, the

Shinto war demon *Oni*, which had a human head on a hawk's body. In the *Bamboo Books* I discovered a Chinese mermaid, the *Ling yu*, and countless other creatures that I dutifully recorded.*

One morning, in the Latin American section of the library, I unearthed a Patagonian bestiary by an eighteenth-century missionary, Joaquin Alvaro, who crossed the pampas on foot in 1756. Instead of converting the natives to Christianity, he recorded their stories about the reputed fauna of the region, strange elusive animals, most of which—but not all—had died out long before: man-sized sloths, enormous birds (like the rukh) that feasted on dust, fish that swam in boiling lakes. Having traveled to the Far East, Alvaro claimed there were dragons at the remote heart of Patagonia composed of a single element—fire, water, stone, air—like their Chinese counterparts.

The ghost dragon, for example, which frequents hospitals, nursing homes, and battlefields, feeding on the spirits of the newly deceased. It is invisible; only murderers can see it, just after committing their crimes.

Mostly, though, I used this time in Honolulu to circle back to more familiar terrain, early natural historians like Pliny the Elder, Diodorus Siculus, and Aristotle. I had become proficient enough in Greek and Latin (having studied each for eight years) to read them in the original. I veered away from the Christian Physiologus and the monks who were his pious successors. Gradually they became less interested in the animals than the moral precepts that could be attached to them. The turtledove, for example, was presented as a symbol of a widow's chastity first, a flesh-and-blood bird second. Certain creatures

---

*SHANG YANG
A one-legged bird that nests along rivers.
Carrying water skyward in its beak, it injects the clouds until they burst.

SHAN HUI
A mountain dog with a human face and a serrated tail.
It feasts on nettles and sleeps in cemeteries.

HEMICYNE
A dog-headed man who lives in a cave by the sea.
Formerly a fisherman, he will drown any fisherman he sees.

(dove, caladrius, panther) were declared to be stand-ins for the Savior, others (wild ass, wolf, serpent) for Satan. Christian dogma attempted to contract and sanitize, to make black-and-white, the bright complex tapestry on which these animals lent themselves to freer allegory. Soon the monks began eliminating the fantastical beasts altogether.

I wondered how many such animals the conventional bestiaries had omitted; not just the ones Noah banished from the ark, but the other amazing stragglers and hybrids, from every continent, that had eluded history.

Aristotle was intrigued by fantastical animals, and while completing his *Animalia*, wrote a book about them, *Peri Mysterion* ("Mysteries"), which inspired the first compilers of the *Caravan Bestiary*. The original disappeared in the fire at the Great Library, but traces of it were said to have survived. Hoping to find them, I turned to the chroniclers who annotated the *Animalia* and all of Aristotle's other works. Most of these medieval texts were only available on microfiche; the originals were in Europe. In one of the most obscure, least promising tracts, written in 1382 by a prelate from Languedoc named Guy Pelletier, I stumbled on the crucial clue that marked the real starting point of my search for the *Caravan Bestiary*.

In his rambling *Commentarii*, Pelletier used Aristotle as a springboard for digressions about his soldiering in the Eighth Crusade as a young man. I quickly grew bored with him, and was about to remove the microfiche of his book from the viewer when I came on his description of the Battle of Smyrna, in October 1351. The Crusaders had triumphed, despite heavy casualties, and Pelletier attended the signing of the peace treaty that followed and provided biographical sketches of the diplomats who conveyed Pope Clement VI's terms to the Saracens. Prominent among them was a French knight named Martin Lafourie.

Because he was a wily and skillful negotiator, Lafourie drafted the greater part of the treaty. Emissary of His Majesty King Philip VI, he was renowned for having advanced the interests of France in Afrique and the Levant. A brave soldier in his youth, Lafourie was so well-

traveled as a diplomat that some at Philip's court in Paris had never encountered him. It was rumored that on a mission to the Knights Hospitallers in Rhodes several years before, he recovered and carried away that rare and dangerous Bestiary called the Caravan. *He neither acknowledged nor denied this, and did not reveal where he might have taken the book.*

I nearly jumped out of my chair. I reread the passage, closed my eyes, and read it again. I was stunned by my good luck.

At the Hamilton Library in Honolulu, on June 2, 1972, from an incidental passage in a forgotten text, I had moved the whereabouts of the *Caravan Bestiary* forward a full century, to the 1340s, and established its last confirmed location on Rhodes.

Michael Brox had been wrong when he said the bestiary was burned in Spain in 1191; and there was no telling if Niccólo Cava was correct to insist that the book had ended up in Italy, locked away by the Church; and Madame Faville had been right about Rhodes, but wrong to assert the bestiary was destroyed. Now I had discovered something that eluded all of them: the strong possibility that a medieval diplomat named Martin Lafourie visited Rhodes and "carried away" the bestiary. Back to France? When, and how? And from whom, or what, did he "recover" it? The book still may have been destroyed after Lafourie obtained it, but the fact it had already lived on for another hundred years gave me hope it might have survived even longer, and might still exist. Before leaving the library, I checked the catalogs, but there were no references to a Martin Lafourie. I knew I would have to dig deeper than that. If he were that easy to find, Brox, Cava, or Faville would somehow have learned of his connection to the bestiary.

Night had fallen, and a warm wind was swaying the palms as I walked down Kapahulu Avenue. I felt both exhilarated and tired and I wanted to celebrate my find. I went into a package store, bought a chilled bottle of Dom Perignon, and headed for the ocean.

On the beach, I popped the cork. I took a long swig and turned toward Diamond Head, past the hotel terraces with their burning torches, and the zoo, and the natatorium. I walked the length of Kahala Beach, until the lights of the city melted away behind me.

Rounding a promontory into a sheltered cove, I heard music and laughter. There was a bonfire. A large party of people my age or younger wearing shorts or bathing suits. Dancing, drinking. I hesitated, then joined them. A guy in a cowboy hat handed me a can of beer from a cooler. I gave him the champagne. A girl passed me a joint. I took a hit. The girl smiled and I took another hit. She drank some champagne. A big man in a chef's apron was barbecuing on a grill. Two girls in bikinis were sitting in the sand playing guitars and singing a medley of slow songs. Their faces glowed in the firelight. They had beautiful voices.

Carlton, the youngest guy in my unit, used to sing all the time. He was from Minnesota. He had wanted to move to Louisiana and work on an oil rig in the Gulf. His family was poor, and someone had told him he could make real money down there. Suddenly I couldn't remember what he looked like. I panicked. I had this crazy thought that if I didn't remember him, no one would. Then I told myself it wasn't that crazy. With the others dead, I was the last living person to have seen Carlton alive, when we evacuated our base. Murphy, too. All of them.

The girl touched my arm. "Hey."

I looked at her more closely. She was stoned, but not that stoned. She had a nice smile. Beautiful teeth. Long black hair. She was Hawaiian.

She passed back the champagne, and after I drank again, there wasn't much left. I gave it to her to finish.

"You a sailor?" she said.

"No."

She cocked her head. "Lots of sailors, they get out of the navy and stay in the islands."

"I can understand that." I took another hit off the joint.

She smiled. "What's your name?"

"Xeno."

"I'm T.J. Do you dance, Xeno?"

"Sure."

I pulled off my boots and rolled up my jeans. She put her arms around me and we started dancing slowly. I hadn't danced or been to a party or held a girl like her close in a thousand years.

Just then Carlton's face came into my head. A moon face. Brown eyes. Thin lips. Every detail clear. So it was all right again.

The party grew louder, and we kept dancing, and her skin felt soft and her breasts against my chest and her hands on my shoulders and her hair smelled so good I didn't want to stop, and we didn't stop.

O N MY LAST AFTERNOON in Honolulu, I watched a mermaid swim through a cloud of convict tangs, yellow with black stripes. The mermaid's long hair was dyed green. Her outfit was skintight Lycra, silver with iridescent scales. She wore a V-shaped mask and every couple of minutes sucked oxygen from rubber tubes, strategically placed among the plants. She navigated deftly with her rubber tail, climbing the walls, turning figure eights, hovering upright.

The aquarium guidebook stated that the mermaid was an invention of sailors who mistook the dugong, a pale marine mammal, for a semihuman creature.

In fact, the earliest mermaids were bird-women, with human heads, claw feet, and tail feathers. They inhabited secluded meadows and sang haunting melodies. *Ker-Sirens*, the Greeks called them, "souls that carry off other souls." Spirits of the dead with license to travel in and out of the underworld.

Eventually they gravitated to the sea. They grew fish tails, but kept their wings. They sang across the flashing waters, luring seamen onto rocky shores.

Finally they took to the water themselves, fish from the waist down. A comb in one hand, a mirror in the other, they danced atop the waves. Their earrings were half-moons, their bracelets human bone. When they came ashore to dance with men, they concealed their tails and dyed their hair black, leaving a single clue to their identity: that the hem of a siren's dress is always wet.

The Polynesians had an identical myth, in which the dead became sirens, beautiful singers who diverted mariners into turbulent seas, and when they'd drowned, dispatched their shades to Reinga, the deep-sea netherworld.

I walked down the promenade to a pier where men were fishing. There were pails at their feet with live bait and baskets into which they dropped their catch, yellowfins and lemonfish with glittering green fins.

I bought a taco and a Coke from a vendor and sat on a wooden bench. I had called Mr. Hood to say goodbye and thank him again for his help. He was excited about my discovery of Martin Lafourie. "You're on your way now," he said. And I was. My flight was at nine o'clock, my bags were packed. The sun felt good on my skin. I was wearing a Hawaiian shirt, orange with purple palms. I unbuttoned the shirt, but because my scar was still livid, did not remove it. Three months out of the army and my hair was back to shoulder-length. I had grown a moustache. My sunglasses were a shade lighter than a blind man's.

I remained on the pier until dusk. Gulls wheeled overhead, their wings tipped with fire. A new group of fishermen arrived, and bathers came to the beach after work.

As I got up to leave, the mermaid from the aquarium appeared in her street clothes: a cotton dress and sandals. She wore a seashell necklace. Her hair was still green, combed back wet. As graceful as she had been in the water, on land she seemed disjointed, slightly pigeon-toed. She had plain features and pale skin. She walked to the beach and removed her dress, beneath which was a blue bathing suit. I would have thought the last thing she wanted to do was swim, but she dove right into the water, swam about fifty yards underwater, emerged briefly, then continued on beyond the buoys and disappeared.

I scanned the harbor for a long time, until I risked missing my flight. The moon had risen by then. But she didn't reappear.

Perhaps, I thought, hailing a taxi, that wouldn't happen until morning, when she had to return to work.

IN SAN FRANCISCO, I found two letters that had never reached me in Vietnam: one from my father's lawyer, which had first been forwarded from Boston to San Francisco, and one from Lena. The letters must have been held at Central Command in Saigon until some clerk, discovering I had been hospitalized and discharged in Honolulu, sent them back to San Francisco.

Pericles Arvanos's letter, postmarked in Athens in March, was, as usual, all business: because I had left school, and had not been using the Boston apartment, he requested my current address. He also wanted to know if my allowance should be wired to another bank: the one in Boston reported that my checking account had been inactive for months. Apparently my blip had grown so faint on my father's radar screen that it actually caught his attention. Of course my father had no idea I'd been sent to Vietnam. I'm sure he would have thought me a fool, putting myself in a position to be drafted and nearly killed. To his credit, I had never heard him wax patriotic, about the United States, Greece, or anyplace else. He was apolitical and unsentimental, as indifferent to flag-waving as to religious piety. During the Second World War, he had served briefly as a seaman in the merchant marine, running U-boat blockades in the North Atlantic; later he insisted it was just like any other stint at sea, except the pay was worse.

In truth, I preferred the letter from his attorney to another cryptic postcard. Fortunately (as it turned out) I didn't reply at once, though I had already decided I didn't want any more money from my father. All those years, there had been a disconnect between the financial support he provided and the emotional support he withheld. I had one pressing financial need—the tuition for my final semester of college—and that was already covered by my veterans' benefits.

Lena's letter was devastating. I tried to phone her, but the Morettis' number had been disconnected. I would have to wait to see her; I had already booked a flight to New York for the day before Thanksgiving, with a brief stopover in Chicago. On the flight east, the American continent below me for the first time in a year— the desert, the Rockies, the lights of cities like mica—I reread her letter.

Carl was still nosediving. Picking up in the morning and drinking into the night. He was suspended from the police force. Irene took a job at Alexander's, demonstrating vacuum cleaners. Every half hour she poured dust onto a square of carpet and vacuumed it. Mrs. Moretti also had to get a job, working for an insurance agent in a walk-in storefront. The widow of a Fire Department captain who dies in the line of duty receives a decent pension, but not enough to offset a large mortgage, loans, and lots of medical expenses. Mrs. Moretti couldn't hold the job, anyway. Her hands shook. Her hair was turning white. She started smoking again after twenty years. Lena was a junior now at Brooklyn College, living at home. With her aunt and mother out working, she ended up doing the housework and seeing her cousins off to school. She was dying to get away. She had been accepted as a transfer student at Georgetown, but couldn't afford the tuition. As for Bruno, he had graduated from Penn in three years. They awarded him a B.S. and an M.S. at the same time and put him on a fast track for his Ph.D., with instant tenure awaiting him. He was a prodigy. He lived in special housing and got shuttled around with other disabled students, but he was doing what he always wanted to do. Something Lena could only dream of.

At O'Hare Airport I made a phone call and was excited to hear a familiar voice on the other end of the line. An hour later, my Checker cab pulled up in front of a big brick house on a colorless street in Cicero. I walked up the flagstone path to a door flanked by dusty evergreens. When I rang the doorbell, a dog barked. A gray-haired woman with thin lips opened the door. She wore a blue woolen dress. The dog was a German shepherd that sniffed my hand.

"Xeno," Evgénia said, embracing me.

In the ten years since I had last seen her, she had married and been widowed. After I went to boarding school, I rarely heard from her. That first year there were birthday and Christmas cards, and then nothing. A letter I sent to her Brooklyn address was returned. Several times over the years I wanted to contact her, but didn't act on it. Then, when I was drafted, I felt a more urgent need to find her, but didn't learn her address until I was already in Vietnam.

She was running the failing nightclub on LaPointe Street she had inherited from her late husband, a fellow Albanian named Zoran Melkind. Melkind had been a bookie in the postwar years. Then he opened a nightclub. When he died of a stroke, Evgénia learned how much they were in debt.

"I made my choices and I have to live with them," she said over a pot of black tea. "Zoran Melkind and I had some good years, but he wasn't honest with me. I came out here soon after you went away to school. I worked for two families. At the second, Zoran was the kids' uncle. He asked me out. I could have been a domestic the rest of my life. I wasn't so young anymore. So when he proposed marriage, I accepted." She patted my hand. "I'm sorry. Here you were a soldier, who lived through God knows what, and I'm telling you my troubles."

"You always listened to my troubles."

"Well, we have other things to talk about. Let me get my bag and we'll go out for lunch."

As a child, I had never visited Evgénia's home. Walking through her house now, I saw familiar touchstones: an aquarium filled with fantails; jade plants and potted palms; and alpine photographs. The furniture was dark and heavy. In the living room there were black-and-white shots of the tallest mountains in Albania: Gramoz, Jezérce, and Korab, whose twin peaks were home to the two-headed eagle on the Albanian flag. The Albanians call their country Shqipri, "land of the eagles," and when I was a boy Evgénia told me that this two-headed eagle, the largest in the world, divided his time between the two peaks of Mount Korab. He had golden plumage and coal-black eyes. When he looked at the sun, his eyes turned into diamonds. Before he died, he drank from a river of fire and went up in flames—like the phoenix—leaving only the four diamonds behind in his nest. The man who found them, Evgénia concluded, would live forever.

ON THANKSGIVING DAY Lena and I had dinner at a Moroccan restaurant on Broadway. Lena was a strict vegetarian now. But she didn't eat much. Bruno was being driven up from Philadelphia, and the next day we would all celebrate Thanksgiving at the apartment Mrs. Moretti and Lena had moved into. It was in a run-down neighborhood in Kingsbridge, a block from Van Cortland Park.

Lena was wearing a black sweater and jeans. Fastened with a black barrette, her hair shone brightly. She was twenty-one now, a year and a half younger than me, but we both seemed older. It was a clear cold day and we had walked for hours, through Central Park, up along the Hudson, and back across town. Lena was like a sister to me, and from the moment we'd met at Grand Central, as she waved smiling and hurried through the crowd into my arms, I wished that weren't the case.

She had brought me up to date on the previous few months.

"Irene finally split, taking the kids to her parents' house in Bayside. After that, Carl drove Mom and me crazy. He brought home other drunks. Fought with the neighbors. Totaled his car. Mom pleaded with Irene to help, but Irene wouldn't come near him. Then one day he disappeared. A week later, a woman from a real estate agency knocked on our door, all cheerful, to inform us that Carl had sold his half of the house. The new owners would be moving in the first of the month. Mom said it was time for us to get out of there, too. She sold our half and rented this apartment. It's cramped, but, hey. For Mom, life's simpler. For me, it's difficult. I have no privacy. No social life." She pushed aside her plate. "I have to get away, Xeno. And I need to make sure I have the credits for veterinary school. But, as a transfer student, I would only receive a token scholarship from Georgetown."

The waiter brought us a pot of mint tea, and I filled our cups.

"I can give you the money for tuition," I said.

"What are you talking about?"

"You know I've been getting an allowance from my father. I don't need it anymore. I'll instruct his lawyer to wire the money to a bank account in Washington, where you can draw on it."

She looked at me in disbelief. "You're serious."

"Once my father sends the money, it's mine."

"But what will you live on?"

"I have some money put away. And I get veterans' pay now. Lena, your family took me in when I was a boy. Without all of you, I don't know what I would have done." I took her hand across the table. "Let me give something back, now that I can."

The next day, when we told her, Mrs. Moretti was also hesitant. "I can't let you do this," she said to me.

Bruno stepped in gently. "Mom, it's between Xeno and Lena. He knows what he's doing."

Bruno had, literally, become the man of the family. Physically he looked as if the wind could carry him off: his wispy hair and transparent skin, the tweed jacket that swam on him, his shoes with the corrective heels; but his voice was forceful, confident. And, despite his youth, it carried authority. University life agreed with him. He was thriving, despite his infirmities. In that competitive, rarefied world, even in the company of senior faculty he was nearly always the smartest person in the room. He knew it, and they knew it, and few doubted that, in time, he would also become the most accomplished person in the room. The only question was whether his health would hold up.

Mrs. Moretti hugged me. By now, her hair was completely white. Though thin, it was carefully coiffed. And she had put on a festive green dress. Pinned to her breast was a gold brooch Mr. Moretti had given her, a salamander with lapis-chip eyes. "Xeno," she said, on the verge of tears, "you'll always be a member of our family. Thank God you're home safe."

"I'm happy to be here—more than you know."

"But you look so tired. And you're white. Bruno told me about your wound. Did the army give you decent care?"

"It was fine. I saw a doctor on my own in San Francisco. He checked me out."

"That's good." I could see her mind was wandering. "Did you bring your medals, like I asked you?"

She examined them closely. "Frank would've been so proud of you."

She fell silent. In the short time I'd been there, I saw how difficult it was for her to focus on anything. "My cousin Nat was in the V.A. hospital in Newark after the war," she said abruptly, coming back from wherever she'd gone. "He was wounded in Sicily."

After dessert, Bruno and I took our coffee to the window. There was a pan with bird feed on the fire escape and two pigeons were pecking. While I sat on the sill and he in an easy chair, his bad leg propped on a stool, he told me about his continuing research into extinction and its earliest indicators. His main interests had remained the same since childhood and were now his life's work. His fervor was as great as ever, stoked by the sheer volume, and sophistication, of the information available to him. Facts that I found overwhelming led him to concoct ever more practical means of action; even then, as a doctoral candidate, he was revising the statistical models and methodologies in his field.

"Until the eighteenth century," he said, "an average of .25 animal species per year became extinct. In the nineteenth century, it jumped to one species per year—and that was considered a big jump. Today the rate of extinction is one thousand species per year. By 2000 it will be 40,000—110 per day. And that's a conversative estimate. In our lifetime, the hippopotamus, the gorilla, and the polar bear may all be gone. Twenty percent of the birds, twenty-three percent of mammals. Fifty percent of the turtles—an animal so durable it can live for centuries. As for plants, one a day now becomes extinct, and that will double in twenty-five years." He shook his head. "In any other branch of science, figures like these could only be termed catastrophic. But when we say that, we're accused of crying wolf."

"Why, when you've got the data?"

"Oh, it's not the data. People don't want to hear the word

'catastrophe.' To them, that's drama, not science. In fact, in this situation, it couldn't be more scientific."

There was dismay, not bitterness, in Bruno's voice.

"All we can do is save as many species as possible," he went on. "I don't want to spend my life writing postmortems—or obituaries. Ever hear of the wisent?"

I shook my head.

"It was the European bison—but even unluckier than its American cousin. The last wild wisent was hunted down in the Bialowiecza Forest in Poland on February 19, 1921. The last sea mink, a shy, beautiful creature, was harpooned off Greenland on April 2, 1860. The one surviving Réunion Island sheldgoose, a multicolored ground bird, died in captivity on Christmas Day, 1710. It's obscene when we can pinpoint the last member of any species, and the exact date of its death, which is the death of all those that came before it. Most species die off anonymously. A species down to its last hundred members is on a precipice. Right now, I'm tracking a couple that are teetering: the wild Bactrian camel and the nomadic Saiga antelope, which roams the desert steppes from Iran to Mongolia. The Chinese poach it for its horns, which they grind into aphrodisiacs. You know what tipped us off to the Saiga's disappearance? The disturbance in the food chain. A proliferation of the sagebush and saltwort it feeds on, and the fact its main predator, the red wolf, was attacking domestic sheep. Only later were Saiga herds sighted that should have been forty strong and instead were down to six head." He sighed. "But enough. I want to know what you're doing. After all you've been through—are you really okay?"

"I'm going back to school. To get my degree. As for the war, I'll give you the short version."

The war Bruno was fighting interested me more. The human race had yet to render itself extinct; perhaps the animals were just a dry run. Once you believed animals were insensate things, disposable, of utilitarian value only, it wasn't so hard to move on to people.

Riding back to the airport in Chicago, I had passed the ruins of the old stockyards. They were demolished the previous summer, but at twilight, with dust clouds sifting into the smoky sky, it was as if the wrecking balls and bulldozers had just finished their work, leveling the vast holding pens, cattle walks, and slaughterhouses, where blood ran ankle-deep on the killing floors. The air was dense with the spirits of the animals that had passed through there. Someone like my grandmother, who could detect an ailing pigeon in a crowded park, would have been overwhelmed in that place. The blood heaviness was still palpable, misting over the lake, clouding the car windows, streaking the horizon. I felt as if I would choke on it.

"Science is on the march in Vietnam, too," I concluded sarcastically, rising from the windowsill. "They're napalming whole villages, Bruno. Entire swaths of jungle. Frying every living thing by the square mile."

He was staring past me, out the window. Since he was a boy, when he was truly upset he grew silent. Finally he reached for my arm and pulled me down and embraced me.

In the living room Lena was sitting alone on the sofa, immersed in the Georgetown course book.

I was happy to see this. But I was also sad. It was not the first time Mrs. Moretti had declared me a member of the family; but it felt as if I had officially cemented my role by helping Lena out financially. I would always be like a sibling to her. As it was, I had long feared that if I initiated a relationship with her which didn't work out, my ties to the family, and my friendships with her and Bruno, would evaporate.

I was taking the last shuttle to Boston, at ten. After I said my goodbyes—and promised Bruno I would visit him in Philadelphia—Lena walked me downstairs. We stood in front of the building, the wind buffeting us, the Broadway subway screeching on the elevated tracks a block away. She looked so beautiful at that moment. I didn't want to leave her. I wished we had more time alone. I noticed then that she was wearing her gold locket, engraved L.M.; either she had slipped it out of her sweater or had just put it on.

Following my gaze, she smiled faintly. "You were admiring my mother's brooch," she said. "My father gave it to her, but told her not to wear it until he died. She's worn it every day since."

That seemed a mysterious request for a straight-ahead type like her father. "Why was that?"

"I asked, but she wouldn't talk about it. At my father's forty-day mass, I asked one of the men from his squad. He told me that some firemen wear a salamander amulet. My father's amulet was pinned inside his slicker when he died. He gave my mother that brooch years ago." She shook her head. "My mother's not altogether with us anymore. You saw it, I know you did."

"She's taken a lot of hits."

"I know. But I still have to get on with my life."

She put her arms around me, then rose up and kissed my cheek. "I'm glad you're back safe, Xeno. Thanks for everything."

I turned up my collar and walked to the subway. The wind stung when I rounded the corner. Inside I felt empty, but also relieved to be leaving. I was exhausted, physically and emotionally. Mrs. Moretti was right about that. The Morettis were the only family I had; seeing them for Thanksgiving was like an official homecoming—with all the mixed feelings that entailed. I felt as if I had arrived from nowhere and was headed nowhere. In between, it was a shock to be with people who had known and cared about me my entire life. Perhaps that was why my visit with them, like my recent encounters with Mr. Hood and Evgénia, was quickly falling away from me—as if it already belonged to the distant past. Time had become so elastic that a single day could feel like a month, a month like an hour. I didn't know if this was a product of raw fatigue or an unconscious attempt to put the war behind me.

Only when I was on the subway did it hit me that, for the first time I could remember, there were no animals—no monkeys, lizards, parrots, not even a cat or dog—in the Moretti household.

As for the salamander, eventually I learned that it meant "fire dragon" in Greek. Aristotle said that it repelled fire. Pliny claimed it was the only animal that sought to extinguish fires, which was why, in the Revesby bestiary, it was called "the fire-fighter."

NATHALIE WORE a red bandanna around her head, Apache-style. Her hair was long now. Three bloodred streaks—war paint—flared off her cheeks, like wings. She was at war. Her scarf was an American flag. Her wraparounds were opaque. Beneath a leather jacket she wore a skull-and-crossbones T-shirt. The seat of her jeans was stitched with multiple patches: the hammer and sickle, a clenched fist, a mushroom cloud, the peace sign, Edvard Munch's scream. In the twenty-four hours I had been in town, I hadn't once seen her smile. And that included the thirty minutes we spent in bed.

We were on the Blue Line, en route to Government Center. The subway cars were packed with people heading for the rally. The city expected a crowd of ten thousand, and forty thousand would show up. Nathalie's small contingent, the Trotsky Worker-Student Alliance, was going to rendezvous near Faneuil Hall. I was one of five vets opposed to the war who would join them. A former lance corporal named Smoltz had gotten my name from Nathalie and contacted me. I had my medals pinned to my denim jacket. It was the first and only time I wore them. After the rally, everyone was to march across the bridge into Cambridge, first to MIT, then Harvard, to protest their research contracts with the Defense Department and the CIA. Several hundred cops and state troopers had been called in by the mayor. They were in full riot gear, armed with tear gas and rubber bullets.

As we emerged into the crisp air and the tumult of the crowd—bullhorns, chants, police sirens—Nathalie turned to me. "We need you—I need you—to do something."

What she needed me to do was throw my medals onto the steps of the courthouse where the government was trying three antiwar leaders for sedition.

I looked at her. "Why didn't you tell me that before?"

"Before what?"

"Before we came down here."

"You mean you won't do it?"

"I mean I would've liked some time to think about it."

"You have time." She glanced at her watch. "Twenty, maybe thirty, minutes."

She said this without a trace of irony.

Smoltz was waiting for us beside a red white and blue van with curtained windows. The curtains were American flags adorned with skulls instead of stars. Smoltz was short and muscular, with a Mohawk and eyebrows that met over his nose. One of his eyes was off, so it didn't feel like he was really looking at you. He wore a sleeveless leather vest and steel bracelets. His Purple Heart was pinned to his vest.

His handshake was like a vise, and lasted too long. "Honored, bro," he said.

He introduced me to two other vets, a skinny helicopter gunner on crutches named Tomansky, who had a Bronze Star, and a black Marine with a missing ear who said his squad had given him the name Cork "because I floated down the Kang River on a tree trunk." The fifth vet hadn't shown up.

"He's on a bus for Portsmouth," Cork said, holding out his arm and mimicking someone shooting up. "His sister's gonna take care of him."

Nathalie's group was assembling around us. They wore red armbands. A girl in a trench coat and beret wore a skull mask. Her boyfriend, whose hair was even longer than Nathalie's, had painted UNCLE $AM across his bare chest. Off to the side, a pair of middle-aged men in tweed jackets and flannel shirts stood tensely, conversing with Nathalie. They were the real Trotskyites, hard-core organizers from a splinter branch of the American Communist Party. That was as far left as you could go in the antiwar movement, and I wondered how Nathalie had arrived there so fast. Just a year earlier, she had

preferred staying in bed all day, sipping her hookah and perusing ancient maps. When I asked her about it, she grew testy, insisting she
had always held strong political beliefs. Perhaps remembering who
she was talking to, she added that her sister's death had been a brutal
wake-up call. Then she reverted to the rote sloganeering I had been
hearing from her all day: "The only lasting action is political action."

Around us the action never let up: speakers on a rickety stage ex-
horting the crowd in two-minute bursts; a band jamming on a flatbed
truck; Hare Krishna initiates ringing bells; "bikers for peace" revving
their engines. Some divinity students released 44,000 bloodred
balloons—one for each American soldier killed in Vietnam—into the
piercingly clear sky. Everyone looked up, except the police. Visors
down, they squeezed their batons and scanned the crowd. The state
troopers were lined up on side streets, ready to converge on the
square. Barricades had been thrown up. Instinctively I checked them
for a way out of there if things turned ugly. I didn't see any way out.

From behind one barricade vitriolic counter-demonstrators were
taunting the crowd: *America—Love it or leave it.* They were buttoned-
down pro-war students who didn't want to fight themselves. Young
Americans for Freedom, they called themselves. I hated them when I
was in college, and I hated them even more now.

Nathalie sidled up to me. "Well?"

"No," I said.

"You won't do it?"

I shook my head.

"What the fuck is the matter with you, Xeno? You told me yourself
you hate the war."

"I do."

"And that those medals don't mean a goddamn thing to you."

"They don't."

"So?"

The balloons were still visible, sailing in the wind toward the river.
I was thinking about Murphy, torn in half in that forest.

"It's not that simple."

"Jesus."

"The answer is no. I'll march. I'll sing. But not that."

She turned on her heel and returned to the men in tweed jackets. A stocky man with a black beard, my age, joined them. He was wearing a lumberjack shirt and combat boots. Grimacing, stoop-shouldered, he seemed to be carrying a tremendous weight. Nathalie spoke hurriedly to the three men. They glanced at me, and the bearded man's grimace turned to a scowl. Then he turned his back on me, and Nathalie did the same.

I should have left right then—not the rally, but the company of Nathalie and her friends. I wanted to be at the rally, to express my anger about the war. I had no idea what Murphy and the rest of my late comrades would have wanted me to do about the medals. I didn't care. But whatever I did, it would be on my own terms. This could have been my big chance to purge myself of Operation Phoenix, but I didn't see it that way. My shame over the medals was a private matter: I wasn't going to try to exorcise it with a public act. The other vets could deal with their demons, and ghosts, as they saw fit.

Nathalie's bearded friend took the podium. His voice was high-pitched, his gestures broad. "I'm Tannen," he hollered. No first name. After a rambling diatribe about the judge in the sedition trial, he introduced the other vets, who one by one ascended the courthouse steps and tossed their medals at the door, Tomansky slow and solemn on his crutches, Cork and Smoltz pumping their fists.

After a few more speeches, the crowd marched across the Memorial Bridge into Cambridge. I dropped back and walked beside a group called Doctors for Peace. At MIT, several hundred students broke away and surrounded the physics lab. They broke windows and hurled paint, chanting *MIT, CIA, how many kids did you kill today?* The cops moved in, but just when it seemed the students would disperse—a moment that yawned wide, then snapped shut—they stormed the building instead.

Some marchers hung back, roaring in solidarity, but most of us surged on toward Central Square. Behind us we heard police whistles and sirens. Then tear gas wafted up the avenue, burning our eyes.

At Harvard Square the cops were waiting for us. They were spooked by what had happened at MIT. Behind Plexiglas shields, they had encircled the Square. Reinforcements in rigid columns appeared on Brattle Street. An amplified voice ordered us to break up at once. Until then, the crowd had been restive, but unafraid; now panic set in. People at the center tried pushing their way to the periphery. Brandishing a permit, one of the march organizers approached a police captain. The captain threw the permit to the ground. The organizer started cursing him out.

What happened next was reported in the newspapers as a riot. From where I stood, it was the police who rioted. Batons whirling, they charged the crowd. People ran in all directions. They were clubbed and kicked, some were trampled. Most poured into Harvard Yard, or rushed screaming into the MTA station, but I ducked down Plympton Street. I saw a girl dragged by the hair. A man on crutches thrown against a wall. Another girl with a bloody face. Then I saw Nathalie. A big cop had her cornered by the steps to a basement apartment. He was swinging for her head and she was barely dodging the baton. She didn't see me come up behind the cop until the last moment—and he didn't see me at all. I shoved him and he plunged down the steps headfirst, hitting some trash cans, making a terrible racket. I grabbed Nathalie's hand and we ran, never looking back, across Mount Auburn Street, down an alley, through a parking lot, to the river. Following the cinder path, we stopped to catch our breath near an old boathouse.

"Thanks," Nathalie said, leaning against a tree. Her war paint was smeared, her bandanna was down around her neck.

"Are you okay?"

She nodded. "I couldn't believe you were there. That was quick thinking."

"I wasn't thinking. We're lucky another cop didn't see it."

"He was a pig. They're all pigs."

I thought maybe the cop had broken his arm or leg.

"Maybe he broke his neck," Nathalie chimed into my thoughts. "It'd serve him right."

I looked at her. "Then your Trotsky pals could add another medal to my collection."

"You don't seem upset about it."

"I'm not."

She refastened her bandanna. "I guess you learned to do that in the war."

"Do what?" I asked, but I knew what she was saying.

"Go after people. Fight."

"I went after him because he was going to hurt you. We should get out of Cambridge. Are you going home?"

She shook her head. "After the march, we planned to drive out to Walden Pond for a candlelight vigil."

"You think people will show up?"

She stiffened slightly. "Everyone who can. Will you come with me?"

I was surprised. "I don't think so."

"Come on."

"Because I helped you out?"

She took my hand. "Because I want you to."

In bed that morning, we had turned away from one another, Nathalie curling against the wall while I stared out the window, down the narrow block of brownstones, parked cars, and spindly trees. I felt as if I had been away forever. The entire city seemed smaller, alien and self-contained: as if I were looking into a diorama. Nathalie's studio was sparsely furnished. Cheap curtains, no rug. In the fridge, there was skim milk, cornflakes, and a tin of coffee. After dressing in silence, we ate some cornflakes.

Now, as we walked back to the bridge, I put my arm around her. The encounter with the cop had brought us closer than making love. But only on the surface, and not for long.

We headed north on Route 1 in her old Saab. Dusk was falling. Between clusters of suburban houses, the woods were dense. As always, Nathalie drove hard, weaving through traffic, chain-smoking. We had lapsed into silence again. Nearing our destination, she turned to me suddenly.

"I don't know why you wouldn't throw your medals, but I'm sorry I sprang it on you."

"Forget it."

She hesitated. "Would you throw them now—after what just happened?"

"I'd do exactly what I did before." I lit a cigarette with the dashboard lighter. "It has to do with me, not you. Not politics. I have to deal with it in my own way."

We followed a winding road through the Lynn Woods to Walden Pond. Among the few cars in the parking area was Smoltz's van. Neither he nor any of Nathalie's other comrades had been arrested. A few dozen people were milling in a picnic area. There were lighted candles on a redwood table, but no vigil. Joints were being passed, and bottles of wine. Cork was sitting alone, sipping from a flask. The girl with the skull mask was arguing with her boyfriend, who had a black eye. Someone else's blood was spattered on her trench coat. Tannen was holding court beside a statue of Thoreau. People were agitated and loud, but his high-pitched voice was the most audible.

He saw us, but didn't return Nathalie's wave.

She fell into conversation with a furtive woman named Deirdre who was speaking into a portable tape recorder. Deirdre had recorded a running commentary during the riot, of which this was the coda; later, she would transcribe and publish it in the *Boston Phoenix*.

I wandered off by myself. Night had fallen. The wind was cold. Familiar scents washed over me—soil, foliage, timber—but, like the sights and sounds of Boston, they seemed a part of the distant past. I climbed a slope behind the picnic area and peered through the trees at the pond. It shone silver beneath the moon. The shadow of an owl slid across the surface. Pines were reflected, inverted, along the far shore. After a few minutes, someone came up behind me, the dry leaves crackling underfoot.

It was Tannen. "You're not welcome here," he said, stepping up close.

I just stared at him.

"Did you hear me?" He reached out suddenly and jiggled my medals. "How many people did you kill for these?"

I slapped his hand away.

"How many?" he demanded.

I felt a hot rush up my spine. "Fuck you."

"Get out of here!" he shouted, pushing me in the chest.

I grabbed the front of his jacket and backed him into a tree.

"Let go of me," he cried.

I pressed my forearm into his throat. "You want to know how many? Thousands—tens of thousands! If you touch me again, I'll kill you."

His face was red, his eyes bulging.

"Stop it," Nathalie screamed, hurrying up the slope. Smoltz was right behind her, and then Deirdre, recording everything.

I released Tannen, and he stumbled, gasping.

"You're an animal," Nathalie said through her teeth. "They made you into an animal."

Our eyes locked. "That's right," I said, walking past her, past all of them, across the slope into the woods. Within minutes, their voices were swallowed up by the darkness.

I walked on, into deeper forest. I skirted a ravine filled with brush. I crossed a shallow stream where many animals—raccoons, a fox, a bobcat—had left tracks when they came to drink.

I had no idea how much time had passed, or how far I had gone, when I stopped to rest beneath an enormous pine. The moon lit up the passing clouds. The wind had died down, and my own breathing filled my ears. I remembered as a child, in bed, listening to my breathing and feeling there was nothing more to me than that. As if my body had slipped from this world and left my spirit behind—perhaps to join those animal spirits that my grandmother said filled our apartment. I had wished I could remain that way, weightless, invisible, freed from shame and fear.

Years later, I learned that among the Seminole Indians, when a woman died in childbirth, the infant was held over her face to receive, from her final exhalation, her parting spirit, to protect him from within. On the Hawaiian island of Niihau when a woman died in those circumstances, a bird named *makuahine 'uhane*, "the mother's spirit," flew out of her mouth and alighted on a tree, to watch over the baby and give it courage. I hoped maybe that was the bird whose shadow appeared in my mother's photograph, and that though I never saw it, it was watching over me.

The moon rose higher and stars filled the sky. I listened to the owls' hooting. And the sharper cries of the ravens. I unpinned my medals and hung them from their ribbons on a pine branch. The Silver Star glinted and the Purple Heart spun in the breeze. Then I set off again, toward a clearing visible through the trees.

Those woods were filled with ravens. I knew that ravens adorn their nests with bright objects. And that on the fortieth day of the Great Flood the raven was the first bird Noah dispatched from the ark, to bring back some sign of land. Soon he did the same with the dove, who first returned with an olive leaf, and the second time it was released didn't return at all, which meant the earth must be dry.

The raven is never mentioned again. Its fate is left ambiguous. But to me it's clear: the raven kept flying as long as it could, and then drowned.

I WALKED OUT of the cypress grove in the Parc Montsouris onto the rue de la Santé. It was hot, and the trees on the sidewalk barely deflected the noonday sun. Following the rue Saint Jacques back to the Seine, I crossed the Pont d'Arcole into the Marais and circled around to my apartment off the rue Perrée. I stopped first to buy fruit and a bottle of wine, then went into a café for an espresso and called France Telecom from a pay phone to find out why my home line still hadn't been activated.

I had flown to Paris a month after earning my college degree. After returning to Harvard, it took me a year, including summer school, to complete my credits and graduate with honors in classics. I wrote my thesis on Aelian. His *On the Nature of Animals* is as much mythography as natural history, a source of endless wonders: a hyena can render a man mute by stepping on his shadow; a horse which treads on a wolf's paw print will be paralyzed; the Corocotta, a rare speckled hyena, can imitate the human voice in order to ambush a man; and rats on the Aegean island of Gyarus eat iron ore. He also describes an Ethiopian tribe that worshiped a dog as their king. They prostrated themselves before him at dawn and dusk, built him a lodge, prepared him special foods, and provided him with a harem of bitches. The tribe obeyed the dog's wishes: when he whimpered, they knew he approved of their actions; when he barked, it was clear he objected. After his death, they deified him. Because my thesis won a prize, I was offered a graduate fellowship, but turned it down. If one day I felt differently, I could return to academia and pursue the subjects that interested me. But I wasn't taking any more detours. I knew that better than ever now. I had waited, and prepared myself, a long time for the day when I could fully pursue the *Caravan Bestiary*. And as Bruno pointed out, if I did find it, a lot of doors would open, whether I wanted to walk through them or not. Meanwhile, I needed my B.A. to get a job and earn enough cash to subsidize my search. Using the university's research facilities, I had been able to map out the itinerary I wanted to follow after graduation: the archives to be visited, the people to be interviewed. What little trail there was wound through Europe, not America, and it didn't take me long to decide I wanted to live in Paris.

After returning from Vietnam, I would have gone abroad even if I weren't searching for the bestiary. I didn't intend to maintain even a nominal home in the States, as my father had. I didn't renounce my citizenship; I just took another step away from Operation Phoenix, the government that concocted and concealed it, and the jingoism that permitted its execution—a renunciation of the sort Nathalie had urged when she wanted me to flee the country two years earlier. Except now, I told myself, I was leaving on my own terms, not running away. I had found this apartment after staying in a hotel for two weeks. On the fifth floor, it consisted of a small kitchen and two quiet, airy rooms with high windows that overlooked the Square du Temple. In the war I had learned that you only carry what you need, and I didn't need much. At first I had a bed, a desk, a table piled with books, and some folding chairs. No radio, no TV. A map of the Mediterranean was tacked to the wall over my desk.

Once settled, I began scouring the city's assorted libraries for any mention of Martin Lafourie, just as I had in Cambridge. He remained my best, and only, real clue. I also wanted to read everything I could find by my predecessors (I felt I had earned the right to call them that after my discovery of Lafourie), Brox, Cava, and Faville. Among the books I found right away were: *Nicholas of Cusa and Roman Cosmology* by Michael Brox; *The Illuminated Books of the Alpine Monasteries* and *Guillaume Heinault & Henri Metz: The Techniques of Illumination* by Madame Faville; and a bizarre monograph by Niccolò Cava entitled *Empedocles's Theory of Evolution*. Of course only Madame Faville's books had any relation to the *Caravan Bestiary* (I learned about the monks' writing instruments, vellum, and methods of transcription), though she never mentions it specifically. It was more difficult to track down some early essays by Cava and Faville that pertained directly to the bestiary, presenting their respective theories about sources that predated Physiologus. For Cava, it was obscure chroniclers like Tatian, a second-century heretic whose animal catalog has disappeared, and Ctesias the Cnydian, court doctor to King Artexeises II in the fifth century B.C., who set out to write a treatise on falconry and ended up cataloging the animals of Central Asia. Madame Faville was also intrigued by Horapollo, a fifth-century A.D. Egyptian who at various times was a grammarian, clairvoyant, spy, and high priest in the great Temple of Isis. In Book II of his famous study of hieroglyphics, *Hieroglyphica*, he wrote eighty-six chapters on animals that became the European template for allegorizing animals.

I wished I had more intimate knowledge of Madame Faville, Brox, and Cava so that I could understand the origins of their passion for the bestiary. How much of it was scholarly, and how much (as with me) was rooted in their personal histories? Such information about Brox and Cava seemed nonexistent; neither was famous enough to have a biographer. I couldn't even find their likenesses—no daguerreotypes, not even a sketch. I had better luck with Madame Faville. A 1920 photograph on one of her book jackets showed an attractive, enigmatic young woman with long hair and wide-set eyes, her blouse with the high starched collar at odds with her arch smile.

I spent my evenings at the Bibliothèque Nationale and the medieval library at the Sorbonne. By day I took what jobs I could find. For three unhappy months I helped edit a classics journal. I cataloged material for an archaeological society (another three months). Then I joined a team of translators working under two editors on the sixteen volumes of Livy's *History of Rome*. None of these jobs was lucrative, but they did allow me to hold on to my modest savings, which consisted of the final year of support checks sent by my father's lawyer. Lena hadn't needed the money for graduate school; she had already received a full fellowship to the Penn veterinary school. Because my own tuition was covered by my veterans' benefits, I was able to squirrel away that other money. But after a year I had grown impatient. My job as a translator, boring from the start, had begun eating up more and more of my time and energy. I decided to live on my savings for as long as possible, and put everything into my research.

I had felt at home in Paris right away—with the language, the food, the welcoming solitude. As I settled in, I bought a Turkish rug at the Porte de Montreuil flea market and at the Marché Paul-Bert good secondhand furniture—a large blue sofa, a bureau, some proper chairs—and a set of beautiful Chinese prints of the six Celestial Dragons, which replaced the map over my desk.

Every morning at nine I had breakfast in a tea shop off the Place des Vosges and rode the Metro to one of the libraries. I began reading through biographies of King Philip VI and histories of his court. Lafourie appeared, first as a minor official, then as one of the king's trusted diplomats. He was usually associated with foreign assignments that concluded in treaties or trade agreements. After being involved in the annexations of Montpellier and the province of Dauphiné, he served briefly as the ambassador to Genoa. But there was maddeningly little detail about the man himself. And no mention of a bestiary. Philip died in 1350. The end of his reign was calamitous: the Black Death wiped out three-fifths of the French population, and the Hundred Years War began when the English king claimed Philip's throne. To finance his armies, Philip impoverished the country. By then, Martin Lafourie had disappeared entirely from the histories. I assumed he, too, had been a victim of the Black Death. Then I saw a new name cropping up in situations where Lafourie's once had: a certain Duc D'Épernay, who served as a roving ambassador, first for Philip in his final two years, and then for his successor, John II.

I looked up the Duc D'Épernay in a peerage of the Valois dynasty, and the blood rushed to my head.

Duc D'Épernay—formerly Martin Lafourie, Knight. Born Auxerre, 1304; died Paris, 1371. Title conferred by King Philip VI on 6 March 1349 in appreciation of M. Lafourie's long service to the crown, especially his role in the purchase of Dauphiné in 1349.

That was why the name Lafourie had disappeared. But would I have any better luck trying to research the Duc D'Épernay? At first I found no more personal information about Lafourie the duke than I had about Lafourie the knight. I looked in vain for a memoir or a biography, and started picking through collections of letters written by his contemporaries, but that seemed very hit-or-miss.

I had befriended a research librarian at the Sorbonne named Sylvie. She was a soft-spoken young woman, alert, funny, with long brown hair and a good figure. We went out to dinner one night on the Ile St-Louis, and after a bottle of wine talked about Vietnam. She had stronger feelings than most people. One of her uncles had been killed at Dienbienphu in 1954. "It was a bad war then," she said, "and it's worse now." She propped her elbows on the table and leaned closer. She had long lashes, and one of her bangs kept sliding over her right eye. "I've met Americans who protested the war, and others who came here to avoid it, but never anyone who actually went. You were drafted, yes?"

After a stroll around the island, and some more brandy at a café, she told me she had a boyfriend, but that he was on a trip to Brussels. I walked her home, up near the Pantheon, and kissed her good night. When I asked her out again, she said with a shrug that the boyfriend was back. At the library she was of great help. I had told her about the *Caravan Bestiary*, and where I stood in my search for it; I told her too about Faville, Brox, and Cava, and how I had discovered Martin Lafourie's later incarnation. This was manna for someone in her profession, and she listened avidly.

That afternoon we did a quick search for information about D'Épernay and came up empty.

But two days later, when I entered the library, she beckoned to me from the front desk. "I thought you would never show up. We're going to the archives, three floors down," she whispered, leading me to a small elevator behind the stacks. "It's a restricted area—you need special approval—so be quick, and look casual."

"Seems like contradictory advice," I said, drinking in her perfume, which filled the elevator.

"This is no joke," she said with a knowing smile.

The low, cavernous room we stepped into was suffused in a light more brown than yellow. The air was so thick with dust that I left faint footprints on the wooden floor.

The long narrow aisles were barely illuminated by low-watt bulbs suspended inside little cages. All the books were oversized and very old. I followed Sylvie to the end of one aisle and halfway down another. She climbed up a stepladder and took a leather-bound book off the top shelf, where it resided with dozens of others just like it.

"None of these books can leave this room," she said, handing me the book. The spine read *Chronicles of the Court of Philip VI* in silver letters. "You'll have to look at it down here. I don't know why I didn't think of this before. This is Volume 16 of a forty-volume set that covers the reigns of all the kings of France from Charles IV to Louis XII. The books contain legal documents, treaties, proclamations, but also correspondence between high officials."

"Including D'Épernay."

"Of course. I put a marker at page 93."

"How can I thank you, Sylvie?"

She smiled. "Maybe that dinner . . . Charles is in London this weekend."

She went back upstairs, and I sat down on the stepladder, beneath one of those lightbulbs, with the big book in my lap. On pages 93–96 there was a letter dated May 27, 1368, in Paris, from the Duc D'Épernay to the Compte de Briand, finance minister to the late King Philip. Before I finished reading the first page, I burst out laughing: it would be a champagne dinner with Sylvie.

Dear Friend,

In service of His Majesty, I traveled often between France & Egypt, & on one such mission had an encounter which I confided to no one but the King. It concerned a book about which many have heard, but few have seen. In my travels I have handled other rarities, plum-sized pearls from Ceylon & chimes stirred to music by light & rose windows tinted by a blind glazier, but none so wondrous as the illuminated book filled with all manner of unnatural &

fantastical beasts refused entry to the ark by Noah when he set sail in the Great Flood. I acquired this book from an Antiquary's widow on the Island of Rhodes & presented it to the Doge of Venice, to whom I was a royal Emissary in the year of our Lord 1347. Now, as we know, the first bestiary, called the Book of Life, was a natural history of all the beasts delivered unto the Earth at the Creation. Only God Himself saw the original, but its offshoots were transcribed & scattered in monasteries throughout Christendom. Over many centuries, divers monks and scholiasts attempted to consolidate these bestiaries, but one fugitive volume eluded them & came to be called the Caravan Bestiary *after an Alexandrian Greek smuggled it by Caravan across the Libyan Desert. Compiled by many hands, this book of lost beasts, that were left to their fate in the Flood, was composed in Aramaic, & appended in countless tongues—Armenian, Arabic, Coptic, Greek, Latin, Provençal & our own French. Many times the book has surfaced & been lost, & in pursuit of it, men have suffered torture, imprisonment, & death at the stake. The book itself avoided the Inquisition's fires. But by the year 1255 no man alive had seen it, or could claim to know of men deceased who had, & so it was said to have disappeared forever.*

The King had sent me to Rhodes to conclude an agreement with the Governor, Jean Longueville, for the services of the Knights Hospitallers in Alexandria, where our agents required protection and accommodation. Afterward, I had several idle days before I set sail for Venice to complete my mission. Rhodes is renowned for its silversmiths. They fashion their wares on two streets, perpendicular in the maze of the town, and there I purchased much jewelry and plate. In the town there is also a Mapmaker, a Cypriot named Pelotes, who fled the strife on his own island to settle on Rhodes. He took a Rhodian wife who bore him two sons, one a Vintner, the other a Mapmaker apprenticed to his father. Together they charted the coast of Africa for the Knights, & Sicily for the Prince of Agrigento, & all those Islands of the Greeks & Turks near to Rhodes. From Pelotes I purchased several Maps, some for our Ministry, some for myself. Now, Pelotes' wife had an elder sister, Marika Leonides by name, who was the aforementioned Antiquary's widow. After Pelotes learned of my interest in antiquities, & seeing how free I was with my purse, he sent me to her. The widow was sickly, bent & bleached with age, with a rattling cough. Yet her mind was clear, & she welcomed me warmly, & was exceedingly kind. She was childless, with no relatives but her sister and brother-in-law to care for her. She was much in need of funds, not least of all for the Surgeons who were bleeding her. She still possessed a few of her husband's most precious wares, which were her bulwark against Poverty and Dependency. She shewed me marble tablets of the Romans, discovered in the Nile's banks, & gold bracelets hammered for the Ptolemies, & an Onyx Dagger found in the Pharaoh Pepi's tomb. Then she drew from concealment a book of Prayers, 200 years old, which she said was the property of Anacletus II, the Antipope, a Roman of Jewish blood, as you may recall, whose rival, Innocent II, fled to France. If genuine, this was a rare volume, indeed, but not so rare as another, which she brought out after swearing me to an oath of secrecy. This was the Caravan Bestiary, *the name bestowed on it by her husband himself. Miraculous to behold, this book was of enormous value, if not to me, then to the Crown. I told the widow so, for I was in no way inclined to haggle with such a sickly woman, and one so kind. I inquired after the price, & she quoted me sixty gold pieces, a tremendous sum, but fair, & so I brought it to her the next morning & she gave over the book in a scarlet pouch. Of its history she could tell me only that her husband had acquired it eleven years earlier, two years prior to his death, from a Greek named Panayoita Fondaros, a dealer in Silver & Gold who had obtained it from an Arab trader. Fondaros carried it to Alexandria from the Atlas Mountains by Caravan. When I asked the widow why her husband had not sold the book before his death, and why she herself had not sold it afterward, she replied that her husband did not trust those of his customers with wealth enough to purchase the book to be shewn it. "Nor have I, sir," she declared. "But with my days running down, I have no choice, & no fear, & no doubts either now in trusting one such as you, of whom my brother-in-law speaks so highly. My husband often said that when the propitious moment arrived, I would know it, & that has happened." So I took away the* Caravan Bestiary *to Venice, where pursuant to His Majesty's interests, I made a gift of it to the Doge, Andrea Dandolo. And that becomes the larger part of the story.*

In October 1347 Doge Dandolo had occupied that high office for four years. By complex means—circles within circles of Electors—the Venetians choose their Doge. Dandolo was thirty-six years of age when so honored, the youngest Doge in 300 years, beloved of his people, & an extraordinary man in his own right. More cultivated in the Arts than his predecessors, Dandolo was truly a scholar, close friend of the poet Petrarch and the painter Veneziano Paolo. In his youth he was acquainted, too, with the painter Giotto and the poet Dante Alighieri. Dandolo was the first citizen of Venice to be awarded a Doctor's degree, at the University in Padua, where he was a Professor of the Law. He authored several books, among them a true History of Venice, from its founding to his own day, & a History of the World from the Creation to the Year of Our Lord 1280.

This is the nature of the man with whom I dined at the Ducal Palace on a warm October night, who, after the other guests departed, invited me to his private quarters. As I sat drinking wine with him on his terrace overlooking the Grand Canal, I confess I did not fully appreciate, or endeavor to plumb, the extent of the Doge's learning, except insofar as I might appeal to it to ensure the success of my mission. That is how fixed I was upon the latter. The King had charged me with securing safe passage for our commercial vessels in the waters east of Sicily, at that time controlled by the Venetian fleet. In return, I was authorized to offer the Venetians a portion of the profits the cargoes on those vessels generated. I never negotiated with a Venetian who was less than formidable, & Dandolo, despite his years, was no exception. Yet, knowing his passions were more scholarly than mercantile, during the long voyage from Rhodes I was inspired to a plan of action which I thought might advantage me. And so, at the opportune moment, I brought out the Greek's book of beasts in its scarlet pouch and informed the Doge that it was the original of the hitherto unobtainable Caravan Bestiary, *which I was hereby presenting to the Venetian Republic and its Doge on behalf of King Philip of France as a token of his gratitude. Holding the book before him, the Doge expressed surprise that such a treasure truly existed, but once he was assured that this was no counterfeit, he fell silent and began gazing at it, page by page, never lifting his eyes. He was clearly bedazzled, transported from that place, so that all other considerations fell away from him. Suffice to say, before the night was out, he signed a missive to the King, guaranteeing the safety of His Majesty's ships in the southern sea lanes, & thanking him for his great gift, which at that moment the King did not even know had been given in his name. As I was rowed back to our Embassy, through myriad canals, I smiled at the thought that when I arrived at the Doge's Palace I was greeted by a Head of State, but when I departed it was a Scholar who bade me farewell.*

Like D'Épernay, Doge Dandolo would have been familiar with the Gnostic belief that the Bible and the first bestiary comprised the only true universal history, but only if the Bible included the Apocrypha (easy to do) and if the bestiary had reincorporated the fugitive bestiary (not so easy). The privileged reader of this universal history might be rewarded with a supreme *gnosis*, something akin to encountering a parallel universe, in which the rarest substances, and subtlest connections, have been restored; in which all that is inexplicable has come clear, and knowledge of "who we were, who we have become, and where we are going"—the Gnostic credo—is within our grasp.

At the same time, it was maddening that, while he called the bestiary "wondrous" and "miraculous," and conveyed Doge Dandolo's intense delight, D'Épernay did not offer his own appreciation of its contents, or even a material description of the book: size, binding, color, and specific entries. Nothing but that scarlet pouch. This despite the fact that, during the month the bestiary had been in his sole possession, he must surely have examined it. Maybe his correspondent, Briand, was not someone with whom he would share his deeper reactions. Even so, it was clearly not the bestiary, but his transaction with the Doge that most interested D'Épernay. Which may be the reason he concluded his long letter to Briand with a curiously hurried postscript, informing him that, while passing through Venice ten years after these events, and three years after Dandolo's death, D'Épernay was granted an audience with another doge, Giovanni Dolfin. He asked Dolfin about the *Caravan Bestiary,* and the Doge said he had never seen or heard of it. D'Épernay believed him, and was only mildly surprised—"having witnessed Dandolo's lust for the book." He concluded that Doge Dandolo had treated the bestiary as a private possession—not a gift to the Republic. Presumably it stayed in his family when Dandolo died, but it could have passed into other hands entirely, inside or outside of Venice.

D'Épernay didn't say; for him, the trail ended in October 1347—a more than interesting date, as I learned that afternoon, because just three months later Venice would be one of the first European cities ravaged by the Black Death. It arrived from the Crimea, on merchant ships carrying flea-infested rats. Within a year Venice lost three-fifths of its population—just as France would nine months later. Trying to cope with this catastrophe, Doge Dandolo had little time or inclination for his scholarly pursuits. At the height of the plague, with Venice on the verge of becoming a necropolis, he dispatched the Dogaressa and their children to an alpine retreat near Castelfranco. Had he taken similar precautions with his artistic treasures, including the *Caravan Bestiary*? That was one possibility. For suddenly, instead of a lot of nebulous ideas about where the bestiary might or might not be, I could proceed from a fixed point in time, unknown apparently to anyone before me, and a specific array of sources: the personal and public records of Doge Andrea Dandolo and his descendants from 1347 on.

As I PREPARED to leave for Venice, I read what I could about Dandolo, and his tenure as doge, at the medieval library. I was having trouble sleeping because of the pain in my side. One night, I had just poured myself a stiff brandy and stretched out on the sofa when Sylvie called.

"Did you see *Le Monde* today?" she said with some urgency.

"No." After the war, I stopped reading newspapers. I had no stomach for politics, the Cold War, the daily catastrophes. "What is it?" I said.

"It's from the obituaries."

I wasn't expecting that.

"I'll read it to you: 'Ferdinand Deschalles died in Narbonne on May 3 at the age of eighty-four. The cause of death was heart failure. He was a graduate of the University of Lyon and a medic in the First World War. A surgeon at the Hospital of Saint Mary for forty-five years, he was Chief of Surgery from 1947 to 1960 and was elected to the National Academy of Medicine in 1954. He is survived by his wife Felicité, a daughter, Margot Fernot, of Tulle, three grandchildren, his brother Roger Deschalles, of Lyon, and his stepsister, Amanda Faville of Sauvigny.' "

"My god."

"Yes, it's her," Sylvie said.

It had never occurred to me that Madame Faville might still be alive. I had so associated her with Brox and Cava—men of the nineteenth century—that I hadn't thought of her living deep into the twentieth. She must have been close to ninety.

I immediately wrote her a letter, saying it was important I meet with her, telling her something of myself and my interest in the *Caravan Bestiary*. Two days later I received an invitation to join her for tea that Friday, at three o'clock.

Sauvigny was in the Loire Valley, west of Moulins. The appointed day was warm and sunny, and I made the drive from Paris in two hours. Madame Faville lived just outside of town, at the end of a long gravel driveway beside a field of lavender. Her house was well kept, white with tall windows. A maid led me down a hallway lined with bookshelves. I spotted titles in French, Italian, and German, and on the right-hand wall, hundreds of art books.

Madame Faville was sitting by the window in her library, a small, compact woman with blue eyes. Her white hair was combed back. Her hands were shaky, but her gaze was clear and her face barely wrinkled. I recognized at once the striking young woman in her photograph. She wore a long green dress and a black shawl. The library overlooked a garden with long beds of tulips and zinnias and several fig and cherry trees. There were three birdhouses on metal posts the squirrels could not climb. While we spoke, a portly gardener came into view every so often, raking leaves.

"Mr. Atlas," she said. "Please sit." She indicated the sofa across from the desk.

"Thank you for inviting me. May I offer my condolences for your brother."

"That's kind of you." She adjusted her shawl. "I didn't really think of Ferdinand as a brother. I hadn't seen him in years. His wife knew he and I never got along. I can't imagine why she included me in the obituary, except that she was always very correct." She smiled. "And now I see that is how you found me here."

"Yes."

"It's all right," she said, noting my discomfort. "I'm eighty-eight years old. I haven't published a word in twenty-five years. There is no reason you could have known I was here."

"I should have known."

"What matters is you're here now."

I looked around the room: a desk so neat it was obviously not in use; more books, floor-to-ceiling; two globes, one contemporary, one of the medieval world; and a dozen drawings and paintings on the wall, many immediately recognizable—a Braque, a Miró, watercolors by Dufy, sketches by Klee. A pair of Burmese cats—so black I hadn't seen them at first—were curled asleep together on an ottoman. Hanging behind the desk were two framed photographs identical in size: a bearded middle-aged man smoking a pipe in that same garden, and a slender man with intense eyes and a broad forehead on a mountain trail, outfitted for climbing.

"The two men in my life," Madame Faville said, following my gaze, "one for forty-one years, the other for fourteen months. The one with the pipe is my late husband, Armand Faville. A professor of physics. The mountaineer is Spengler. In my youth I climbed with him in the Dolomites and the Alps. Oswald was not particularly athletic, but he loved to climb. Like him." She pointed up to my left, where a third Burmese was nestled onto the topmost bookshelf, staring down at me. "That's why he's named Oswald," she added drily. "Now, Mr. Atlas, your letter was very polite, but also cryptic. It surprised me that anyone would be interested in my unsuccessful search for the *Caravan Bestiary*—or would himself be searching. But, then, when I was your age it made perfect sense: a prize so chimerical, only one copy in the whole world and no one can find it. So of course you must try. It becomes like a quest for perfection, or ideal love— doomed from the start. Because the bestiary no longer exists." She studied my face. "Do you disagree?"

"I don't know."

"Are you an idealist, then—a seeker of the perfect, the divine?"

I smiled. "I wish I were. But I do have some new information. I wanted to share it with you."

"Why?"

"Because of the work you did. I was able to build on it. It inspired me."

"I wish it had inspired *me*," she said. "Perhaps you think I can give you some information now? I'm happy to, though it will be fifty years out of date. I only hope, for your sake, that whatever you've dug up is not old stuff that's been recycled."

"I don't think so. I would like to know what you think about Michael Brox and Niccólo Cava."

"Ah," she nodded. "You are a serious pursuer. But first tell me more about yourself. In your letter you didn't say how you came to be interested in the *Caravan Bestiary*."

"It would have been a very long letter."

"I have plenty of time now, if you do."

I told her about my grandmother, and Mr. Hood, and my search up until Honolulu. "You see," I concluded, "the day I first learned of the *Caravan Bestiary*, I also heard of you."

"From your teacher."

"You've always been a part of it for me. I went on to read every book of yours I could find."

"You are among the few people who can claim that distinction."

"Tell me, aside from the fact it was chimerical, and you were young, what made you search for the bestiary?"

She smiled. "Two words. Fame and glory. It would have made my career, just like that," she said, snapping her fingers. "I wish I could say my motives were as esoteric and spiritual as yours."

"I don't altogether believe you."

"Suit yourself," she shrugged.

"Well, I've been especially curious about your interest in Horapollo."

"He's a marvelously contradictory figure: no one has ever pinned down who or what he was exactly. Christians and pagans alike claimed him. In the end he declared he was a direct descendant of the god Osiris. You must know that you can see a well-preserved manuscript of the *Hieroglyphica* in Florence."

"At the Biblioteca Laurenziana."

"I went there in 1922. The manuscript was brought to Florence from the island of Andros exactly five hundred years earlier by a bandit scholar named Cristoforo Buondelmonti. The authoritative edition, in Greek, was published in 1505 and in the next century alone went through more than thirty editions and translations, not including the adaptations."

"I know he drew on Aristotle's *Mysteries*."

"Yes, whatever parts of it survived into the fifth century. He also had access to early Gnostic texts before they were destroyed by the Church. I was convinced that the compilers of the *Caravan Bestiary* owed more to Horapollo than to Physiologus. That was my theory, unprovable of course if I didn't have the bestiary."

"That was the thesis of the book you never finished?"

"Yes," she sighed, sitting back. "That's no mystery. And, as you can see, I am not some mysterious figure. Just an old woman who has retired to the country."

"You're considerably more than that."

"I am flattered you think so, Mr. Atlas. But how can I help you with regard to Brox and Cava?"

"Is there anything worth knowing about their searches? You must have read their writings long ago. I'm just catching up. I was planning to go to the University of Vienna to read Brox's essay. You wrote that there's nothing there."

"There isn't. In 1923 I spent two stifling days in the Hauptbibliotek wading through that essay. German prose thicker than Spengler's, but without a trace of wit or subtlety. Brox just kept expanding his stale conspiracy theory, that the bestiary was burned in Seville. Except now he insisted that Pope Clement III himself participated in the burning."

"Do you think Brox's murder was connected to his search?"

"It's possible. He was a theologian, supposedly very high-minded, but I know for a fact he made deals with wealthy collectors, shady types. They underwrote his expensive travels. They may have wanted the book in order to sell it whole, or a page at a time, on the black market. Perhaps he led them on, or was double-dealing. Perhaps they led him on, then double-crossed him. Who knows? He was quite a womanizer: it could have been a jealous husband."

"Do you know why he was in Turkey?"

"I have no idea. He had concocted an elaborate route that the book supposedly took to Spain. Turkey was one of the stops, but so were a host of other countries."

"And Cava?"

"Italy Italy Italy. And the Vatican. He too was a conspiracist, even more tortured than Brox. Dozens of church officials were supposedly involved in suppressing the bestiary."

"The book *is* considered heretical."

"Of course. And maybe it is locked away in a vault hundreds of meters below the Sistine Chapel. But Cava had no proof, just theories that became increasingly paranoid. He and Brox hit dead ends long before I did. You want to know what I learned from them? That such desperation in others should set off warning bells about what you yourself are doing. That said, tell me about this new information of yours."

I leaned closer to her. "You were right about Rhodes, Madame. The bestiary did end up there around 1255. But it was not destroyed. Let me read you something I discovered last year, from a tract written in 1382 by a former Crusader named Guy Pelletier."

I took out my Hawaii notebook and read her the passage in French.

When I finished, her eyes were wide, but she merely nodded and said, "Read it to me again."

I did so, slowly, and she shook her head in amazement. "So he claims to have known in October 1351 that this Martin Lafourie had the book 'several years earlier.' "

"1347, to be exact."

"You were able to trace Lafourie, then."

"Yes. Did you ever hear of him?"

"Never. Nor Pelletier. Where did you find this tract of his?"

I told her, and she smiled broadly. "Two Frenchmen. I looked all over France and Italy for something like this, and you found it in Hawaii, of all places. I congratulate you, Mr. Atlas, on a tremendous discovery. And I apologize. Because so many others failed—because I failed—was no reason to assume that you could not have succeeded."

"You didn't fail. And I got very lucky."

"I am not going to argue with you. Just tell me the rest, please."

"I'll let you read it for yourself."

Sylvie had smuggled Volume 16 of the *Chronicles* up to the second floor of the library and photostated D'Épernay's letter. I took the pages from my briefcase and passed them to Madame Faville, telling her their source.

She listened carefully, then put on her reading glasses. "In a basement at the Sorbonne," she murmured, shaking her head.

It was a thrill for me, watching this old woman's face light up as she read through D'Épernay's letter. Occasionally she paused, and read a sentence over again, mouthing the words. She nodded, grimaced, wrinkled her brow. I didn't know how much active thought she had given the *Caravan Bestiary* over the previous decades, but at that moment I could see her reconnecting with her youthful self, the memories of her own search, the small triumphs, false leads, possibilities pursued or abandoned, until finally it ended for her. On Rhodes, in 1255.

She looked up when she was finished, not with tears in her eyes, but laughter. "It's incredible, Mr. Atlas."

"Please call me Xeno."

"Xeno, I think we ought to have a glass of cognac. I have a fine bottle in that cabinet, if you would do the honors."

I got out the bottle and two glasses. She watched me pour, then raised her glass. "Congratulations."

The cognac was very smooth.

"With what you know, I wonder why you didn't go directly to Venice," she said.

"I had to see you first. I wanted you to know."

"Thank you," she said softly, reaching for my hand. "Now go to Venice, for both of us."

F ROM THE PUBLIC GARDENS I walked down the promenade, past the bronze statue of Garibaldi, to the vaporetto station. The wind was strong and salt coated my lips. It could have been the same wind that had tousled Garibaldi's hair and made him turn up his collar as he gazed across the choppy waters of the canal.

I had so immersed myself in the private correspondence and public records of Doge Andrea Dandolo that I had begun to feel I was living in the Venice of 1347 rather than 1975. In fact, the city's essential maze hadn't changed: a Venetian of Dandolo's time, transported to the twentieth century, would have had no trouble finding his way around. The names of nearly every *calle, campiello, ramo, rio, fondamenta, salizada,* and *piscina* (that wonderful menu of Venetian byways) remained the same. I walked them endlessly, and some evenings, as the mist off the canals darkened, felt as if I might turn a corner and meet up with Dandolo himself. As Lafourie had noted, he was not cut from the usual mold: he was not just the youngest and best educated, but one of the most popular doges, nicknamed *il conti,* "the little count." A trim, handsome man with intense eyes, his likeness is well preserved in the statue atop his sarcophagus in the Basilica and the mosaic portrait above the baptistery altar at Saint Mark's, both of which I had visited that morning. After ruling for eleven tumultuous years, Dandolo died at forty-seven, his health shattered. Among the crises he faced were a belligerent Ottoman Empire, ballooning debt, widespread piracy, and a naval war with the rival republic of Genoa— all of which paled beside a catastrophe soon after he was elected that no Venetian, or European, could have imagined.

I boarded the No. 51 vaporetto to San Giorgio Maggiore and

crossed the Giudecca Canal as ceremonial gondolas, carrying gold statues of dragons and winged lions, rounded the tip of the Dorsoduro from the Grand Canal. It was the day of the August regatta. Teams of rowers in black-and-white-striped shirts were preparing their sleek boats for the first race. Spectators lined the Zattere, jamming the parapets around the old Customs House. Vendors were selling candies and cakes, pennants and balloons.

I circled the gardens beside the Teatro Verde and walked up the gravel path flanked by walnut trees to the Biblioteca Fondazine in the Villa Ziane. For weeks, I had been following the same daily routine: for nine hours, breaking only for lunch, I planted myself at a reading table piled with leather-bound books and scroll maps. There were few other visitors. The cavernous room was so quiet I could hear only the scratching of my pen in my notebook. Occasionally a footfall echoed on the marble floor. Or I'd hear someone climbing the tightly spiraling steel stairways to the mezzanine and upper tiers. A giant oil painting depicted the victorious fleet returning from the Battle of Lepanto. And on the domed ceiling there was a mural of the third doge, Orso Ipato, clutching a trident in the prow of a longboat. He wore a flowing red robe and a gold cap. His profile—the hooked nose and strong chin—was one I had often seen while wandering the city: on tradesmen, waiters, a fishmonger near the Rio San Giustina.

In three months I had filled three notebooks. When the library was closed on Sundays, I typed up my notes, first in my hotel room, then in the tiny apartment I sublet near the Campo San Polo when I realized I would be in Venice, not for weeks, but months. After lunch on Sundays, I often took the motonave to Torcello. The population of fifty seemed woefully outnumbered by the island's ghosts, the multitudes wiped out by malaria five hundred years before. I strolled through the marshes, then sat in the cool light of the ancient cathedral. I loved the animal traceries on the marble panels before the altar and the mosaics depicting the Last Judgment on the counter-façade: on the left, destined for Paradise, sipping nectar from a crystal fountain, children and animals (lions, foxes, deer, and peacocks); on the right, the damned—corrupt officials, murderers, and infidels—

disgorged in hell by sea monsters and prodded into the fires by avenging angels.

Deciphering the florid handwriting of medieval scribes, I had now read through nearly all the surviving private correspondence and public records of Doge Andrea Dandolo. I followed up every reference to Dandolo I could find. I spent weeks exploring the remaining records of his immediate descendants. I knew as much about him, perhaps, as anyone alive. He was my only lead, and I had to follow it. But I still hadn't found what I was looking for: specific clues as to the whereabouts of the *Caravan Bestiary* after his death in 1355.

The fourteenth century, which commences with Dante's descent to the underworld, held few surprises for someone of my own century: endless wars, religious fanaticism, famines and epidemics, cutthroat imperialism. The Venetians were at the center of that world, pouring huge sums into their foreign adventures. The swift galleys the navy shipwrights constructed at the Arsenal were feared throughout the Mediterranean. The Venetian government employed a vast network of spies, at home and abroad, and was so layered in secrecy that no part of it ever had complete knowledge of any other. And all of this was under Dandolo, the most enlightened doge of his time. But, in the end, his reign was defined, not by war or intrigue, but the Black Death. At its peak, the disease claimed sixty Venetians a day. The bodies piled up. Every physican but one fled the city. Dandolo would reward this man for his bravery with an annuity of five hundred gold ducats.

A handful of physicians, the so-called plague doctors, were lured from Ravenna and Florence. They specialized in treating the Black Death until they succumbed to it themselves. They wore an elaborate costume: a huge bird mask, with protective spectacles and a beak ingeniously honeycombed with vials of medicinal herbs and tonics; thick gloves; a scarf dusted with powdered oyster shells; and a canvas coat soaked in wax. They carried a stick with which to raise the bedclothes of the sick. And a tuning fork whose vibrations dispelled toxic vapors. All of this paraphernalia was intended to prevent their contracting the plague, and of course it failed.

It was one of these doctors, across the centuries, who enabled me to pick up the trail of the *Caravan Bestiary* again. He, and Dandolo's eldest daughter, Beatrice. I was sifting through a packet of her letters that had been well preserved in a leather box. The letters were unremarkable, though well written, and I was nearly done skimming them when I came on one that brought me up in my seat.

On March 14, 1367, a week after her mother's death, Beatrice Lungasti, née Dandolo, informed her husband Fabrizio, a sea captain stationed on the island of Chios, of a curious request her mother had made on her deathbed. The former Dogaressa instructed her daughter to seek out a Dr. Armando Bendetto of Ravenna, saying she had entrusted a packet to him for safekeeping when the Doge sent the family to Castelfranco to escape the plague.

Mother informed me that Bendetto was one of the finest physicians to lend his services to the Republic at that dread time. He snatched from death my father's cousins, Pietro Dandolo and Timoro Carpaneri, who had been stricken with hellish fevers. In gratitude, Uncle Pietro gave him 3,000 ducats. After two months, exhausted, Bendetto returned to Ravenna, where the plague was just taking root. He took my mother's packet, but once the plague abated, and for years afterward, she had no word from him. He was such an honorable man that Mother could not fathom his silence. After my father's death, she tried to locate Bendetto, but her efforts, feeble on account of her ill health, came to nothing. She regretted that she had not previously confided in my sisters and me and enlisted our help. With your experience of the world, Fabrizio, perhaps you will have better luck. On your return to Venice, kindly put in at Ravenna and inquire after Bendetto, but do not tarry, for I miss you terribly . . .

Lungasti did as his wife asked, and learned that Bendetto had died several years earlier after a long illness. Bendetto's widow, a woman half her husband's age, was a great beauty. Upon Bendetto's death, she had opened the Dogaressa's packet and was disappointed to find that it contained, not jewels or gold, but an illuminated book of strange beasts. The Latin text was penned in sea-blue ink. Books did not interest the widow. She stored it away with her husband's medical texts and forgot about it—until Lungasti's arrival. He was smitten with the widow and she with him. They became lovers. He extended his stay in Ravenna. One night he asked about the packet, and without hesitation she dug out the bestiary and made him a gift of it. To placate his wife, Lungasti sent it to her by courier. If he knew how rare it was, he didn't let on. Nor did he ever return to Venice. He and the widow moved to Sardinia, where thirty years later he died, a trader in silks. For the rest of her life, embittered and solitary, Beatrice Lungasti rued the day she had dispatched her husband to Ravenna, complaining that she had exchanged him for a book of beasts. And that this was her father's ill-starred legacy, born of the Black Death.

Upon Beatrice's death, the bestiary was passed on to her son, then his daughter, and then her daughter, Serena—Andrea Dandolo's great-great-granddaughter—who married another doge, Andrea Gritti, in 1508. No one knows which of these people, if any, actually read the *Caravan Bestiary*. It had acquired the status of a family heirloom, and as such was passed down along with other books, keepsakes, and domestic fineries which it far exceeded in value.

From the records of Andrea Gritti's dogeship, his letters, and a biography written by two of his contemporaries, I was able to piece together in a couple of weeks the next stage of the *Caravan Bestiary*'s odyssey.

Andrea Gritti was nothing like his scholarly predecessor, Dandolo. Nor did he fit the austere profile of most doges. He was a womanizer, a carouser. A spy in his youth, he fathered at least three bastards on Turkish women and one on a nun who was his favorite mistress. He died at eighty-six, in December 1538, after feasting for two days on grilled eels and drinking a dozen flagons of cold wine. It was fifteen years earlier that he played a small but decisive role in the history of the *Caravan Bestiary*.

Gritti had shown as little interest in the bestiary as in the Bible beside which it was shelved in his wife's library. Then, one stormy night in November 1523, a nobleman and Knight Hospitaller named Antonio Pigafetta paid his respects at the palace. Pigafetta was the most uniquely traveled Venetian of his time, outstripping even Marco Polo. A member of Ferdinand Magellan's original crew of 270 who set out to circumnavigate the globe, Pigafetta had become a celebrity as one of the eighteen survivors who actually completed the voyage three years later, putting into port at Seville in a storm-battered ship, starving and half-naked. Magellan himself, hacked to death by tribesmen on the island of Mactan in the Philippines, was not among them. With a sharp eye and prodigious memory, Pigafetta had become the unofficial chronicler of Magellan's voyage. Much celebrated, he made the rounds of the European courts—Portugal, Spain, France—before touching down in his native city. He presented Doge Gritti with a handwritten copy of his journal, filled with the marvels of unknown places: Brunei, a city built over salt water, like Venice; the island of Mindanao, where the warriors ate their enemies' hearts raw, sprinkled with lemon juice; Tierra del Fuego, where eight-foot giants walked barefoot on ice and worshiped a volcano; Java, whose trees, harder than iron, produced leaves that came alive (they had feet and tails) when they fell to the ground. Pigafetta claimed to have kept one such leaf in a cage for nine days before it escaped. On the Malay peninsula he encountered a fish with a pig's head, in Borneo parrots with mirrors for eyes, and in Loçan an "armored mule," thickly plated, with hooves that shot sparks and iron teeth that dripped rust. On Sumatra he heard tales of the Garuda, that once a year flew to the sun and back.

In his *Memoirs*, Pigafetta recounts how, as a token of his appreciation, Gritti gave him the *Caravan Bestiary* to pass along to his Grand Master, Philippe de Villier. Having just been driven from Rhodes by the Turks, the Knights Hospitallers were temporarily headquartered in Italy. De Villier served Pope Clement VII, with whom Gritti wanted good relations. Making De Villier a gift like the bestiary could only help. But he never received it. Recognizing its worth, and knowing De Villier would see in it only something to peddle, Pigafetta kept the original of the bestiary and had a copy made for De Villier. Sure enough, De Villier took the copy to Prince Mehlenberg of Bavaria, who promptly purchased it for two thousand florins. Mehlenberg liked to bring distinguished scholars to his alpine estate. Among his other houseguests at that time was the Swiss naturalist Konrad Gesner. Gesner was famous for having translated the Lord's Prayer into the world's 130 known languages and compiled the first dictionary of the Gypsies' language. Now he was embarked on his masterwork, a comprehensive *Historia Animalium*, in which he combined fact and fantasy as freely as Pliny the Elder. He promised to supply his readers with all the facts recorded, speculated on, or imagined about every animal known to man. Not surprisingly, Gesner was fascinated by the *Caravan Bestiary*, which he read under the watchful eye of Mehlenberg. Gesner mentions it but once in the *Historia*, but he pilfered from it extensively, as I discovered in the library at the Villa Ziane, reading Edward Topsell's 1658 English translation. I came on descriptions of the catoblepas, that massive black bull with dragon scales and Gorgon eyes that turn men to stone; the Indian leucrotta, the swiftest animal on earth, with a lion's torso, stag's hindquarters, and horse's head; and the Assyrian pazuzu, a harbinger of disease, with its human head, bird's wings, and lion's paws.

Pigafetta meanwhile took the original *Caravan Bestiary* to Malta. Then he returned to Venice for good. I was sure he must have brought along the bestiary, but upon his death it disappeared again. If not the book itself, I thought the key to its whereabouts must be in Venice. When I met a Hungarian count named Vartan Marczek at the Armenian monastery on the island of San Lazzaro one October morning, I wouldn't have guessed that he was the one who held that key.

It was the first time I had visited San Lazzaro. My guide, a young monk, introduced me to Marczek, and we exchanged pleasantries before I continued my tour. Marczek was standing on a bench with outstretched palms, feeding bread crumbs to the peacocks that roamed the garden. With his skullcap and flowing hair, he gave a good imitation of Saint Francis of Assisi. But Marczek was no saint.

O VER THE NEXT MONTH I redoubled my research efforts, making day trips to Padua and Treviso, staying for several nights in Vicenza, riding the *rapido* to Genoa, pursuing leads that didn't pan out. It was no longer Dandolo, but Pigafetta about whom I sought information. I discovered his exact place of birth (Vicenza), his parents' names (Vitali and Zara), the Venetian sestiere in which he'd grown up (Santa Croce), and the fact his father had been a nautical engineer at the Arsenal; but what I needed, and couldn't find, was information about his later years.

One afternoon, exhausted and bleary-eyed, I left the Villa Ziane and, on a whim, rode out to the Armenian monastery. San Lazzaro was one of the most peaceful places in the lagoon, and I thought a few hours there would help clear my head. The garden was empty. Bees were humming in the flowers, bitterns dipping through the reeds. I entered a small courtyard and came upon two monks dozing in the shade. Then I saw Count Marczek, book in hand, a pencil in his teeth, pacing around a bubbling fountain. I had been spending so much time alone, and had met so few people in the city, that I was immediately glad to see him. To my surprise, he remembered me, and invited me to join him for a cup of tea.

He spent most days at the monastery, reading in the library, feeding the peacocks, fishing off the pier with the monks. He wore the blue robe and slippers offered to guests of the abbot. Fifty years old, he had long gray hair and a thick moustache. From the waist up, he was built like a wrestler—barrel-chested, bulging neck muscles—but his legs were thin and his feet small for a man six three.

We fell into conversation, and over the next few weeks became friends and continued that conversation, talking away the afternoons before boarding the last vaporetto back to the city at dusk. Vartan Marczek was a raconteur of the old school, an excellent companion. He seemed to have been everywhere and done everything. I felt in him a kindred spirit, and a model, like Mr. Hood: someone with a deep and eclectic curiosity who had maintained, and refined, his enthusiasms into middle age. Like Mr. Hood, he was also generous with his time and knowledge. I felt lucky to have encountered both these men so early in my life. Though their temperaments and personal codes were different, other dissimilarities could be deceptive; that is, while on the surface Marczek might appear to have led a racier life, I knew Mr. Hood had been places Marczek could only imagine.

In the city Marczek tied his hair back in a ponytail and donned a wide-brimmed black hat, checkered scarf, and yellow cashmere coat. He wore a ring set with an oval of Pliocene amber in which an ant had been entombed. We went out for long dinners. Marczek was familiar with restaurants unusual for Venice: Afghan, Brazilian, the cuisine of Macao. He knew the names of maître d's, waiters, coat-check girls. Gondoliers lounging at various *stazia* greeted him. He bantered with the hawkers at the Rialto Bridge, who called him Barone. He seemed to have countless acquaintances. Yet he made his home in Paris, and before this extended stay, he had seldom visited Venice for more than a week or two at a stretch.

For the past five years, Marczek had been writing a biography of Lord Byron for a French publisher. Previously he had published a biography of Georg Buchner and a bestseller entitled *Three Fascists: Céline, D'Annunzio & Junger.* It was the latter's success that enabled him to keep his publisher at bay while he dawdled, digressed, and complained that he would never finish the Byron book. In fact, he was nearly finished. A part of him didn't want to be.

"I don't want to leave him. For all his imperfections, I am smitten, like so many before me. As with any biography, there is the illusion that the whole, the real, story lies clearly before you, from birth to death, if only you approach it from the correct angle. Now, at the end, I can only wonder what I missed and how much I skewed that angle."

He took notes in Hungarian—his native tongue—and wrote his text in French. He was an autodidact who could also speak English, German, Italian, Albanian, and Armenian. I had a facility with languages, but I was a piker compared to Marczek. He claimed that the blood of nearly every European nationality ran in his veins. His mother was half Czech, half Albanian, and his eyes lit up when I mentioned the Albanian lore I had learned from Evgénia: for example, the country's "true name," Shqipri, and the eagle myths created around the twin peaks of Mount Korab. He had inherited his title from his father.

"An earldom represented the lowest rung of royalty in the old Hungary. Still, my father had plenty of money to go around. But what the communists didn't confiscate, he pissed away on women and gambling. He fled to Austria and secured a license to export beer to Hungary. When he died a few years later, he bequeathed me that license, which was worth a good deal more than his title, at least until the Hungarian government banned all imported beer."

Marczek lived in a sprawling, drafty apartment off the Campo San Silvestro. Through tall windows, past the cupola on the Palazzo Barzizza, he had an eastward view of the Grand Canal. The furniture was sparse. Pyramids of books were strategically placed on the Persian rugs. When weather permitted, he worked at a table on the *altana*, the wooden platform on the roof where Venetian ladies once bleached their hair in the sun with a mixture of alum, Damascus soap, and burnt lead. Puffing Havana torpedoes, Marczek pecked away with two fingers on his pale green Olivetti. Researching Byron's life, he had spent two years in England, six months in Greece and Albania, and now a year in Italy. These labors, and his library and archive excursions, were one side of his life—one I could relate to—but I sensed there was another, very different side, and I soon came to know it.

He threw elaborate parties, famous for their revolving sets of guests. Foreign academics, local literati, art restorers, models, musicians, con men, a Kabuki troupe. Strangers brought other strangers, and there were evenings when Marczek wasn't acquainted with a single one of the dozens of people milling around the apartment. I believe he liked those times best. For all his outward sociability, he was an introvert, immersing himself for years in the lives of other men, and these parties were his way of letting go and stepping out of himself. He had a girlfriend named Oso. She was Japanese, twenty years his junior. She designed glassware. She had close-cropped hair and puffy cheeks and a full figure which she showed off with tight silk dresses and four-inch heels. She and Marczek conversed in Italian, and he liked to cook for her.

The first time Marczek had me over to dinner, Oso mixed us martinis. While he was cooking, she and I went up to the altana and watched the sun set across the lagoon. Back in the living room, she put on a record. Deep flute music filled the apartment.

"It's a shakuhachi flute," she said, joining me on the sofa. "In medieval Japan it was carved from tough root bamboo because the komuso, the priest-warriors who played it, were not permitted to carry swords. The flute is three feet long, and they used it both as a sacred instrument and a cudgel."

"So they could attain satori and also bludgeon their enemies."

"Exactly," she smiled, spearing the olive in her glass.

Marczek's inclinations as a biographer seemed to draw him to people whose lives were less a continuum than a jumble of conflicting incarnations. There was a former stunt pilot who had become an herbalist; a Bulgarian poet who—"like Rimbaud," he boasted—sold armaments in the Third World; and, most outrageous, a defrocked Coptic priest named Talmet. Nearing sixty, he had lost his collar because of sexual indiscretions with married women in his parish. His bishop in Alexandria turned a blind eye until Talmet seduced a woman in her daughter's bedroom—while the girl lay beside them. Talmet was short and compact, with restless blue eyes and a pallid smile. Soft-spoken, attentive, he seemed utterly sincere—and maybe he was. The kind of person you wouldn't mind confessing to if confessions were something you did. He had become an astrologer to the rich. His workplace was impressive: a glass dome built atop the Palazzo Bernini by an amateur astronomer in 1870. While the stars blazed overhead, Talmet cast your horoscope. He also made housecalls. Once a month he held a séance. There were only twelve seats at the round black table, including his own. The waiting lists were long. Talmet had become rich himself. He was a collector now, a patron of the arts. But his true passion lay in patronizing the city's call girls.

"He would have been happiest," Marczek observed, "if he lived around 1600, when the courtesans here were members of the ruling class, as accomplished in music and poetry as they were in bed. He shares the Tantric belief that sex clears the channels of the body so the spirit can roam."

Talmet also had a taste for opium, which Marczek shared to a lesser degree. At that time, opium was readily available in Venice by way of Turkey. One rainy night during the *acqua alta*, when Saint Mark's shimmered like a lake and planks had been laid down on strategic byways, Marczek and I pulled on rubber boots and went off to meet Talmet at a private club.

Outside the Doge's Palace we passed the statue of Saint Theodore, perched on a crocodile, spear in hand. Theodore was the original patron saint of Venice. The crocodile was his emblem. Venetians whose family histories go back a millennium celebrate the feast day of Saint Theodore, not Saint Mark. In a letter to Mr. Hood, updating him on my search, I asked if he knew that these Venetians claim it is Alexander the Great, not Saint Mark, who is entombed in the saint's basilica. Supposedly the merchants who claimed to have smuggled Mark's body (by all other accounts, it was cremated) from Alexandria to Venice had, in fact, carried off Alexander's remains, which disappeared from their mausoleum at the same time.

The club was on the Rio dei Servi, near the Ghetto. The owner was a plump Libyan woman in a man's suit. In the lounge some well-dressed men were drinking at a glass bar. There were private rooms, one of which we entered. It was lit by floor lamps with red bulbs. It took my eyes a moment to adjust. Then I saw Talmet on a couch with two African women. They were sharing a hookah. The women wore silk robes and hoop earrings. Their eyes were bloodshot. A familiar scent, the smoke was so cloying it closed up my throat.

Talmet greeted us with a raised hand.

We pulled up chairs and he passed the hookah. He introduced the women as Efazah and Sela, from the Ivory Coast. The opium went right to my head and I lost track of the conversation. Everything slowed down. The air was red and hazy. After a while, Talmet went over to a large bed with Efazah and Sela. Sela dropped her robe and lay down. She had small breasts and wide hips. Efazah unzipped Talmet's fly and began working with her lips and fingers to make him hard. They all seemed far away, their features blurry. Time passed—a few minutes that seemed like an hour—and Talmet was naked himself, on top of Sela.

Marczek and I exchanged glances and stood up.

"Is that what he always does?" I asked, as we stepped back into the rain.

"The African girls?"

"The exhibitionism. As in screwing a woman with her daughter present."

"I wouldn't know."

"Or maybe it's just another Tantric belief."

He shrugged. "This is the first time I have played witness—and I have smoked with him there before."

I wasn't sure I believed him, but what difference did it make? Going out on the town with Marczek was a welcome distraction from my work. Usually the entertainment he provided was not so sleazy. I doubt he was surprised on this occasion, but I was sure he wasn't embarrassed. Short of murder, and doing harm to a child or an animal, he thought most everything ought to be permitted. "Because it will happen anyway," he explained with irrefutable logic.

In the end, however, this part of his life interested me less than our evolving conversations at the monastery. My classics background intrigued Marczek; the more esoteric our conversations, the better. He picked my brain, just as he did anyone's who was a specialist in some field. We might talk about the saltworks of ancient Venetia or Plutarch's methodology as a biographer. But, increasingly, Marczek told me about Byron's Venetian exploits. Byron lived in Venice from November 1816 to December 1819, when he turned thirty-one. His vices made Talmet's pale in comparison: serial adultery, promiscuity with both sexes, incest. Byron had been driven into exile by scandal, specifically the fact he had fathered a child on his half sister. In Venice, unconstrained, he slept with countless women, from high society and low. A powerful swimmer, he often swam home from his late-night trysts by way of the Grand Canal, pushing before him a plank on which a candle burned while paddling with his free arm.

But Byron was no mere libertine. In the afternoon he bathed or rode his horse on the Lido. He took a season box at La Fenice, which in his letters he called "The Phenix." From midnight to dawn, with iron discipline, he wrote the initial cantos of his masterpiece, *Don Juan.* Then, after a few hours' sleep, he sailed to San Lazzaro to study Armenian, a notoriously difficult language. He wrote his publisher that he was doing this in order to sharpen his mind in the midst of his dissipations. A menagerist from his youth, he established a lively group on the ground floor of his villa: two monkeys, a silver fox, a bear, a mastiff, three cats, a Spanish-speaking parrot, and a pair of wolf cubs named Romulus and Remus. In his journal he noted that the bear liked to sing folk songs in Veneto dialect, the fox told him stories, and the monkeys danced on the terrace by moonlight. He transcribed one of the fox's stories: a princess named Lucina each night took the form of a nightingale to evade her suitors until she lost all memory of her human life and flew deep into the forest, never to be seen again.*

But it was Byron's Armenian studies that grabbed my attention. With the monks, he had compiled the first English-Armenian grammar. In the oblong library, where we sat beneath an oil painting of the poet, Marczek stunned me one day when he unknowingly revealed that, in performing this obscure task, Byron had been a crucial link in the history of the *Caravan Bestiary.*

---

*The nightingale is called Lucina because she heralds the dawn, like a lantern (lucerna).

I HAD NEVER DISCUSSED the *Caravan Bestiary* with Marczek. Over the years, there were only a handful of people in my life with whom I had. From my first notebook entries as a schoolboy, it had been a very private quest. I certainly wasn't the only person in the world who knew about the *Caravan Bestiary*, but I was proprietary about what knowledge I did possess. Whether or not the bestiary was something so grand as one missing element of a universal history, the key to a *gnosis* of massive proportions (in our times did that mean a vertiginous glimpse of millions of shards briefly unified?), I had also, for better or worse, treated it as a missing piece of my personal history. Maybe that was the point. The dream of finding it—the dream that it existed at all—may have been nothing more than that, yet it sustained me at times when my lack of a family, my choice of lovers, my duller pursuits could not. My search had always been a refuge: the notion of a parallel world, and the creatures that might inhabit it, helped me to tolerate the harsher disappointments—and worse—of this world.

Now I was about to confide in Marczek. As we sipped the monks' black tea, he was telling me how Byron came to San Lazzaro, first as a tourist, then as a student of Armenian, and finally in the unlikely role of grammarian. The grammar was his idea, and his delighted host, the abbot Pasquale Aucher, an expert linguist, agreed to collaborate.

"For weeks," Marczek explained, "Byron sat here compiling declension and conjugation tables and vocabulary lists. His principal contribution was to set down in plain English the intricate, shifting rules of Armenian syntax that make Hungarian look easy. He wrote a preface as well, which was found among his papers after his death. It reads like a polemic and was never published. He declared that the

Scriptures place Paradise in Armenia and that it was 'in Armenia that the Flood first abated, and the dove alighted.' In slaughtering Armenians, he added, Persians and Turks 'alike have desolated the region where God created man in his own image' and where Noah went aground in his ark." Marczek chuckled. "For a man caricatured as Lucifer in London newspapers, he sounds like a reactionary Christian. Though he agreed with Byron's sentiments, Father Aucher thought them too incendiary for a grammar, and so he quietly scotched the preface. Byron was furious, but he still underwrote the book's publication in England. In gratitude, the monks gave him access to the monastery's collection of rare illuminated books, the largest in Venice. Father Aucher took him on a tour of the library, showing off its treasures. A first edition of the *Divina Commedia*. A copy of the *Lives of the Saints* that belonged to Machiavelli. Then he showed Byron an exceptionally beautiful book, large and thick, bound in purple, with gilt-edged pages. A golden sun divided into quadrants was embossed on the front cover; within the quadrants were a dragon, a phoenix, a manticore, and a tortoise. On the back cover, a nine-tailed fox, haloed by stars, was etched on a silver moon. This is how the abbot himself described it:

It is a book of fantastic beasts, those excluded from the Ark, and others, more obscure yet, still to be found across the World, hidden in shadows or basking in light.

"What's the matter?" Marczek asked.

I shook my head. I couldn't believe that, after all those years, I had just heard the *Caravan Bestiary* described—size, color, cover adornments—by someone who had actually handled it.

"You've heard of this book?" Marczek said.

I nodded and gazed around the room. "So this is where Pigafetta left it."

"You know about him, too?"

"I know quite a bit about him." I could barely contain my excitement. "Vartan, I've been trying to find the *Caravan Bestiary* for ten years."

For once, Marczek was speechless.

"I'll explain," I said. "But, first, what else can you tell me?"

"I'll start with this: the abbot provided clear directions to the book's hiding place."

"Here?"

"In this room." He stood up. "I'll show you."

After all this time, I thought, is it going to be this easy? The answer was no.

"I'm afraid the book's been gone for some time," Marczek said, "but according to the abbot, it was concealed for several centuries in a hidden drawer in an oak desk."

He led me to a desk I hadn't even noticed before, in a dark corner of the library.

"Here, behind the nautical atlases," he said, sliding the atlases aside, tripping a latch, and pushing open a panel. He pulled out a wide deep drawer, about five inches high. It was empty. I put my hand in and ran my fingertips over the wood. They came away coated with fine dust. Knowing the bestiary had been shut in there all that time gave me a chill; if I never got closer to it than that, I would still be grateful.

Marczek was watching me. "This book means so much to you," he murmured.

"I need you to tell me everything you know about it. And everything you think Byron knew."

He sat back, gathering his thoughts. "No other biographer has even mentioned it, so far as I know. The Armenian grammar is well known. But this bestiary is not even a footnote."

"How did you learn of it?"

"Last month the abbot and I came on a box of papers Byron accumulated while laboring over the grammar. Between a fractured list of irregular verbs and a draft of his preface, he left a four-page, unfinished letter to his friend Douglas Kinnaird in London. That letter, dated November 1819, tells an amazing story, which I've been fleshing out ever since. According to Byron, Father Aucher told him the bestiary had been entrusted to the monastery three hundred years earlier by a Knight Hospitaller. The knight was journeying from Malta to Armenia when he fell ill and stopped in Venice, his native city. He was a famous mariner, who had in fact come home to die. Neither Father Aucher nor Byron had ever heard of Antonio Pigafetta. Aucher discovered the record of Pigafetta's visit here in the official journal of one of his remote predecessors, an abbot named Father Léon. Léon wrote that on the night of January 9, 1535, in a biting wind, Pigafetta crossed the lagoon in a *caorlina* rowed by six oarsmen. He wore a black cape and hat. Fifty-one years old, he was sickly, and looked far older. The great event of his youth, the Magellan voyage, was far behind him. He prayed in the chapel with the monks. He declined supper and requested a pot of tea while he wrote through the night at a table in a visitor's cell. At dawn he presented Father Léon with a long letter and a red velvet pouch adorned with his personal seal, a pair of lions back to back. Then he returned to the city. His letter began with the declaration that he was entrusting this pouch to the monastery, which he called the Venetian outpost of Armenia, the land of Eden and the Flood. He said the pouch contained a *most perfect work, which must be preserved and protected*. What Léon found inside was the *Caravan Bestiary*.

"Three centuries later, aided by Léon's distant successor, Byron sat at that oak desk working through the bestiary's Greek. He was intrigued by the book's premise and enamored of its vivid illustrations: the same gargoyles, griffins, and dragons that had always fascinated him on the parapets of British churches. He recalled the fabulous monsters in Ovid's *Metamorphoses* and Ariosto's *Orlando Furioso*. It is no coincidence, Xeno, that the chimera and the manticore appear in *Don Juan*. Still, Byron had scant knowledge of bestiaries. He told Kinnaird that the only bestiary he ever saw, at the Cavendish Library in Cambridge, was so imbued with moralizing that—predictably— it repelled him. Until he translated Pigafetta's notes, Byron had no idea how rare the book before him was. Writing in Veneto dialect, Pigafetta provided a brief history of the *Caravan Bestiary* and recounted how it had come into his possession. He explained that because he deemed it a 'living book,' worked over by many hands, he had no compunctions about inserting an appendix of additional animals real and fantastical, but 'unknown in Christendom,' that he had encountered circumnavigating the globe."

"I know about the ones in his journal of the Magellan voyage," I interrupted him.

Marczek smiled. "Evidently he saved up some others for the bestiary: the ocean bird that slumbered underwater—"

"That's the rukh."

"And the 'invisible monkey' of Java, so green it blended into the jungle foliage. And the bai ma, a white horse with one eye and eight legs. Pigafetta noted that the *Caravan Bestiary* had been an integral part of the first bestiary, the long-lost Book of Life. An astronomer in Lisbon told him that the *Caravan Bestiary* was initially compiled at the Monastery of Saint Jacob at the foot of Mount Ararat in Armenia, where Noah landed in the ark and founded a city called Ani. What do you know about Ararat?"

"It's seven miles high. Snow-covered. Part of Turkey now."

"In Pigafetta's time, the ark was still visible on top of the mountain, six hundred feet long, embedded in dark ice. A lone monk had supposedly scaled the mountain and returned with a petrified plank, which was displayed at the monastery. Many of the entries in the bestiary were provided by pagan sources—Persian magi, Indian shamans, and Tibetan sorcerers crossing Asia along the Caravan Route—so the monks who recorded them were branded heretics, and the bestiary was repeatedly 'lost' as it made its way across Christian Europe. Pigafetta said the *Caravan Bestiary* was initially translated from Aramaic into Armenian, and once in Europe, expanded in Greek and Latin. Even these later entries had pagan roots, drawing on the Greek historians and Egyptian storytellers.

"All of this impressed Byron enormously. He never expected to stumble on such rich material while working on a grammar in a monastery: the mysterious book, its arcane history, Pigafetta's selflessness in the face of death. Byron had already written two verse dramas steeped in Venetian history; in his letters he mentioned wanting to write a third—with Antonio Pigafetta as its protagonist—and until now, no one knew why. But here's where the story gets really interesting. Byron urged Father Aucher to complete Pigafetta's interrupted mission by arranging for the bestiary to be transported to Armenia.

He thought Pigafetta had been honoring, not just the book, but Armenia herself, in undertaking such a mission, and that his last wishes ought to be respected. In Byron's translation, Pigafetta cites a dream in which he clutched the bestiary while descending a snowy mountain *among thousands of divers animals.* Certain the mountain was Ararat, Pigafetta took this as a sign that the bestiary should be *returned to the site of its creation, rather than knocking about the world like forgotten cargo. For the sake of completeness, it must be so,* he added cryptically. Byron saw the repatriation of the bestiary more as an issue of nationalism, not mysticism: first and foremost, the book belonged to the Armenians. Father Aucher agreed, and when Byron finished translating Pigafetta's notes, the abbot enlisted a young monk named Adolphus Sarkas to be the courier. Aucher had written to the Metropolitan Zakalian in Ani and informed him that Brother Sarkas would be bringing the gift of a rare book to the Monastery of Saint Jacob. Here on San Lazzaro, Sarkas was an icon painter. He ground gold, lapis lazuli, and cinnabar into a base of egg tempera which he applied to thin blocks of cedar. He painted the chapel mural and the altar panels of Saint Clement and Saint Mark that you so admired."

"They're amazing," I said. "I've never seen anything like them."

"They would be better known if this weren't the city of Tintoretto and Veronese. Few people come out here."

Unlike the typically austere renderings of the saints, with their baleful undertones, Adolphus Sarkas's panels were detailed with vivid colors—green wings, vermilion robes, yellow hair—the faces radiating light so real it seemed not to be composed of paint. I had seen portraits that lifelike in museums, but never from the brush of an ecclesiastical painter. His mural was equally bold: extending the length of the side wall, it depicted Saint Veronica in her cave conversing with the Angel Gabriel. The composition was perfectly balanced, the perspective calibrated to pull the observer in, so that I felt as if I were standing inside the cave with the two figures. A myriad of elements were working in unison, but three immediately caught my eye: over Gabriel's shoulder, outside the cave, the raging storm his whirlwind had set off; the golden glow of his fiery wings that illuminated the cave; and the black spiders on which Veronica subsisted that covered the walls, red crosses on their backs and their eyes the same amber as her own.

"With a glazier from Murano," Marczek went on, "Sarkas collaborated on the stained-glass window in the dining hall. Clearly the monk had a sense of humor, executing such a sumptuous version of the Last Supper for his brothers to gaze on while they ate. But, all in all, he was considered an industrious member of the community, a loner who expressed his devotion with his craft. Father Aucher thought him efficient, pious, trustworthy. The perfect emissary to the Metropolitan.

"Byron was a shrewder judge of character, and his take on Sarkas was not so positive. Though he admired Sarkas's artwork, he observed that Sarkas had the annoying habit of staring at his feet when he spoke. *Some might deem this a sign of humility*, Byron wrote, *but I think the opposite: his pride is so overweening, he cannot look you in the eye. I have known many such men. However they contain it, in the end their dishonesty must prevail . . .*

"Events bore him out, for apparently Sarkas never reached Ani, or even set foot in Armenia. He got as far as Izmir on the Turkish coast before veering south to Cyprus and Rhodes—then disappearing. And the bestiary with him. It's certain he left Rhodes, but his ultimate destination remains a mystery. Father Aucher waited for him to turn up, or to send a message explaining his actions, but he was never heard from again."

Marczek sat back with a sigh. "That's all I know. Maybe more than I thought I knew," he said drily. "But I'm sure you have a few questions."

"A few hundred."

My head was racing, and I hadn't even noticed that darkness had fallen over the lagoon.

Marczek glanced at his watch and stood up. "The monks would offer us accommodations, but I'd prefer to catch the last vaporetto. Then, over dinner, you can tell me everything I don't know about the *Caravan Bestiary*."

I smiled. "It will be a pleasure."

THE FOLLOWING NIGHT, the twenty-eighth of February, Marczek and I had been invited to attend Talmet's monthly séance as his personal guest. This was an honor, seeing as the other participants paid 200,000 lire each. The séance was to begin at eleven P.M. in the Palazzo Mocenigo, which had once been Byron's Venetian residence.

Marczek and I took a water taxi up the Grand Canal in a soft rain. We passed crowded vaporetti, their glowing windows salt-smeared. At San Samuele, disembarking passengers were indistinct, outlined in charcoal. The invitation said formal attire, so I had put on a black suit and black shirt. In the taxi's cramped cabin, over the roar of the engine, Marczek told me some of the palazzo's illustrious history. The Mocenigo family had produced seven doges and played host to a stream of distinguished visitors. Two centuries before Byron leased the place, Giordano Bruno, the alchemist, was the houseguest of Doge Giovanni Mocenigo. Mocenigo attempted in vain to learn Bruno's alchemical secrets, then out of spite denounced him to the Inquisition as a heretic. Imprisoned and tortured for eight years, Bruno was burned at the stake in Rome on orders of Pope Clement VIII. His ashes were scattered in the Tiber, but his angry ghost returned to Venice to roam the Palazzo Mocenigo.

"Perhaps," Marczek concluded, turning up his collar, "Bruno will appear for us tonight. Unless we're truly lucky and Byron materializes."

A sprawling five-story building, the palazzo was ocher colored, with green shutters and a terra-cotta roof. Its upper windows were brightly lit. Smoke curled from one of the chimneys. After bounding across the canal, we stepped onto the submerged landing, thick with algae, where a footman held open a heavy door. The dimly lit room we entered was spacious, bare of furniture, with a low ceiling. Portraits of the Mocenigo family stared down at us. I also noted an image of Saint Theodore, atop his crocodile, on a marble tile embedded in the wall.

"This is where Byron kept his menagerie," Marczek said, leading me to a stairway, and I tried to imagine those animals coexisting in that dank space. I wondered if any of their spirits would be making an appearance at the séance. My grandmother hadn't required a ceremony to commune with them. One of the few items from my childhood I still possessed was her music box containing the white whisker.

We climbed to the third floor, where the ceilings were higher and the rooms large. The butler took our coats and led us down a corridor to a circular room with drawn curtains. On the black table candles were burning. The ceiling was a mural of the night sky, with the Roman goddess of night, robed in stars, standing astride a pair of streaking comets. A fire was crackling in the marble fireplace. We were the last guests to arrive, but the room was strangely silent. There were nine other people scattered around, formally dressed, sipping tea—no alcohol permitted before the séance, and no conversation. Talmet was not among them. Some of the guests were more ghostly than any ghost: an old couple with yellowing white hair; an ashen, bearded man beribboned with medals gazing at a bust of Giovanni Mocenigo (hatchet-faced, slit-eyed, he looked like an informer); a grim young woman smoking on a couch beside a fat woman in a tiara. The fat woman was so pale she could have been wearing whiteface.

Our hostess, a tall blue-eyed woman with silver hair and a gown to match, glided over.

"Welcome, Count. Mr. Atlas."

Marczek kissed her hand. "Signora Camarelli." After she moved on, he murmured, "Her husband used to control the bauxite monopoly in Italy."

Now he was one of the spirits Talmet hoped to summon.

The lights went down and Talmet entered the room. He wore a burgundy velvet jacket with shoes to match. Stitched on his pocket in gold was a lightning bolt crossed by a dagger—instruments for tearing the fabric of time, and a symbol of life after death. Talmet shook hands solemnly with everyone. When it was my turn, and our eyes met, there was no acknowledgment of the scene I had witnessed at the nightclub. Just a quick handshake and a pat on the shoulder.

The lights went down. I took the seat assigned me, between the beribboned gentleman—a retired general—and the elderly lady. The grim young woman was sitting opposite me. Talmet was at the head of the table, Marczek to his right, Signora Camarelli to his left. The butler tinkled a bell and set a large glass sphere in the middle of the table. It was midnight blue, capped with glittering gold crystals. If all went well, the crystals would shoot rays far out into the night, communication lines to the dead.

Talmet laid his palms flat on the table and fixed his gaze on the sphere. His face was calm. In a role so easy to overplay, he stayed within himself, projecting both humility and command. His body language sent a clear message: I'm indispensable here, but I'll remain detached enough so you can judge the proceedings for yourself. He offered no speeches, and his instructions were simple: join hands, close your eyes, and concentrate on the person you want to contact; he would see to the rest.

He joined hands with Marczek and Signora Camarelli, and the rest of us followed suit with our neighbors. The old lady's hand was dry, the general's damp. Keeping my eyes partly open, I watched the young woman, grimmer than ever, bite her lip. There seemed to be much at stake for her.

I followed Talmet's suggestion and concentrated on my mother. At first, nothing happened. Every few minutes, Talmet compressed his lips and hummed deeply, fell silent, and hummed again. This went on for some time. No one else made a sound. The blue sphere was his only prop; there were none of the special effects or elaborate paraphernalia I had expected. This was more an exercise in collective meditation than theatrical illusion. The fire crackled. Rain pattered the windows. Talmet hummed. And I picked up no frequency on which I could contact my mother. Nor did I feel emanations from the spirits of Byron and Giordano Bruno. I began to drift.

The voice that broke into my reverie was decidedly human. "Michael!" the fat lady cried, pointing at the window.

"Please sit, Signora Starza," Talmet said gently. "If you break the circle, you won't see him at all."

She looked bewildered. "You're right—he's gone now."

"Please join hands again," Talmet said.

And she did.

This was the dramatic high point of the evening. If anyone else spotted a dead relative or friend, they didn't let on. Near the end of the séance, the elderly lady and the general claimed to hear voices. She said her mother had identified the mastermind behind the 1881 assassination of Tsar Alexander II. The general reported that his late wife told him a massive explosion in Antarctica in 2027 would mark the end of the world.

I had erroneously thought that a successful séance must be a collective exercise, everyone sharing in the same sights and sounds, seeking a glimpse into what my grandmother used to call *il Grande Oscurità*, the Great Darkness. I realized that, from Talmet's point of view, this sort of unanimity was beside the point. A convincing outburst and one or two participants hearing voices was all he needed to ensure an influx of clients. Some artful manipulation could always elicit such responses. These were people, I thought, who couldn't take no for an answer, even from Death. Gripped by anxiety and longing, they viewed the séance as a kind of elaborate telegraph office, with Talmet the well-paid operator who knew the right codes. That was why they were willing to fork over 200,000 lire. Only the grim young woman had gone away dissatisfied; wanting urgently to speak to her late fiancé, she was furious when all she got was Talmet's humming and Signora Starza's hysteria.

Champagne and canapés were served afterward. Talmet held court in a chair adorned with the Mocenigo coat of arms, a lion clutching crossed swords. Marczek was sprawled on a divan, deep in conversation with Signora Camarelli. Glass in hand, I wandered down the corridor, studying another set of Mocenigo portraits.

I passed a succession of dark rooms, descended one stairway and climbed another, and at the end of an L-shaped corridor stepped into an enormous, musty room. It was an orangery, many centuries old. The roof was glass, the walls mirrored, and double doors gave onto a wide terrace. There was a fountain centered by a statue of Atalanta, in her tunic, stooping to pick up an orange. The marble floor, itself a faded mosaic of orange trees, was streaked with water stains. A hose was coiled in a puddle beside the planting table. At the time of the Crusades, this room must have housed over a hundred trees, imported from the Holy Land. They grew in wooden planters that could be wheeled onto the terrace in summer. Now there were just two rows of thin orange trees and a lone date palm. Dozens of empty, broken planters lined the wall.

I sat on the edge of the fountain and finished my champagne. Reaching into my jacket pocket for one of Marczek's Cuban cigars, I instead pulled out a handful of letters the concierge had given me when I was leaving my hotel. I had forgotten all about them. There was a laundry bill, a library notice, a letter from my landlord in Paris, and another letter—twice forwarded, ricocheting across the Atlantic and back—from Pericles Arvanos, postmarked two weeks earlier in Athens.

I knew at once what it was. I hadn't heard from Arvanos, or my father, in three years. Once our financial connection ended, there was no social correspondence.

I was at a séance, yet the spirit farthest from my thoughts was the one that might actually have been in transit from this world to the next. He had, however, contacted me so seldom in life that I couldn't expect him to make the effort in death.

My father was dead.

5

M Y ROOM was on the top floor of a hotel on Mount Lykabettos that was ringed with eucalyptus trees. From the balcony, squinting into the sunlight, I could imagine the clean lines of the ancient city, the marble *polis* buried in the helter-skelter limestone of modern-day Athens. The landmarks of that vanished city had been fixed in my mind in New England classrooms long before I set foot in Greece: the Temple of Zeus, the Agora, Pnyx Hill, and the Parthenon rising in a cloud of bright dust. Beyond the sprawl of working-class neighborhoods to the north, I could make out the harbor at Piraeus beneath a layer of smog. Of the many freighters anchored there, one of them now belonged to me.

I had just come from the offices of Pericles Arvanos, where he read me my father's will. It had been difficult for me to travel to Greece, and so long as my father was alive, I never intended to do so. The associations were just too painful. Despite my passion for the language and the history, first and foremost it had been the place where my father lived when he chose not to live with me. I had always wanted to know why he made that choice, and I hoped when our business was concluded, Arvanos might fill me in on that and some other things.

After all the years of transatlantic communications, I was as curious about Arvanos as I was about the will. I knew him only from those letters, and the (comically sinister) mental image I'd conjured up thirteen years earlier—swarthy, corpulent, ham-handed, with a bushy moustache and a deep voice—that in no way meshed with the man before me, who was pale, lanky, stooped, clean-shaven, with a musician's hands and wispy white hair. His beige suit was well cut, his tortoise-shell glasses stylish. His English was excellent, for he had studied law in England as well as in Greece. He was soft-spoken, with an easy, almost slow-motion manner—not the sort of man I would have expected my father to entrust with his business affairs. I could barely imagine them in the same room together. That was my failing; when Arvanos addressed me in earnest, peering past the stacks of color-coded folders on his desk, and I got a closer look at his steady gray eyes, I knew exactly why my father had retained him. He specialized in maritime law, and his dusky office off Constitution Square was decorated with model ships and navigational maps, and an odd assortment of bric-a-brac, notably a stuffed kingfisher and a bronze statuette of a mermaid with mother-of-pearl scales. Across from his desk there was an oil painting of Odysseus's ship sailing past the Sirens: the crew with beeswax in their ears pulling at the oars; the claw-footed Sirens singing on the reefs; and Odysseus, lashed to the mast, straining to get free.

While I was fascinated with Arvanos, however, he seemed to have a strictly professional interest in me. What other kind should he have had? For years, he had been my sole conduit to my father. To him, I was the son of one of his many clients. When I walked into his office, the blinds drawn and cigarette smoke in the air, I was nervous and off-balance. Arvanos was cordial enough, but detached. Some of this, too, owed to the circumstances: I was the one, after all, being informed of my inheritance.

I had not expected to inherit anything. The gulf between my father and me had grown so wide, the silence so resounding. And as far as I was concerned, he had fulfilled his financial obligations by supporting me generously, past the age of twenty-one. Unknown to him, he had even put Lena Moretti through college. Nothing more was necessary.

That said, I was stunned by what he did leave me: not money or securities or land, but a 300,000-ton, 450-foot freighter. The *Makara* was currently under contract to a textile company that brought cargo from the Far East; after maintenance, insurance, and all other expenses, I would receive an income of eighty thousand dollars for the year.

"Next year you can do what you please," Arvanos said, "renew the contract or lease the ship to another client. Your father's remaining cash will be used to overhaul the ship this winter."

He paused, but I remained silent.

"Good ships are always in demand," he continued. "This one should yield you a solid income for many years, as it did your father. Of course you can also sell the *Makara* outright next year. I would estimate its worth at around three million dollars. Even after taxes, there would be a good amount to reinvest."

I tried to read his eyes—for what, I didn't know. Never wavering, they matched his tone, calm and matter-of-fact. Meanwhile, all sorts of feelings were churning up in me: rage, resentment, guilt. I said, "I had no idea what my father owned, and I never gave a thought to what he might leave me."

"He's left you everything."

"By default?"

"Oh no. You are the stipulated beneficiary. He had no other survivors."

"What about his other ships?"

"There are no other ships. The *Makara* was his single largest asset. He bought it thirteen years ago. It was the first ship he owned. That's when I became his lawyer."

"What happened to the rest of his fleet?"

Arvanos poured himself a glass of mineral water. He offered me one. Then he told me the story—framed succinctly as a legal brief— of my father's life in the years he had known him.

"Two years after your father bought the *Makara*, he married a woman named Eléna Louritis."

He paused, studying my face.

"If you're wondering if I knew," I said, "the answer is no. But I'm not shocked. I suspected it. I always asked myself why he was so secretive. I used to think he had a second family here. I came up with all sorts of scenarios."

"There was no family—no children. The marriage was short-lived and unhappy. Eléna came from a wealthy family—the wealthiest, in fact—in the town in Crete where your grandparents were born, Asprophotes. Most of the Louritis family left there long ago, and settled in Irakleion, but they kept their houses and land. Your father met Eléna in Irakleion, courted her aggressively, and proposed marriage. She accepted. She was over forty years old, plain-looking and shy. She had nearly given up on the idea of marriage. But she was impressed by your father's imposing presence, his physical strength. She'd had suitors before, but never one like him, a real seaman. It was impressive the way he had pulled himself up out of the boiler room. Working overtime, taking out high-interest loans, risking everything, really, and never flinching until he got what he wanted: a ship. Eléna's grandfather, the patriarch, had gone to sea as a young man and then made a fortune in shipping. But, unlike your father, he had some capital to start with. His son, her father, assembled a fleet of oil tankers and freighters, thirty ships in all. When he died, her two brothers ran the business. But she inherited a third of it. So, for a time, after she married your father, he oversaw a fleet of eleven ships, including the *Makara*. Your father could never have married into the Louritis family if they knew he had previously been married and had a child."

The look on my face stopped him. He cleared his throat, then offered me a cigarette. I declined, and he lit one himself.

"These people are Cretans, from the mountains," he went on. "They haven't changed their ways in centuries. That is why your father kept your existence a secret. Beyond that, he did not confide in me. I cannot speak for his innermost thoughts. He and Eléna lived here in Athens for two years. Then, as her health declined, they moved to Crete. She wanted to be nearer her family. It was clear that her true loyalty was to them—not a good formula for any marriage. Add to that your father's duplicity, and you see they had a shaky foundation. Eléna insisted they were leaving Athens because of the smog. She had weak lungs. They went to Hydra. There are no automobiles or motorcycles permitted on that island. It's peaceful. Your father bought a house in the town, up high, overlooking the harbor. Many shippers have homes there. That's where Eléna died, of a heart attack. Your father was at sea, as he was much of the time. Before his return, her family took her body to Crete and buried her in their plot at Asprophotes. In her will, all her property reverted to her brothers. Under Greek law, that is not something a husband can contest. So your father was left with the house in Hydra and the *Makara*. For a while he owned a piece of a ferry company. He began to live on Hydra year-round. He always lived simply. He would come to Athens for a few weeks at a time, to do business. He rented an apartment near Vathis Square. Last year he sold the house in Hydra and moved here full-time. He said he was having trouble getting around on the island. He was fifty-seven years old, but he looked older. His arthritis was plaguing him. It was bad in his shoulders and spine, from his early years in those boiler rooms. He died at his apartment last month. It was a massive stroke. There was no warning. He was alone. The land-lady found him the next day." He sat back, laying his palms on the desk. "I'm sorry."

Through the slats in the blinds I watched the traffic crawl toward the city center, so slowly it seemed as if the same cars—gray Mercedes taxi, yellow van, a black sedan—had been there ever since I'd sat down. Though Arvanos had presented the facts in the most orderly fashion, as soon as I took them in they became disordered: the more I tried to fix on them, the faster they flew apart. Trying to imagine my father, who had been so physically imposing, deteriorating to that extent, at that age, rattled me. When I reached for my glass of water, my hand was trembling.

"Where was my father buried?" I asked.

"He wasn't. He was cremated the day after he died. His ashes were scattered in the sea. There was no church service. No wake. Those were his wishes."

Apparently all of my father that was left on this earth were the freighter *Makara* and me.

Averting my eyes from Arvanos to Odysseus and the Sirens, I began to feel ashamed, not for myself so much as for my father. I don't know how Arvanos felt about seeing me before him, a living person, after all those years. But it couldn't have been any more pleasant for him than it was for me. That my father had abandoned me was bad enough; that he had denied my very existence seemed even worse. That was my bad luck. My father's seemed to lie in marriage. He had married once for love and once for money, and lost both wives prematurely. The double life I had imagined for him had turned out to be anything but elaborate. And he had remained a loner to the end.

"Outside of money—the tuitions, the allowance—did my father ever speak to you about me?"

"How do you mean?"

"Did he ever talk about what I was like, where I lived in New York, who I lived with?"

"I knew you lived with your grandmother and a housekeeper. I knew your mother died in childbirth. I received the grade reports from your schools and passed them along." He hesitated. "So I knew what you were studying."

After an awkward silence, I said, "Is that it? Did you have any idea what I looked like?"

"I saw a photo once. When you were a boy."

"Did my father ever say why he never brought me here to see him?"

"No."

"Or why he didn't have me come after his wife died?"

"No."

"When was that, by the way?"

"She died in December 1967."

"So I was seventeen. I guess I should be grateful that he never told me. After working so hard to establish that I didn't exist, maybe he believed it himself."

Arvanos let out a long breath. "I know this: your father assumed he would be rich, and for a while he was. Perhaps he rationalized that his short-term actions would be justified when he passed some of that wealth on to you."

"Excuse me, but I don't buy that. My father shut me out long before he got married, or got rich. I don't care how he dealt with his guilt—if he had any."

"Yet you want to know his motivations."

"Wouldn't you?"

"Yes," he said quietly. "I would. I wish I could be more helpful. And I understand that you are angry."

"Yeah, I'm angry. You've just told me that, in order to marry for money, my father disowned me."

"I'm not here to judge," Arvanos replied evenly. "I was his lawyer. He gave me instructions and I followed them. When it came to shipping, he asked my advice and I gave it. With personal matters, that never happened. We were not friends."

"Fine. Let's leave it at that. Do you know of any friends he had here in Athens?"

"It's not something I would know."

"Or in Hydra?"

He shook his head. "I know the details about his marriage and his dealings with the Louritis family because they overlapped with business matters. I rarely met with him outside of this room. I can tell you little of what he did outside of his business."

"Sure." I felt defeated.

Arvanos leaned forward. "Let me tell you something that might be helpful." This was the only time I thought he deviated from his prepared remarks. "During all the years I sent you your allowance, your father told me to give you whatever you asked for. This was true even when his wealth diminished dramatically. In the end, I was sending you about half his income."

I frowned. "Mr. Arvanos, it was never money that my father withheld from me. And you don't owe me any explanations."

I left his office soon afterward with a sheaf of documents pertaining to the *Makara*, a copy of the will, and two addresses I requested.

I visited the first address early the next morning, a nondescript apartment building on an anonymous street in the Vathi district. It was midway between the Archaeological Museum and the military cemetery. The exterior was white concrete. The lobby was bare, the elevator cramped. The handyman let me look into Apartment 405, so long as I remained at the threshold while he held the door open. The rooms were already empty. Walls had been patched and plastered.

The painters were about to begin their work. Their cans and rollers were piled beside a stepladder.

I noted that, like every apartment my father rented in my childhood, this one had terrible light, slanting in off a cramped courtyard. He had died in the sort of dark room he preferred.

Later that morning I took a taxi to Piraeus and boarded the hydrofoil to Hydra. As we left the harbor, we passed near the *Makara*. It towered over us. Reading its dimensions was nothing like seeing them firsthand. I was still amazed that I owned it. The largest thing I had ever owned was a car; I didn't even own a house. A ship like this seemed far too huge to be the property of anything but a corporation or government, not a single person. It looked well maintained, just as Arvanos had said. Freshly painted, the hull was white with a yellow border, the upper decks blue, the stacks yellow. Two seamen were hosing down the deck. An officer was standing by the pilothouse. Above the bridge the radar antenna was revolving. The *Makara* was registered in Ecuador, and the flag of that country was flapping on the mast: a tricolor centered by a snowcapped mountain and a steamship on a river, over which a condor hovered.

The town of Hydra is like an amphitheater in which the rows of houses, gray or white with terra-cotta roofs, rise steeply, curving around the harbor. It was a warm day. The outdoor cafés were filled, and many boats were anchored at the docks, but still the waterfront felt calm. I was struck at once by the quiet of a place with no motor vehicles. Not even bicycles were allowed on the island. People carrying baggage who disembarked with me hired mules to take it up the hills.

I asked a mule driver about the address Arvanos had given me. He directed me up a series of twisting alleys. As I climbed, the alleys narrowed. The harbor's marble pavement gave onto whitewashed granite. The silence deepened. Distant sounds carried: a donkey braying, a dog's bark. I entered an old neighborhood with large houses. Potted geraniums lined the verandas. Cats sunned themselves on the walls. I passed a widow hanging her laundry and a girl with a basket of eggs. Then there was no one.

I reached a plateau from which the boats below looked like toys.

My heart was beating fast from the climb. But also because I knew this was the place Arvanos had described: the last of three houses off a sunbaked square. I understood why someone with an arthritic spine would have had trouble climbing that hill, or even riding up on a mule. The house was old, but well kept: two stories, white with blue shutters, a garden in back, lemon trees in front. Bougainvillea covered the façade. Grape clusters hung from a trellis. There was a weather-worn coat of arms above the door, from the island's Venetian days: a full-masted galley with a lion in the prow. The front gate was locked. The windows shuttered. The air hummed with insects, and cicadas were clicking in the grass. Far out on the water the boats trailed ribbons of foam. The panoramic view surprised me, the fact he had given himself something so grand. More likely that was his wife's doing.

I sat down on the steps before the gate, shaded by one of the lemon trees. According to Arvanos, my father had occupied this house on and off for eight years. But it was hard for me to place him there: except for the time he took me to school in Maine, I had never seen him outside of New York or Boston. I had so narrow a context in which to situate him that my imagination was stymied: I always pictured him in a vacuum, like a cutout figure without a background. I had never even seen him on a ship, his true home, or at the seashore. Neither those bare rooms in Athens nor this other place he called home were going to provide any more closure than a gravesite. And what exactly had come to an end, after all?

Back at the harbor, I waited for the last hydrofoil to Piraeus. Dusk was falling. The fishing boats went out, churning slowly. I wandered into the marble church with the bell tower that was the largest building in town. All afternoon, I'd heard those bells ringing on the hour. Candles were burning beside the icons. The church had been built by shipowners. The nave was adorned with the busts of sea captains. There was a mural of Christ, cold-eyed and muscular, walking on the waves swinging a lantern. From the chandeliers, tiny silver ships hung on fine chains. And, behind the altar, on the rounded door to the sacristy, Saint George in blue armor was impaling a mottled dragon with his lance. Like all Saint Georges, he was on horseback, but his was a seahorse, with glowing eyes and a mane that was not hair, but sea foam. The saint's helmet was a gold triton and his saddle was studded with nautilus shells. In the vestibule there was a brass plaque that listed the names of drowned sailors and their ships, dating back to 1701; at the bottom were engraved the names of those who had paid to erect the plaque. One of the names was my father's, looking as permanent as the inscription on a tombstone. He might as well have been one of the drowned, not one of the donors—it was all the same now.

Before I left the church, I stuffed a wad of drachmas into the poor box. But I didn't light a candle, not for my father, not for myself.

A FEW DAYS LATER, Arvanos arranged for me to take a tour of the *Makara*. "It's your property, it's an investment, you ought to see it," he said, sounding like my own lawyer, rather than my father's executor. In fact, I had formally retained him now that I had real need of counsel.

A launch from the ship picked me up in Piraeus, piloted by the first mate. His name was Carmine. He was a wiry young man with a shaved head, polite but reserved. It was a humid, overcast day. I had never been on a ship larger than a ferry and never boarded one by scaling a ladder with the sea swirling below. The captain, a man twice my age, welcomed me on deck with a strong handshake and addressed me as "sir." He introduced himself as Marco Salice. He was a Sardinian, shorter and slighter than the first mate, but—to my eye—even tougher. His gray hair was curly, his salt-and-pepper beard neatly trimmed. His eyes were intelligent. The furrows in his brow looked as if they had been carved with a penknife. With a sailor's rolling gait, he took me around: the quarterdeck, pilothouse, radar room, engine room, galley, mess hall, crew's quarters, and the catwalks atop the tremendous three-story holds from which sixty tons of fabric from Singapore and Malaysia had recently been unloaded. It was a complex, orderly world, alien to me in every way. The seamen going about their tasks either stared at me openly or cast furtive glances. Captain Salice kept up a running commentary, detailing the ship's specifications (300 feet long, 80 feet wide, with 220,000 square feet of deck space); engine type (20,000-horsepower Daimler-Hamburg); top speed (17 knots); tonnage (29,000); fuel capacity (2,000 gallons); size of crew (14); guest quarters (for 7); cargo capacity (91,000 cubic feet); date of construction

(1953). He had arranged for our lunch to be served in his cabin, the last stop on my tour. But first he wanted to show me what he called "the owner's cabin."

"Just as it was your father's," he said, "it will be yours now whenever you're aboard."

Arvanos had mentioned it in the most perfunctory way, so I was surprised to enter a stateroom-sized cabin with a gleaming mahogany bed and chest, a large pigeonhole desk, a Persian carpet, and a well-appointed bathroom. For my father, austere in all things, this was opulent.

"Everything looks so new," I said.

"It is new. Your father's health had been declining. He had not sailed with us in two years. He told me he would never go to sea again. Last year he had the cabin refurbished. No one has stayed in it since then."

Amazing as it seemed, he had evidently had it refurbished for me. What other conclusion could I draw?

"Let me know if there is anything you would like modified," the captain said tactfully.

I shook my head. "It's fine."

"There is also an envelope for you, in the desk." He hesitated. "Perhaps you would like a moment here alone."

"Thank you."

I walked around the cabin. I peered out the two portholes. I opened the closets and drawers, which were empty. As was the medicine cabinet. In his will my father had ordered that his material possessions be auctioned off or destroyed. Obviously that had included the contents of this cabin. I sat down on the bed. It was a hard mattress, the kind he liked. Beneath my feet I felt the humming of the ship's pumps and engines and its powerful generators.

I sat at the desk. It felt massive, immovable, like an upright piano. Two oversized books were shelved beside it: a volume of nautical maps and a world atlas. I rolled the desktop back and found a five-by-seven manila envelope on which my name was printed in my father's hand.

I should have known that he would have considered this ship, not the houses ashore, to be his true home. If he left a trace of himself anywhere, it would be here.

Inside the envelope was a single photograph of my mother and father, the first I had ever seen of them together, taken the day they were married. They were standing in front of the Bronx County Courthouse, near Yankee Stadium. The sunlight was bright. Their shadows loomed on the broad steps. Patches of ice shone on the sidewalk. Some pigeons had just taken flight. My father was wearing a black suit and a wide checked tie. His overcoat was folded over his arm. His hair was slicked back. He had his other arm around my mother. Standing beside him, she was not as small as I would have thought. But she did look so much younger than him. She wore a double-breasted coat over a white dress. The wind was ruffling her long hair. The two of them were smiling, squinting into the light. I had never seen my father look that happy.

He had left me something he had never been able to give me in life: an image of himself happy. As to why this girl had made him so happy, even at this late date he was not willing to share that information. Nor to tell me that he loved me: just that he had loved her, to the end.

I T WAS VARTAN MARZCEK who had said to me, "You're from the most hard-assed people in Europe: Cretans and Sicilians. A couple of islands too big to be islands. And too tough. No hammer breaks their stones. They make the rest of Greece and Italy look soft by comparison."

I was in Sicily, a town called Fornace in the mountains fifty miles southwest of Messina. It lived up to its name, for even in October it was hot as a furnace. On top of which there was a severe drought. Dust coated the one road in like snow. The pine forests were dry as tinder. The stream that skirted the forest was reduced to a trickle.

The residents were suspicious of visitors. Fornace was my grandmother's birthplace, so I had hoped to feel at home. Maybe if I had mentioned my lineage sooner, people would have been more welcoming. But even when I did identify myself as the great-grandson of Emmanuel Azzaro and the grandson of Rose Azzaro, it barely registered. All the Azzaros had either died off or moved to Catania and Messina to find work.

I did get a response finally on my third day in town when I struck up a conversation with an old man. I was renting one of the four rooms at the only pension in town, and he was at a café next door. He had a brown, lined face and a wild thatch of white hair. He was wearing a blue work shirt, with old wine stains washed in, and frayed suspenders. I bought him a grappa and smoked one of his Corso cigarettes, the harshest tobacco I ever tasted.

"I knew your grandmother's cousin, Mariella. She married a boy from Triano and died there a few years later. She had two children."

He shrugged. "I don't know what happened to them. In America, did your grandmother have many grandchildren?"

"Not too many."

He smiled wryly. "A lot of money?"

"Not too much."

He stuck a toothpick in his mouth alongside the cigarette. Two of his front teeth were gone. "She never came back here," he said. "Her father never came, either. None of them who left came back."

"And there are no Azzaros left here?"

He shook his head. "None."

I signaled the waiter—a skinny schoolboy in an apron—for two more grappas.

The old man leaned forward. "But, you know, there is a cousin of yours here now."

"A cousin who is not an Azzaro?"

He nodded. "I don't know her name. But she's your cousin."

"Where is she?"

"At old Garzas's house. His son rents it out." He gave me directions. Then two of his cronies joined him, and that was the end of our conversation.

After lunch, I walked to a small stone house at the other end of town, close to the forest. A cat was sleeping by the front door. Chickens were pecking in the yard. A rooster was perched on the fence. His plumage was red and orange, his coxcomb gold. Eating my landlady's bean soup the previous night, I heard her tell her nephew a story. An old shepherd in his hut woke from a restless sleep and overheard his rooster and his dog discussing the fact their master was soon going to die. Distraught, the shepherd ran outside to question them, but in the darkness tripped on a stone, hit his head, and died. "He should have gotten to his knees and prayed," my landlady concluded solemnly.

In Sicily it is well known that animals converse. If you understand their languages—a rare gift—you can avoid many tribulations. My grandmother told me this.

The woman who answered my knock was about my age, thin and pale, with brilliant red hair and black eyes. I had only seen hair like that once, on my cousin Silvana in the Bronx. Was it possible I had another such cousin?

She looked at me in disbelief when I said, "My name is Xeno Atlas."

Standing frozen on either side of the doorway, we scrutinized one another. Then she beckoned me in, and in clear English said, "I'm Silvana Conti."

But by then I knew she was my American cousin, Uncle Robert's daughter whom I had seen long ago at my grandmother's funeral.

It wasn't just her red hair. To my astonishment, Silvana had the face of Uncle Robert's sister as she might have looked had she lived past twenty—a face I knew only from photographs, most recently the one on the *Makara*.

She looked like my mother.

M Y DOCTORS told me to go somewhere quiet, with clean dry air, like Utah or Arizona. Instead, I came here. I wanted to be close to Nana."

That was what she called my grandmother.

"They said my chances of recovery were good, but I had to get away."

She had nearly died of tuberculosis. It was a virulent strain, resistant to antibiotics, and in the end they had to remove half her left lung. She was hospitalized for two months, and convalesced for several more.

"I've never been sick before, and that made it harder."

We were in the grape arbor behind her house, where the shade was densest. She had brewed a pot of tea. The cat had come around and was sleeping beneath the table. Ants were scurrying along the flagstones. The scent of wild thyme was blowing in from the fields. Silvana was getting tired. In the three hours I had been there, we had begun to sketch out our respective histories.

Instinctively we each worked backward from the present. Our childhood years—the circumstances that had kept us apart—were too painful to approach head-on. The only surprising thing was that we were able to discuss them at all after such a short time together. But my grandmother had been right: Silvana and I were very much alike. It felt as if we had known each other for many years—and in a way we had.

She was a draftswoman. She worked for a camera company in Atlanta. That was where she had gone to college. She had picked up a slight Southern accent, which took me aback at first.

"I don't design the cameras or projectors," she said, "I draw the blueprints to the designers' specifications. I could always draw things true to life."

She was being modest: in fact, she could precisely render the workings of complex instruments, framing them three-dimensionally. Having previously worked for an electronics company, she said the assortment of lenses, shutters, and spools that comprise a camera were far easier to draw than the circuitry of a stereo receiver.

"People often ask if I wanted to be an artist—as in: am I a frustrated painter? The answer is no. If anything, it's surgeons and engineers who always fascinated me. I like to see how things work. But I'm not an inventor myself."

She had been married briefly.

"To a man like my father," she said pointedly. "That was what was wrong. We got married right out of college. He was a devout Catholic—a zealot, as it turned out. I left the Church to get divorced. That was the one good thing that came of my marriage. My father never forgave me. But we were already estranged. He was a worse zealot. The most unforgiving person I ever knew."

I sipped my tea, thinking of those Sundays when my grandmother went to visit my uncle and his family: Uncle Robert's balding head and brown suit, his boxy gray sedan reflecting flashes of sunlight. For Silvana and her siblings, he had made my mother and me into mysterious, forbidden figures, objects of curiosity.

I must have looked pained, for Silvana said, "I'm sorry. Here I am telling you, of all people, about my father. You must have hated him."

"I did," I said, "inasmuch as you can hate anyone you've never met face-to-face."

Staring at Silvana, I couldn't get over it: her forehead, cheekbones, even the curve of her lips were so like my mother's. Everything seemed the same except that shock of red hair. And her eyes were darker. Silvana's resemblance opened up another grim angle onto my uncle: what kind of man could look at his daughter and see his sister's face so clearly, yet continue to keep me out in the cold?

"Did he hate my mother, too?" I asked.

Silvana cocked her head. "He liked to say that he loved your mother until it hurt. Hurt whom? I used to think. He claimed he would have done anything for her. His little sister. The flower of the family. Then she ran off and married without permission—a common seaman, and a non-Catholic, to boot. As if the Contis were royalty. He would have done anything for her, but he never tried to understand her and he certainly wouldn't forgive her. I always felt he was jealous of your mother because she did what she wanted and he was trapped. A trap of his own making. My—our—grandfather also died young, and my father claimed that he had been expected to fill his shoes, to be responsible for the family. In fact, no one expected that, or thought him capable of it—certainly not Nana. He got caught up in this delusion, which in his mind justified his prejudices, his false pride, all his suppressed rage. Yet he saw himself as deeply religious, the bulwark of the family. When your mother died, he acted as if he had been vindicated. If only she had listened to him, everything would have been different: she would have lived, would have thrived."

"Instead, she was bad. And so I must be bad."

"Yes," she said softly. "I'm afraid most of us were bad."

"What did your mother think of all this?"

"She was afraid of him, like everyone else. Righteousness can be as effective as a blackjack."

"Grandma wasn't afraid of him."

"No. But she really stepped out of our lives when she went to live with you. What influence she had on my father disappeared." She hesitated. "I resented that she went. That must sound awful."

"No. Sometimes I hoped you and the other cousins did resent it. I felt it was the only advantage I had over you." I shook my head. "It was an impossible situation. Everyone knew that."

"Not my father," she said angrily. "That's the worst part. He didn't know it. He died not knowing it."

I hadn't expected her to be so vehement. "When did he die?" I asked.

"Three years ago. Of leukemia."

I couldn't bring myself—even perfunctorily—to say I was sorry, because I wasn't.

Sensing this, she changed the subject. "Why did you come here, Xeno?"

"The same reason you did: to be close to Grandma. I'd always wanted to visit. I needed a reason. Then my own father died a few months ago."

"Oh, I—"

I put my hand up. "Please. I hadn't seen him in years."

"I had stopped seeing my father, too, but still it was hard."

All I could think was that these were the two men who had perverted the course of my childhood, and I was glad they were dead. They were dead and I was alive. And if that made me an unforgiving bastard like my uncle, that was all right, too.

"I visited here once before," Silvana said, "with my parents when I was thirteen. Nana had died three years earlier, but I felt her presence." She smiled. "Maybe my father did, too. He hated it here, and we left after a single day."

She poured me more tea, then picked a cluster of grapes and rinsed it under a spigot. Watching her move, I saw she must have been strong, with a fuller figure, before her illness. Despite her thin arms, her hands were steady, her grip firm. Her leg muscles were taking shape again. She held herself erect. She was someone who wouldn't easily reveal her pain.

She felt my eyes on her and blushed.

"You've recovered well," I said awkwardly.

"I'm getting there. In the spring I was down to ninety pounds, and falling. I've been making lots of vegetable stew—yams and blue turnips—to regain my strength. And all the bread and pasta is finally sticking. I've been eating big meals, but I may not have that luxury for long."

We fell silent. The cat came and went. We picked at the grapes. The minutes ticked away. I was as unselfconscious as I would have been if I were alone.

"When I was a kid, I used to ask Nana about you," she said.

"What did she say?"

"That you were special, like your mother. Energetic. Fearless."

"I wish that had been true," I said ruefully.

"She showed me pictures of you."

"I would have liked to see your picture."

Silvana thought about this. "Maybe she thought it would have made things more difficult for you."

"Maybe." I wasn't sure she was referring to the fact she so resembled my mother.

"Once I saw you," Silvana said brightly. "At your window."

"From your father's car?"

"How did you know?" Her smile faded as she realized that, for me, this could not be a pleasant memory.

"I saw you, too," I said. "Then again, at Grandma's funeral."

Her eyes widened.

"My nanny brought me to the church, but we didn't stay long."

She shuddered. "That's terrible."

"It was a long time ago."

"After Nana died, we lost track of you. I figured you lived with your father."

"No. He parked me in a boarding school in Maine. My childhood officially ended when Grandma died."

"I am sorry." She squeezed my arm and stood up. "But I'd better rest now. This is the most talking I've done in months."

"I stayed too long."

"Not at all. Can we meet in town tomorrow for lunch?"

At the door she took my hands. Hers were cold and small. I could feel the bones so clearly. "I wouldn't want you to forgive my father for what he did," she said. "But please forgive me."

I wrapped my arms around her. "I feel so lucky to have met you after all these years."

T HE NEXT DAY at noon, when the heat was fiercest, Silvana walked into the square, wearing a broad white hat, her face in shadow. From a distance, she looked even thinner. She carried a hand-bag so flat I thought it must be empty. She reached into it for a small canister and sprayed something into her mouth. When I got up close to her, I saw that she didn't look quite so pale; she had put on some makeup: penciling her eyebrows, reddening her cheeks and lips. Still, even the short walk seemed to have winded her. For my part, I was tired, having spent a restless night pacing my room, smoking, and fi-nally downing three grappas at the bar before getting a few hours' sleep.

We had lunch at a restaurant with tables in front, beneath a broad shade tree. We ate salad and cheese. I ordered cold wine, she drank mint tea. I told her I had spent the morning at the church, scanning the registries of births, marriages, and deaths in the basement archives.

"I unearthed some interesting family items," I said.

"So fast?"

I had only told her about my chosen field in a cursory way, and I said nothing about the *Caravan Bestiary*. "I've spent a lot of time in li-braries and archives."

"You looked up Nana?"

"Uh-uh. Her grandmother, your namesake."

"Oh." She placed her fork down and sat back with a sigh. "She was another person not to be mentioned in our house. My father said she was a witch. An anti-Christian."

"Yet you were named after her."

"That was Nana's doing. A minor scandal. I was the eldest, so out

of respect, my parents asked Nana to offer up the name at my christening. They told her they had chosen her own mother's name, Maria.
You can't get more Christian than that," she grinned. "But when the
priest turned to Nana, that's not the name she gave. And once he pro-
nounced 'Silvana' aloud, that was it."

"That sounds like something Grandma would do."

"So, what did the archives reveal?"

I took out a piece of paper and sipped my wine. "Silvana Parese
was born on July 1, 1840. She married our great-great-grandfather,
Gabriel Azzaro, on March 5, 1857. She was sixteen, he was twenty-
five."

"They were married in the Church?"

"Yes. Did you know she was the runaway daughter of a priest?
'Una fuggitiva,' Grandma used to call her. In the baptismal records, I
found certificates for their two sons, Angelo and our great-grandfather,
Emmanuel. And I found the death certificate for Gabriel Azzaro,
dated December 27, 1872."

"Silvana was a widow at thirty-two. When did she die?"

"I couldn't find out. I checked every year from 1880 on, though
I'm sure she lived to be well past forty. It was easier to check deaths,
because they're recorded in annual rolls as well as individual certificates."

"How far forward did you go?"

"To 1955. Unless she lived to be over 115, what are the possibilities? That she died elsewhere, her records were lost—"

"Or her burial was not sanctioned because she was a witch."

"Yet they allowed her to baptize her children. And her husband
was given a church funeral."

"Maybe they only learned about her after her husband died,"
Silvana said.

"Maybe. But what did it mean, exactly, when they called her a
witch? You know, she had some extraordinary gifts. She was a kind of
idiot savant."

"How so?"

"Aside from the fact animals flocked to her in the wild, she had a gift of tongues. One day she began spouting pre-Homeric hymns in Greek, despite the fact she was illiterate in Italian. And ancient Greek hasn't been spoken around here in two thousand years."

"Nana told you all this?"

I was surprised. "Who else?"

She was lost in thought. "What else did she tell you about Silvana?"

"That she could communicate with the animals in their own languages. A gift the people here prize enormously."

"In other words, maybe she wasn't such a pariah."

I shrugged. "I just don't think it was black and white."

Whenever the conversation returned to my grandmother, I discovered how little Silvana really knew about her. At least, compared to me. I had assumed my grandmother told all her grandchildren about her relationship to the world of animals, which began with her connection to her own grandmother. That essential part of herself, which she shared with me, she had apparently withheld from others. I didn't understand why she would have done so with Silvana, to whom she had bequeathed that name, and with whom she insisted that I—and, by extension, she herself—would be so simpatico. I suspected that it had to do, again, with Uncle Robert. He would have been repelled, even as a teenager, by this aspect of my grandmother's life, and would have objected strenuously to her sharing any of it with his children. Her response, I saw now, had been to erect a wall between herself and him—and his family. For the first time, I grasped how much it had benefited her to live apart from them. Frigid as her relationship was with my father, under his roof she could say and do whatever she liked, spiritually or otherwise. Certainly he didn't care, even when he was around. And so I became the only grandchild privy to her innermost beliefs. Silvana and the other cousins had nuclear families, but I had my grandmother, even more than I—or they—realized at the time.

It was nearly siesta. I called for the check. People passing on their errands had taken notice of us, many staring openly. After all, we were the only two foreigners around, we were relatives, and we had roots there, as they would have learned by now. The old man who had told me about Silvana appeared, lugging a roll of chicken wire.

"*Ah, due cugini,*" he called out by way of greeting.

"*Cugini germani,*" I replied, letting him know that we were not just cousins, but first cousins.

"*Germani,*" he repeated solemnly, for to Sicilians this was an important distinction.

"You're leaving tomorrow, then," Silvana said as we stood up.

"Yes. I have to be back in Paris."

My business in Paris could have waited. Maybe I would regret that I hadn't prolonged my visit to Fornace. But while meeting Silvana had been cathartic, it had also been draining. Especially on top of my father's death. And it was far more unsettling at this second meeting that, with the hat covering her red hair, I really felt as if I could have been looking at my mother.

"How long will you stay here?" I asked.

She thought about it, her eyes wandering, then returning to mine. "Maybe a long time."

I offered to walk her home, and she suggested a shortcut through the woods, to avoid the heat of the open road.

I was amazed to be entering the woods Silvana the dryad had roamed, which my grandmother had brought to life in her bedtime stories—and to be doing so with another Silvana. It felt like a place previously accessible to me only in my dreams. My grandmother had actual memories of these woods, but from so early in her life they must have seemed like dreams. As a boy, I had pictured the woods to be like one of the illustrations in my book of fairy tales: tangled vines and gnarled roots which at any moment could turn into serpents; fleshlike mushrooms; flowers glowing like suns; a waterfall that emptied into a pool of moonlight. And, most importantly, the animals, each more fantastic than the next, visible everywhere: chimeras and hippogriffs, man-sized ants, one-wingèd birds and two-headed owls. Caves of bats with glittering eyes. Dragonflies trailing fire. Tigers romping with manticores, armadillos with basilisks.

Of course, the forest before me was nothing like that. At first it looked like any other forest, but with truly ancient trees: towering oaks with broad trunks and interlacing branches. Their leaves were dark, their acorns plum-sized. The underbrush was thin at the forest's rim, and the ferns green, despite the drought. There were boulders lined with moss, and hollow tree trunks orange with toadstools. As always happened when I walked into a forest, I felt that the world of men, of everyone and everything I knew, was falling away from me. Usually I was alone. This time I'm glad I wasn't.

Silvana was a few feet ahead of me. She was sure-footed on the rough ground, as if she were accustomed to it. We didn't exchange a word. The silence was complete, all the way to the treetops, which were so high and dense the sky was no longer visible. There was no telling if it was blue, or cloudy, or if a storm was blowing in, for the weather could change rapidly in those mountains. And so, ten minutes into our detour, we were surprised by a downpour—doubly unexpected because it hadn't rained in so long. Thunderclaps were followed by sheets of rain. And a whiff of sulfur, as if lightning had struck nearby.

Silvana leaned against a tree and tilted her head back. She removed her hat, which, like her dress, was already drenched. Her long hair spilled down her shoulders. I took off my jacket and draped it around her. I thought it would be dangerous for her to get chilled. She didn't seem to share my concern. Drawing that burnt air into her lungs, letting the water run down her cheeks, she stared around her and began laughing.

The forest was changing before our eyes—as if the rain could alter the very chemistry of the place, setting in motion, and revealing previously hidden elements. Colors deepened. Sounds emerged, playing off each other: birds fleeing, bees swarming low for shelter, the wind quickening in the heavy leaves. The rain itself seemed equally composed of water and light. When it struck the ground, silver dust rose and brushed my skin, like the mist containing the spirits of animals when I was a boy. My body felt weightless, my head was buzzing, and I saw animals begin to appear—just flashes at first: tantalizing glimpses of a muzzle, a tail, a bared fang, a luminous wing. In and out of the mist they slipped. Bits of a tapestry that existed whole in another dimension, visible only to other spirits. I hadn't seen anything like it since my grandmother died. I turned to Silvana, to determine if she saw it, too.

"Silvana," I whispered.

But her eyes were closed now.

I heard faint howls in the distance. Then again, a little closer.

"Silvana!"

A snout, a hoof, a patch of black fur blurred past me in the mist.

Silvana was so still now she could have been asleep. Her head resting against the tree. Water streaming from her hair. Her white hat dripping in her hand. The rain seemed to have washed all strains of illness from her face, so she looked young, fully at ease for the first time since I'd met her.

Those howls were louder now, over the farthest ridge of trees.

Then something large stirred in the brush ahead. I approached the spot cautiously, twice glancing over my shoulder at Silvana, who hadn't budged. I was wet to the skin. My pants were clinging. My shoes sank into mud. The rain smelled like iron, filling my eyes to overflowing.

In the brush where I had seen movement there were paw prints in the mud, narrow and not too deep. They led away from me, winding deeper into the forest.

The howling trailed off.

I followed the tracks. Again I saw something move, behind some trees. And, again, when I reached the spot, there was no sign of an animal, just those paw prints continuing on.

The rain was drumming harder than ever, tearing through the foliage, rattling branches, echoing off the oak trunks. If that howling resumed, I couldn't have heard it.

I set out once more, then heard a cry behind me and spun around. I had left Silvana about a hundred feet back, but she was gone. Instead, there was an animal by the tree. A red fox, with a ring of white fur around its neck. Rising onto its hind legs, its muzzle twitching, it stared at me with its black eyes.

I stared back, the hair on my neck bristling and the fox's long tail ticking off the seconds—eight, nine, ten—before it darted into the trees. I watched it race deep into the forest, a streak of flame burning through the mist, then looked down at the tracks I had been following and remembered that line from the Hereford bestiary: *The fox can leave tracks in one direction while traveling in another.*

The fox disappeared. The rain poured down. The tracks were washed away. I found my jacket at the foot of that tree.

As for Silvana, I would never see her again.

6

In Paris, I redoubled my efforts, searching for information about the *Caravan Bestiary*. Over the previous ten years I had filled twenty-six notebooks with entries, drawings, maps, and clippings. In addition to new animals, the twenty-seventh notebook chronicled my research into the final whereabouts of Adolphus Sarkas, the last man known to have the bestiary in his possession.

As in Venice, for many months I had been putting in ten- and twelve-hour days, poring over obscure source materials, cross-referencing even the most tenuous lead. I had a hunch that from Rhodes Sarkas did not travel to North Africa, or double back into Asia Minor, but fled deeper into the Aegean, to Crete, another island with Venetian roots. I realized that Cava, Madame Faville, and Brox had all been partially correct: Cava with his assertion that the bestiary had been in Italy for centuries; Madame Faville for focusing on the Greek islands; and Brox for traveling to Turkey (which I didn't think a coincidence), before he was murdered. But following Sarkas's trail after a century and a half was like chasing after smoke. And I no longer had Sylvie to assist me at the Sorbonne's medieval library; in the pile of mail that had been held for me at the post office, I found a postcard from her in Brussels, where she and her boyfriend Charles had moved and gotten engaged.

At the reference library of the Musée de la Marine in Chaillot, I spent a month reading the captains' logs of ships that sailed the southern Mediterranean between 1818 and 1830. Then, at the Greek embassy, examining microfiche of Cretan and Rhodian census rolls and customs records that the cultural attaché had obtained with great difficulty, I was indeed able to confirm Sarkas's arrival on Crete in the fall of 1819. An "A. Sarkous" was listed in the manifest of the *Fontana*, a ship out of Rhodes that docked in Irakleion on September 3. On Rhodes, the harbormaster had stamped a joint customs declaration from the eleven departing passengers, who had scrawled only their initials, the last of them "A.S." However, no "Sarkas" or "Sarkous" was listed in the census rolls, which included foreign residents of a year or more as well as permanent citizens.

I went to the Maritime Bibliothèque and read all the historians and chroniclers who touched on Crete at that time. Not surprisingly, I came up empty. I felt deflated, having to face the obvious fact that Sarkas was a thief on the run, an obscure figure desperate for even greater anonymity; not the sort of person who would make himself readily available to a census taker or any other official. I realized I would have to search through private, not public, documents—no easy task, especially since the ones I most likely needed were archived in Venice, not Paris. For a while, I worried I might have to return to Venice. But after exchanging a flurry of faxes with the librarians I knew at the Villa Ziane, and visiting the Société Italienne on the rue Marbeau, I got lucky.

In the otherwise dreary diary of Giorgio Zetto, a wealthy Venetian doctor and former consul that the head librarian put me onto, I found Sarkas mentioned twice. Zetto had retired to Xaniá, on the northwest coast of Crete, because of ill health. It was there, on October 4, 1819, that he met Sarkas. He identified him as an Armenian monk returning from a pilgrimage to Jerusalem—an obvious lie—and a painter of note, whose work he admired. *Father Sarkas can render animals—of sea, sky, land, and ether—with frightening clarity.* In his second entry about Sarkas, on November 15, Zetto wrote: *He claims to be embarked on a mission conceived by angels, which one day all the world shall know. His only fear is that Death will claim him first.* That was Sarkas, grandiose and elusive. Zetto's next observation is what one would expect from a doctor turned diplomat, a man as coolly observant as Byron, whose complaint about Sarkas he echoes: *The monk's humility is tempered by an evasive glance, for he never would meet my gaze.* Zetto does not describe the exact nature of Sarkas's "mission" or of his animals, but I had little doubt their "frightening clarity" and that reference to "ether" connected them to the *Caravan Bestiary*, from whose pages Sarkas may have copied images onto canvas. I sent the head librarian at the Villa Ziane several new queries, but had yet to receive a reply. And my researches in Paris were turning up nothing new. Again I despaired that, close as I might be to some bigger breakthrough, the channels of information had become too rarefied, the possibilities too thin; not to mention the fact that, even if I learned all I needed to about Sarkas, I might still discover that he was many links back in the chain, that after traveling to Crete with him, the *Caravan Bestiary* had continued its journey with someone else, and someone after that—as it had done for centuries—and could now be anywhere in the world, or nowhere at all, and to pick up its trail I would have to start all over again.

And I knew that wasn't possible.

B RUNO EASED his electric wheelchair into the shade of a peach tree. He was wearing a seersucker suit and a madras tie. The blue lenses of his Ray-Bans shone beneath the brim of his Panama hat. His white shoes, to the soles, were unblemished, for they seldom touched the ground. We were in the horticultural orchard outside his laboratory at the University of Pennsylvania. It was a warm spring afternoon. Starlings were chattering. Water splashed into a fountain filled with carp. In the tropical greenhouse, toucans and parrots occasionally took flight. I had come to the States for ten days, to visit the Italian Archives at the Library of Congress (cross-referencing, in vain, "Sarkas" and "Zetto"), and for a variety of personal reasons, one of which was to see Bruno.

At twenty-six, he held an endowed chair—the youngest person in the university's history to receive that honor. Many people served him: a team of lab technicians and researchers, an administrative assistant, various graduate students and gofers, and the maid who cooked his meals and kept up the three-bedroom house provided him by the university. He had an elastic budget and a sizable expense account. He was in touch with a network of fellow biologists, in the United States and abroad, who were undertaking similar or parallel research, and when he traveled to conferences, he enjoyed all the amenities. Officially he reported to the university president. In fact, he reported to no one. Nor would he so long as he continued doing groundbreaking work and attracting grants that swelled the university's coffers.

There was no question all of this had gone to his head, the sickly, disabled son of a fireman from the Bronx. How could it not have? Especially at his age. I was as impressed as anyone with his accomplishments, his stamina and brilliance; but I also had known him his whole life, and in the few hours since my arrival in Philadelphia, I was surprised to see just how imperious and vain he had become. A vanity that extended beyond his newfound affectations of dress—silk shirts, gold cuff links, a luminous Rolex—to his dealings with practically everyone he encountered. He could maintain a glacial reserve or affect a formal tone that was foolproof as distancing techniques: so far as I could tell, no one liked him. His intellectual confidence had devolved into arrogance. And he seemed to take perverse pride in his decrepitude. It may have started as a defense, but over time it had been integrated into the pose he assumed: a celebrated scientist who had had to overcome handicaps that would have stymied the best of men. He had suffered indignities for which he now demanded compensation. Respect and admiration were no longer enough: thus the pleasure he took in playing the improbable role of dandy and in indulging his newfound appetite for truffles, pâté, and exotic fruits after years of bland functional food. Others had to help him get around, but until he was flat on his back for good (as would happen soon enough), his shirts were going to be custom-made and his meals haute cuisine.

When you looked past the fancy clothes and flashy accoutrements, it wasn't a pretty picture. I hadn't seen him in a while, but it might as well have been decades; for every calendar year, he looked to have aged five years. He couldn't have weighed more than 120 pounds. He sat awkwardly, his knees touching, his feet pigeon-toed. His right eyelid drooped worse than ever. Because of his kidney medication, his eyes were hypersensitive to light; unless he was in a dim room, he wore thick dark glasses.

All of this, like his vanity, was readily discernible; not so his anger, which, though submerged, had increased exponentially. His afflictions had always made him ornery and fatalistic; it was frustrating to have such a capacious mind anchored by so frail a body. The broader anger he felt now was a natural outgrowth of his life's work, in which he was pummeled with reports of human cruelty and callousness toward other creatures. Things were always worsening in that area, and all his life he had kept himself informed of those horrors. His idealism was long gone. What had remained unchanged, and pure, was his love of animals. Still the best part of him, it was also what drove him to keep going, despite his frustration—and protestations.

"Extinction has made me a big shot, Xeno," he said, peering at me over his glasses. "There's something unsavory about that, don't you think?"

He didn't wait for me to answer. He could answer his own questions, after all, better than anyone else.

"Even worse, what we're doing here is not working. It may even be counterproductive. We're losing the race."

"But you've saved so many species."

He shook his head. "Not enough."

"And if you were doing nothing?"

"Nothing would be different."

"You're just tired."

"I am tired. But what I'm saying is true. In science, problems always outrun solutions. But not at this pace. And these aren't theories falling by the wayside, they're living things. I used to tell you about these animals when we were kids. Fifteen years later, I still put up a poster every week of the next animal that will disappear. I saw you looking at it."

"The white monkey."

"It's called the douc. One of the most sociable primates. Very intelligent, with a musical voice. It used to thrive in the rainforests of Laos and Vietnam. Maybe you saw one over there. You wouldn't see it today. Ninety-five percent of the doucs were killed by Agent Orange and napalm. It used to group in families of twelve. Now, to avoid hunters, it travels in pairs. Some hunters eat it, others kill it for its fur, but most shoot it for target practice and leave the carcasses to rot." His voice was rising. "It's no different over here. Cowards who pick off grizzlies from helicopters or pay to shoot a penned tiger—or even a giraffe. You can fight pollution and sprawl, but killing for pleasure—how do you deal with that?" He smiled crookedly. "Maybe we need another Flood. When life began, the earth was entirely ocean—a chemical soup, bombarded with ultraviolet light. Shift a few molecules and everything could evolve differently. Maybe you end up with a planet of insects, or worms. Maybe that's an improvement."

His rant was interrupted by his administrative assistant, Naomi, who emerged from the lab. She handed him a sheaf of computer printouts, which he initialed. Naomi was a knockout, in her mid-twenties, curly black hair, bright blue eyes. She wore all red: leather miniskirt, V-necked blouse, zip-up boots.

Diverted, Bruno calmed down. He watched me follow her retreating figure up the steps to the lab. Pollen was swirling around us. Bees were humming, and mayflies. "Wonderful, isn't she? Her current beau races motorcycles. Weekends he skydives." He chuckled. "Still, I have my hopes."

That night at dinner he opened up to me about his private life, which, for once, was offering him solace from his work, and not the other way around. We had eaten on the screened-in porch off his living room, crickets on the damp lawn, a full moon rising. His housekeeper had prepared mushroom risotto and fennel salad. We were finishing our second bottle of Barolo. This was another of Bruno's newly acquired tastes. I had never known him to drink. He didn't have the weight to absorb the alcohol, which was bound to mix unpredictably with his prescription drugs. He was high, slurring consonants, when he announced to me that for the first time he had a real girlfriend.

"I used to pay the girls from escort services to go down on me. It would take them forever. All channels of energy to that part of my body were blocked. You could have brought in a girl with a Ph.D. in the *Kama Sutra* and it still would have taken forever."

"What's her name, Bruno?" I said gently.

"Marisa. She's from the Ukraine."

"Pretty name. Am I going to meet her?"

"Of course. She's in Boston. She gets back tomorrow."

"Where did you meet her?"

"She's a sonogram technician in the medical school. I had to go in for some tests. She smeared Vaseline on my abdomen and ran that gizmo around on it." He was fumbling through his wallet. "I have her picture here."

She was a brunette with a pageboy haircut. From her narrowed eyes and angular face, it was clear she had Mongol blood. She was smirking, a glint in her eye. I couldn't tell if the beauty mark high on her cheek was real or artfully applied. "She's pretty," I said.

"You know what she did that no one else knew to do?"

"Bruno, you don't need to tell me."

"But I want to. You're my oldest friend. I'm not being crude: it's an important development for me. And if I can't tell you, who can I tell?" He leaned closer. "She has a great body. A no-nonsense attitude. She came into my bedroom, and without a word took off her clothes and laid me out on the bed and climbed on top of me. Nobody had ever done that. Hand jobs, blow jobs—nobody had ever just started fucking me. It changed everything."

"So you're in love," I said, trying to deflect him from further detail.

"I don't know about that," he said brusquely. "We're having good sex—at least, I am, for the first time. Falling in love—you're such a romantic, Xeno."

I was taken aback. I didn't know if it was the pain or the painkillers that had eaten away so much of him, leaving such a bitter residue.

After the plates were cleared, Bruno stood up slowly, bracing himself on the arm of his chair. "Let's go outside. There's a nice breeze."

We sat on his lawn on a white bench between two pin oaks. Bruno had grown quiet. I felt I could hear his mind at work. When he spoke again, it was to an entirely different subject, his voice subdued.

"You were lucky not to have had an extended family. I've had to watch my family dissolve. My father, my uncle, my aunt splitting with my cousins. Then my mother coming apart at the seams. And Lena, too."

"I did have an extended family, Bruno. All the people you just mentioned."

"I'm sorry." He gripped my arm. "Forgive me. But sometimes I feel like they were ghosts all along. That they never really existed. That none of us did, back in that world. That house. The get-togethers, the comings and goings. Ghosts."

"What are you talking about?"

He removed his sunglasses and squeezed the bridge of his nose. "Maybe I'm saying that I'm afraid of my memories."

I had known that when he was ready he would fill me in on what had become of his family since my last visit to New York. Except for a few letters, I had been woefully out of touch, absorbed in my own affairs. I realized he had been waiting until the very end of my visit to open up.

First, he told me about his mother.

After a slew of dead-end jobs, living alone after Lena left, Mrs. Moretti had married an appliance salesman named Sal. He took her to Atlantic City for their honeymoon and the first night dropped two thousand dollars at the blackjack tables. His money. Then another three thousand the second night. Her money.

"He pissed away her savings in four months," Bruno said. "I warned her before she got married, after I met this guy. 'I will not be a widow forever,' she shouted at me. Salvatore was going to be her savior. Instead, he took off when the money was gone. She spent three weeks in the psycho ward. When she got out, I rented her an apartment on Staten Island, near her cousin Maureen. I begged her to come down here, but she refused. And Lena couldn't take care of her anymore. Maureen is also a widow. She owns a florist's shop. Mom tried working there—for three days. She began to isolate. She was wasting away. Then, just before Christmas, she had a stroke." He let out his breath. "It was a blow, Xeno. That woman suffered more than I want to know."

It was a blow, and I felt it myself at that moment. I had held on to my own memories of Mrs. Moretti, her many kindnesses, the crinkly lines beside her blue eyes, the scent of her perfume. Listening to Bruno, I was reminded of my grandmother's most important gift to me: her belief that we must pursue the beasts of this life, rather than allowing them to pursue us. If they consumed us in the end, as they had Mrs. Moretti, at least we could confront them first on our own terms. This knowledge enabled me to survive my childhood without embracing the corrosive elements—cruelty, dishonesty, envy—that ate away at so many people I knew. Eventually it translated into my quest for the bestiary, which I had come to realize was all about seeking the beasts outside myself in order to understand those within.

"Then there's Lena," Bruno said. "After my mother died, she really snapped. Not that things were going so great before that," he snorted. "Sure, I'm pissed, too, about some of the same issues she is. Maybe even more pissed. I've dedicated my life to animal rights. But I can't condone violence."

"What happened?"

"Lena dropped out of veterinary school two years ago. We had a huge falling-out, and she hasn't spoken to me since. I doubt you've heard from her . . ."

"I haven't." This was not a big change; over time, our correspondence had dwindled. After she graduated from college, we drifted apart. I knew she had been living with a guy in Philadelphia, a fellow graduate student, while I was enmeshed in my own affairs in Europe. But I didn't know there had been a rift with Bruno. And I couldn't imagine her quitting school after all her struggles to get in.

"She said she was disillusioned with the program here," Bruno went on. "Sickened by the way the university treated its lab animals. She called it criminal. Forget the fact that *I* run a lab," he said angrily, "and have to deal with all the other university labs, including the veterinary school's. She joined an animal rights organization, but after a couple of months quit that, too. She claimed the legal system was rigged against them, that every suit and petition was doomed before it was filed. She moved out west, to Portland, and hooked up with a radical group. They did violent interventions, sabotaging labs and rescuing mistreated animals by breaking and entering. As a partially trained vet, she was recruited to treat these animals. That was the plan. Lena never participated in the 'fieldwork'; she just saw animals that were brought in. Then one night she crossed the line and joined a raid on a mink farm. Her comrades clubbed a security guard, released the animals into the woods, and set fire to the pens and the gas chamber. The state police rounded up her entire group the next day and charged them with arson, larceny, assault—you name it. Lena was the getaway driver, and because she had never left their van, and had no criminal record, most of the charges against her were dropped. The judge handed her the lightest sentence, four months in state prison, on a count of conspiracy, while the others got six years. But he also imposed a far more damaging long-term penalty, refusing to reduce the felony charge to a misdemeanor for purposes of sentencing. This means she cannot obtain a veterinary license anywhere in the country, even if she completes graduate school. In fact, it will be tough for her to get any kind of responsible job."

"That's terrible."

"Before she broke off with me, I told her she was playing with dynamite. These people weren't protesters, they were vandals. No matter how strong your beliefs, violence is counterproductive. You have to be detached," he snapped. His chin dropped to his chest. "I know. People get frustrated. They blow up. Lena blew up."

"Where is she now?"

"Quebec, last I heard. She served her sentence in Oregon, then left the country."

"Do you have an address?"

"I do. But she's moving around." He hesitated. "Are you going to try to see her?"

"Yes, of course."

"I was hoping you would. Maybe she'll listen to you." He shook his head, and his voice hardened again. "She says she won't come back to the U.S. for a long time. Maybe never. Maybe that's good. She told me she could never be happy here. And she's probably right."

I FLEW TO QUEBEC from New York late the next afternoon. There was a long layover after I arrived at JFK from Philadelphia, and I took a taxi to the Bronx. I hadn't been there in years, and I had been thinking about it ever since my father died—and since my visit to Fornace.

Everything looked smaller in the old neighborhood: the grocery store where I used to accompany Evgénia, the florist, the Rexall drugstore, and Bellmon's Wine & Liquors across from my old building. The building itself was sorely in need of repairs: the façade crumbling, window frames peeling, the front steps cracked. My grade school had cages over the windows and a security guard at the door. The griffin that had visited my fire escape was gone, as was his partner and the First National Bank itself on whose parapet they had perched; the bank and adjacent buildings had been demolished to make way for a housing project.

I visited the Church of Saint Anthony of Padua, whose name suddenly meant something to me—conjuring up elaborate fountains and marble palazzi—now that I had actually visited Padua. I asked the rector what he could tell me about my cousin Silvana; knowing little, he directed me to a parishioner who knew the Contis, a Mrs. Tascone, the wife of a wine importer. She told me that four years earlier, Silvana Conti had contracted tuberculosis and entered a sanatorium down south.

"She recovered enough to travel to Sicily after her release," Mrs. Tascone said, "but she never returned. She held on for a while, then passed away this year. My people are from the next town, and they let me know."

When I left Fornace, I knew that the next time I opened my grand-mother's silver music box, the white whisker would be gone. I knew it just as surely as I had known I would never see that red fox again, even in my dreams.

I WAS IN MONTREAL, booked on a flight to Paris that night. In Quebec City the previous day, I had gone to the address Bruno gave me, a residency hotel that rented by the week. The clerk remembered Lena, and informed me that two months earlier she had gone to Paris. She had left no forwarding address. So it turned out that when I flew home, I would be following Lena's trail.

First, though, I was seeing Evgénia, who had written me in Paris and invited me to visit the next time I crossed the Atlantic. I had been planning to do so even before Bruno told me about Lena.

Her debts paid off, Evgénia had moved to Montreal the previous year and opened an Albanian restaurant called Shqipri on the rue Richelieu, by the river. There were thick red rugs embroidered with wolves and bears, a quartz statuette of a two-headed eagle, and a painting of Scanderbeg, the folk hero who resisted the Turks. And of course her alpine photographs adorned the walls. She lived on the second floor with her dog Yuri, in a two-bedroom apartment with bright windows and a brick fireplace. Beside the zebra-striped sofa there was an aquarium even larger than the one in her house in Chicago—fifty gallons, at least—filled with fantails.

"It's the first place I ever owned by myself," she said after we took a long walk by the river with Yuri.

She poured us both a glass of red wine and had the cook serve up a sampling of the house specials: baked okra, pepper salad, barley cakes soaked in honey.

"I'm glad you got to see me again, here," Evgénia said.

Through the window the pedestrians were melting in the fog. The first customers were being led to tables by the maître d', a young

Albanian woman named Reza in white jeans and a black headband. My plane to Paris was at nine. Evgénia and I had another hour to catch up.

I told her about the *Makara*, my father's death, my travels.

After listening intently, she said, "It's funny. I never thought you would be like him. I mean, you're not, really. It's just that you seem so rootless. No wife or children, no real home."

"I have a home."

There was an awkward silence.

"And you're still looking for that book?" she said.

"Yes."

A boy in a blue jacket, a book bag over his shoulder, entered the restaurant. He was about ten, with long black hair and a serious gaze. I was startled when he ran straight to Evgénia and she embraced him.

"Xeno, this is Philip, Reza's son," she said. "Philip, this is Xeno."

He looked at me, his mind elsewhere, and we shook hands.

"I've known Xeno since he was a little boy," Evgénia went on. "He was good at history, just as you are."

"What kind of history do you like?" I said, finding my voice.

"Oh, British and Canadian." He turned back to Evgénia. "Is Mom in the kitchen?"

"Remind you of someone?" she smiled, as he hurried off.

"I can see he reminds you."

"He's a good boy. Reza is divorced, so she leaves him with me when she goes out." She leaned over and kissed my cheek. "Of all the children I cared for, Xeno, you were like my own."

She walked me outside and I hailed a taxi. The driver put my suitcase in the trunk.

"You're only twenty-six," Evgénia said. "Who knows, you may end up with five children. And find your book, too."

A book that might no longer exist, I thought, as Evgénia, waving, receded through the rear window of the taxi. And if that was so, what would I do? Maybe I was more like Madame Faville than I thought, and it was glory I was after, not enlightenment.

7

D ID YOU THINK I tried to kill someone?" Lena said sharply.
She was wearing a striped smock and rubber gloves and had
just finished cleaning the cages of four dozen formerly white, now fur-
less, rabbits that had been rescued after a successful lawsuit against a
cosmetics company by the organization she worked for, International
Refuge. We were in the basement clinic of their headquarters on the
rue de Siam, in Passy. In their cages, dogs were barking, cats howling.
There was a tiger cub abused by a drug gang; monkeys that had survived a gruesome psychological experiment after being injected with
LSD; and a scrawny goat, branded with hot irons, that had been rescued from a voodoo cult.

"I made mistakes," she went on. "That's why I'm here. But I never
hurt anyone."

"I didn't say you did."

"You didn't have to."

I took her arm. "Lena, I'm not judging you."

"Then stop looking at me like that," she said, pulling away.

I had spent several weeks tracking her down at the clinic, and from
the moment I walked in the door, she had been angry with me. First
surprised, then angry.

She stowed the smock and gloves in a locker, put on a blue raincoat
over her plain blue dress, and led me to the elevator. I returned my security pass to the guard, and we went out the back door, onto a gray
side street.

"You want to find some real killers?" Lena went on. "Visit the biol-
ogy labs: they maim and vivisect animals by the hundreds. With the dogs
they sever the vocal cords first. They experiment on pregnant animals,

shelter animals, newborns. So-called wildlife preserves? Poachers
have the run of them. The food industry? You don't want to go there."

At twenty-five, she had the same choirgirl face, but her eyes were
as fierce as her voice, their deep gray at once more opaque and less
mysterious than when she was a girl. Her enviable reserve had been
eroded; now she just seemed defensive, wary, coiled at her center. At
least, that was the side of herself she was showing me. I hadn't seen
her in three years, and though thinner and paler, she was still beautiful. She wore no makeup. Her blonde hair remained thick, but it was
carelessly combed. Her fingernails were bitten down, and she had a
bruise on her left forearm. One of her front teeth was chipped.

"That happened in prison," she said, catching my glance. "A bull
dyke hit on me. That's what I've become, Xeno. What my father used to
call 'the dregs.' I haven't fixed the tooth because I don't want to forget."

We stopped at a drab café. There were four metal tables on the
sidewalk and we were the only customers. A nearby wall was covered
with graffiti in Arabic. Two boys were kicking a ball against it.

Lena downed her espresso. "So here I am. The French have no
problem allowing me to be employed. Their animal rights organizations have real clout. I read about International Refuge in prison.
Then I sent them a letter. Looking back, I caught a lucky break when
I was busted. Not because I saw the error of my ways," she added defiantly. "I've never regretted that night. I'm still trying to do what I
know best, and it's nice to get results." She shrugged. "You can't stop
all the suffering, but you also can't give up."

"It sounds like you're doing a lot of good over here," I said.
"Would you ever want to do it back home?"

She tilted her empty cup this way and that. "I couldn't go back if I
wanted to. I violated my probation." She nodded at my surprise. "I'm
afraid Bruno doesn't know that part of the story," she said drily. "The
judge put me on probation for two years. In Portland I was supposed
to report in twice a week. Forget it. Even before prison, I'd been itch-
ing to leave the country. I took a bus to Vancouver, then flew to
Quebec. So now I'm an expat—like you," she smiled, not pleasantly.

"The difference is, I'm also a fugitive. I could be extradited to Oregon from any of the other forty-nine states, and they'd put me back in jail. The FBI isn't going to come after me here—this isn't a case for Interpol. Maybe in a few years it will all blow over. Meanwhile, I have a job. A place to live. The French don't give a damn what you did in America."

Her voice was so hard. "Lena, what can I do?"

"Do? Nothing. You've helped me more than enough," she added with a frown. "You put me through college, remember?"

"I didn't just mean money."

"What then? Please, don't tell me you came here to rescue me."

"Why would I want to do that? You seem fine."

She wagged her finger mockingly. "Maybe this is a bit of a problem—you know, because when you were a kid you wanted someone to rescue you."

That smarted, coming from her. "It's not the worst vice: it's what you do for a living now, right?"

"That's different," she snapped. "Bruno is into numbers and you're into magic, but there are animals out there being wiped out. *Real* animals, not imaginary ones."

"Would you tell me, please, why you're so goddamn pissed at me?"

"I'm not pissed at you."

"Come on, Lena. We've known each other too long."

She flushed. "Maybe we have." She pushed her chair back and stood up. "Too long." And she walked away.

"Lena!"

I threw some money on the table and hurried after her, but she had disappeared in a taxi.

My hands were shaking. My first impulse was to follow her, but I decided it would be better if I waited and called her the next day at International Refuge. It turned out I didn't have to.

That night, at two-thirty, I had just fallen asleep when my buzzer rang. She was at the door in her blue raincoat, the collar turned up. Her hair was windblown, her eyes tired. She barely managed a smile.

"How did you find me?" I said, tying the sash on my bathrobe.

"You're in the directory."

Ushering her in, I tried to gather my thoughts—and to read hers. But her expression revealed little.

I took her coat, and she looked around. By now, one wall of my living room was lined floor-to-ceiling with books. Papers were stacked on the desk. Through the window, a blue mist hung over the Square du Temple. The small pond at the end of the park shone like a mirror.

Lena walked to the window and stared down. I switched on the lamps and waited, but she didn't move.

Finally she said, "Have you lived here long?"

"Less than a year."

"I read the plaque across the street that says the Square du Temple was once a separate country."

"Yes, a kind of ministate, like Monaco."

Beneath her calm I sensed she was nervous, gathering her thoughts before she said what she came to say.

"It belonged to the Knights Hospitallers," I continued, trying to give her more time, "and was separated from the rest of the city by a drawbridge. The Knights built a fortress, a church, a hospice, even a prison. The prison lasted up until the Revolution. Louis XVI spent his last night in it, and for a while Marie Antoinette was a prisoner."

"They were guillotined here?"

"No. They were taken to the Place de la Concorde."

Only after moving into my apartment did I discover that I had my own connection to the Square du Temple. In 1524, during his triumphal tour of Europe, and after visiting King Francis at Fontainebleau, Antonio Pigafetta was an honored guest of his brethren, the Knights. He regaled them with stories of his great sea adventure. Whether or not he permitted them a look at the *Caravan Bestiary*, he certainly had it in his possession, just a few hundred yards from my building.

"Do you want a drink, or coffee?" I asked.

Lena turned around. "Coffee would be nice."

She sat on the sofa and I went into the kitchen to put the kettle on. I nearly poured myself a whisky. Instead, I made the coffee very strong.

When I rejoined her, she looked me in the eye for the first time. "I'm sorry about this afternoon."

I pulled a chair up to the sofa. "Forget it."

She let out a long breath and again tried to smile. Then she covered her eyes. "Oh, Xeno."

I leaned closer. "Lena, tell me what's wrong."

She shook her head. "Why did you fall so out of touch? Where were you?"

I hadn't expected this, and it knocked me off-balance. Since we were children, there had been no one in my life like Lena. I had fallen in and out of love with other women, but I had loved her more than any of them. Even when we were separated by an ocean or a continent, and barely communicating, she had never seemed far from me. She was so much a part of my innermost self that, even if I wanted to dislodge her, I wouldn't have known how. I wished I could tell her that just then, and break through all the barriers between us. But having been like a brother to her for so long, I had given up on the idea she could also be in love with me. To preserve what we did have, I had remained silent. The truth was, I feared I would push her away if she didn't feel the same way.

When she reached out to me, I took her hand, and she pulled me down beside her. "I shouldn't blame you," she said. "I'm the one who's been hiding out."

"I've done my share. Maybe it's time to stop hiding."

She lowered her eyes and gently took her hand away, ostensibly to lift her coffee cup. "Bruno told you about my mother?"

"Yes."

"And Sal?"

I nodded.

"I bet he didn't tell you about the photo."

"I don't think so."

"In the apartment on Staten Island, when she started to isolate, she wouldn't even answer the phone. Maureen told us the only talking she did was to a photo of my father, taken on his last birthday. He's standing under the big oak where we used to play. Remember?"

I remembered that the first time I saw Lena she was on a swing suspended from the oak's lowest bough, holding a white cat her father had rescued from a fire.

"At night," Lena went on, "my mother placed the photo on a pillow beside hers. She heard my father's voice. He told her how to find him when, as she said, *I cross over to the other side.* And he told her to listen to Camilla, the eighty-year-old woman in the apartment below. Camilla was from the West Indies. A former midwife, she was an herbalist and faith healer. Apparently her favorite herb was marijuana, which she claimed speeded all healing, but only if one believed that Jesus still walked the earth, saving souls. She meant, literally. She gave Mom doctored snapshots that depicted a man who was the image of Jesus: bearded, long-haired, with a thousand-mile stare. He was wearing a white suit at the bazaar in Calcutta, crossing a public park in Berlin, exiting a nightclub in Tangier. Always in a crowd, but anonymous. Jesus in mufti," she added drily. "Camilla prescribed reefer for my mother's migraines. And it *worked.* It didn't cure the migraines, but it took away her anxiety. Mom was getting high to the very end, and I believe she died happier because of it. Materially she was broke. She left me only one thing."

She opened her handbag and fished out the salamander brooch she had shown me years before.

"It seems it's easier for you to talk about your mother than yourself."

"It is right now," she said. She was examining the brooch. "I know your grandmother taught you that animals have souls. Do you still believe that?"

"I do."

"Bruno doesn't."

"When it comes to Bruno and animals, what matters is that he has a soul."

"That's true." She closed her eyes, and when she opened them again, her voice softened. "You once told me the book you're searching for is all about the psyche."

"What else could it be about? All our imaginings about animals, the mythmaking, our intense projections into their world. First, we set them up as our gods; then we made ourselves their gods and began treating them badly. Many of the animals I've studied were driven to extinction before entering the human imagination."

She closed her eyes again, as if she was thinking—and maybe she was—but I soon realized our conversation was over. She tilted her head back and yawned, tucking her legs up under her. "I'm so tired. I should go home."

"It's late. Stay."

I didn't have to ask her again.

"Go into the bedroom," I said. "I'll sleep out here."

"No, I like it right here," she said, stretching out on the sofa.

I got the quilt off my bed and put it over her. "Good night," I whispered.

But she was already asleep.

I stood in the kitchen and had that whisky. Then I switched off the lights and returned to my bedroom and lay on top of the sheets. Around four o'clock I woke up. A shaft of lamplight was streaming in from the living room.

Lena was at my desk, poring over a book. She had the quilt wrapped around her. She looked up as if she had been expecting me. "This is amazing," she murmured.

Opened before her was a facsimile of the Mortford bestiary, compiled at the monastery of that name in Wales. The illustration she was pointing to was the avasphinx, a sphinx with a bird's head and a leopard's body, from the XI Dynasty in Egypt.

"You were always partial to sphinxes," I said.

"Not like this."

"All the sphinxes represented sun gods, but this one was also a phoenix. The pharaohs had its statue placed in their burial chambers, to deter the wiliest demons."

Under the desk lamp, her hair shone, and I wanted to stroke it.

"Have you been up long?" I said.

"Long enough to appreciate the work you've done." She indicated the stacks of notebooks and folders. "It's incredible." She looked up at me. "I didn't really understand."

I was touched.

"I hope you don't mind that I pried," she said.

"Not at all. I'm glad you did."

When I woke at dawn, she was gone. The quilt was folded neatly on the couch. There was an envelope beside it on which she had written:

Xeno, thanks for everything. Bring this tonight . . . 10 o'clock?

Inside the envelope was the gold locket with her initials that she had worn since she was a girl. I clicked the catch and the front flipped open, revealing a tiny image. It was my face, cut out of a photograph taken in my late teens.

That night, we met for a drink at a café near her office. At five A.M. she was flying to East Africa on a mission for International Refuge that had been scheduled weeks before. She had to pack and get some sleep, so we only had an hour.

I took out her locket, and she searched my face, waiting expectantly.

"You made me so happy," I said. "All these years I hoped you knew I felt the same way."

"I thought I did," she smiled faintly. "But so many things were in the way."

I raised my hands and put the locket around her neck. As I fastened the clasp, she leaned forward and kissed me. We were suspended like that for an instant, before she closed her eyes and I held her close and kissed her again.

THE NINE DAYS she was in Africa felt interminable. The fact it rained much of the time didn't help. I threw myself into my work even more than usual. Then, on a brilliant spring afternoon, she was at my door again. She was tanned, and her hair was combed back. She was wearing a trim red jacket and black jeans. Makeup, too, and perfume.

"I got back this morning," she said, embracing me. "Sorry I was incommunicado. Mostly I was in the wild."

"How did it go?"

"Fine. After Madagascar, we went to Niger. I was laid up with a fever for a couple of days. I'm okay now."

"You look beautiful."

She smiled, and between the coral bands of her lipstick, the chipped tooth stood out.

"So the trip was a success."

"You know, we operate in increments. Two steps forward, one step back. Madagascar is an isolated ecosystem. Hundreds of unique species have been jammed into shrinking pockets of rainforest. Some have been reduced to 'bushmeat.' Lemurs like the indri—our most direct ancestor—and cats like the fosa are being hunted to extinction. It took years to push through a ban on the hunting. Now we're trying to get them to enforce it."

"Sit down. We'll have something to drink."

"I've been cooped up for days. Would you like to go for a walk?"

We circled around to the river and crossed the Pont d'Arcole to Notre Dame. The usual crowd jammed the plaza. Many cameras taking the same picture. Tour guides with their rote recitations, provincial

priests on pilgrimage, beggars. A boy in a wheelchair was selling cru-
cifixes. An African band was playing the Marseillaise on steel drums.

Lena and I climbed the north tower to the Galerie des Chimères,
where the gargoyles, facing outward, protect the cathedral from evil
spirits. Claws extended, fangs bared, they were intended to be more
fearsome than any beast the mind could conjure.* On the parapet to
the south tower, between a particularly fierce pair, we gazed over the
city: the Hôtel de Ville, the Petit Pont streaming with pedestrians, the
gold Dôme des Invalides blazing, and, just below, the Seine green as
jade, swollen with rainwater.

"I missed you," Lena said.

"I missed you, too."

"But I had time to think." She leaned back against the wall. "We
have so much history together, Xeno. I've been asking myself: 'How
do we do this? Where do we start?'"

I put my arms around her. "How about right here?"

She smiled. "I knew you'd say that."

"This is more than most people ever get."

She hesitated. "Sometimes I think if you get too happy, it's taken
away."

Her hair was blowing. Up there, the din of the city became a low
hum. The two gargoyles peered down at us.

"That's not going to happen to us," I said. "We won't let it."

She rose up on her toes and I kissed her.

A few hours later, as evening fell, we lay in bed in my apartment.
On the way there, I bought her a bouquet of white lilies from a vendor. Now they were in a vase by the window. Their scent filled the
room. A candle burned beside them, gilding the thick petals. Lena's
head rested on my shoulder, her arm on my chest. I ran my fingers

---

*THE GARGOYLE
A dragon that rose from the Seine in the 7th century to ravage Rouen.
Saint Romain killed it with a green sword.
Where the gargoyle fell, a spring of angels' tears began to flow.
One sip can cleanse a man's soul.

through her hair. I still couldn't believe she was beside me. We had traveled so many miles and been so far apart.

After making love, we remained locked together, drenched in sweat, and then eased apart. Her thoughts had obviously been following a parallel path; pressing her palm to my heart, touching my lips and my cheek, she murmured, "Is it really you?"

I held her into the night, feeling her chest rise and fall as the candle flickered out and the darkness expanded around us. Her body was as beautiful as I'd always imagined: full breasts, small hips, shapely legs. There was a faint hollow between her breasts, a gold shadow. Through all those hours we never said a word. Just when I was certain she had fallen asleep, she slipped from my arms and stood up with a shiver and crossed the room. Her skin shone silver, then white, before she melted into the darkness. There was a long silence. The bathroom door opened and closed. I heard water run in the kitchen. A glass clink. There was another silence. Then a floorboard creaked in the hall.

I felt a cool rush as the sheet was lifted and she curled in beside me.

"I was afraid I would never see you again," I said hoarsely.

"You were dreaming," she whispered, kissing my cheek.

It certainly seemed that way when I closed my eyes and images from the past began flooding my head.

Steaming avenues bleeding tar. Antennas cluttering rooftops. Ragtag crowds streaming from the subway. I recognized individual faces. The blind man playing a mandolin on his fire escape. His sister from Mexico City selling corn cakes from a cart. The hustlers at the pool hall drinking Cuba Libres at dawn. The seminarian with a glass eye arrested for shoplifting. The Jewish shoemaker's son selling fireworks. The daughters of a bus driver, murdered on the job, turning tricks. Our mysterious neighbor, the Irish nurse, whom my grandmother claimed to have seen levitating at the Laundromat.

Denizens of that world, Lena and I had escaped it—or, unawares, been expelled. It didn't matter which. Like its inhabitants, we, too, were destined to be grains in the great hourglass, as Mr. Hood, expounding on the flow of history, once described the billions of human beings that have preceded and will follow us, some embracing this world, most rejecting it, before, without exception, it swallows us up again.

Beside Lena, I felt far removed from the hourglass—from the dead, the unborn, and even the living. We were as alone as we would ever be, like the stars on some remote latitude that shine on no one. We could shine for one another, with no need or desire for anyone else. We were very lucky just then, and we knew it.

"Hold me closer," Lena murmured the next morning, her breath warm against my throat.

But I was already holding her as close as I could.

W E SPED OUT of the city on my new motorcycle, taking the western autoroute past Versailles and Chartres to Courville, a river town at the edge of a forest. The speedometer ticked past 150 kph, but Lena shouted into my helmet, "Faster!"

I had not owned a motorcycle since I returned from Vietnam. Every so often I rented one to ride out of the city. After Murphy rode behind me the day he was killed, I had not been able to take anyone on the back of a bike. Friends, girlfriends, co-workers, no one. But the previous week I had bought a black 750cc Dugatti, so precisely tuned that, even at high speed, its four-hundred-pound frame barely vibrated.

Lena loved speed—another thing about her I hadn't known. I bought her a black helmet with a tinted visor, like my own. She pressed up against me and locked her arms.

"You're still in such good shape," she laughed, as we weaved through traffic. "For a desk jockey."

"Thanks."

Buildings, bridges, factories flew by before we exited the autoroute and rode across open countryside, in and out of small towns, down long roads where the poplars lining the shoulder felt close enough to touch. We stopped at a restaurant with a sky-blue awning where we lingered over lunch at a white table.

Except when Lena went to work, we had been inseparable for a week. That Saturday I had picked her up at an unfamiliar address on the rue de Rivoli, a professional building. It was only when our waiter brought us bread and uncorked a bottle of wine that Lena looked me in the eye and smiled broadly.

"I fixed it today," she said, and I saw that the dentist had done a fine job capping the chipped tooth and matching the color to the enamel of her teeth.

I smiled, too. "It looks beautiful," I said, taking her hands in mine across the table. "You look beautiful."

Two days later, after she had been working late, we met at the Japanese garden in the Bois de Boulogne. It was a quiet, out-of-the-way place. The miniature Shinto temple was weather-beaten. The carp pond, filled with leaves, had been drained. Vines covered the water wheel. I was waiting for Lena on a stone bench beneath the maple trees.

She was preoccupied. At first, she wouldn't discuss it. She made small talk about a film we'd seen the previous night. Finally she said, "I have to return to Africa—West Africa. Not now, but soon."

"For how long?"

"It depends. We're trying to head off a disaster in Senegal. There's a wildlife preserve the government has decided to dissolve—their word. They want to clear the land for cattle grazing, which is bad enough, and set aside a section for hunters. Turkey shoots with big game. Many of the animals have dropped their defenses with humans. Other animals will be relocated to the country's other, already over-crowded game preserve—who knows for how long—or to foreign zoos. Some will end up on the black market, for their fur or their organs. Most will die in captivity."

"There's no way to stop this?"

"No. We thought we could do something through the UN, but the Senegalese government is impervious to all pleas. They presented a single offer: International Refuge has until July 30 to get out any animals it can. After that, all bets are off."

"So you have two months."

"Yeah. The catch is we have to provide transportation and find homes for the animals. It's a huge undertaking, but doable. We've already lined up game preserves in Kenya and South Africa. Most of the animals—monkeys, water buffalo, zebras—will travel overland in trucks. They can handle the heat and the rough roads. It's transportation for the big cats—leopards, cheetahs, caracals, and two prides of lions—that's giving us fits."

"What do you need?"

"A transport plane that can make a couple of trips in a short span. We petitioned the UN, but that's going nowhere because of countries that don't want to offend Senegal. Greenpeace owns two planes, but they're too small. The U.S. said no. The French have large transport planes, but also a delicate relationship with Senegal. It goes on like that."

"Could you do it by sea?"

She nodded. "It would be slower but better. A large ship could transport all the animals at once. Still, it's not feasible."

"Why not?"

"Because it's even harder to get a ship," she said wearily.

I looked at her. "I have a ship."

8

O N THE SECOND OF JULY we embarked from Piraeus in a green
rain. The sea was smoky, the anchored ships like ghosts as we
headed for open waters, sailing south by southwest.

In the mess hall, Lena and I joined Captain Salice for breakfast at
one of the two long tables. Plates and silverware were laid out on a
long counter. The cook emerged from the galley through swinging
doors and set down a steaming pan of scrambled eggs and hash
browns. He was a small, heavyset man who wore high-top sneakers
and a red apron. Nodding to the captain, he rang an old brass bell to
summon the crew.

"That bell originally hung in a Bulgarian church," the captain said
to me. "My predecessor gave it to your father."

My father.

I could never have imagined that his old cabin would be the first place
Lena and I called home together. That night, after twelve hours in the
hold, overseeing the workmen, she sat cross-legged on the bed, immersed in her graphs and checklists, while I sat at my desk, rereading
my notes on Sarkas. I was restless, still awaiting additional information
from the librarians at the Villa Ziane. I had faxed them another request,
and instructed the radioman to find me the moment they replied.
Before I disembarked at Crete on the return voyage from Senegal, I
wanted to narrow the range of my search as much as possible.

Before falling asleep, Lena and I lay propped up in bed, leafing
through a book of photographs of the churches on Crete. It was a
comprehensive study, with interior and exterior shots, close-ups of
murals, mosaics, and frescoes. The Greek text was dry, but straight-
forward, and I translated it for her as we went.

The night before we left Paris, I had stumbled on a line in Giorgio Zetto's diary that I previously passed over. Two words in a throwaway sentence: *After hearing about Sarkas's church when we visited Signor Algrete, I want to learn more, but no one has seen Sarkas for days.*

Sarkas's church. At first, I assumed Zetto meant the Armenian Orthodox Church. But as a Roman Catholic, and a Venetian who surely knew the monastery on San Lazzaro, why would Zetto suddenly "want to learn more" about Armenian Orthodoxy? Would he really have been interested in hearing Sarkas discuss its liturgy? And even if he was, why would the renegade monk accommodate him? I never found evidence that Zetto saw Sarkas again; this diary entry, on March 14, 1820, was his last mention of him. Then in Athens I thought: what if Zetto was referring to a physical church in Crete with which Sarkas had become associated in some way? Before we sailed, I bought *The Churches of Crete* in a religious bookstore on Stadiou Street.

"What are you looking for, exactly?" Lena asked.

"I don't know. Something that may only make sense when I learn more about Sarkas."

"Such as?"

I closed my eyes. "I don't know that, either."

THERE WERE ONLY three Americans on board, but on the Fourth of July we celebrated with Egyptian firecrackers and cognac. The captain ran up the American flag beneath the Greek. The cook baked me an apple pie.

I was thinking of the barbecues at the Morettis'. The pungent smoke off the grill, the pitchers of lemonade, the cans of beer nestled into a tub of ice. The backyard filled with firemen and cops, their wives and kids. The younger kids running with sparklers, the rest of us setting off ashcans and cherry bombs in the street. In the evening the men playing poker under the oak tree, drinking shots now, fireflies dancing around them.

Apparently Lena was revisiting the same memories. Wearing red shorts and a blue T-shirt, picking at her pie, she broke a long silence. "This was my father's favorite holiday. He'd be upset with me, leaving the States the way I did."

"He'd also be proud of what you're doing now."

"Maybe *I've* been upset about the way I left. I don't want to go back; I just hate that I can't," she added sharply. She looked out at the sea. "Daddy would be happy if he could see us now, Xeno."

The *Makara* was carrying a full crew and eight passengers, including me: Lena and four colleagues (a vet, two animal handlers, and the director of their African office, Dr. Lucapa, an Angolan lawyer), and two unexpected guests, Vartan Marczek and Oso.

We would put Marczek and Oso ashore at Safi in Morocco, where she had business with a famous glazier, before they traveled to Essouaria to stay with friends. When I heard about their trip, I offered them passage—an invitation Marczek couldn't resist.

I had met up with him again in Paris, and he invited me to a party in his honor at his publisher's swank apartment on the Boulevard Raspail. He had turned in his Byron biography. We drank champagne and smoked cigars on the terrace. I brought him up to date on my researches. He listened intently, his great head bowed.

"I have no doubt you are closing in on Sarkas's final destination," he said. "And on the bestiary itself. I can feel it. I thought of you recently when I came upon a line in Augustine: 'If we find in the depiction of an animal an uplifting or penetrating symbol, we should not worry whether that creature really exists, or ever existed.' Compiling or reconstituting a bestiary, Xeno, is a constant re-creation of Creation. Like Pigafetta and Byron, you're leaving your own mark on the *Caravan Bestiary*."

We were sailing due west now, north of Malta, south of Sicily— closer to Tunisia than Italy. The Ionian Sea was a deep purple on which whitecaps remained impossibly poised. The light penetrated everything, and the dome of the sky was like bright blue quartz.

One morning I spotted a phalanx of dolphins. They darted dangerously close to the prow, raced the ship, then peeled off and leapt above the waves. The second mate told me he once saw a dolphin skim the water vertically, propelling himself with his tail fin, aware of the amazement he inspired. No wonder Aelian, Pliny, and every other ancient naturalist—a cold-eyed bunch—wrote of these animals with such delight.

When Lena wasn't toiling in the hold, she was meeting with her colleagues. They had sent and received dozens of radio messages and faxes, to and from Paris, Dakar, and London. I still hadn't heard from the Villa Ziane. I was resigning myself to the fact I might hear nothing at all during our voyage.

In Paris, Lena was stunned at first that I would offer up use of the *Makara*, in effect underwriting a major portion of the mission. "I know you love animals—"

"If I could do more, I would."

She took me to see the Director of International Refuge. After conferring with his board, he set up a meeting with their attorney and an attaché at the Senegalese Embassy. Pericles Arvanos sent me the insurance certificates. Visas and permits were obtained.

Arvanos and I had a testy phone conversation. He thought I was crazy. He spelled out how much money I would lose, and how much everything would cost: $175,000 for construction and another $30,000 to dismantle the modifications later.

"Then there is the $180,000 contract I will have to break with Alta."

Alta was a Turkish tobacco company that had commissioned the *Makara* to carry six tons of long-leaf tobacco from Istanbul to Buenos Aires.

"Take it out of operating expenses," I said. "It's only two months. Imagine the ship is in dry dock."

"Imagine?" I could picture him shaking his head. "Dry dock does not entail losing hundreds of thousands of dollars. Anyway, your mind's made up. Tell me: after you've deposited these animals in Kenya, the *Makara* will return to Piraeus, correct? She can be reoutfitted in August and carry cargo again in September. Unless you have other plans."

"Not at the moment."

It wasn't just that he disapproved of what I was doing; it felt as if he was conveying my father's disapproval, by proxy from the beyond. I didn't mind Arvanos's concern—he was my lawyer, after all—but I wasn't interested in his approval.

"Please send me the necessary papers as soon as possible," I said, cutting short our conversation.

"Of course. It is your ship."

It was my ship. And it felt that way for the first time.

After inheriting the *Makara*, I had tried reducing it in my mind to the monthly check I received from Arvanos. The irony of his reprising his old role—sending me my youthful allowance—was not lost on me. He worked for me now, but obviously I had been comfortable with that old template. It had helped make the ship into an abstraction, an investment impersonal as stocks and bonds, rather than what I now found it to be: a self-sufficient world, with its own codes, taboos, and humor, and an unusual group of seamen: the machinist who could play simultaneous games of chess blindfolded; the Algerian boatswain who had a wife and ten children. And the man who oversaw the engine room, Hasan, a Turkish Cypriot, who informed me that his prosthetic left foot was carved from a walrus tusk and his little finger from a triton shell.

Lena and I had flown to Athens and hired a team of carpenters, welders, and electricians to adapt it for this mission. In four weeks they constructed a dozen cages, partitions, storage bins. They installed sunlamps and air conditioners. We needed refrigerators large enough to hold enough raw meat for the journey back up around Africa, across the Mediterranean, through the Suez Canal, and south to the Kenyan port of Mombasa. Eight days' sailing in all.

I had the passenger cabins painted and properly furnished. It was obvious my father had seldom taken guests on his voyages. I kept my own quarters as he had refurbished them. I tried to make them my own by stocking the bookshelves and hanging some Piranesi prints. I also brought many of my notebooks. My father knew enough about me to surmise that a desk would be an important item. This one, with its reassuring bulk, was good to write at.

After watching her go nonstop for weeks, I persuaded Lena to take a day off. We rented a car and drove north to Delphi, which she had always wanted to see. It was one of those places her aunt, who traveled to Egypt, told her about when she was a girl. We visited the site of the oracle, and Lena wanted to know how it worked.

"The high priestess of the oracle was called Pythia," I said.

"A vestal virgin?"

"Far from it. She oversaw elaborate orgies. At the summer solstice she was required to give herself over to a stranger. In her ceremonial role, she sat alone in the Temple of Apollo. There was a chasm beneath the floor from which ethylene gases escaped. Inhaling them, she fell into a trance and muttered her prophecies in a secret language which only her priests could interpret. The priests then sold the prophecies to various supplicants."

"They had to pay?"

"Through the nose. The oracle was only open for business a few days a year, so it was a seller's market."

She laughed. She liked to talk about what she called my work, which was my knowledge of ancient history.

We visited the amphitheater, then climbed the steep path to the stadium, which I told her had been carved right out of the mountain in the fifth century B.C.

"Does it have a name?" she said.

"It was called *Marmaria*, which means 'struggle.' It accommodated seven thousand spectators."

Twenty-five centuries later, we were the only ones there. The dust was hot beneath our feet. The cicadas were loud. Yellow flowers grew from cracks in the stone. We sat on the wall and gazed across the plain below to the Gulf of Corinth, a gold crescent suspended in haze. For the first time since leaving Paris, we were truly alone, even if only for a few hours. Before leaving Delphi, we mailed Bruno a postcard and signed it *Love, Lena & Xeno.*

PREVIOUSLY I had only seen the Rock of Gibraltar in photographs. Through binoculars I spied two of the famous Barbary apes (actually tailless monkeys, Lena informed me) perched on a ledge. There are four colonies on the Rock, comprised of the last free-ranging monkeys in Europe, two hundred of them. I remembered that it is also home to the peryton, but try as I might, I didn't see a single one.

Gibraltar is one of the Pillars of Hercules that intrigued the ancient Greeks. The pillars held up their sky. The other six pillars, notably Mount Acha and Jebel Musa, lie fourteen miles across the strait, at Ceuta in Morocco. The pillars are the gateway to the Atlantic—the end of the Greek world. Their mariners feared that if they ventured beyond the pillars they would slide into the void. *Ultima Thule*, they called it, represented on their maps by the blank spaces beyond Ocean (the self-devouring, world-encircling serpent Nathalie had worn on her jacket) and populated by monsters that preyed on unsuspecting travelers. Eventually they passed through the pillars and made their way into bestiaries—the most elusive and frightening into the *Caravan Bestiary*: the manticore, the gorgons, the monoceros (a horned stallion with razor teeth), and fiercest of all, Echidna, who had a beautiful nymph's head on a serpent's body. Her teardrops were venom, her blood lava. With her husband, hundred-headed Typhon, she produced the most grotesque monsters in Greek mythology.*

---

*ECHIDNA
*Among her offspring: the Chimera, the Hydra, the Nemean Lion & the Sphinx;
the dogs Cerberus and Orthrus and the dragon Ladon, all multiheaded;
and Ethon, the eagle that tormented Prometheus chained to his rock.*

At dusk we slipped into Ultima Thule, survived intact, and steered southward, leaving behind the last straggling gulls from the coasts of both continents.

Marczek prowled the ship in his slippers, his yellow scarf fluttering. Curious, as always, he engaged passengers and crew: Mr. Lucapa (who discoursed on river diversion and animal famine) and Hasan (whose prosthetic parts fascinated him) and, most of all, Lena, who discussed this rescue mission. Prone to seasickness, Oso kept to their cabin unless the sea was exceptionally calm.

Sixty miles off the coast of Morocco, on this, his last night aboard, Marczek regaled Lena with tales of his ill-fated years as a beer importer in Hungary. We were all exhausted and after dinner we uncorked several bottles of wine and sat on deck. Lena was curious about the life I had led abroad, and Marzcek was the first of my friends she met. She took to him at once. He had that effect on women. We both missed him when he was gone.

When we returned to our cabin, Lena pulled me close, her lips glued to mine. We slipped out of our clothes and she took my hand and led me to the bathroom. The shower stall was small, but there was just enough room for us, the water pouring down our backs.

Later, she fell asleep in my arms. Around midnight, I got up and checked in again with the radioman, but he just shook his head. I drifted to sleep imagining the immensity of the sea beneath us, its myriad currents, the creatures gliding in the deep darkness known only to them.

Dakar. Through a driving rain, its jagged skyline was a blur of pink and brown. Fetid winds and thunderclaps greeted us as we entered the harbor.

Nearly everyone went ashore. Captain Salice and I escorted two Senegalese customs officers on their inspection of the ship. After they left, the captain and I remained in the pilothouse. Rain streamed down the windows. The captain rolled a cigarette, picking the stringy tobacco from a pouch with his thick fingers. "I have never had a live cargo," he said matter-of-factly. "They will be loud at night, you know."

The big cats had been driven to the city from the game preserve, eighty miles to the north, in a caravan of trailer trucks.

> 7 cheetahs (including two cubs)
> 11 lions (including 6 cubs)
> 4 caracals
> 5 leopards

One by one their cages were lifted high into the air by cranes and lowered into the bowels of the ship. The cats crouched low, anxiously staring down at the uplifted faces of stevedores, policemen, and sailors on the dock. Among the International Refuge contingent, in yellow slickers, Lena was cross-checking her manifest with the one provided by the authorities.

By seven o'clock we had refueled, taken on stores, and set sail.

That first night, the cats were even louder than I expected, the mournful yowls of the leopards and the lions' roars. Some of the seamen were spooked, but I found these sounds comforting. They brought back memories of the animals my grandmother used to mimic in the dark, reminding me that they were all around us: they in our dreams and we in theirs.

The hold was now a world unto itself, and for the next couple of days Lena was down there constantly.

Two nights out of Dakar, when she was asleep, I went there alone for the first time. It was 4 A.M., and after a long nightmare, I couldn't get back to sleep. The smell was overwhelming: shit, piss, raw meat. And the body heat of the cats, confined at such close quarters. We had erected a labyrinth of partitions, but couldn't filter the crosscurrents of scents that excited some and paralyzed others. A week after being rounded up, netted, and tranquilized, they found themselves caged for the first time in their lives—in a rocking ship, no less, with human beings in alarming proximity.

I was amazed to be that close to them: gazing at the lions' golden eyes and the cheetahs' whiskers, delicate as Japanese fans, and the leopards' bared fangs, sharper than any dagger. Many of the cats were asleep. In that suffocating air I thought I could hear their hearts beating. My grandmother would have been able to distinguish those heartbeats according to the species—maybe even the individual cat.

In a corner, away from the other cages, I found a solitary cat Lena had never mentioned. Nor had I seen him listed in the manifest. A panther. Black, with topaz eyes and silver whiskers. He circled his cage, clockwise, then counterclockwise . . .

He showed no interest in me. I half expected him to rise up on his hind legs, with a human smile, and break into speech, like the panther who stood at my hospital bedside in Honolulu, and before that visited my grandmother's deathbed, speaking to her in his strange language about "the lost animals" turned away from the ark—the first mention I ever heard of them. But this panther remained a creature of the jungle, silent, self-contained, gliding on all fours; if he had something to communicate, it wasn't going to be through speech.

Suddenly I didn't want to be alone with him anymore.

I returned to my cabin and poured myself a raki. Careful not to wake Lena, I searched for some entries in my notebooks. The first, from one of my oldest notebooks, was based on a passage in the Hereford bestiary in which the panther was identified, not as a carnivorous cat, but as Jesus himself: gentle, gracious, with breath so sweet it drew other creatures to him. In the archives on San Lazzaro I had discovered an alternative biography that went to the other extreme, which I recorded in detail in my final Venetian notebook:

THE PANTHER

He is Satan, who in the guise of a panther stowed away on Noah's ark to ensure that all of man's innate sins and vices survived the Flood, as they must. The only animal onboard without a mate, the panther lurked in shadows, scavenged food, never slept.

The Armenian chroniclers praised Noah as a skilled mariner. Only later did he devolve into the mean-spirited farmer who scapegoated his son Ham for stumbling upon him naked and drunk and then the ambassador for a god who coldly declared after the Flood that every beast of the earth, sea, and sky should live in fear of man, and that every moving thing that lives shall be meat for him.

Every civilization has a flood myth and a Noah, though he is usually more benign and heroic: in India, he is Manu, guided by the god Vishnu in the form of a whale; in Babylon, Ea, a merman who built the human race a colossal ark and calmed the waters; in Greece, Deucalion; in Chaldea, Xisuthros, whose story matched the Hebrew Noah's: after forty days of rain, he set sail on the floodwaters with his family and a pair of every known animal (16,000 in all).

Noah only provided sanctuary to those creatures sanctioned by his god. All others that were refused entry to his ark (the animals of the Caravan Bestiary) *resurfaced later; because no one could determine how or where they had survived the Flood on their own, they were feared all the more.*

In that same notebook I had described Ani, the city Noah founded near Mount Ararat where a thousand churches sprang up, including one (unknown to anyone) that had an altar constructed with beams from the ark. The man who discovered it would gain immediate entry to paradise. Similarly on the island of Paros there is a Church of One Hundred Doors, built by the Emperor Justinian, of which ninety-nine are known. The man who finds the one hundredth door will supposedly step through it into the Kingdom of Heaven.

In the back of that notebook I had pasted two photographs taken by a Russian explorer in 1921: one was of the enormous, decayed ship preserved in a ridge of dark ice atop Ararat; the other was of a black marble statue at the foot of the mountain. No one knew who erected this ancient statue: a panther on his hind legs, his eyes glittering, and—apparent to all—the trace of a smile on his face.

When we were back in the Mediterranean after a long night of rain, the air smelled clean and metallic. Lena and I leaned against the railing on the starboard side.

"This voyage will lead to more interventions," she said, "with other organizations lending support. Locana is already hearing from people—a guy from the Swedish Naval Ministry and some UN honcho who didn't return his calls in the spring." She patted the railing. "We can thank the *Makara* for that. And you."

Stars were filling the sky, brighter than I'd ever seen them—in Maine, or even Vietnam. Scorpio was directly overhead. Libra beside it. The wind picked up. We watched flying fish skim the waves. Lena rested her head against my shoulder.

"If this wind carried us off," I said, "it could set us down anywhere in the world and we'd be all right."

"Yes, we would," she smiled.

When we fell asleep later, she was breathing softly. At four-thirty I was awakened by a knock at the door. I slipped on my robe. It was the radioman.

He handed me a piece of paper. "It just came in, sir."

I read and reread it, pacing the corridor.

For months I had been thinking that where Adolphus Sarkas's journey ended, a part of my journey must also end. Now I would find out if that was true.

9

W E WERE IN a square in Xaniá, studying a map of the town. The heat was stifling. The cafés were busy. Shoppers drifted by, buying loaves hot from the oven, examining the fruit. The old quarter had barely changed over four centuries. The Venetian lion was everywhere: statues, coats of arms, door knockers. There were a few benches under the trees and a flower bed that needed watering. The sea shone at the end of a long street. The wind was kicking up yellow dust. The buildings, too, were ocher, not white. With their ornate balustrades, stately windows, and arched gates, they made me feel as if we were in Venice, not Crete. Lena, who had not been anywhere in Europe except France, had awoken early and wandered the narrow streets, their names a jumble of Italian, Greek, and Turkish.

The *Makara* was on its way to Piraeus. As planned, I had disembarked in Irakleion. After remaining in Kenya with her colleagues for two days, resettling the animals, Lena flew to Irakleion via Cairo. I rented a car and met her at the airport. We drove to the northwest shore of the island. The highway was lined with oleander bushes in full flower. We opened the windows and turned up the bouzouki music on the radio. It was a relief to be on land, on an open road. I had finally come to my father's island, but I didn't plan on visiting Asprophotes, his ancestral village. I felt no tugs in that direction.

My destination was Skalos, a small island twelve miles off the coast. I'd learned that it was four miles in diameter, rugged and dry, and practically uninhabited. Fishermen stayed in beach shacks for short stretches, and there were a few reclusive goatherds, but no houses or electricity, and only one scheduled launch a month from Xaniá. Once there had been a small village, but it was abandoned early in the nineteenth century when the island's largest spring dried up.

I got the break I had been waiting for with regard to Adolphus Sarkas when the librarians at the Villa Ziane informed me that he died in Xaniá on February 2, 1822. The cause of death was "fever" (which could mean anything). Three days later, he was buried on Skalos in the cemetery behind the church. I wondered if this was the church Giorgio Zetto mentioned in his diary. The librarians didn't know why Sarkas's grave was on Skalos, but they did provide a piece of unexpected information: the name of the witness on the death certificate. Nicanor Simonides. It would have been easy to assume he was a municipal clerk or casual acquaintance if not for the fact the certificate noted (as the law required) that Simonides was also the person arranging Sarkas's funeral and settling his affairs. Simonides had taken on the role of an executor or next of kin, which suggested he was far more intimate with Sarkas than Zetto. But who was he?

After breakfast, Lena and I had split up: she went to the harbor to hire a launch and buy supplies, and I visited the public records office. There was a single clerk. After a long wait in which he sifted through several file cabinets and disappeared into a back room, he told me that Nicanor Simonides was born in Xaniá in December 1779. There was no record of his death.

"If he died anywhere in Crete," the clerk sighed, "it would be noted."

"So he was abroad."

"He could have been in Athens—or Moscow. Anywhere but here." He shrugged. "Unless the record was lost."

"Do records get lost?"

"Some were, after the First World War." He looked at his watch. "I must go for lunch now."

This meant the office would be closed. He put on a beige jacket and straw hat and walked out with me, locking the door. On the street, in sunlight, I looked at him more closely: a man in his thirties, prematurely bald, stooped. But he assumed a different persona once he was out of the office; low-key and conversational, he was suddenly offering up useful information.

"The Simonides family is one of the oldest in Xaniá. They may be able to help, if you call on them." He stroked his chin. "The family has several branches. I would try Petros Simonides first. I'll walk you a bit—it's on my way—and then give you directions to his house."

I thanked him, and a few minutes later we separated in a warren of streets shaded by eucalyptus trees. Petros Simonides's house was on a dead end that looked as if it had once been fashionable. The house was white, three stories high, and typically Venetian, with tall shuttered windows and irregular balconies. The paint was peeling in the eaves. Potted geraniums flanked the front door. A young woman answered my knock. Her black dress told me someone had died. It could have happened a week ago, or a year. Depending on who it was, she might be wearing black for the rest of her life.

"I would like to see Petros Simonides, please."

She looked closely at me. She wasn't friendly. She had short black hair and pencil-thin eyebrows. Her eyes were a pale gray that was like no color at all. For a moment, from her silence, I thought he was the one who had died.

"Who should I say is here?"

I told her, and shutting the door, she disappeared. I heard a dog bark within, many rooms away.

I never saw her again. An old man in a black cardigan and wire-rimmed spectacles opened the door and looked at me inquiringly.

"Excuse my intrusion. I'd like to ask you about an ancestor of yours named Nicanor Simonides."

He studied me more closely, but said nothing before ushering me in. In Crete it was considered rude to turn away a respectable stranger, whether he needed a bed for the night, a meal, or a glass of water. But that didn't mean you had to answer his questions.

Simonides led me to a sitting room off the parlor. It was stuffy. The furnishings were drab, the drapes faded by sunlight. The rug was worn in front of the sofa and easy chairs. He offered me coffee. "Or perhaps you would like brandy?"

"Coffee is fine."

"And a sweet," he said, and it wasn't a question.

A few minutes later, another woman in black, heavyset, middle-aged, brought in a tray with two demitasse cups and a dish of candied fruit. Looking me over impassively, she handed me one of the cups with a napkin.

I told Simonides I was a scholar trying to learn the fate of a man named Sarkas. I explained to him about the death certificate. I gave him the dates. He listened carefully.

"Your Greek is good," he said, "for an American."

"My father was Cretan."

He nodded approvingly. "Where from?"

"A small village. Asprophotes."

"In the mountains. I know it." This information seemed to reassure him. "Getting back to your question. Yes, I know who Nicanor Simonides was. Actually, there have been several of them over the years. The one you're talking about was a priest, you know."

"I didn't know," I said, concealing my excitement. "An Orthodox priest?"

"What else? My brother can tell you about these things better than I can."

I had a sinking feeling. "Oh. Where does your brother live?"

"Why, here in this house," he replied, as if it were an absurd question. "I can get him if you like."

"I would be grateful."

He shuffled out, and I finished my coffee, thick as mud. A few minutes later, the dog trotted in, a boxer who stopped short when he saw me, then sniffed my shoes. He must be old, I thought, not to have smelled me from the parlor. A man followed, who was quite old, older than Petros. He too wore black, a jacket and a wide tie. His moustache was white and he had liver spots on his hands. His gaze was steady, though. He sat down in an easy chair, the dog at his feet, and introduced himself as Alexander Simonides. I realized his brother wasn't going to return.

I apologized again for intruding. He offered me the fruit, and I took a date. Then he picked out an orange slice for himself.

"Petros told me your people are from Crete."

"My father's people, yes. This is my first time on Crete."

He was surprised. "You never visited with your father?"

"No."

"So he never came back from America."

"Oh, no, he came back. But he didn't bring me."

He thought about this, then put his hands on his knees and shifted his weight slightly. "You wanted to ask me about my great-grandfather."

I repeated what I had told Petros about Sarkas and his death.

He looked at me with renewed curiosity. "No one outside our family has ever asked about Nicanor Simonides. Sometimes I wonder why," he added cryptically. "Why are you so interested in this man Sarkas?"

"I'm doing research on a book compiled in the Middle Ages. For a while, it was in his possession."

"What kind of book?"

"A bestiary." I saw he had no idea what that was. I used the original Greek word, *physiologos,* and he shook his head. "It's a book about animals," I said. "With beautiful pictures."

"Ah."

I remembered how in the fourteenth century the bestiary had lain unrecognized in the widow Bendetto's closet in Ravenna and then been passed through many generations of Doge Dandolo's family. It had become an heirloom, a packet in a trunk. If Sarkas had passed the bestiary on to Nicanor Simonides, or if Simonides had simply taken it, I wondered if that could have happened again, with this family.

"Have you ever seen such a book?" I said.

"No."

"Or heard of it in your family?"

His eyes narrowed. "No. Why should I?"

"I thought perhaps if it came into Nicanor Simonides' hands, he might have passed it on to his descendants."

"That's not possible," he said with surprising vehemence.

"Why not?" I thought I had offended him.

He leaned forward. "Will you be putting any of this in a book of your own?"

"No, I'm not writing a book. Whatever you tell me is just between us."

He seemed satisfied, but paused to formulate his words. "Nicanor Simonides was a scoundrel," he said. "Through generations of Simonides, there's been no one like him."

I was stunned. "What did he do?"

"He deserted his family. His wife and two sons. He disappeared the same year you say this man Sarkas died, 1822."

"Why?" I imagined some scandal—embezzling church funds, an illicit affair.

"Nobody knows. He was the priest at the Church of Saint Stephen, by the harbor, and thus responsible, too, in those days, for the Church of Saint George on Skalos, which was part of the parish. His eldest son was my grandfather. All Grandfather remembered was that his father told the family he had to undertake a holy mission and would be gone for several months. He wouldn't tell his wife what this mission was or where he was going. Then he didn't come back. And she didn't hear from him again. Not a single letter, nothing." He grimaced. "Some people said maybe he was in an accident or fell ill. Others that he got the call again—from God, you know—as he had for the priesthood, but that this time he became a monk or a hermit. My great-grandmother scoured his papers. She found only one thing out of the ordinary, tucked away in a trunk: an Armenian grammar."

Now it was my turn to lean forward. "Did he speak the language?"

"Not that anyone knew. She was convinced he went there."

"To Armenia."

"But it made no sense. My grandfather always said she had nothing else to grab on to. He didn't think the grammar meant anything." Simonides shook his head. "Grandfather never forgave him."

"And you never heard of Adolphus Sarkas, Mr. Simonides?"

"Not until today."

So there were two churches which might have been "Sarkas's church," both connected to Nicanor Simonides, to whom Sarkas had entrusted his remains, his final affairs—and what else? For a moment, I thought of telling Simonides' great-grandson that Sarkas was Armenian, that he had been a monk in the Orthodox Church, that he too had once set out on a mission to Armenia. But what would this have accomplished? Alexander Simonides was an old man, and the history that had been passed down to him was bitter and confused enough without my injecting further confusion at this late date.

Instead, I said, "So Nicanor Simonides conducted the services at the church on Skalos as well?"

"Correct. Sundays he conducted the morning service in town, and in the afternoon went to Skalos. When the village on Skalos was abandoned, he maintained the Church of Saint George for a while."

"It hasn't been used in a long time, then."

"Not since he disappeared. It was locked up soon afterward."

The heavyset woman appeared in the doorway and nodded to him. Her sharp black eyes stood out in a face that was otherwise tired, pasty.

"I must go now," he said, standing up.

We shook hands. I thanked him for his hospitality. At the front door, the dog by his side, he said, "Mr. Atlas, I've told you a few things—would you tell me something?"

"Of course."

"Why didn't your father bring you to Crete with him?"

I looked him in the eye. "I'm afraid my father was a bit of a scoundrel, too."

THE PILOT POINTED to a strip of land across the water. "That's it," he shouted over the motor.

The launch was bumping over the waves, belching smoke. The pilot wore a soiled cap and a striped vest. The stubble was white on his brown face. Long ago a fishhook had torn away a piece of his cheek. Rope burns had scarred his hands. In Xaniá, his shrugs in response to my questions made clear his disdain for Skalos. When Lena had approached him on the docks the previous day, he told her—by way of his grandson, who spoke English—that she must be mistaken, surely she didn't want to go to Skalos. Replying that it was exactly where she wanted to go, she negotiated a good price for his services. When we boarded the launch, and he saw we had no fishing tackle, he was even more baffled. English birdwatchers also visited the island on occasion, but that was it. At the same time, he didn't pry.

When we were close enough to the island to make out the jagged coastline, he broke his silence. "There's nothing on Skalos. The goatherds who live there aren't even Cretans," he added contemptuously, "they're Gypsies."

He meant Gypsies with a capital *G*.

"Romany," he emphasized, to make sure I understood.

"Have they been there long?" I said.

"As long as anyone can remember. But they're always on the move. One day they'll leave Skalos, too." He shrugged. "Who knows, they may already be gone."

"No one has seen them recently?"

"I wouldn't know. There used to be a lot more of them, but during the war many fled to Kos to hide out from the Germans. They never returned. And none of them fought."

A crucifix and a small Greek flag hung inside his salt-streaked windshield beside a photograph of his nine grandchildren.

"I was in the Resistance," he went on. "There were thirty Germans for every one of us, and they came here like beasts, not soldiers— shooting children, hanging women, cutting off people's hands—but we never surrendered." He put a cigarette between his lips and turned back to the sea. "There is nothing good about war, even if you sur- vive."

"What's he talking about?" Lena whispered.

"The evils of war."

She was surprised. "Did you tell him you fought in Vietnam?"

I shook my head. "That's not a war that would interest him. More to the point, he said the only people we may encounter here are Gypsies."

Like the meltemi, the wind shearing the tips off the waves had a name: the sirocco, a hard, sand-filled wind that blows across the Mediterranean from Africa. It draws up moisture from the sea, but not before raining down more sand than water on the small islands off Crete, like Skalos.

The moment we were ashore, climbing the slope from the crum- bling dock, sand filled our shoes and stuck to our lips. We put on our sunglasses and pulled our hats low. My knapsack contained a flash- light, a compass, and a pocketknife. In my khaki jacket I had a note- book and a map. Lena carried a camera, sandwiches, and a canteen. It was eleven o'clock. The launch was going to return for us at six.

"Make sure you're here," were the pilot's final words to us. "We can't sail through those reefs once it's dark."

We climbed one hill, then another, before following a goat path through a rocky field. Thorns snagged our jeans. Thistles crunched beneath our shoes. To protect herself from the sun, Lena had put on a long-sleeved shirt. She walked with the sure step of someone who spent a lot of time in rough country.

The entire island was hilly. Much of it was bare. We saw no sign of human life. The vegetation grew in clusters: scrub pines, cacti, sea grapes, and wild thyme. The goat path branched off into small clearings. Heading toward the eastern end of the island, we saw a pine forest, outlined against the sea. According to my map, the ruins of the village Simonides mentioned were on the southern shore; the Church of Saint George was on higher ground, beside the forest.

When Lena and I had rendezvoused at the harbor in Xaniá the previous afternoon, I told her about my interview with Alexander Simonides. As we walked to the Church of Saint Stephen, she said, "So you think this priest took the bestiary to Armenia after Sarkas bequeathed it to him?"

"It's a strong possibility. It's hard to say if he and Sarkas were confidants, confederates, or just opportunists who used one another. What we do know is strange enough: a Cretan priest arranged the funeral of a stranger and then ran out on his family, his parish, and his homeland. His wife believed he went to Armenia, of all places. That can't be a coincidence. On his deathbed, did Sarkas repent and confess to Nicanor Simonides? Did Simonides promise to put things right and carry the bestiary to Ani, completing the 'holy mission'? If so, it may have been tucked away at the Monastery of Saint Jacob in Ani until 1840, when it would have been destroyed."

"Why do you say that?"

"Because in 1840 there was a volcanic eruption and the monastery burned to the ground."

She stopped short. "My god. And you knew about this?"

"I knew there had been a fire, but until I talked to Simonides, I thought the bestiary had been spared because Sarkas never reached Ani. But what if Nicanor Simonides did go there? Or maybe he set out with the best intentions and then yielded to temptation himself and absconded with the book. I doubt he got the call to be a monk. That would have been a reaffirmation of his faith, not a reason to act dishonorably. And why flee to Armenia when Greece is filled with monasteries? Anyway, if Simonides didn't go to Ani, the book may still exist."

"And if he didn't take it at all?" Lena whispered, as we entered the Church of Saint Stephen.

"Then it could still be here in Xaniá—or, far more likely, on Skalos. Because Sarkas had himself buried there, I feel certain the church on Skalos was the one Zetto was referring to as 'Sarkas's church.' The fact it was closed up soon after Sarkas's death is interesting, too, don't you think?" We were now standing in the nave of the church, which was empty. "Since we also just learned that this church, too, was overseen by Simonides, I thought we ought to check it out—just in case."

First and foremost, Adolphus Sarkas was an artist. In veering off, becoming a thief and a renegade, relinquishing his holy orders, he had changed the course of his life, and of the bestiary; but I doubted he would have stopped painting, no matter what his circumstances. His renderings of animals—*of sea, sky, land, and ether*—had been powerful enough to jolt Giorgio Zetto, whose diary was otherwise short on enthusiasms. Yet, after months of digging, I had discovered no references in any other source to the paintings Zetto saw. But I wondered if Sarkas might have also created formal ecclesiastical art for Nicanor Simonides—as he had for Father Aucher—here in the Church of Saint Stephen. If so, it had not been noted by the author of *The Churches of Crete*, who relegated a single workmanlike paragraph to this church, providing its date of construction (1514; rebuilt 1735), size (60 by 54 meters), height (49 meters), building materials (Naxian marble and mountain oak), and notable events (the christening of one Cretan governor, the wedding of another, and the funeral of Admiral Christos Valiotes, who defeated the Turkish fleet off Cyprus). But there was nothing about artwork.

For good reason, I realized, after examining the church's icons and murals. They were pedestrian depictions of Saint Nicholas distributing alms, a pensive Virgin Mary, Jesus with the disciples in Gethsemane, and Jesus crucified, many times over: all of these standard issue in every Orthodox church from Serbia to Siberia. There was no sign of Sarkas's brilliant, distinctive style. And no way of knowing if the *Caravan Bestiary* had passed through there in 1822, in transit to

Armenia, or to Skalos, whose Church of Saint George wasn't mentioned in *The Churches of Crete*—not even a footnote.

Lena and I walked on across Skalos. The sun beat down hard, but until we reached the pine forest, there were no trees large enough to offer shade. Twice we stopped to empty our shoes of sand. Horseflies circled our heads. Lizards skittered through the weeds. The island felt so deserted I was beginning to think the pilot was right: maybe the Gypsies were gone altogether.

At the top of a steep hill we were startled by the clatter of goat bells before we saw the goats themselves. There were four of them, with shaggy white fleeces, eating tufts of spiky grass on the downward slope. The one male, with curved yellow horns, looked up at us, chewing slowly.

Mopping my neck, I looked around. "I guess we'll find out soon enough who put those bells on their collars."

Beyond the next hill, we came on three more adult goats and two kids, also wearing bells. For these animals a pail of water and a block of salt had been left beneath a scrub pine.

We were just a few hundred yards from the forest now. We crossed a shallow ravine. The goat path widened from there and, just short of the forest, forked right, to the ruins of the village, and left, up an incline, to the Church of Saint George. We turned left and had gone about a hundred yards when the church steeple appeared through a break in the trees.

"There it is," Lena said, squeezing my hand.

We continued on, the path increasingly clotted with weeds, when suddenly a man stepped out of the forest up ahead. He was in his forties, wearing baggy pants, a shirt worn through at the elbows, and a wide-brimmed black hat. Tall and muscular, he was brown-skinned, darker than the darkest Cretan, with large hands and feet. He carried a knife in his belt and a staff in his hand. He stared back at us, then put a finger to his lips and descended the path quickly, nimble as a goat himself.

He carried the odor of his goats, and of tobacco. I didn't understand why he wanted us to be silent until he pointed to a grassy slope where a flock of snowy egrets were picking for insects.

"Wait," he said, "they will fly off as one." His Greek was strangely accented—the final syllables dropped too quickly, the consonants high-pitched.

"The birds are beautiful," I said, "but that's not why we're here."

"No?" He seemed disappointed. "I know all about the birds. I can guide you."

"No, thanks." I extended my hand. "My name is Xeno. This is Lena."

"I'm Sampson," he replied, and we shook hands. His hand was rough and unexpectedly cold. He had a tattoo on his wrist, but I couldn't make it out clearly because of his shirt cuff.

One of the egrets flew off, but the others remained on the slope.

"You see," Sampson said, "they didn't follow because he is not the leader."

When I translated this for Lena, she smiled pleasantly and murmured, "Not true."

Sampson had obviously developed a line of patter for the birdwatchers.

When he sensed we weren't buying into it, his smile faded and he turned suspicious. "So why are you here?"

I pointed at the steeple.

He squinted at me. "The church?"

"We're tourists. We heard it was interesting."

"Who told you that?"

"Alexander Simonides, in Xaniá."

If the name meant anything to him, he didn't let on. "He must not have seen it for a long time," he grunted. "There's nothing there. Anyway, it's locked up. My father is the caretaker."

"Caretaker?"

He nodded. "My father, Rumen."

"I didn't know there was a caretaker," I said skeptically.

"Well, there is. And now I have to see to my goats," he said abruptly, and started down the path. "Goodbye."

"What did he say?" Lena asked, and I repeated it while we climbed the remaining stretch to the church.

It was bigger than I expected, and better preserved. The architecture was Venetian. At one time, it would have been brightly whitewashed, with blue mosaics around the door and marine talismans, dolphins, and miniature galleons adorning the terra-cotta roof. The building's stone and mortar were still intact. Only the steeple showed signs of crumbling. The windows were boarded up with splintering planks. The rear wall was covered with red bougainvillea. The rusted padlock on the door must have accommodated a giant skeleton key.

"Let's try to find Sarkas's grave," I said.

Circling around to the cemetery, we soon discovered this would be impossible. The dust lay an inch deep, and on the few tumbledown gravestones that remained intact the elements had worn away names and dates. Somewhere beneath all that dust was Sarkas's dust.

I turned back to the church. There was a small door on the rear wall, nearly concealed by the bougainvillea. "We're going in," I said, gripping the doorknob and putting my shoulder to the door. The hinges creaked and the door opened. A wave of stale air washed over us. "Get out the flashlight."

Lena shone the beam into the darkness: there were piles of rubble, shattered tiles, mounds of sawdust. Mice scurried into the shadows. My head grazed the low ceiling, and clouds of dust rose beneath our feet. We went through an arched doorway into the sacristy, where the ceiling shot up twelve feet. The cobwebs were thick. There were bat droppings beneath the beams. A cross taken down long ago had left an outline on the back wall. Below it, a shelf remained intact on which a line of books had been reduced to dust. A baptismal font was lying on its side. A gutted cabinet was pushed against the wall. In the corner there were brass hooks where Nicanor Simonides would have hung his vestments.

Three plain wooden doors led out of the sacristy. We went through the middle one and found ourselves directly behind the remains of the altar, facing the pews. Icons were painted on the three doors: Saint George and Saint Christopher flanking the Crucifixion. I took the flashlight from Lena and examined the images beneath layers of grime. Then I shone the light on the mural of the Ascension above the altar and on the domed ceiling from which Christ Pantocrator, copper-skinned, olive-eyed, gazed down sternly. I was disappointed. Like the icons in Xaniá, these were dull, standardized pieces of work. My hope that this was "Sarkas's church" was fading. If those wondrous animals Sarkas painted were not in either the Church of Saint Stephen or the Church of Saint George, Giorgio Zetto must have seen them in some other church in northwestern Crete (there were hundreds, many long gone) or on canvases that could be anywhere. As for the bestiary itself, if Simonides did not take it, if, instead, either he or Sarkas hid it away in this church, it must now be dust, like those books in the sacristy. Either way, here on Skalos or in the monastery in Ani, the bestiary must have been destroyed.

Lena sensed my disappointment. "Let's look around some more," she said.

"Not many more places to look," I replied, shining the flashlight over the heaps of debris that covered the pews.

Just then, the double doors in front were flung open. Sunlight flooded in, blinding us. A man was silhouetted in the doorway. He was shorter than Sampson and wore a top hat. Stepping inside, he closed the doors behind him and lit a candle. "Can I help you?" he called out, starting up the aisle.

Only when he reached the first pew could we see him clearly. He had a white moustache and long white hair. He was about seventy. His face was creased, his throat wrinkled. Though his clothes were rough, his outfit was far more elaborate than Sampson's: striped pants, a black cutaway with satin lapels, and high black boots. His elbows were patched and the top hat was dented now.

"Your light . . ." he said, and I lowered the flashlight. "I speak English. Are you English?"

"American." And I told him our names.

"I'm Rumen. What is it you want?"

His directness was disarming. Though I could have told him any number of things, I chose the truth. "We were looking for the grave of a man named Adolphus Sarkas."

"The cemetery is in back," he said drily. "It's all one grave now."

"I thought we might find some sign of his paintings in here."

"Paintings?"

"He painted icons and murals."

"These?" he said, pointing behind the altar.

"No, these aren't his. He also painted animals."

His eyebrows went up. "Oh?"

"Lost animals. Most no longer exist, some never did. Sarkas had a book I've been searching for, filled with such animals." I took out my notebook. "I'll show you."

He walked up to us, and to my surprise smelled, not of goats, but spices. Cinnamon, rosemary, myrrh.

Lena held the flashlight over the notebook and I showed him a drawing I'd done on the *Makara* when we passed the Straits of Messina: the Greek sea monster Scylla: six-headed, with three rows of teeth, and from the waist down composed of barking dogs.

Rumen studied the drawing.

"Scylla devoured sailors whose ships strayed near the whirlpool Charybdis," I said. "Once she was a beautiful Nereid, but in a fit of jealousy Circe used witchcraft to turn her into a monster."

He looked up with a small smile. "These islands are filled with witches."

I turned a few pages and showed him the opinicus, a griffin with the usual lion's torso and eagle's wings, but also an unexpected camel's tail. "And here is the simurgh," I said, flipping to the Persian phoenix, with its lion legs. "An immortal bird."

Rumen lingered over this image. "Like the *famash*," he said, the candlelight carving shadows into his face. "That's what my people call it." He held out his wrist, and tugging at the cuff, revealed a tattoo: a red bird with rainbow wings and sea-blue eyes.

"A phoenix," I said, peering at him in amazement.

"So you're searching for a lost book with lost beasts," Rumen said.

"Have you ever seen such a book here?"

"No."

"Adolphus Sarkas brought the book to Xaniá."

"How did he come by it?"

"He was a monk. His abbot ordered him to carry the book to another monastery. Instead, he stole it and fled."

"A monk." Rumen looked at Lena and me as if he were seeing us for the first time. In a measured voice he asked, "Why do you want this book, mister? To sell it? To keep it for yourself?"

"Neither. If someone else hasn't claimed it, I would give it to a library or museum so other people could see it."

He studied our faces, scratching his cheek with his little finger. Finally he seemed to make up his mind.

"Now let me show you something," he said, gesturing for us to follow him.

Lena and I exchanged glances and my mouth went dry as he led us back into the sacristy. He went up to the gutted cabinet and, handing Lena his candle, gripped the cabinet on either side and slid it away from the wall. At first I saw nothing. Then he took back the candle and held it close to the wall, revealing a door about four feet high by two feet wide. Thinking it must be a closet, I wondered if the *Caravan Bestiary* could have survived in this place after all. I sucked in my breath as Rumen took a key from his pocket and unlocked the door. It swung open without a sound. He thrust his candle into the doorway, and we saw, not a closet, but a small landing from which a flight of stairs disappeared into a well of darkness.

Neither Lena nor I scared easily, but for several seconds we stood frozen.

"Come," Rumen said, stepping through the doorway and starting down the stairs.

From the landing, we couldn't see the floor below. Cool air rose up to us. And silence. The stairs were steep and narrow, but less rickety than I expected. Lena was several steps behind Rumen, and I was just behind her. There was no banister, so we descended gingerly. Rumen's candle and my flashlight lit the way down many steps. We were in a room with a high ceiling.

At the foot of the stairs, Rumen's candle revealed the emblem of a phoenix chiseled into the stone wall, identical to the phoenix on his wrist. He lit two more candles in holders that flanked the stairway. The stone floor was swept clean.

Walking beyond the candles' glow, Rumen struck a match and raised it to the wall and an instant later a kerosene lantern bathed him in light. We were in a cavernous chamber, larger than the church above. It felt like a separate entity, a church within a church.

"Originally this was a hiding place from pirates," Rumen said. He saw I was studying the emblem on the wall. "The old Christians called Christ 'the Phoenix' because he was resurrected. But the Egyptians worshiped the phoenix long before that."

"At the golden temple in Heliopolis."

"You know, then," he said, proceeding along the left-hand wall and lighting another lantern. "Sentinels guarded the temple. Members of a brotherhood, from India, who wore the sign of the phoenix. They were Romany. They used to have many members," he added ruefully. "Now, just a few." He continued on, lighting one lantern after another, nine in all. "There are no books here," he declared, and my spirits sank. "There is only this."

He pointed to the opposite wall, now fully illuminated, on which Lena and I became riveted, trying to take in an enormous mural, at least fifteen feet high and sixty feet long. It made me dizzy at first. But I knew at once that it was the work of Adolphus Sarkas. I had never seen anything painted quite like it, except the murals on San Lazzaro.

"My people have always called this 'the monk's mural,'" Rumen said. "It has been good luck for us. For nearly one hundred and sixty years, we have watched over it."

"And you didn't know Sarkas was the artist?"

"I didn't know his name." He shrugged. "That makes no difference to me."

It made a difference to me, for this was "Sarkas's church" after all. He had left behind the mural. It was surely the reason he had been buried there. Whatever their final arrangements, Nicanor Simonides had provided Sarkas with this space where, on a grand scale, he could transpose images from the *Caravan Bestiary*. I couldn't imagine what I saw before me originating anywhere else.

In those first moments I felt the way I always thought I would if I ever had the bestiary open before me. A mixture of joy and exhilaration—and trepidation that, after all those years, the bestiary could not possibly fulfill my expectations. Many people were standing beside me just then—my grandmother and Evgénia, Mr. Hood and Madame Faville—but, most importantly, Lena, who was there in body as well as spirit.

"It's so beautiful, Xeno," she said, taking my arm.

As our eyes adjusted to the lanterns' light, the mural came alive. Colors brightened. Forms deepened. It seemed three-dimensional. It was as if we were gazing through a vast window into another world, as fresh as the day Sarkas painted it, as shimmering as the world itself must have appeared at the time of the Great Flood.

The mural was a broad seascape flanked by two shores: on the right, beneath a ghostly moon, a desert dense with cactus; on the left, a sunlit orchard encircled by gardens. The sea, emerald green with blue wavelets, stretched away to a silver horizon. The sky was filled with tattered red clouds. Powerful winds were blowing.

At the center of the mural, a phoenix with spectacular plumage was flying high into the sky. Its wings trailed streams of fire. Directly below the phoenix were not one, but two arks, filled with animals, sailing in opposite directions.

One was Noah's ark, overflowing with familiar members of the animal kingdom in pairs: bears and oxen, snakes and lizards, falcons, pigeons, turtles, and bees. Mermaids and dolphins swam nearby, helping guide the ark to shore.

The second ark stunned me. I could barely take it in at first. It was crowded with animals from the *Caravan Bestiary*. I recognized most of them: manticores, griffins, hippogriffs, basilisks, perytons, rukhs, a variety of dragons, the chimera, and a number of creatures I had never seen before.

Was this second ark the bestiary's great secret? It would explain why Sarkas used the Flood to animate, and backdrop, the creatures he had seen in the book. But I was amazed that, in all my research, of the concrete and the apocryphal, from D'Épernay's letter to Zetto's diary, I had never encountered a reference to a second ark.

The pilot of the first ark was a thin man with a weathered face. Despite navigating the ark for one hundred and fifty days and nights, he looked calm. His eyes were wide and bright. He stood on the bridge beside a tall, imposing old man in a blue cloak who gazed straight ahead, his white hair blowing out wild. A master of sea and land, he held a trident in one hand, a pruning hook in the other. This was Noah, and his ark was on course for the lush shore. The animals that swarmed the three lower decks and craned their necks through the many windows were also looking to shore.

On the bridge of the other ark there appeared to be a second, identical Noah. But when I looked closely, I saw only a bright shadow, a play of light in the paint which, from certain angles, took Noah's shape momentarily, then dissolved. The pilot standing erect beside him remained palpably visible, a fearsome figure wearing a black, high-collared robe. In the manner of Anubis and Horus, he had a panther's head atop a human body. His bloodless hands gripped the wheel. His topaz eyes scanned the desert shore. Rather than being a stowaway on Noah's ark, here Satan was the pilot of the second ark, charting his own course. Certainly his passengers were more unruly, swarming the decks and roof, howling into the wind. The fiercest of them—dogs like Cerberus and harpies with outsized talons—were confined to the brig, clawing at the barred windows, gnashing their teeth.

To see all these creatures at once, intermingling, when I was used to studying them singly, made them all the more monstrous. Especially the unfamiliar ones: a cyclops bull with a leopard's tail; a crocodile with centipede's legs; an eyeless bird with four sets of wings; a burly ape with transparent hands and feet. I would have loved to know their names and origins, but Sarkas had only copied images, not text. He had portrayed many of the animals on the second ark as agitated, verging on violence. Rightly so, considering their destination, and the fact they looked more like prisoners than passengers.

Of course the notion of a second ark would have appealed to the compilers of the *Caravan Bestiary:* how else could these fantastic, exiled beasts have survived the Flood? I felt, however, that the moonlit desert with its cactus maze was Sarkas's contribution, his conception of the limbo they inhabited before entering the human imagination.

Rumen, who had been watching us all this time, pointed to the second ark with a dry laugh. "Some say the first Romany were on board with the mongrels and outcasts, beings of mysterious origin who feared neither God nor the Devil and believed there was no difference between the two."

"What do you believe?" I asked.

He gave us a sly look. "I believe that, as a chosen people, the Romany must have been on both arks."

"Have you shown this mural to anyone else?"

"Before you, no one ever asked about paintings or knew about the monk. He and his friend the priest did a good job of keeping it secret. The few people who come to this island never pay attention to the church. They have heard it is a shambles, and nothing they see on the outside makes them think otherwise. Isn't that what you heard in Xaniá? Sampson has been down here, of course, and my brother, Neptune. And before us, my father was the caretaker, and before him, his uncle. When I am gone, my eldest son, Noah, will take over." He smiled and drifted across the room. "Noah is a popular name among the Romany, you know."

Lena turned to me. "If they knew the bestiary wouldn't be here, why were Sarkas and Simonides so secretive?"

"Heresy, for starters. A second ark, with that cargo . . . if the Church had known of this mural, they would have destroyed it. The real question is why Sarkas painted it in the first place."

I thought of several possibilities. I knew Sarkas had lived in Xaniá for three years. Considering the mural's scope, he must have worked on it right up until the end. I could only assume that sometime before November 1819, when Giorgio Zetto first saw the mural, Sarkas had decided to take the *Caravan Bestiary* to Ani. He may have painted the mural in order to preserve the bestiary's essence, an homage of sorts,

in the way he knew best, images, not words. Another, cruder possibility
is that the mural was his advance payment to Simonides after the latter agreed to transport the bestiary to Ani. At that point, Simonides
may have fully expected to return to Xaniá. Or perhaps there was another explanation too tortuous for me to intuit with the little I knew
about both men. What seemed indisputable was that these two churchmen had taken great pains to conceal a remnant of the bestiary in a
place where they could savor it with impunity.

"How could this mural have remained undiscovered?" Lena asked.

"Up the coast, Knossos was buried for four thousand years," I said.
"This country is filled with ruins, statuary, frescoes that were hidden
for millennia. What are a couple of centuries compared to that? And
it isn't really undiscovered, is it. The Gypsies have known about it for
a long time."

Rumen rejoined us.

"I promise you I won't reveal the location of this place," I said to
him, slipping off my knapsack. "This is as close as I'll get to the book
I've been searching for, and I'll only share that information with a few
friends."

Rumen was unperturbed. "You don't have to promise anything.
If you tell others, what happens will happen. I'm a caretaker, not a
policeman."

"I don't want to tell anyone."

He shrugged. "Whatever you say, mister."

I rummaged in my knapsack and took out my camera. "And I don't
plan to return myself. But I would like to take some photos—for myself, and my friends."

"Go ahead," he said.

I used three rolls of high-speed film. Sixty-nine shots of the mural
from every angle I could manage without a stepladder, tripod, or
floodlights. I took a set of overlapping shots from left to right; after
the film was developed, I would enlarge and juxtapose them in order
to piece together the entire mural. I got close-ups of the animals on
the second ark, of the phoenix, of both Noah and his shadowy twin,
and of the grim second pilot.

When I was down to my last three shots, I asked Rumen if I could photograph him.

He shook his head. "No," he said, without explanation.

So I snapped one of Lena at the foot of the mural, and she snapped one of me, and I saved the last shot.

Lena and I lingered in that chamber for hours. We walked back and forth beneath the mural, identifying animals, studying the finer touches, comparing notes. One of many details that caught my eye: that there were nine mermaids with bright shining manes, eight of them dark-haired, one a blonde. Another was Sarkas's illustration of the animals whose threefold incarnations—on land, sea, and in the air—are celebrated in the *Caravan Bestiary*. He had chosen the horse, painting (in close proximity) a grazing stallion, a seahorse riding the surf, and a wingèd horse like Pegasus rearing in the sky. Nearby was the phoenix, the only animal that freely inhabits the four elements, including fire. Rumen waited patiently on a stool in the corner, flipping his worry beads. Finally we, too, sat down on the floor against the opposite wall and gazed at the mural. The more I drank in Sarkas's creation, the more I was in awe of him. However low his personal morality, it did not diminish my admiration for his painting, and I would always be grateful that he had preserved the bestiary in this form. I was astonished at the enormous energy he invested, working anonymously, literally underground, knowing few people would enjoy the results, and in the end realizing he himself would not live long enough to do so. Maybe he preferred that the mural remain as unknown as its artist—at least for a time. I hated to think what would happen if the floodgates were opened to museum curators, art historians, religious fanatics, tourists—to the Church, worst of all, which still owned that building and its contents.

Finally Rumen pocketed his beads. "You must go now," he said.

I kept my eyes on the mural while he extinguished the lanterns: the sea, the arks, the animals gradually swallowed up by the darkness. He took his candle and I switched on my flashlight and Lena and I followed him up the stairs. He locked the door and pushed the cabinet over it. We followed him back to the altar, down the aisle, and out of the church. Rumen shut the doors and clicked the padlock in place.

"Thank you," I said, shaking his hand. Like Sampson's, it was cold and rough.

He made a small bow to Lena, who thanked him, too.

"Good luck," he said, and descended the steps and disappeared into the forest.

Lena and I went around the church. All the shade in the cemetery was bleached away. Puffs of dust rose, as if the bones below were stirring. We walked down a line of fallen gravestones and entered the forest. I felt the presence of animals in the shadows. Then the wind picked up through the trees, tinged with salt. A sparkling blue band appeared and we stepped from the forest onto a beach, a white crescent flanked by boulders. The horizon shimmered. We put down our knapsacks and removed our shoes.

"I'm going in," Lena said.

She stripped off her blouse and jeans, then her underwear. Her body glowed in the sun. Her arms and legs were tanned, which made her breasts look even whiter. She waded into the surf and dove cleanly, surfacing fifty feet out, filling her lungs, and continuing on with long steady strokes. I knew she was a strong swimmer. When we were children, she won trophies at the Y. It had been that long since I had seen her in the water. Sweating in the mezzanine above the pool, our eyes smarting from chlorine, Bruno and I had watched her compete. She was a long-distance swimmer. Her best event was the 800 meters. I remembered her red bathing suit and the matching cap her father had given her, initialed FDNY across the front.

As she swam out, a cloud obscured the sun. The sea turned gray. She stopped finally, a dark circle rising and falling. Then the cloud shifted and a shaft of sunlight lit her hair up gold. She beckoned to me. I took off my clothes. The water was cold. I started swimming, every so often raising my head to find Lena among the waves.

Later, poised to snap the last shot in my camera, I was puzzled to find it had already been taken. When the film was developed, there were all the photographs of the mural and then one of Lena and me in the sea, shot from the beach. Everything was as I remembered it: the clear water, the heavy clouds, her shining hair. We remained in the sea the rest of the afternoon, naked, weightless, riding the swell, before swimming in at twilight and returning to the dock where the launch was waiting, the pilot at the wheel, his cap pulled low, his cigarette glowing when he raised it to his lips.

Glossary

A Selection of Fabulous Beasts
from the *Caravan Bestiary*

Amemait

A beast of the underworld, out of Egypt. With the head of a crocodile, torso of a lion, and hindquarters of a hippopotamus, it is known as "the Devourer" because it consumes the hearts of the wicked after death, to assure the destruction of their souls.

Amphisbaena

A two-headed serpent, one head at either end of its body, each with fangs and eyes of fire.

Bai-ma

A white horse with one eye and eight legs that appears wherever an infant is stillborn and roars like a tiger.

Baku

A threefold beast—with a lion's head, tiger's feet, and horse's body—which, when invoked, will consume one's bad dreams.

Basilisk (Cockatrice)

A desert serpent with a star set in its forehead, like a coronet. It befouls air and water. As with the gorgon, its glance turns men to stone, but if reflected in a mirror or shield, will destroy the basilisk itself.

Bi-bi

A wingèd fox that lives high in the mountains and honks like a goose.

Bo

A horse from the plains of Central Asia with a white body and black tail, and the teeth and claws of a tiger. No weapon can harm it.

Bonnacon

A horse with the head of a bull and enormous horns that excretes fire and can scorch the land for miles, reducing whole forests to ashes.

Caladrius

A pure white bird known for its powers of divination. Brought to a sickbed, it will turn its back on a patient with a mortal illness, but face the patient who can avoid death, drawing the vapors of the illness into its own body and dispersing them as it flies toward the sun. Its dung is a powerful curative.

Catoblepas

A buffalo with the head of a hog and a poisonous tongue, it wallows in the mud of riverbanks. It always faces downward. Anyone who glimpses its red eyes perishes.

Centaur

Half man, half horse, they were fierce warriors and dedicated orgiasts, unruly and unpredictable. The lone exception was Chiron, a healer and astrologer, who tutored a pantheon of heroes, including Achilles, Theseus, Ajax, and Hercules.

Cerberus

The hound with one hundred (some say fifty, others three) heads that guards the Gates of the Underworld, on the far bank of the River Styx, terrorizing the souls of the dead.

Chimera

Only one chimera ever walked the earth, devastating the countryside in ancient Lycia. Part lion, goat, and serpent, it spewed flames and was killed by Bellerophon upon his wingèd horse, Pegasus.

Crocotta

A speckled hyena that imitates the human voice in order to lure men to secluded places and kill them.

Dipsas

A hooded asp whose bite causes the victim to die of thirst.

Echidna

Half serpent, half woman, with fiery eyes and a hunger for raw flesh. The wife of Typhon, she bore a host of monsters: the Chimera, the Hydra, the Nemean Lion, and the Sphinx; the dogs Cerberus and Orthrus and the dragon Ladon, all multiheaded; and Ethon, the eagle that tormented Prometheus when he was chained to his rock.

Emorroris

An asp, its name derived from the Greek αἷμα, "blood," because, when bitten, its victim hemorrhages to death.

Garuda

Half vulture, half man, with red wings, a white face, and a golden body. His mother, Vinata, was the sister of Kadru, the Goddess of Serpents, and he consumes a serpent daily. Vishnu, one of the three major gods in the Hindu pantheon, rides on his back.

Gorgons

Three female monsters—Stheno, Euryale, and Medusa—with nests of snakes on their heads instead of hair. Medusa is the only mortal gorgon, and the sight of her turns men to stone. Perseus manages to behead her only by looking at her reflection in his shield.

Griffin

The offspring of an eagle and a lion. Guardian of treasures, with gold talons and powerful wings. Able to fly to great heights with incredible weight on its back: men on horseback, oxen, even mountains.

Gullinbursti

A wild boar forged of gold by dwarves who are master smithies. It can travel on land or water and fly high in the sky, its path lit even in dead of night by its glowing bristles. At times, it is harnessed to the chariot of Freya, the Norse goddess of love.

Hippogriff

The offspring of a griffin and a horse. It lives in the icebound regions near the North Pole.

Hydra

A multiheaded offspring of Typhon and Echidna that dwells on the island of Lerna. If one of its heads is cut off, three more grow in its place.

Hypnale

An asp whose bite is a fatal soporific. Cleopatra's means of suicide. (From the Greek ὕπνος, "sleep.")

Jaculus

A flying serpent that hurls itself onto its prey from trees. (From the Latin for "javelin.")

Keres

Birdlike creatures with women's heads, deadly talons, and large wings. They tear apart corpses and are always present on battlefields, drinking the blood of the wounded and directing the fates of whole armies. Spirits of the dead, they are licensed to travel in and out of the underworld.

Kitsune

From Japan. A trickster fox that can metamorphose into any human form it wishes, but always keeps, and must conceal, its bushy tail. Most often, it assumes the body of a beautiful woman and coils its tail beneath the obi sash of her kimono.

Kujata

A huge cosmic bull, with thousands of eyes and ears, that stands upon the behemoth Bahamut, beneath whom are successive seas of water, air, and fire atop a serpent large enough to swallow the universe. On the kujata's back is a mountainous ruby on which an angel stands, holding the earth.

Ladon

A hundred-headed dragon that guards the apples of the Hesperides near Mount Atlas, on the African side of the Strait of Gibraltar. Hercules' eleventh labor was to slay it and bring back three of the apples.

Lamia

Beautiful women from the waist up, serpents from the waist down. They roam the African deserts, and in the way of mermaids, beguile travelers with their musical voices (that resemble whistling winds) in order to feast on them. They possess the ability to vanish at will.

Leucrocotta

From India. The swiftest animal on earth, with a lion's torso, stag's hindquarters, and horse's head.

Long

A benevolent Chinese dragon. Overseer of clouds, seas, lakes, and rivers. Bringer of rain. It is an amalgam of many animals, with a camel's head, a stag's horns, a snake's neck, an eagle's claws, a fish's scales, and a bull's tail.

Makara

An amphibious creature, crocodilian but with a snout that resembles an elephant's trunk. It originated in India as a composite beast—elephant and snake—that represented the duality of good and evil.

Mandrake

A root with the form of a man, it inhabits the divide between the plant and animal kingdoms. It is said to have originated in the dank soil at the foot of gallows, where hanged men fell. When torn from the ground, it screams like a man, and those who uproot it perish instantly.

Manticore

A lion with a human face, three rows of razor-sharp teeth, and a tail studded with poisonous darts that it can shoot at its prey. In India it is believed that the manticore was the ancestor of all man-eating cats: lions, tigers, and leopards.

Mermecolion

The "Ant-Lion," attested to by Aelian, Strabo, and Physiologus himself as the improbable offspring of a lion and an ant. It is a lion in its foreparts, an ant in the rear. A beast so fantastical that, by definition, it cannot survive. Half its body will not tolerate meat; the other half cannot digest grain; therefore, it starves to death.

Naga

From India. A large serpent, hooded like a cobra, that has dominion over oceans, rivers, and rain. Guardian of treasures, it lives in sumptuous palaces on the seafloor. It can confer invisibility on men underwater. Female nagas, naginis, are semihuman and beautiful, like mermaids, and often fall in love with mortal men.

Nine-tailed Fox

A fox that lives for a thousand years, at which point it sprouts nine tails and ascends to heaven. A trickster and master of illusion, by moonlight it can transform a hut into a palace and assume any human shape.

Nue

A fourfold beast—badger, monkey, tiger, serpent—that is visible only by moonlight. At death, it dissolves like snow.

Pazuzu

From Assyria. A harbinger of disease, with a human head, bird's wings, and lion's paws.

Peryton

A high-flying bird with the head and forelegs of a deer that casts the shadow of a man. It originated on the continent of Atlantis and now nests in caves on the Rock of Gibraltar, subsisting on soil and salt water.

Phoenix

A large bird with iridescent wings, eyes blue as the sea and feathers the color of fire. Sustained by air alone, it neither eats nor drinks. It resides in paradise, nesting in the date palm, and every thousand years dies and is reborn. Its song is so beautiful it was the basis for the first musical scale.

Rukh

A bird with a wingspan of 300 feet that can lift an elephant and fly for a thousand miles without pause. In the Indian Ocean its half-submerged eggs are often mistaken for islets.

Salamander

The smallest dragon in Creation, part animal, part mineral, according to Marco Polo. The mineral is asbestos. Thus it is said to live in fire. The Great Khan sent the Pope a pouch of salamander skin to protect the napkin of Saint Veronica, imprinted with Jesus' face. The Emperor of India had a suit tailored from a thousand salamander skins.

Serra

A sea monster that can out-race ships by rising out of the water in flight, beating its enormous fins like wings.

Simurgh

The combination of a huge bird and a lion. The Persian incarnation of the phoenix.

Sphinx

A lion with the head of a man, a woman, a ram (criosphinx), or a bird (avasphinx), it is the guardian of temples, treasure houses, and tombs.

Talos

A living giant composed of bronze, with melted lead running in his veins, created by Hephaistos to serve as the guardian of Crete.

Typhon

A hundred-headed, wingèd monster with a serpent's tail, his eyes spin like fiery wheels and flames shoot from his mouth. He is the husband of Echidna, father to her monstrous brood [see Echidna], and the son of Tartarus, a god who dwells in the deepest chasm of the underworld.

Uroboros

The serpent that encircles the world and devours its own tail. (From the Greek for "tail-devourer.") It also appears in Norse mythology, with the name Jormungard.

Zaratan

A sea turtle so enormous that sailors often mistake it for an island—far larger than the rukh's egg. Sometimes it is so large, and has been afloat for so long, that it is covered with valleys and forests, themselves populated with all manner of animals of normal dimension—including the turtle.

About the Author

NICHOLAS CHRISTOPHER is the author of four previous novels, *The Soloist, Veronica, A Trip to the Stars,* and
Franklin Flyer; eight books of poetry, most recently,
Crossing the Equator: New and Selected Poems, 1972–2004;
and a book about film noir, *Somewhere in the Night.* He
lives in New York City.